BOOK II

The Crowns of Croswald

The Girl with the Whispering Shadow

D.E.NIGHT

The Crowns of Croswald: The Girl with the Whispering Shadow by D.E. Night

Published by Stories Untold Press.

Editor: Jessie Chatigny
Cover Design: resn.co.nz

Publisher's Cataloging-in-Publication Data

Names: Night, D.E.
Title: The crowns of Croswald: the girl with the whispering shadow / D.E. Night.
Description: Pembroke Pines, FL : Stories Untold, 2019. | Includes 33 b&w illustrations. | Series: Crowns of Croswald series ; no. 2. | Audience: Ages 9-12. | Summary: In a tale of magic, intrigue, and danger, Ivy Lovely searches for the enchanted Kindred Stone. Along the way, her friendships grow deeper and she confronts the Dark Queen.
Identifiers: LCCN 2018963924 | ISBN 9780996948661 (pbk.) | ISBN 9780996948678 (hardcover) | ISBN 9780996948692 (epub) | ISBN 9780996948685 (mobi)
Subjects: CYAC: Magic—Fiction. | Coming of age—Fiction. | Private schools—Fiction. | BISAC: JUVENILE FICTION / Fantasy & Magic. | JUVENILE FICTION / Action & Adventure / General.
Classification: LCC PZ7.1.N54.G57 2019 | DDC [Fic]—dc22
LC record available at https://lccn.loc.gov/2018963924

Printed in the United States of America.

STORIES
UNTOLD

Dedicated to two of the strongest women
I know: my grandmothers.

Mama Yay, your storytelling ability
has sparked the scrivenist in me.
And to the real Harriet Smiles,
I only wish I could hear your voice
at the Hollow Shaft.

Contents

Prologue

A Dark Homecoming

Chapters

1. Catching a Cabby 10
2. Scriven This 24
3. Belzebuthe 32
4. Fyn's Place 44
5. The Gracious Greeleys 52
6. The Tour of All Tours 62
7. The Birthday Party 71
8. Fishing for Stars 85
9. Quinton's Brews & Hodgepodge 99
10. The Hex 105
11. Moonsday 120
12. A Potions War 131
13. Spelling 137
14. The Dorms 145

15. The Uncommon Flicker 155
16. The Magic Inside Creatures 163
17. The Carriage Accident 168
18. The Oath 177
19. Back at the Ball 196
20. Quogo Below 206
21. Invisitaurs 220
22. Shadows, Spices, and Scaldrons 229
23. Quo-no 240
24. Dungeon to Den 250
25. A Book Out of Place 267
26. Splitting Shadows 280
27. The Occulyst 290
28. The House in the Tree 300
29. The Empty Nest 319
30. Star Solo 330
31. Battle for Belzebuthe 338
32. The Rubble 359
33. Graduations and Goodbyes 367

Acknowledgments 373
About the Author 375

Prologue
A Dark Homecoming

THE air in Belzebuthe was so thick with magic that she felt as if she had to force her limbs through the atmosphere, especially when she had been gone a while. It always took a few days to adjust and the feeling never failed to surprise her, to say nothing of the ever-present chill in the air. The cloud cover was as thick as ever, further disguising and protecting the Town, but it seemed to be colder than usual for early summer.

All hairies in their lanterns were at rest, and the only light was from the low-hung stars that were particular to Belzebuthe. Even those did nothing to lighten the girl's confusion. This town had been kept hidden by more than a dozen spells, including one forbidding the mention of its name, the name a key to finding the Town itself, for generations.

As she made her way down the familiar cobbled streets, her shadow pulled her back, stretching behind her. She shivered: Her elaborate feathered gown was drenched and clung to her legs. As she reached the door of the home where she grew up, she realized that she didn't have her trunk or anything else with her. No key. She lifted her hand and heard a warm and welcoming voice inside before she could knock.

"They're home! And so early! I'll get the door!"

The door was thrown open and Easel Leelangraf enveloped his daughter in his loving arms. Only when he peered around her did his enthusiasm fade to a questioning look.

"Where's your brother?" he asked, his thick brow rising. "Is he all right? I thought you'd be on the morning cabby together."

Easel ushered in his only daughter, back from her first year at the Halls of Ivy, into the warm foyer lit by aging hairies in rusty sconces. She dropped the hood of her periwinkle cape, and her long, black, curly hair tumbled down over her deep-caramel skin.

"We heard about the Ball," Easel said. "How frightening! I'm just so glad, so-so-so glad, you're safe. And your brother?"

"He's fine. Everyone's fine, only a few broken chandeliers and some waterlogged furniture. Nothing a little magic can't fix." The girl made light of the disaster on purpose—still no one knew what to make of the reclusive Dark Queen's appearance at the Masquerade Ball. No one seemed to remember exactly what had happened, only that a boat had defied logic and become lodged in the ballroom of the Halls of Ivy. The image of the crushed walls, the sailing ship at a wild angle, the pooling water: she knew it would all appear in her dreams that night. Her dreams had become more and more strange—and frightening—as of late.

Forcing herself back in the moment, in her father's warm embrace, she said, "He'll be arriving tomorrow. He stayed back to sort out a few things with his friends—probably his little club thing. He told me to tell you not to worry. I just—I just wanted to be home."

"Oh, how we've missed—ooof!" Easel had nuzzled his daughter under his chin then jerked his head back quickly. "What is that, that awful smell? A mix of sour fruit and pond water?" Only one thing in his experience as a matteler smelled like that. "I know that everyone has been in her presence… I just didn't think that the smell of the Dark Queen would be so strong on you."

Her mother interrupted, "Never mind your father, dear. He just got home from a moon-long exploit. Still got his head, rather his nose, on the job. And he's off on another the day after next!"

"Do you have to go already?" she asked sadly, talking to her father while accepting her mother's warm embrace. She had always been a daddy's girl and didn't want to think about having only a few moments with him before he went off again. He was a lead investigative matteler, a scrivenist appointed to keep order in the world of scrivenry.

"Duty calls, darling. Let's make the most of the time we have—malts at the Melted Milkshake tomorrow afternoon? Your favorite."

Her mother smiled softly. "And for now, Easel, how about some tea around the fire? And let's get you, my dear daughter, into something dry."

Sybel Leelangraf's well-used quill danced, letting loose a flurry of sparkles, and her daughter's dress dried as she spun in a circle. The dress went from soggily clinging to her legs back to its fluffy, twirling silhouette of gray tulle and feathers.

"That's better," Sybel remarked.

"You wouldn't happen to have any of the cranberry cake left over, darling Sybel, would you?"

"Despite your best efforts, there is cake left," Sybel smiled wryly.

As her mother left for the kitchen, the girl and Easel settled in the living room. The cramped space was warm and cozy, decorated in greens and dark yellows. The bay window let in only starlight, but the warmth of the fire was enticing. Dried herbs hung from the woodwork of the ceiling, giving off a familiar scent of sage and rosemary and who knows what else. Easel created his own herb blends to aid his keen sense of smell, all for his job. He could sniff out a spell or potion like a wolf did dinner. His uniform—a midnight purple, almost black—and matching military cap with the matteler insignia—was in the closet as he made himself comfortable in his robe and slippers.

Easel drew up a footstool opposite the aging velvet couch where his daughter sat and asked in a low voice, "Now what happened at the Ball, my dear? I want to hear it from you."

She faltered.

"Something is troubling you."

"It's just—you ask how the party was, but the truth is I didn't attend." It was true; she had every intention of going but, once dressed, was too tired to go.

He looked at her quizzically. "And where did you go, if not the Ball?"

"To sleep. I was… I was tired."

"And your clothes? All wet because…?"

The girl just shook her head in confusion.

"Hmmm…."

"Not that I've been getting very restful sleep these days—I've been meaning to send a mendlott and ask if you have any remedies for a sound sleep. Dormdaze tea doesn't seem to cut it anymore."

The sound of teacups rattled from inside the kitchen.

"That is strange. Concerning. I'll look into it, love. Don't tell your mother; she'll worry." He sighed and pressed his hand to his daughter's forehead, checking for fever. Nothing. "Just—just take care of yourself."

She was barely making it through her strange days lately, on sleep that felt like it depleted rather than restored her. *I don't have enough energy to take care of myself.*

Sybel joined them and the three sat at the hearth. The girl held her mug of blue tansy tea, letting it warm her hands. Peering into the mug, she saw the indigo liquid bubbling softly.

"How did you find the party?" her mother asked, a much lighter conversation than her father's. "Did you dance with any boy in particular?"

"Mother," she ducked the question bashfully.

Her father gazed intently out the window, his mind wandering like thick drifts of fog.

"What? When I was your age, I met your father—"

The girl made for a quick change of subject. "Catch anything on your latest hunt, Father?" Her father's stories of daring chases after evil always thrilled her.

"Tell her, Easel. Tell her what you were tracking!"

"What was it?" the girl asked, her dark-brown eyes widening.

"Shades."

"What's a shade?" she curled in her chair, knowing that if her father's team of mattelers was dealing with it, it had to be terrible.

"A shade of life. Not quite human. No blood. Composed of water. The terrible thing is that we don't even really know what they are exactly or where they've come from." He took a long breath in. "They've been appearing and then vanishing in Belzebuthe, like they're being hurled from the heavens. Then they dissolve, probably due to one of the Town's elimination spells. But the very idea that they can get through the barriers even for a moment is quite disturbing."

The fire dimmed, the room darkened, and an eerie chill drifted through the room, even with the window closed.

"They seem to be related to the strange disturbances in the cloud cover. How it's been colder overall this year, even now with the summer moons. The snows have not gone away." This made the girl shiver in her seat.

Sybel interrupted in a hushed tone, "There's been talk of the Dark Queen manipulating matter in the clouds above Belzebuthe and trying to find the Town itself. Oh my stars, what if the time in which we scrivenists may practice magic freely is over?"

"Now, Sybel, don't scare the poor girl. The Dark Queen still has no access to our town. I'd smell it from a mile away if she did." But his wife caught him flaring his nostrils at their daughter, breathing her odor in again.

"Well, the agreement to not broach the Halls uninvited has been broken, hasn't it? Who knows what's next?"

"We are working on the mystery of the shades. We'll know what they are and what they mean soon enough." He motioned to her cup. "Finish up that tea—should help you sleep, darling."

By the time she made it up to her room, she was too tired to change and fell into a deep sleep at the foot of her tiny, fluffy bed.

Deep and long, but far from restful.

She awoke with a start, a shrill, urgent voice ringing in her head. The words were incomprehensible, but the voice had the feeling of being too close, like it was eavesdropping on her inner world. Her mind was full of dark dream images; she needed to sketch them before the images slipped away. Still in her ball gown that had never been to a ball as far as she knew, the girl grabbed her favorite pen and proof pad and hastily drew upon the pages.

The sketches had a frantic feel about them; if she hadn't watched her own hand do the work, she wouldn't have thought she could have conjured such images. She had no recollection of ever seeing such things: a windowless corridor with a blocky spiral staircase, liquid-filled glass enclosures framed with brass, a candle held aloft casting terrifying shadows.

She shivered. Why couldn't she have nice dreams and draw pictures of hairies twinkling or pretty stones? *Ugh.* She looked to the timepiece on her wall and something on her narrow windowsill caught her eye.

A quill. *A quill?* It rested ever so peacefully.

The quill was jet black and had the texture and sheen of fine satin. It was obviously not hers, as she had only finished her first school year. She examined it without picking it up. Not her father's—too long. Not her mother's—hers was scarlet. She was sure she'd never seen this quill before.

Chapter One

Catching a Cabby

THE bright rays of Croswald's morning sun speckled through the canopy of trees that lined the long narrow path leading to the school's grand gate. It was a perfect early summer morning with a lace-like mist clinging to the ground. The path, like the Halls of Ivy itself, was completely empty except for two girls. After the fiasco of the Ball, most students had left late the night before, collected by terrified parents. Royals went home to their castles, and sqwinches scattered in cottages and row homes throughout the land of Croswald. Even the graduation ceremony had been canceled: Diplomas and quill certificates were to be sent by mendlott to the graduates.

"Cheer up, Ivy. You'll be back soon enough," Rebecca Connell, a sqwinch *and* royal, said to her best friend.

Ivy Lovely sniffed, holding back tears. "But he, Derwin, my family's scrivenist," she could hardly believe the words she was saying, "said that the Halls aren't safe for me any longer, that I have to leave. What if I'm never invited back?"

The Halls of Ivy had been the only place where Ivy had ever felt welcomed and understood. Who would have thought that a year of magic school, studying scrivenry and stones, could be so eventful? For the first time in her life, she was able to do the things she loved: learn and read and sketch and explore. As she stood shoulder to shoulder with Rebecca, Ivy reflected on the year's memories, both good and bad. How had it only been a year? And all of it was threatened, to say nothing of how her own life and the lives of nearly everyone she cared about were threatened the night before. She shivered at the thought: the Dark Queen's evil cackle in the ballroom still rang in her head.

Part of the reason the Halls felt like home is that it really was. Built hundreds and hundreds of years ago as Ivy's family castle, the gray stone towers of the Halls of Ivy stood tall and proud against the cliff, looking out over the town of Ravenshollow below.

Ivy certainly couldn't return to her life as an orphaned scaldrony maid in Croswald's least magical castle, tucked amid fields of magic masking slurry flowers. She had been kicked out of there, too, though under different circumstances.

Each year the Halls closed in the most dramatic of ways—once the last student, the last professor, and all the groundskeepers left, the school transformed from the lively, bustling place that it was fall, winter, and spring, to a dark, drawn-in place. The ivy it was named for rapidly overtook the castle's walls with woody, gnarled branches, losing the bright green leaves the moment it finished its growing work. The brightness of the castle turned dark, and where jostling students and lecturing professors once filled the castle, now it was quiet, not a soul in sight, not a hairie lit in its little fairy lantern. Every summer the place would revert to the same abandoned castle from where Ivy's ancestors had once been cursed away. Ivy had barely begun to process that her family had been royal, let alone that she was in the queenly line.

Looking at Rebecca's face, Ivy could tell that her friend didn't harbor her same fears—Rebecca knew that *she'd* be welcomed back for another three years of study. After all, she was from one of the oldest royal families *and* had the tingle of magical scrivenist blood to boot.

Ivy could feel warmth radiating in her pocket from the precious stone hidden inside it. It was a segment of the Kindred Stone, smooth and faceted on one side, rough on the other. She fiddled with it in between the soft fabric of her skirt, assuring herself it was still where she last placed it—the pocket that Rebecca had helped make extra deep. Her conversation with Derwin Edgar Night rang in her head. "This is your destiny."

Ivy shivered at the memory of the Dark Queen's vacant black eyes. *I suppose there are worse things than not having a home to go to... worse things like the evil Queen trying to murder you. All because of a silly rock.* At that instant, the stone heated up. Ivy drew her hand out quickly with a yelp.

"What are you squealing about? What's the matter?" Rebecca looked at her curiously.

Ivy pulled the stone from her pocket. It glowed brighter than any she had seen before.

"It's so temperamental, almost like it can sense what I'm thinking."

"Of course it can sense what you're thinking! It's like any stone linked to a royal. I didn't know my love of minks would cause such a problem for me," Rebecca sniffed.

Ivy smiled at the memory of her first encounter with

Rebecca and her friend's involuntary transformations into a mink imprisoned in a utility closet. All due to the Hellexor Stone, the gem of transformation, that was set into Rebecca's crown.

Tossing her hair, Rebecca said, "It does make for a silky mane of hair though! Tell me again: What kind is that stone?"

"Only the supposedly mythical stone containing Princess Isabella's magic. Apparently the first magical stone *ever.* Oh, and it controls Croswald's future, and whoever has it the Dark Queen wants dead," Ivy rolled her eyes at the sheer ridiculousness of giving her such a thing.

"Seems to me something like that is best left in a Forgotten Room."

"Right?! Some scrivenist I have. I meet him for one day and he tells me my whole life is about to change, that I'm to protect the most precious stone in Croswald, and that I'm the rightful Queen of Croswald. Then he just vanishes without so much as a hint as to how to find him again!"

"Ugh. If the Queen is after it, it seems best not to tempt her to follow you."

"But I just can't"—she paused—"*abandon* it. I just wish Derwin could have stayed. So many questions." Ivy bit her lip. "Here, look at this letter. He delivered it right before he left."

Dear Ivy,

I can hardly express the pride and joy I feel at being set free by you from that terrible ship in that cursed bottle. Thank you.

I know that we spoke of so much and that it must be hard for you to take in. But please trust me: You must not come back to the Halls. The only place safe for you is the Town. Not only will the Town be safe, it is where you will begin seeking the second segment of the Kindred Stone. You must find the remaining two pieces of the stone and reunite them with the one you have now. It is your inheritance and our only hope of dethroning the Dark Queen. She is more dangerous than ever before. I, too, must go away. Winsome's quill is missing–I cannot let it fall into the wrong hands. Heed my words and stay tucked away, Ivy.

By the light of the moon, your devoted scrivenist,
Derwin Edgar Night

P.S. You'll be staying at 418C, Scattered Street, The Town.

Rebecca skimmed the scrap of parchment and looked up. "A town that doesn't have a name and a street called *Scattered*? Are you sure he wants you to find this place? What are you supposed to do without his guidance, especially when you can't continue your studies?"

Ivy knew that she could count on her friend to know exactly how she felt. After holding back her tears all night, all morning, she finally let go and cried, sobs wracking her body. Rebecca held her tightly.

"Are you sure this letter is the only instruction he left?"

"Yes. He said he'd be in touch through mendlott, and that I can study along with the Compass Startus when school begins again. Though I don't think sending me school assignments through a notebook is nearly as good as being in person. And of course, the place I'm supposed to go is unmentionable, unfindable, except by secret transport that hides itself in a storm that I'm not even supposed to talk about! Look at me, half confessing everything!" Ivy had barely wrapped her mind around the idea that the Town was findable only by those who knew its name: Belzebuthe.

Rebecca put a halt to Ivy's ramblings. "If Derwin were here, then he could have a say. But I think you're best off with your best friend! Plus, the woods around our castle are so fun to explore!"

"I don't think I'll be doing any exploring," Ivy said wistfully.

"Oh, right, the Queen. Well, our castle walls have got to be the sturdiest in all of Croswald. Father himself had them spelled. And my sister is dying to meet you. Plus, you'll love Frederick, my family's scrivenist. He's in charge of the dragonry."

"Don't tempt me! Humboldt might not like living with big dragons." Humboldt grumbled in his habbitry at Ivy's ankles. "Sorry, Hum. Not every dragon can be majestic. Although your cranberry crumb cakes *are* majestic."

Humboldt was a rescue, a scaldron that served as an oven in the kitchen where Ivy had worked.

Rebecca giggled, "Humboldt would be safe. I'm almost one-hundred percent sure."

Before Ivy could reply, Rebecca's family carriage came up the hill and pulled up next to them. A large, gregarious man, clad in scrivenist plum from head to toe, stepped out and wrapped Rebecca in a warm embrace.

"Ivy, this is Frederick Faddacky, my family's scrivenist. Wacky, but quite wonderful."

Ivy chuckled, "I'm Ivy, Ivy Lovely."

"A pleasure to meet you!"

"Ivy had the most influential Compass Startus this past year. Of course, I'm not sure she intended it to be so. A bit of illegal adventuring, etcetera."

"Well, then I can imagine why the two of you have become such good friends." Frederick smiled widely at Ivy and bowed. "It's a pleasure to finally meet a friend of Rebecca's, especially one who is staying with us! It's—dare I say—lovely? Oh, the scrivenist fun we'll have! I'll teach you, and maybe you can teach me a thing or two, Ms. Lovely."

Ivy could see that Rebecca, and now Frederick, were going to be difficult to say no to. She laughed: the aggressive welcome of these two went a long way to erase the confusion and abandonment Ivy had felt just moments ago.

"Well, I can't think of anything more fun than a summer with Rebecca. It's just—"

Frederick interrupted, "If only Rebecca's mother approved of the root roller, we'd get home much quicker! Alas, a carriage it will have to be."

"A root roller?"

"Best form of transport: discreet and accommodating, passed from root to root underground."

Before Ivy could ask anything else, Humboldt's excitement had grown with Frederick's, and the little domesticated dragon was puffing with smoke. With a burp, he set on fire a skirt hem that hung out of one of Rebecca's many trunks.

"Oh no!" Ivy exclaimed, waving at the little flames.

"Ha! Look at him go. Just doing what he's meant to do, little dragon. I'll bet he's a good little cooker. Maybe we can set you to work at Castle Connell. Just for fun, though." Frederick patted his head, extinguished the flame with a wave of his quill, and turned to Ivy to say, "Rebecca told me about how you grew up, Ivy. There's honor in service and hard work—it'll help shape you as a scrivenist."

Ivy blushed.

Frederick peered up at the sky and opened the carriage door. "Rain's coming. Best be on our way."

Ivy reached for Rebecca's arm and said tentatively, "But Derwin told me—he said I'd be safe in the Town."

Overhearing, Frederick leaned back and said, "I know the place, Ivy. I'm sworn to its secrecy—its safety, really. I won't reveal its name or location, but if you are meant to go there, you will."

Ivy's frustration began to mount again. *Why wouldn't Derwin assure himself of my safety and guide me to Belzebuthe? Why not leave this piece of the Kindred Stone where it's best left forgotten while I search for others?* Her heart was already picturing the fun she'd have with Rebecca during the summer moons, but her gut knew that she shouldn't go to Castle Connell.

She turned to Rebecca once more. "Wherever I go, the Queen is headed. I couldn't forgive myself if something happened to you or your family. Or Frederick. Derwin says that the Town is the one place she'll never find me. If anything should happen, I just—I want you to know where I'll be." Then, as an afterthought, she said, "Of course, I'll need to figure out how to get there first."

The rain began to thrum as it pelted the carriage, stirring up the dirt into mud. The unexpected shower was building momentum, more and more like a weeping shadow. The weather clearly reflected Ivy's mood.

Then, a wave of realization washed over Ivy's face. "Wait! The weather!"

She spun, taking in the rain that was now coming down in sheets only yards away. In a panicked rush, she grabbed the habbitry, lantern, and satchel from Frederick before he loaded it up.

Ivy shouted, "The rain… the rain!"

"Have you lost your mind, Ivy?"

"The storm, though!" Ivy looked around wildly, finally catching a glimpse of the cabby beast through a dark cloud. "There it is!"

"Ivy! Stop it. What are you doing? You'll catch a cold. You're not seriously thinking about staying here?" Rebecca shouted.

"The cab—er, never mind, I'll be okay. I promise. I'm sorry, I'm sorry about all of this. I'll explain later! It's just—I have to go!"

"Ivy!" Rebecca squealed.

But with that last word, Ivy was off and running to chase after the cloud. She peered up into the sky, but the cold rain was coming down too hard to see anything at all. She rubbed her eyes on her already soaked sleeve and shivered. But then the storm shifted and quickly started traveling west.

"No, wait! Nooo!" she called. "Please!"

Ivy ran along the cobblestone path between the now-dormant oranstra trees, crossing through rough patches of old pines until she reached a large pasture on the other side of the school's property. The cloud stalled as if waiting for Ivy to catch up.

The storm was so localized, what else could it be but a cabby? If only she had Rebecca's Hellexor Stone and could shapeshift into something, anything with wings! Ivy felt a pang of panic. Had she just turned down an offer to live with her best friend for the summer—the first time she'd be a guest in a castle—on a hunch, a hunch that was about to be proven untrue?

The rain cloud quickly outpaced her, leaving Ivy panting for breath. She made it to the top of a small rise. The wind was still, the large pasture deserted, and the cabby was out of sight.

"Come back," she whispered, feeling utterly hopeless.

Suddenly, a spray of dirt tickled the back of Ivy's elbow. She held still. The presence of a being standing above her loomed large. Warm breaths huffed down on her. Biting her lip, she turned slowly in her crouch. There was no one.

But there *was* someone—because she felt (and smelled) its breath still. Again, dirt was kicked up, like a horse ready to go, only she couldn't see the horse. And the breath was coming up from far over her head. Humboldt sensed the presence, too, but was strangely calm. It was unusual for Hum, who was typically pretty jumpy.

She stood slowly, ready to meet whatever invisible creature was there. *If it wants to hurt me, it would have—*

But she didn't have the chance to finish her thought. A firm push buckled her knees from behind and she was swept up into the air like one of the Jester's juggling pins. While she was in the air, head down, she caught sight of giant cloven-hoof footprints that were pressed in the mud next to her own. Then she was tossed up again.

"What the—" she yelled, equal parts angry, bewildered, and afraid. She screamed for help, half laughing and half crying. On the final toss, Ivy landed securely on shoulders of some sort, an impressive nine feet in the air. Ivy was sure it wasn't a horse. For one thing, the hoofprints showed it ran on two legs. For another, she watched an invisible arm (knowing the impossibility of such a thing) scoop up her things. Ivy scanned with her fingers, as if she were in total darkness, feeling broad shoulders and matted fur. Ivy watched her hands feel a head that she couldn't see. She barely had enough time to grab the long, curved horns, like a bull's, before the creature took off with a jolt.

If Ivy's friends saw her now, she was sure the sight of her and her floating possessions would be enough to give them plenty of material to record in their proof pads. They sped down toward the ivy-covered wall at the edge of the Hall's property. To Ivy's concern, they didn't seem to be slowing down, only going faster. She screamed and squeezed her eyes shut.

But then a feeling of weightlessness, a tickle in her tummy, overcame her. Ivy opened one eye and saw they were speeding up the ancient stone wall! The invisible beast could climb! And she felt like they were flying. Once they reached the top of the wall, Ivy spotted the cabby storm hovering over a town in the distance, farther than Ravenshollow.

Without hesitation, the creature leapt off the wall and sped through an opening into the trees. Ivy's heart pounded uncontrollably, her skin tingling. They ripped their way through a tangled growth of vines as they fell down. Ivy surmised that the creature had long, sharp talons as she watched deep cuts in the wood's bark appear.

Ivy wasn't even doing the work, but still she was winded with excitement and effort. The weight of her body crunched forwards and back with each long stride, and the stone jiggled in her dress pocket. She gripped thick, dreadlocked strands of fur. The beast's musk was strong—woodsy and mossy—but she could feel a paw steady her back when they went through rough spots. And by now, she could tell that the beast was following the path of the cabby!

The cabby was near: The smell of wet earth, the sparkle glinting off the moss-covered trees, and the dew were easy evidence of that. Ivy couldn't believe how fast they had traveled. They had already crossed behind and beyond Ravenshollow and the cabby was directly ahead. But then the beast stopped abruptly.

"Over there!" she pointed. The beast stood still, hesitant for the first time. "What are you waiting for? Come on! It's right there!"

Ivy squirmed and leaned forward, trying to urge the beast on. They were going to miss it! To be so close, then to have all hope vanish again in seconds! She knew she had to get to Belzebuthe.

But what Ivy couldn't at first see, the beast could smell. On a hill between the cabby and Ivy stood a small convoy of dark, tall, menacing figures atop unicorns as black as death, with snarling wolves at their sides. It could only be the Dark Queen's henchmen, the Cloaked Brood. Ivy gasped.

In a panic, she kicked and pushed against the beast. Was it

just delivering her directly to the Brood? Her shrill scream captured the Cloaked Brood's attention. Soon the sound of their black unicorns' thundering hooves and the wolves' howls echoed in the valley.

The invisible beast made a sharp right away from the roaming group and the cabby. Ivy's adrenaline was pulsing and the rain whipped past her ruddy cheeks. Faster and faster they fled, but the Cloaked Brood was closing in on them.

Then the invisible creature unexpectedly stopped short and Ivy and her things went flying forwards, tumbling over its head and landing straight in a mud puddle by an ancient, uninhabited cottage. She pulled her head up just in time to hear the beast's roar. The rain bounced off its form—an upright bison?—and it took off back up the hill. The Brood followed suit, leaving Ivy and her mud pit behind. They hadn't seen her! She could hear the shouts of the Brood and the beast's strange keening traveling farther and farther away.

"You okay, Humboldt?" she panted. His black-and-white face was now splotchy with mud. "Hairies?" The furry, glowing fairies blinked sporadically and shook the muck from their wings.

But then the rain was picking up—*the cabby!* Ivy dashed to the center of the downpour.

"Hellooooooo?! Can you hear me up there? I'm looking for the Town!" she yelled towards the sky.

Suddenly the cabby careened into view. Three miniature houses towed by an enormous gray beast that was producing the weather itself. Ivy was equal parts relieved that it was indeed a cabby and terrified because the flying cabby beast was barreling straight into the small cottage next to them. Humboldt yelped, and Ivy snapped out of her blank stare and leapt back into the muddy ditch.

With a resounding boom, the rhino-like beast crashed into the old gray cottage, reducing it to a pile of soggy matchsticks.

Chapter Two

Scriven This

THE beast was uninjured, as cabby drivers and beasts are quite accustomed to crash landings. With a whistle, the driver hopped down from the harness at the top of the beast, sliding down the slippery gray skin from which the storm emanated. The driver pulled open the door of a compartment, one of the three little cottages that the beast towed in its storm.

The driver was a sturdy-looking gray woman who came out in the traditional scrivenist attire, plum tweed from head to toe. She wore a cap topped with an umbrella which was cranked fully open. With quick motions of her quill, she started the restoring spell, fixing what the beast's landing had destroyed. The quaint cottage would have to wait until the cabby took off again, but the shrubs and grass were already growing back as Ivy ran up to the cabby driver.

"I've been following you for miles! Surely there's a better way to go about this?"

"The Cloaked Brood was too close, dearie. We had to wait until they were long gone, out of sight. You understand."

"Are you certain they're gone?"

The driver shrugged, "For now at least, but let's hurry along. Off to the Town, are you?"

"Yes. Yes, please."

"Compartments are quite full, so you'll have to stow away all your belongings, Miss."

"But I'll keep the scaldron and hairies with me," Ivy clutched Humboldt's cage close to her chest.

"The *scaldron*?" the driver asked in disbelief. But seeing the girl's resolve, she shrugged and relented. "Well, all right, but no funny fire business"—this she said to Humboldt—"and you'll have to stow the satchel at least," she said to Ivy. "No room!"

At that, a trunk dropped down from the top of the third cottage, and the driver dropped Ivy's satchel inside.

"Off we go!" she hustled Ivy, Humboldt, and the hairies into the compartment. A blast of hot air hit her and Humboldt, and instantly they were dry. Ivy's long, chocolate-brown hair was poofed to full volume and she twisted it around itself to try and contain it a bit.

Just like the Halls of Ivy admission cabby, this little cottage-like building was larger inside than expected. Still, the little living room was full to the gills—each of the mismatched chairs had a scrivenist in it, some facing the little potbellied scaldron that kept the compartment from freezing over.

Ivy set her eyes on a seat all the way in the back (which wasn't a long way back) in the last row that faced out the back window. The view was terrible, due to the beast's storm-making to mask the cabby's journey, but Ivy was just glad it didn't face anyone else. She felt uncomfortable enough brushing past strangers as she made her way to the empty seat, trying not to bump into her fellow passengers and keeping Humboldt from view.

As far as she could tell, she was the youngest person in the compartment and the only sqwinch, not yet a full-fledged scrivenist. Everyone else seemed at ease, calmly reading papers and sipping pear nectar as if they hadn't just been through a crash landing into a cottage the size of a cabby compartment. *I've got to figure out how to get a cabby the normal way*, Ivy thought. It seemed preposterous to travel in such a way, though now that Ivy had met the Dark Queen, she understood the urgency of keeping Belzebuthe—both its location and its name—secretly safe from her.

Her feelings were in stark contrast to the calm everyone else seemed to be experiencing. She didn't even know for sure where she was going, let alone what to expect when she got there. Was this really what Derwin's letter had meant? And would she really be safe? And what about the other pieces of the Kindred Stone? Ivy gripped the one segment tightly in her pocket. It had become quite the reflex since Derwin had dropped it in her hand only a few days before. What if she never made it back to the Halls of Ivy? What if she never saw Fyn again? That thought surprised her a little. A bit of a different flavor, but what was Fyn up to this summer? Would she have to wait all summer to see him again?

"That should be everyone, folks," the driver droned on the cabby's intercom. "Straight to our destination without a further delay."

"You look like you need a warm-up." A familiar face beamed at her. It was Professor Royal, who was wearing a navy tweed traveling cloak and had her ash-blonde hair tied back neatly. She pulled a tiny cord above their heads and a delightfully wooly pair of socks descended. *Witchy warmupps!*

"Those should help."

Ivy was too surprised to take them and so the kind professor did instead. Then she handed the socks over to Ivy. Ivy took off her shoes and slipped the warmupps on—instantly she was warmer.

"I can see you are surprised to see me. Surprised that I know of Belzebuthe, even though I'm a royal? I'm off to visit old friends, the family of my childhood scrivenist, the woman who inspired me to teach. Looks like cabby travel is new to you, as it would be for most sqwinches."

New felt like an understatement. Looking into Professor Royal's long-lashed eyes, Ivy longed for the comfort of the Halls with a sudden pang. Even just being with Rebecca or Fyn, this whole adventure would be better.

"It might seem strange, but it gets better. You'll see." Professor Royal yawned, "We'll have plenty of time to talk later but, if you don't mind, I'm in need of a quick cat nap." And then she leaned up against a pillow that had dropped from the ceiling and was soon asleep.

Ivy settled in. The only thing missing was her old lumpy sweater, stowed in her satchel above. It really would go a long way towards making her comfortable. But then, just as she had the thought, it was accordion-armed into her lap.

"Thank you," she said in a whisper as she shrugged the custard-colored sweater on. The arm then brought down a hot cup of tea and biscotti to her. The cabby storm raged, but it felt calm inside.

Ivy didn't feel like she could sleep. She glanced around; everyone else seemed to be dozing off, despite the wild weather.

She tried to amuse herself by staring out the window, but there was nothing to see but storm clouds. She reached into her pocket and tentatively pulled out a folded sketch that Derwin had given her. It was one of Winsome's sketches of her parents during the wandering years. They had died so soon after her birth that the sight of their faces was still novel to her. It made goosebumps rise up on her flesh. What would it have been like to talk to them? Did her mother bite her lip raw when she was nervous, like Ivy did?

The scrivenist on her left, a gentleman with a gray tuft of hair, snorted in his seat, and his copy of *Scriven This* dropped down to the floor. After carefully tucking her sketch away, Ivy looked right, then left, and then picked up the paper.

She felt a wave of nerves. Would news of the Dark Queen ravaging the Ball be in the paper? Would everyone know who she was in a matter of days? She wished she could hide in the slurry fields for a moment, then took a breath and read the headline:

Suspected Break-In at the Quill Keep Has Belzebuthe in a Frenzy

Surprised, Ivy read on.

Belzebuthe, 8th Day of the Sixth Moon–In the wee hours of this morning, an unidentified person made mincemeat of the entryway to the Quill Keep. One quill contained on one of the uppermost floors has been reported missing. An inside source says the quill once belonged to the long-dead Daryl Debnick. According to the Quill Keep's historian, Wisteria Greeley, Debnick is best known as the scrivenist to Princess Isabella before her untimely disappearance. His later work focused on the mastery and creation of dreadful creatures, among them the rabies that infect balding hairies and the orbis, the infamous hunter of those in the now-defunct queenly line. Debnick was disbarred in 1697.

This quill is highly dangerous, as are all quills in the Quill Keep. The mattelers beseech the public to come forward with any information as to the whereabouts of this quill and any information regarding suspicious activity the night of the break-in.

Quill description: As black as a high-gloss Portal Stone, this quill has a medium-sized feather. Quite contrary to its history, the quill appears elegant and sophisticated. In the moonlight, it sparkles angrily. Beware.

Reward: One Hundred Ketzels & One Ounce of Moondust

A gravelly voice next to her said, "First time it has ever happened, to my knowledge, and I've been living in Belzebuthe for thirty-three years."

Ivy turned wide-eyed to the gray-haired gentleman. "Oh! I'm sorry, I thought you were, um, done with the paper."

He continued, not needing nor taking note of her apology, "The most protected place in all of Croswald. How did the perpetrator get away with it?"

As he mused, Ivy noted his unique scrivenist uniform: midnight purple with a curlicued "M" embroidered in gold thread on the left chest pocket. The scrivenist pulled out his quill and touched the sketch of the damaged thirteenth floor with its tip. The detailed sketch shimmered and the scrivenist narrowed his eyes in concentration.

To her right, Professor Royal stirred. She whispered to Ivy sleepily, "He's pulling out the facts. Having an internal conversation with the historian, searching the crime scene in-depth."

"What do you mean?"

"It's called teledetecting. He's a matteler, the investigative scrivenist sworn to protect us and chase down evil and errant magic. See the insignia to the left of his lapel? Anyway, his specialization must be teledetecting. Basically, he can travel somewhere without actually being there by way of mentally entering a sketch. He may gain new information not initially gathered in the scene investigation, or re-interview victims and witnesses. But he can only travel to the room pictured."

There was so much that Ivy didn't know about scrivenry. At times she felt deeply hindered by her upbringing behind the slurry fields. The scrivenist continued to explore the Quill Keep in his mind; Professor Royal dropped off again. The cabby continued to rattle and roll, and Ivy took to gazing out of the storm-filled window again. She brought out her proof pad and began sketching quietly. Because there wasn't much to see outside, she found herself sketching the Halls of Ivy, a place she'd sketched for so long from her dreams and now had a year's worth of adventuring to capture.

But then there was a jolt. Even the teacups rattled. A hush came over the group. Seconds later, the cabby dropped what felt like several yards. Ivy's stomach caught up in her throat. The matteler to her left stood.

"What is this nonsense?" he demanded, directing his voice to the ceiling, presumably the driver.

Then there was a flash of light—lightning?—that

illuminated the entire compartment. In the flash, Ivy saw dark shapes shifting in the thick clouds behind the window. She gasped. It was too familiar, too much like the Bearded Cloud that she and Fyn faced leaving the Hollow Shaft.

The reedy voice of their driver piped down into their compartment, "Seats, please!" All humor had fled her voice.

With a rumble and a rattle, the cabby beast bellowed loudly. The storm turned from rain to sleet to snow. The window went completely dark. Ivy felt as if they were spinning. So were her thoughts.

As if answering her unspoken musings, the matteler sputtered as he fell back down into his seat, "What is Belzebuthe coming to? The Quill Keep and cabbies no longer safe? If safety can't be found here, then where?"

But with that, the cabby took a sharp left and grazed the outer wall of the Town below.

Chapter Three

Belzebuthe

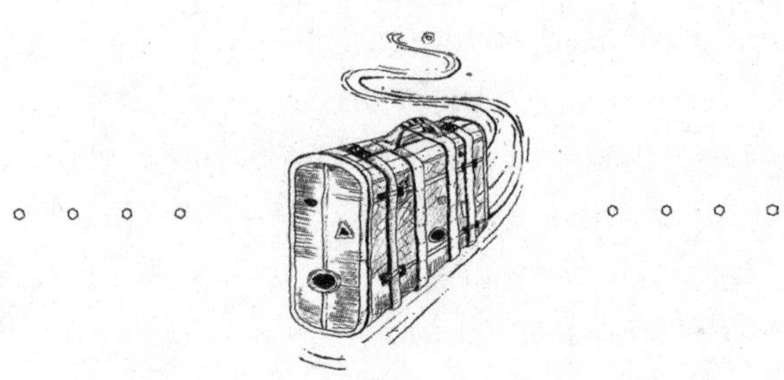

IVY'S window offered its first non-cloud view when it scraped up against a thick, stone wall covered in frosted lichen. She involuntarily let out a little shriek, which drew knowing glances from the other, more experienced riders around her.

"There now, Ivy," said Professor Royal, "just a little crash landing. That terrible Brood can't find us here."

The cabby careened onto the landing deck, screeching to a halt. The doors of the compartment popped open as if there was nothing unusual about crashing into the Suitcasery building that framed one side of the deck. There was a rustle as everyone stood to exit. Ivy pretended to know what she was doing and gathered her hairie lantern and Humboldt in his cage.

Stepping out into the cabby's dwindling storm, Ivy was surprised at the darkness. Certainly, they hadn't been in the cabby long enough for night to fall. Professor Royal whispered in her ear, "Always dark here, love. Usually cold, too. Part of the disguise."

But her surprise at the dark was quickly shifted over to shock at the stars. The *stars!* They were the brightest, largest stars she had ever seen. Her mouth was agape and even Humboldt seemed to be stunned. The stars seemed so low—actually beneath the layer of fog—that Ivy felt as if she could reach out and grab one. Meanwhile, Ivy had gone from being relatively warm to completely drenched and freezing again.

The cabby deck was elevated above the streets of Belzebuthe. Ivy went to the ledge, looked over, and was surprisingly charmed by what she could see down the way: Old world Gothic buildings with carefully wrought iron balconies squeezed in tight along cut-stone facades. Directly below, little pubs and cafés were tucked underneath dark apartments and row homes. Windows were long and narrow, with artful shapes and intersecting ornamental flourishes. Copper downspouts lined the edges of the buildings to drain off the moisture of the ever-present damp and frequent rains and snows.

Ivy rummaged through her pocket for the scrunched-up letter she had sat on for the past several hours. *418C Scattered Street, The Town.*

Her worry over finding Scattered Street was eclipsed by the growl from her stomach, brought on by a delicious scent that wafted over to her. Something sweet. Humboldt rattled in his cage, his small, scaly black-and-white face looking up at her. A little drool was collecting at the corner of his wide mouth.

"Hungry, too, Hum? I agree. Let's get a snack before we find out whatever's waiting for us at Scattered Street."

Ivy was grateful for the warmth emanating from Humboldt as she followed her nose. There was a little food cart across the cabby deck, as far from the beast's storm as possible. It was oval shaped and had three wheels at the bottom, a hitch for towing, and its smooth walls were painted a cheerful, rusty orange. The little white awning did its best to shield the cart owner from the cabby's rain. The cart was labeled Plumlie's Puddings & Stuff and seemed to be fairly popular.

Last in a line was a sqwinch holding a leather sack that was nearly bursting with reading material. Ivy stepped in line behind him and, after hesitating, finally tapped him on the shoulder.

"Excuse me?" she asked. The sqwinch turned around with an expression of curiosity. He was about Ivy's age and only a fraction taller. He had short, shiny black hair and dark, penetrating eyes. There was something about him Ivy liked almost instantly. He was vaguely familiar—a handsome second year at the Halls of Ivy? "Is the line always this long?"

"Plumlie's is the absolute best!"

But soon the stars took her attention again. He saw Ivy's eyes flit up to the sky.

"Enchanted stars," he pointed.

"Excuse me?"

"The cloud layer here is too thick for a normal star to shine through. The scrivenists here missed starlight—legendary inspiration, you know—and so they created these enchanted ones that hover just above."

"It's such a strange place, Belz—I mean, the Town."

"Don't worry. The name Belzebuthe isn't a secret when you're physically here or on the cabby. It's obvious everyone *here* knows its name. Not like at school." He paused, then launched in, "You're studying at the Halls of Ivy, aren't you? I recognized you immediately. Surprised to find that we were headed to the same place, but I was stuck on the other side of the cabby. Plus, it's a little intimidating after what happened with the Dark

Queen at the Ball. Everyone's talking about you: the girl who stood up to a queen. You don't even have a quill! Remarkable, really."

Ivy smiled, graciously accepting the compliment, though she still hadn't sorted out her own feelings about the Masquerade Ball. She felt a little undeserving of the attention, considering what had happened was hardly intentional.

"I was as surprised as you were." Surprise was too mild a word. Stunned at the result of a miracle was more like it. "Do you live here?"

"Around the corner." He sighed, "Not a lot of families live here full time, but when both your mom and pop are mentor scrivenists, it's kind of inevitable that you be born here. I haven't done much exploring beyond this fog. The Halls of Ivy are a breath of fresh air for me."

"I thought this was mostly a place for scrivenists to further their studies."

"Is that what you're doing here?" he asked pointedly.

"I actually can't explain what I'm doing here. Other than the fact that someone told me here is where I needed to be, and the cabby picked me up in the middle of the woods." She just didn't know how much was safe to share.

"Well, you're here now. I'm Glistle, by the way." He shot a dazzling grin at Ivy and she wondered if he was as conscious of his good looks as was Damaris Dodley.

"Next please," called the middle-aged man behind the counter.

"I'll have one box, please. The larger. Thanks!" Glistle dug deep in his pocket for three brums. Turning to Ivy, Glistle said, "They sell all sorts of puddings; however, I'm not a fan of anything too mushy. These candies, though," he offered Ivy a look, "they're called cracker hats: chocolate waffle cone on the outside, smooth chocolate cream on the inside. You ever try one?"

"No," Ivy replied bashfully, looking at the top-hat shaped confections, dusted with powdered sugar. The purple and silver box Glistle held had nine cracker hats all lined up in rows of three.

Wasting no time, Glistle unceremoniously popped one into his mouth.

"Delicious, but also a sly way for parents to correct bad behavior, accounting for the fortunes and warnings inside. My parents used to give me one every night. Things like, *Touch a quill that isn't yours and your fingers will blister up.* There are worse ones. *If you speak the word Belzebuthe, your tongue will turn black. If you speak of a cabby outside Belzebuthe, your brain will go all foggy on you.* But I'm old enough to know these things are full of fudge and the warnings are pretty useless. Do you want to try one?" He held out the cracker hat with the popped lid.

"How can I not after that description?"

Ivy bit into the treat: its crunchy, slightly salty crust gave way to a deliciously fudgy center. Then she peered into the box, right where her cracker hat had been, and read her message: *If you leave Belzebuthe, the Dark Queen will hunt you.* Ivy gasped in fear and almost choked on her bite. She gave the rest of the snack to Humboldt, who happily chomped it down.

"Calm down, there. You scared? It's only supposed to work on children. I've seen this one before." He recited his message with a mouthful, *"Your future quill will disown you if you share Belzebuthe's secrets."*

"They're terrible," Ivy muttered.

"We'll have to argue that point another time. I've got to run." Glistle threw another treat down to Humboldt and squashed the rest of the box into his bag. "My dad's leaving town for a bit, and I want to catch him before he goes. Maybe I'll see you around?" This last bit was shouted over his shoulder as he dashed off into the crowd.

The vendor at the Plumlie's cart peered at Ivy and said, "Well?"

"Um, no, thank you. Sorry," Ivy apologized as she backed away. She looked around for Professor Royal but had lost track of her.

Then there was a whirring noise; Ivy spun around and saw luggage flying from the rooftops of the cabby's carriages. Each satchel and suitcase hooked itself onto a thick cable that was reeling quickly away from the cabby over the passenger's heads and through a door in a wall—the exit, on the very same wall they had crashed into in their landing. The whirring grew louder as the belt picked up speed, whipping along belongings, Ivy's satchel included.

"My—my things!" Ivy yelped.

The thought of losing her Compass Collectis and Compass Startus—the books that catalogued everything known in the scrivenist world and held all her learning, respectively—sent Ivy into a panic. As far as she knew, these were her only remaining ties to the Halls of Ivy, the only way she'd be able to develop her abilities while she wasn't welcome at the Halls.

"Excuse me!" Ivy pushed past the line that was queuing up at the exit. Toting the scaldron habbitry and hairie lantern made for awkward progress. People meandered underneath the cable with the bags moving quickly overhead. "Pardon!"

She ran, cutting the line, and saw that once inside the Suitcasery building the people were moving calmly downstairs but the baggage made a sharp right, down a hallway. Cords and cables snapped and pulled like so many whips and tethers near the ceiling. Dozens of suitcases, satchels, and bundles of apothecary jars rolled and tumbled precariously along. Afraid to put Humboldt and the hairies down—she wasn't going to make the same mistake twice—Ivy ran after the luggage. Humboldt squawked and squealed; clearly, he was enjoying himself. He loved a good chase.

At the top of the seventh floor, the conveyor belt ran into a copper gutter, which ran along the atrium's interior wall and disappeared through a hole in the wall. At that moment a large black trunk was jammed into the hole, blocking the others. With a scrape from the trunk and a groan from the cable, the bag made it through.

She dashed to the door next to the hole. *What is this madness?* she asked herself, but before she could answer she was standing inside a living room. A small family of scrivenists was having dinner at their table. Oddly, they hardly seemed surprised to see a panting stranger holding a scaldron in a habbitry burst into their home.

"That way," the mother pointed with a sigh.

"So sorry, please excuse me! Do enjoy your dinner!"

Ivy chased the luggage train down a tiny narrow hall and out the back of the apartment, onto the fire escape, down a floor, and into the next apartment.

"Please don't be another family eating," Ivy whispered in embarrassment before pushing the door open.

It wasn't a dinner scene, but it was a dark bedroom where a tiny old man was snoring terribly loudly. Ivy crept by the bed that nearly filled the room as quietly as possible. Tiptoeing into the hallway, she saw that the conveyor belt was funneling into a giant, vertical silver pipe.

"No—no—no!" she lurched to grab her satchel, but it was already down the chute. "Rats!"

Ivy ran down the public stairwell, keeping her eye on the thick silver pipe running down the center. The tube vibrated with magic, shimmering and even activating the stone in her pocket. Humboldt continued to squawk every time the cage bounced off her bruised legs.

Rounding a corner, she bumped into a scrivenist making her way to her room. "Not again!" the exasperated woman hollered. "This is the third one this week! These baggage chasers are as thick as stew."

"Sorry!" Ivy shouted over her shoulder.

At the bottom of the atrium, the luggage was spat from the pipe's trumpeted end and caught some sort of pulley system. All sorts of luggage were hanging on to the moving contraption like a pot rack that extended the length of the corridor and out the back.

Gasping for breath, Ivy ran and pushed out the door. In the alley between the buildings, she looked up to find all the cabby's luggage, gently rotating within arm's reach on something that looked suspiciously like a laundry line.

"Hello again," said Glistle. "Was beginning to wonder where you'd gone."

There it was! Her worn, brown leather satchel, wedged in between a set of magenta luggage that had at least six pieces. Ivy looked around, mouth agape. Every scrivenist who had traveled in Ivy's compartment was here, as well as those from the other compartments. They had merely walked calmly through the queue as she was meant to. Each stared at her with varying looks of amusement, disinterest, sympathy, or superiority. Glistle grabbed his trunk and a small velvet pouch and he was off with a wave.

"Sorry, dear," said Professor Royal, who had appeared alongside her, in a low voice. "I thought you knew about the Suitcasery's system, seeing as how you had your satchel stowed."

"Well, I know about it now," Ivy sighed, trying to catch her breath. "What is it all about? Why can't they just hand us our bags on the deck?"

"For safety, of course," Professor Royal said, a tad disbelieving that Ivy could be so naïve. "You really don't know much about Belzebuthe, do you? This is the last safe place for scrivenists to fully practice their art. Magic without the watchful gaze of those who might feel threatened by it."

"So, what does that have to do with my bag?"

"The system of spelled pulleys, chutes, and pipes disables any tracking spells and identifies and eliminates curses. That way, only safe people can find the Town."

Everything in her satchel was perfectly fine, despite the wild ride on the conveyor belt, to say nothing of the stormy cabby journey. Her Compass Collectis was in order, and so were the books by Derwin Edgar Night, the very ones that she had pondered over nearly a year ago when Rimbrick the dwarf gave them to her in this satchel. The cabby riders gathered their luggage and set off on their business in the starlit twilight.

"Um, Professor Royal?" Ivy asked, right as she was about

to leave. "Is it—what time is it?"

"Just before dinner." Then, seeing Ivy's confusion, she kindly said, "It's tough to tell the time in Belzebuthe without a timepiece! You might pick yourself up one from Counter Clockwise. Can I help you get somewhere?"

"No, but if you could point me in the direction of Scattered Street, I'd appreciate it."

"To the left, three blocks down. Can I walk you?"

Despite Professor Royal's kindness, Ivy couldn't bring herself to accept. "No, thanks. I've got it from here. Enjoy your visit!"

"You do the same, dear."

Ivy found that her eyes had adjusted to the dimness of Belzebuthe and the low light was actually quite beautiful. Everything was bathed in a silvery glow that highlighted the elaborate brick and stonework on the buildings, even casting shadows. She had to tell herself not to reach up for the stars—they hung so low! But she was trying to not make a bigger fool of herself than absolutely necessary.

Her outfit had been just right earlier this morning for a summer day at the Halls, but certainly not for Belzebuthe's completely different weather system: A light snow was now falling. The Town was awash with scrivenists in their tightly buttoned jackets, quills twitching. Her light slippers were clearly not as up for the weather as the thick combat boots laced on every other person she saw, and she was more than a little self-conscious.

Everyone looks happy to be home, she thought. Though she was glad to have made it to the very place Derwin said was safe for her, she didn't know what she was doing. If she had ended up here a year ago, the now-familiar, distinct sensation of being different would have crumpled her self-confidence. Now, it was tough, but she remembered Winsome Monocle's guidance: *Different, yes, but different for good reason.* She straightened her spine and blinked back tears. Winsome had been her best teacher and, as she found out near the end of last year, her own family's scrivenist.

To her right, residences were squeezed in tightly together. The steeply pitched rooftops were slick with snow and rain, but that didn't deter the dozens of cats that stared down at passersby like gargoyles. There was a shopping district, and Ivy could tell that the magic contained on that one street would make all the shops in Ravenshollow pale in comparison.

The people were surprising. Umbrellas floated and trailed their owners like airborne pets without leashes, protecting them from the drizzle. Above each storefront was a giant, multifaceted hairie lamp. *The hairies are so much more active and beautiful than those in Ravenshollow!* Perhaps it was because this town needed the light even more. Or maybe it was because these hairies seemed to be even more luminescent. She spun in a slow circle, admiring the beauty of the place. Once on Scattered Street, Ivy counted off the building numbers as she went. *I've got to be close.*

And then finally, there she was: number 418. A hairie lantern illuminated the stairway that led up to the tall, narrow brick building's double door. Little snow flurries gathered on the two juniper bushes that rose out of pots to frame the door. She climbed to the entrance and pushed in. Inside, four narrow apartment doors were labeled A through D.

Ivy twiddled Derwin's letter in her hands nervously as she

caught her breath in front of the door with 418C on it.

"This is it," she spoke softly to Humboldt and her hairies, setting them down.

Ivy gave the door a knock. But second thoughts overwhelmed her. She turned, grabbed her critters and started to stumble back out the door, letting her anxieties carry her away.

But, with a loud creak, the door opened and a surprised voice called out.

Chapter Four

Fyn's Place

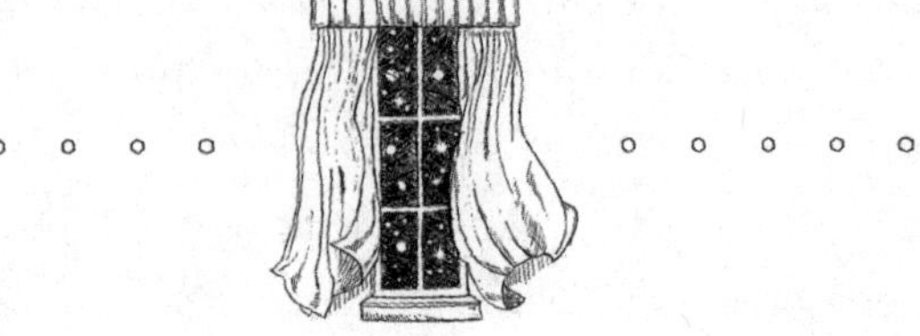

THAT voice. Ivy had recognized it immediately—cheerful and strong. Even with its now very shocked tone. A flush crept over her usually pale cheeks. She held her breath as she turned, and, there in the doorway stood Fyn Greeley. Fyn gazed at Ivy like she had three heads. His tall frame was only a head shorter than the door. He pushed back his brown, shaggy hair in surprise, accidentally dropping a velvet pouch embroidered with the letters QQC. Ivy's eyes were arrested by the strange feathers inside.

"Ivy! I didn't expect—what are you? I mean, hi! Hello!"

Ivy bent to pick up the pouch, but Fyn got there first.

"I got it, thanks."

Ivy was still reeling with surprise. She peeked past Fyn at the dark brown, mahogany wraparound stairwell leading to upper floors. The tall, narrow window opposite the front door was draped by thick navy curtains, revealing a sky full of stars. It was evident that Fyn himself had barely been home for minutes, just long enough to answer the door. Had he been in a different cabby compartment? The camel-colored leather of his Compass Collectis was easy to spot amongst the clutter that lay pushed up against the foyer wall. The foyer was clad in a dark wood—what little wall space existed was a dark yellow. Perhaps it had been wallpaper, but it was aged beyond recognition now. Rather than feeling off-putting, the overall effect was warm and comfortable, if a little disorderly.

Fyn cleared his throat. "What—what are you doing here anyway?" he asked with a cocked head and a half smile.

"Oh, I—uh… well…." Ivy glanced down at the wrinkled letter clenched in her hand, the hand that wasn't holding Humboldt, wondering the same. She double-checked the address listed and placed Humboldt's cage on the floor beside her hairies.

"This letter—" Ivy started to say, but her vision started to go a little hazy at the edges. "From Derwin…."

Fyn's voice came through the fog and said, "Forgive me! I haven't even invited you in. Just so surprised to see you, that's all." He ushered her in, bringing in Humboldt and opening his habbitry door.

Ivy felt like her legs were made of Plumlie's puddings. The day's excitement, on top of sleep deprivation and not knowing anything about what she should be doing, was catching up to her.

"Are you all right?" Fyn asked, steadying her shoulder.

"I—it's been a long couple of days. Not enough sleep, I guess."

"It's warmer at the hearth. You could do with a change of clothes, too. It's a bit wet on the cabby deck."

Fyn grunted as he hefted a heavy housecoat from the hall closet. "Here. It's mother's and will beat out Croswald's coldest day."

The housecoat swallowed Ivy whole. She learned two things from trying it on: Fyn was thoughtful and his mother was about the size of a shorehorse. That, or she loved oversized sweaters as much as Ivy did.

"Ahhh… warm. Thanks."

"No problem."

Fyn rolled back doors to reveal a rustic dining room with a farm table of raw wood adorned with a hand-stitched runner. Around it stood mismatched dining chairs. One wall was made up entirely of cabinetry: from tiny, box drawers at the bottom to open shelving showing chipped china.

"You hungry for anything?"

"Starved."

"Have a seat. Please. Get comfortable."

Ivy sat in the corner chair with a view of the kitchen. In the kitchen beyond the dining room, the ceiling dropped again. This tiny room was a riot of dishes, spices, and vials of every ingredient imaginable. A clump of dough was kneading itself in the corner. Fyn grabbed a plate of muffins and brought it out to Ivy. They ate while catching up.

"So, what really brought you to Belzebuthe? To my place? Though it's great to see you."

"Really, I had no idea you lived here. After the Ball, Derwin told me that the Halls were no longer safe for me. Then he left me this note." Ivy passed it over to him shrugging.

"Huh, look at that. You've got the right address. The real question is why did Derwin send you here?"

"I haven't a clue. But, long story short, I didn't go home with Rebecca. I caught a cabby, even though it felt like it caught me. So, here I am." She paused. "Wait. Were we just on the same cabby?"

"Most likely, but probably different compartments. The cabbies are always pretty full at the end of term. Oh wait, I'll bet it was you that we picked up right after we smashed that cottage?"

"Yes! And I assume people in the know don't have to chase after the cabby to catch it? What's the secret?"

"Well, people from here know to pick up a cabby on the roof at the Halls of Ivy. You just have to use your return ticket—it calls the cabby straight away."

Ivy burst out laughing, "A return ticket sounds amazing, a lot easier than chasing a storm."

Fyn grinned. "We'll make sure you get one next time."

"It's funny how I was supposed to be spending the summer moons with Rebecca and here I am with you. Wait until she hears."

"Spending the summer with me, are you? Peachy."

Ivy felt immediately embarrassed for having invited herself to stay at Fyn's place. How quickly she had assumed she'd be spending the rest of her time here.

"You need a place to stay. Admit it."

"Well...."

"You just did." Fyn smiled. "We have an extra bedroom upstairs. Of course, if you don't want to or if you have another place to stay...."

"Here would be great," she agreed timidly, brushing aside her hair. "Thank you."

"It's just me and Ma. You'll meet her in a bit when she gets back from work."

"What does she do?"

"She works at the Quill Keep. She's a historian studying really interesting quills that don't do anything anymore. Quills from banned scrivenists."

"On the cabby ride, I read about a break-in at the Quill Keep. Could that be true?"

"Wish I had been sitting next to someone with a copy of *Scriven This!* I only found out about it when I got back. I went straight to the Keep, but the mattelers were interviewing Ma. Fortunately, only one quill was taken. A big, bad quill."

"Do they have any idea at all who might have done such a thing?"

"More like *what* could have done such a thing. Weird stuff for Belzebuthe."

The two finished their meal in silence.

"Let's take your stuff up," Fyn said while carrying the plate back to the kitchen.

Ivy only nodded, feeling a combination of nervousness and fatigue welling up inside her. The narrow mahogany stairway twisted around, leading upstairs to the bedrooms. Ivy counted four narrow floors, only two rooms wide each, and the attic room was for Ivy. Fyn pushed it open.

The faded gold wallpaper was a beautiful damask pattern, and there was a miniature fireplace where Humboldt immediately made himself comfortable. A diminutive four-poster bed was nestled along one wall. It was a small, cluttered space, charming but little used. Except for a polished trail that led straight to the small, arched dormer, a thin film of dust had deposited itself upon papers and potion bottles, journals and sketchbooks. One volume, *The Crownerie: Employment Handbook*, was etched with images of stones on the spine.

"It's not much, but—"

"It's perfect. Thank you."

Ivy set the hairies down on the window ledge, and Fyn put her satchel on the end of the bed.

"Used to be my father's office. These were my father's things. Ma has a hard time looking at them anymore. Hope you don't mind the clutter."

"It's perfectly fine. Everything's lovely." Ivy looked downward as she fought for courage to ask about Fyn's father. "What happened to your dad, Fyn?"

"He went out one night and never came back. Don't know much other than that."

Ivy could sense that Fyn didn't feel up to talking about it. "I'm sorry."

"Things are okay. I was pretty young. Just wish I knew him better, that's all."

Their tender moment was interrupted by the unmistakable crash of glass coming from below. Fyn dashed out and looked down the stairwell.

"What was *that*? Your mother coming home already?" Ivy said hopefully.

"If Ma were home, she wouldn't be coming through a window, would she?"

Ivy felt panic rise up in her breast. Fyn whipped out a quill from his pocket.

"Where did you get that? You can't, I mean, you don't—"

Fyn shushed her, holding the quill close to his chest like his life depended on it. Fyn glanced at Ivy and quickly tried to shake off the fear he clearly felt, steeling his jaw.

"I knew I saw feathers in that bag. Quills!"

Fyn lightly flitted the quill, trying to get a feel for it. Then with a whip, he got the tip of the feather to spark and he smiled with exhilaration.

"Are you kidding me? You don't even know how to work it? Now is not the time for games, Fyn," Ivy hissed, following Fyn as he crept down the stairs, which narrowed at every turn.

"What? I just picked it up. Haven't had time to properly acquaint myself."

Fyn's swishes were getting bolder and bolder when he began to feel a tingle travel up his arm. The tingle quickly gave way to a blistering-hot sensation, as if he were picking a pan out of a scaldron's mouth without a glove. Instantly, he let go. A whoosh of lavender light pulsed from the dropped quill and the staircase they stood on shook. The two gripped onto the handrail. Ivy shrieked. They both watched the quill jiggle down the steps out of reach.

Fyn whipped out another quill stored in his pocket, accidentally sliding down a few steps as he did.

"Another one?" Ivy was flummoxed. "What's with all the quills, Fyn?"

"Long story, but I've got a quiver full!"

Fyn spotted the edge of a shadow moving swiftly across the downstairs hall. With another swish of the new yellow-feathered tool, the apartment shook like there was an earthquake underway. Fyn fought to climb down the wriggling staircase steadily, his tripping over steps and bumping into walls adding to the ruckus. There was a snap, and the hairies dimmed as if covered and then brightened back up.

"Enough with the quills," Ivy shouted. "Clearly, it's not helping."

"It's new, don't know whose it was—might have been helpful had I read its geer!" Fyn was struggling to unwrap the parchment that wound around the base of the next quill.

"Its what?"

"Information about its past owner—tell ya later!"

It wasn't only the walls that were jumping. The stone seemed set on leaping from her pocket. Ivy clenched it tightly, using all her might. Then she remembered something that Winsome had taught her in the potions lab: "Spells made with frowns go upside down, Ivy!" She made a conscious effort to relax the muscles in her face and body, keeping only her right hand clasped around the stone. Slowly, with the pace of her even breathing, the stone stilled itself. When she opened her eyes, the stairs had, too.

They had reached the bottom of the stairs where they found the broken window in the dining room; just then they heard a racket back up the stairs.

"How'd they get upstairs so quickly?" Ivy shouted. "Without our seeing?"

Fyn raced back up into his father's office with Ivy not far behind. The office was a mess. There was a slam and whoosh—they had just missed someone dashing out the window, knocking over and breaking the hairie lantern on the way out. Fyn raced to the window, but it slammed in his face.

Whoever it was had spelled the window shut.

Chapter Five

The Gracious Greeleys

THROUGH a cloud of dark smoke, the Dark Queen rose over Ivy with a dagger raised above her head. A terrible mist enclosed just the two of them. Then there was a terrible cracking noise as if the world were being split in two.

Ivy jumped from her bed, the sheets sticking to her sweat. She was ready to defend her life and looked about wild-eyed. But as she blinked, she realized there was no Dark Queen to contend with. Just Humboldt, looking a little sheepish. He had apparently knocked over a trunk full of old books, trinkets, and parlor games—ones Fyn had likely played with his father.

One apothecary jar had spilled, and familiar tiny, tinny voices were now rattling around the bottom of the trunk. "Why, I oughta punch you right in the nose, you big dummy!"

"Spoken word spells. Very funny, Hum." Ivy was relieved to be awake—nothing was worse than that terrible dream, not even the grumpy words that the grouchy spoken word spells slung at her and her dragon. Humboldt had backed into a corner with his tail curled around himself protectively. His pale-yellow eyes flicked back and forth. If it were possible, his black-and-white harlequin spots would have faded.

"Poor thing. You're frightened."

Without even thinking about it, Ivy calmed Humboldt by reaching out to him. Magic naturally slipped from her fingers to him, and he instantly softened and relaxed, faster even than if she had been able to hold him!

Ivy hadn't practiced any of her natural magic since leaving the Halls, in part because she had just been too busy getting to Belzebuthe, but also because the last time she had summoned her magic, in the ballroom, too much had happened. Yes, she had pushed the Dark Queen off for another day, but Ivy was the first to admit that she still had no control over the magic that coursed through her veins.

And yet, here it was again. Her magic. Popping its head into her life without permission, all on its own. Humboldt was now snoring again by the hearth. Ivy sank back into bed, letting her hands delicately dance with each other overhead. Little swirls of white light circled. She pulled the broken apothecary jar up, fragments and spells and all. The books and games joined next. The fragments danced above her, and the small pockets of air eventually stopped grumbling. Ivy took a breath and envisioned the bottle whole again, and it became so with an extra glow of light. Ivy actually laughed out loud. One by one, the little voices were tucked back into the jar, still bobbing along gently overhead. It was… rejuvenating. The act of magic soothed her like a meditation. The bottle, books, and games all settled back into place.

"They were my father's favorite," said a voice so suddenly it startled Ivy, who sat up with a jerk. With a grin, Fyn added, "They always made him laugh."

Ivy didn't know what to say.

"Sorry to surprise you. Heard a terrible thump and came up to check. Door was open." He paused. "How are you feeling this morning?"

"Much better. I desperately needed a good night's sleep, I guess."

"Happy you got it." Then he paused and said, "You're good at magic, you know. It's good you practice."

Ivy sighed, "I'm just afraid of screwing things up, that's all. Causing a mess. Attracting attention. You know, everything I hate."

"Remember the book flying incident?" Fyn smiled. "Anyway, you worry too much about what people think."

"Why do you say that?"

"You'll only be as good as you allow yourself to be. If everyone were afraid to showcase their magical abilities, it would be one boring world, that's for sure!"

Ivy pushed the curtain all the way open with a wave of her hand. She looked away, toward the window, and saw with some surprise that little snow flurries were coming down.

"Weather's been real weird lately. I can't remember it snowing this much at the start of summer." Fyn marveled.

A damp wind whistled around the windowpane. Before she let the curtains fall back, Ivy saw through the flurries a heavy black cloud resting on the horizon.

"Oh! Any word on the intruder, Fyn? Did the mattelers have any idea who it was?"

"They got away. No trace."

"I'm so sorry. I can't believe I slept through the investigation! I should have been helping!"

Fyn shook his head and held up both hands, refusing to allow Ivy any regret. "Ma wants to meet you officially. She's downstairs in the kitchen preparing breakfast."

"Oh, yes, I'd love to meet your mother. I'll be down soon."

Fyn smiled and then closed the bedroom door. Ivy splashed water from the basin on her face, threw her dress on, and went down. She was surprised to find the dining room festively decorated for a party.

Mrs. Greeley was busy pulling something delicious from the scaldron, but cried out, "Ivy! Welcome. I trust you slept well."

Fyn's mother was lovely—her salt-and-pepper hair fell in waves around her shoulders. Her kind eyes were green like Fyn's but framed by soft lines that betrayed her having been through hard times and sadness.

"Pleased to meet you, ma'am," Ivy smiled. "I slept very well. Thank you so much for opening your home to me and allowing me to stay."

"Of course! Hope you don't mind the state of things. All a mess!"

Wisteria Greeley was now icing a cake: She emblazoned *Happy Birthday* in frosting with her quill and set 19 bright blue candles upon it, not yet lit.

Ivy turned to Fyn and asked, "Is it your birthday, Fyn? You never said!"

"Modest boy, I have!" interjected Mrs. Greeley.

Fyn tore into a blueberry muffin. "Mmm, my favorite, Ma!"

"Ha! Everything is your favorite. Do you have a favorite birthday food, Ivy?" Mrs. Greeley asked conversationally. "When is your special day?"

"Oh, well, I—I share my birthday with Moonsday, I suppose."

"Moonsday?" Her face showed surprise. "Plenty of favorites to pick from then. No other feast in the land compares to Moonsday," she laughed. "It's a shame we have to wait till the end of summer."

Ivy was grateful to be kept busy with her mouth full of warm muffin. It was too much to explain she had seen and prepared many Moonsday feasts but had only ever participated in one.

Mrs. Greeley sat, bringing the morning paper with her. Taking in a deep breath, she shook her head as she read, "'The Quill Keep Break-In Continues to Flummox'! No wonder the mattelers haven't had time to think much about ours, especially seeing as nothing was taken! Are you sure it wasn't one of your friends, Fyn? Just playing a practical joke, perhaps?"

"Maybe it was you? You're the connection between both places, Ma," Fyn teased.

"Oh hush! Home and work both a mess is enough for me to deal with, without my son's bad jokes." She rolled her eyes.

Fyn mused, "It's all so strange. Nothing taken from here, only that one window broken. One of the matteler's spellseekers said they smelled something rank up in here. Sour fruit and pond water."

"Sour fruit and pond water? So precise," remarked Ivy.

Fyn turned to his mother. "Still only one quill missing from the Keep?"

"Yes, just the one. Debnick's. Not much for you two to worry about, dears. The orbis hunts only queenly blood."

Ivy stuffed the rest of her muffin in her mouth to quiet a shriek.

"Is the quill still here? Still in Belzebuthe?" asked Fyn.

"Let's hope so. The mattelers are searching every nook and cranny, following every clue." Mrs. Greeley paused thoughtfully. "Never in my twenty-five years at the Keep have I seen or heard anything like it. I was just preserving the records for Debnick's quill the other day—such an interesting character."

It was the second time Ivy had heard the name of the quill's owner, and now hearing Debnick rang a bell for Ivy.

"He lived about two hundred years ago, so the records were in desperate need of upkeep. The last scrivenist to the last heir apparent to the throne. Before the Dark Queen began her rule so suddenly. He had been such a prominent proponent of magical control. And then after Princess Isabella died, apparently, he went on a creative rampage. Not just any scrivenist can create creatures out of thin air, but suddenly he could. Very strange. And then, after the orbis, his ethics were called into question. But before the tribunal, he turned tome. It was decided that his quill should be turned over to the Keep for safety purposes."

"So, wouldn't it be safer just to destroy quills like that?" Ivy was mystified.

"Mattelers investigate the quills in their holding cells later, trying to extract whatever curse patterns or formulas they can."

"Holding cells? Like a jail?"

Mrs. Greeley laughed, "I suppose that's one way to look at it. Really, they look more like aquariums. You can see them flit about in the water, lit by their own magic. That is, if you ever get to see them. Security is quite tight. There are only a few ways to get in, and we were just talking about eliminating even those."

"Oh, with Mr. Leelangraf?" Fyn asked.

Mrs. Greeley nodded, then addressed Ivy, "One of my duties is to observe the quills, take note of their movements and magic. I never imagined something like this could happen!" Her brow furrowed with worry. "And then the house!"

"Let me get you a tea, Ma." He squeezed her shoulders as he went by to the kettle.

"So, Ivy... Fyn tells me you're from school, but nothing else. Why the summer in Belzebuthe? I know you're not from here—I know everybody. Where do your parents live? Won't they miss you this summer?"

Ivy could see Fyn straighten up, even from the back, as if he was concerned about bringing up a touchy, complicated subject.

"Mother, that's not nec—"

"It's fine, Fyn," said Ivy. "I, I actually never met my parents."

"Never met your parents? How terrible! An orphan born on Moonsday." Ivy could see that Mrs. Greeley was beginning to connect pieces of information.

"Yes, well," Ivy paused for a moment, because for the first time ever she knew why she was an orphan. "They died in a carriage accident."

"I'm so terribly sorry, dear. It's awful to lose someone close," her green eyes welled with empathy, "and I can't imagine losing someone you never knew. But perhaps I'm upsetting you. A change of subject is in order."

"I think so," acknowledged Fyn, as if protecting both

mother and friend.

"Let me tell you kids something. The fact that Daryl Debnick's quill is missing is not to be taken lightly. If I know my son, he's probably planning on taking you to the Quogo scrimmage next moon. Fyn, I'll not have you at any Quogo match until that quill is recovered. Do you understand?"

"But Ma!" Fyn protested, pushing back his chair.

"It's not safe! Do you understand the purpose of my work? The purpose of the Quill Keep? Such quills are incredibly dangerous, unreliable, and erratic. The integrity of their shafts is damaged by their owners' corruption. This quill is so old, we hardly even know the havoc it could cause."

"What exactly is so dangerous about Daryl Debnick?" inquired Ivy.

Mrs. Greeley looked intently at Ivy. "He was the single scrivenist who witnessed Princess Isabella's death, the only one to see what escaped the glanagerie bottle, what killed Princess Isabella. He never really disclosed in full detail what he saw."

Ivy and Fyn exchanged a wide-eyed look. No one knew that they had heard this story at the Hollow Shaft, from Daryl's own tome, but Mrs. Greeley was confirming it all.

"And then he just began serving the Dark Queen, helping her solidify her position in those early years. But his powers of creation were extremely suspicious. And then when his orbis turned rogue and began hunting down those in the queenly line, the Society of Scrivenists began to suspect him of more than just being witness to Princess Isabella's death. That and his full-on support of the Dark Queen's rule… it just didn't seem right, all those years ago. Still doesn't now. Especially with those Cloaked Brood being descendants of the first orbis."

"What?"

"Another scrivenist gone bad, Agatha Mudderflog, I think, modified the orbis for use as guards for the Dark Queen. Terrible stuff. Many years ago, before we knew how bad it would get."

"Ma, do you honestly think scaring the wits out of our guest is a bright idea?"

"If it keeps you away from Quogo, then certainly! Anyway, I've got to go to work!"

"Should be an interesting day!" Fyn remarked.

"But I'll be back early to finish preparing for your party, Fyn. Ivy, of course, I'm so glad that you'll be here with us to celebrate! Five o'clock sharp 'til whenever the neighbors tell us to hush."

Fyn groaned, "Except you've probably invited all of the neighbors."

"Don't be a stink, Fyn! Of course I did. When you are grown and throw your own parties, you can make the guest list."

"As long as the QQC is here, I'm happy."

"You certainly love that Quogo fan club, don't you? One last thing, one little gift now, more later. Happy birthday, son!" said Mrs. Greeley, who placed a square, brown-paper-wrapped package in front of Fyn. No ribbon. Fyn looked at Ivy nervously, just hoping it wasn't like the lime-green, frog-printed underpants he had received the year before.

"I figured you could play this with your friends while you take a break from the real thing." It was *Quogo: The Card Game.*

"Oh no!" cried Fyn. "Love you, but this is not the same as getting to go to a real game. Thank you? I guess?"

Mrs. Greeley laughed, gathered her things, and swept out the door and down the street.

Fyn turned to Ivy and said, “You *are* going to a Quogo match while you are here.”

“I mean, if it’s unavoidable, I suppose I can check it out.”

“I know that tone.”

“What?” Ivy smiled.

“Nothing. Nothing at all. Here,” he shoved the card game into Ivy’s hands. “Take this. I certainly don’t need help with my Quogo strategy, but you will.”

For the second time that morning, the game was foisted upon someone who didn’t want it.

“But leave it here for now. Let me show you Belzebuthe!”

Chapter Six

The Tour of All Tours

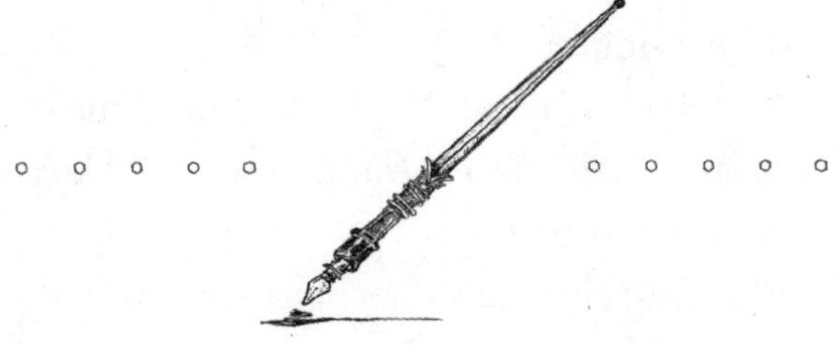

IVY was having some trouble following Fyn's lead, buried as she was in layers of Mrs. Greeley's winter coats. Fyn glanced back and had another good laugh at Ivy's waddle.

"You'll get used to the weather in a bit. Shed some layers," he said, cracking his award-winning grin at Ivy.

The dressmakers and pie shops and taverns gave way to more magical stores, and they glistened like glitter beneath the summer frost. In this part of town, strange tiles adorned the facades of the buildings and windows had tiny panes in intricate shapes. Ivy was torn between the desire to peer into every window and the desire to eavesdrop on the street. She had never been around so many scrivenists, and what they spoke of was fascinating and mysterious. With every conversation under floating umbrellas, Ivy could hear words she didn't know and it set her mind spinning. *What is a quillusion, anyway? What is warthog hair good for?*

Another thing Ivy had to tear her eyes away from, so she didn't walk straight into something or someone, was Belzebuthe's sky. The thick collar on one of her coats blocked her vision to the sides, but she could still set her eyes upon the stars again and again. So beautiful, she wanted to sketch it for hours. The stars were like airborne halos, and the sight immediately brought on a good mood. The coolness in the air was refreshing against her skin.

Then there was something darting in and out of the clouds, veering around under the stars. Something with wheels, something too small to be a cabby. A scraping noise sounded behind them, and Fyn and Ivy turned to see a second silhouette fly out a high-up open window, taking with it a few roof tiles.

"What is that?" Ivy pointed to the flying contraption, something like a giant tricycle—except with four wheels: two large in the back, two small in the front—with a large glass visor over the front.

Fyn looked up and let out a little laugh at Ivy's surprise. "That's a starguster. One of these days we'll ride one. They're unbeatable for a close-up view of the stars. Low flyers, obviously—got to stay under the shield so they won't take you to the moon," he grinned wryly. "It's not cheap to rent one. Later I'll show you another way to see the stars."

The starguster's silhouette hovered past, quickly disappearing higher up into the snow flurries. Ivy made a note to go back and visit the Star Shoppe later. The shop's display was as inky as the sky and had a pint-sized starguster floating midair as if taking off to join the other. Sparkling pinpricks of light floated in the window, mimicking the stars.

"It's rarely open, but worth a visit," Fyn said, following Ivy's gaze.

Fyn was already leading them on, pointing to the shop next door. "And this, this is where my dream summer job would be. The famous Plumes and Fumes, where a scrivenist goes to acquire a quill. The only comparable shop is the Crownerie, where royals are granted crowns in Ravenshollow."

The corner shop had an enormous window that wrapped around both sides of the building with the door at the corner. The burgundy window was full of multicolored quills that danced midair, making magic happen for the sheer joy of it. Beyond the quills hovering in the window, a young red-headed scrivenist in brand new scrivenist gear was scouring the shelves full of quills in inkwells, making the most anticipated decision of her life.

"How will she know which one to pick?" Ivy asked.

"They say you just know. It's like picking a pet from a litter—there's just a lifelong bond that you can sense."

Ivy nodded thoughtfully, thinking about Humboldt, her little dragon rescue, then said, "Fyn, do you ever wonder what your quill will be like? You'll graduate next year. I imagine you're getting antsy."

"Antsy is too calm a word. But yes, I think about it all the time! I think I'm going to have a terrible time focusing on my studies next year. I just want to know what *kind* of scrivenist I'll be! When I was young, I thought I'd be a gemologist like my father, but I just don't have an aptitude for stones… barely made it through Stones and Sorcery. So I don't know. Royal scrivenist? A great honor, but not really me. Quill fabricator? I only hope my quill won't end up in the Keep one day," Fyn teased. "Until then, I'll be working and dying of boredom over there, across the street."

"What's there?"

Across the street stood the narrowest shop Ivy had ever seen. She could easily have touched both sides at once. For a sign, a large tote hung above the door with *Luggage, All Sorts* emblazoned on it. They walked over to the window.

"Bags. Every kind. But just *bags*." He rolled his eyes, "Scalloped quivers for quills, embroidered satchels, large trunks, leather sacks, yada yada. I spend my time in the back, embossing and engraving scrivenists' initials on their luggage. Yep, I'm the guy that does that!" He feigned a thrill.

There was a small wooden desk with tools on it, and then behind was a wall made up of varied trunks and suitcases, like a brown and black and rust quilt.

"It was my father's first job, too, before working at the Crownerie."

Fyn got quiet for the first time since they began their journey in Belzebuthe. Ivy put a hand on his arm. She knew what it felt like to be without a father. He nodded at Ivy, grateful for her touch, but he soon brushed it off and redirected their tour.

"I could get used to your hometown. It really is an enchanting place, Fyn."

"Enchanted and enchanting."

"Exactly the opposite of how I grew up." They both chuckled.

Despite the twilight, Ivy knew it to be noon because her tummy was grumbling louder than a spoken word spell.

"How about lunch?" Ivy suggested.

"It wouldn't be a proper tour without introducing you to Belzebuthe's lunch hotspot: most delicious sandwiches in all of Croswald. Even professors order delivery via mendlott to the Halls. They're that good!"

They soon ducked in through a narrow door with a worn

wooden sign that read, *Bramble's Fritters & Nosh.* The tiny door opened into a large dining hall at least two stories high, with a coved ceiling covered in alabaster plaster. A giant fire twice the width of Ivy's spread arms roared away, cooking up delicious bread in clay pots. The air was warm and dry. The aroma of candied bacon lingered. Candles dripped wax from several heavy wrought-iron chandeliers, lighting the place with a convivial glow. They flickered and cast shadows across the arched ceiling. Drink sloshed out of metal cups that were slammed down on the communal farm tables in between enthusiastic bites.

Ivy's eyes glowed as she looked around—what fun to be eating in a crowd like this! Fyn tossed the server a few brums, and moments later a platter was dropped with a clatter in front of them. It held two small piping hot rolls stuffed with roasted vegetables, thick-cut bacon, and a magical looking sauce.

"Dig in!"

They did. And the sandwiches lived up to their reputation.

After she'd stopped her tummy from rumbling, Ivy ventured, "Fyn, you and your mother, hosting me all summer. I can't say how thankful I am. I'd like to help out, not just take advantage. I was thinking I'd get a job this summer."

Fyn's mouth was full, but he made some hand gestures.

"I know, you're happy to have me. Still. I have a ton of experience in kitchens… maybe I could work here?"

"Bramble's rarely hires. They only ever have family staff."

"Oh."

"But I've heard Quinton's is hiring."

"Quinton's?"

"Quinton's Brews & Hodgepodge. The potion shop we passed. You should feel right at home after your time with

Winsome. The dwarves who run the shop are potions masters."

"Sounds interesting enough."

The quirky waitress set down two glasses in front of Fyn and Ivy, a complimentary drink with each meal. Tiny flares of magic glimmered inside Ivy's bronze-dusted cup, inspiring a sip. It felt like sunshine in a cup.

"Winky Drink. It chases away the foggy blues."

Ivy smiled. "Cheers to a great morning. And an even greater afternoon."

"Cheers!" The two tapped glasses.

On their way home, Fyn spotted friends across the street and ran over to say a quick hello; Ivy ducked in to explore a small bookshop. The sign read *Lie Buries: A Library of All Things Fantastical.*

As Ivy's eyes adjusted inside, it felt like there was a shadow lifting. The place was jam-packed with books; they even sat in lopsided stacks on the floor, rounding the register. The carriage wheel fixture above was lit by hairies only slightly brighter than Ivy's, and it spun lazily. Ivy ran her hands along the book spines with a smile: they were cobwebby and dusty, and even though they appeared to be old, the books were hardly used. The volumes appeared in no particular order: a book about beanstalks nestled next to life on the moon. Authors were randomly stored: Buiton Henry next to Lundon Moose. *How was anyone to find anything in here?*

"Can I help you?" asked a girl with flowing black curls and flawless sienna skin. She scurried down the stepladder from a space upstairs. Ivy peered up and saw a little writer's nook nestled against the upstairs windows, frosted with cold.

"Oh, Gretta! It's good to see you here," said Ivy. "Sorry, I should have announced myself. It's pretty quiet in here."

"Ivy! Now I'm surprised! To see you, well, really anyone in here. Not a hot spot, as you can see," Gretta shrugged. "Most scrivenists are all about discovery and learning real life stuff. Every book in here is a fantasy, and they consider fantasies to be just the same as lies. Hence the name. But these books are written by some of the most creative people I've ever met," the girl said in admiration.

Ivy gave a half smile and nodded. "Thanks again for helping me that night."

"Anytime," Gretta said kindly. "I'll just never forget your hair standing up on your head like that!"

They both giggled.

"What's that you have in your hand?" Ivy asked.

In her inky fingers Gretta held a freshly dipped pen with red head and a floral relief on its iron shank. Ivy had never seen a pen or porcupel like it.

"Oh! Forgot I was holding it. It's a pseudopen—keeps the author's identity a secret so they can be free to write whatever they dream up. Makes you invisible while you're at work writing."

"Are you writing your own book?" Ivy gestured to the ink staining Gretta's fingers. "Or do you work here?"

Gretta shrugged, "Both. Trying to write my own book while I wait for work to walk in. What brings you into Lie Buries?"

The only sound was the scratching of the pseudopens upstairs.

Ivy cleared her throat, "I'm actually in search of a book for a friend's birthday gift. The party's tonight. I'd like to get him something like a mystery."

"You're not talking about Fyn Greeley, are you?"

"Do you know him?" Ivy asked.

"He's a good friend of my brother's. Glistle. If you've been in town, for a minute, he's definitely found a way to introduce himself. Small town. A book is better than what my brother plans on gifting him! Can I make a suggestion? A book, I mean?"

"That would be great. I hardly know where to start."

"Fyn visited the Hollow Shaft unattended last year, didn't he?" Gretta went to a shelf by the door and pulled off a narrow, blue edition.

Ivy was taken aback, but then realized the whole of the Halls of Ivy must know about Fyn and Ivy's adventure.

"This book is about life below Lonefellow Loch, about a boy who never made it out in time and his adventures."

"Sounds perfect!"

As Ivy approached the register, she caught a glimpse of the book Gretta had set her pseudopen down on. Gretta noticed Ivy staring at it. She hesitated for a moment, then, as if she found Ivy trustworthy, she said in a low voice, "I'm thinking about calling it *The Girl with the Whispering Shadow*."

"Your book?"

"More like the beginnings of a book."

"What's it about?"

Ivy noticed that Gretta's face was tired and pinched, and wondered why. Gretta flushed and shrugged, clearly deciding she'd rather not discuss what she was writing after all. "Would you like to see the upstairs? The pseudoroom is absolutely fantastic. It's the only thing keeping us in business."

"Sure."

The small pseudoroom was filled mostly with a rectangular,

communal table in the center. The pseudopens buzzed speedily, furiously writing stories into already bound books. Ivy counted nine pseudopens, and every one of the authors was invisible. Aside from the pseudopens scratching, it was as quiet as a graveyard. Ivy smiled at the scene in front of her. She loved discovery and science just as much as the next sqwinch, but her childhood had taught her that imagination, creativity, and stories could save someone's life.

Gretta led her back downstairs.

"My brother often jokes that I work at the place where I'm the only customer, but that's not true today," Gretta smiled strangely. "Eleven brums, please." Ivy handed over some of her savings. *I really need to get a job.*

Chapter Seven

The Birthday Party

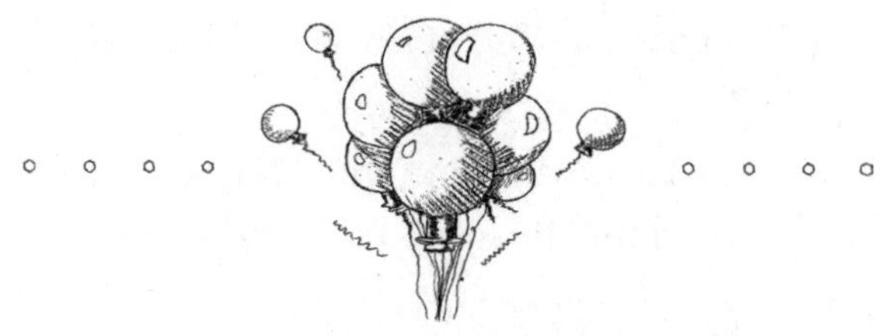

IVY could hear the chime contraption on the door ringing over and over. The walls trembled with party guests' loud laughter and footsteps. Big band music blared up the stairwell.

"Everybody's here, Humboldt," she said as she turned to the sleepy critter. After baking up a little something to go along with Fyn's birthday present, Humboldt was ready to hit the sack. She'd never met a lazier—or cuter—scaldron.

Another door chime.

"I guess I can't hide up here any longer."

Ivy stood and stared at her reflection in the mirror, not yet ready to enter a room full of partygoers, pastries, and peers. She patted down her dress, making sure there wasn't a smear from her cooking. Nothing—simple and clean. Still, a small sliver of anxiety set over her. She took long, deep breaths.

"I can do this," Ivy said to herself. *I can do this.*

She'd never been very good at social events: meeting new people; answering questions, unsure of what she could say and what she should not; sounding like a know-nothing among people who had grown up in magical Belzebuthe; to say nothing of the painful small talk that Ivy loathed. She stopped mid-grimace. *Oh, no! What if they want to talk about the Ball? Or the break-in?* She just couldn't shake the feeling that she was bad luck wherever she went.

Humboldt snorted a whiff of smoke her way. All she wanted to do was to curl up in bed and be alone.

"Fyn says his friends are going to be here—mostly third and fourth years. They'll probably look at me as if I'm the strangest girl they've ever seen. What'll be worse is when they talk to me; *if* they talk to me, I'll have nothing to say. I'll just ruin the party. Again."

Humboldt snorted again. Ivy glared at her unsympathetic pet.

She carefully removed the stone from in her hidden pocket to talk to it. "Do you do anything to calm people's nerves?" She could feel it sparking through her fingertips. "Wish me luck, Hum. I'm going to need it!"

Ivy crept downstairs. Balloons and streamers—all Fyn's favorite shade of light blue—carried up the stairwell and into every lower room. At the top of the stairs overlooking the living room, she tentatively looked out over the crowd. At least three dozen heads bobbed up and down, some dancing, some bald, some in heated debate over some magical matter. Young, old, in between. *Is the whole of Belzebuthe here?*

Scrivenists were dressed in whatever they felt was their best, many wearing the traditional purple garments that signified their scrivenry, but some in completely random get-ups. Their next-door neighbor wore a suit made of a bright balloon-printed fabric. A pair of dwarves wore dungarees and suspenders. Just as Ivy's foot hit the last step, the front door directly across from her swung open. It was Glistle, holding a strange box like an oversized egg carton, but with only six compartments. *Happy birthday* was scrawled across the top.

"What are you doing here?" Ivy asked, trying not to smile too widely. At least now she'd have someone to talk to. After all, Fyn was the guest of honor, and she couldn't expect to keep his attention all night. Even the thought, the idea that she wanted to hold Fyn's attention, sort of freaked her out.

She shook off the feeling as Glistle punctured her thoughts with his reply. "I was invited to the party, of course! Nice to see you again. Do you know, I'm sorry, but do you know where I can tuck this away? It's not heavy or anything, just fragile."

"Oh. Sure. What about inside the coat closet?"

"Yeah. That's good."

Glistle set the carton down carefully and turned back toward Ivy. "Lumbuses don't like to be disturbed," he grinned wickedly. "Fyn told me he had a girl staying with him, but he didn't say it was you!"

"Oh, I—well, it's sort of a long story."

Ivy was unsure of what to say. Glistle looked strangely at Ivy, noting her discomfort and then kindly changed the topic. "So, what is there to eat in this humble abode?"

"Food!" Ivy replied awkwardly.

"You're kidding!" he smiled sarcastically.

"Lots of food, I mean. Shall I show you?"

It came naturally for Ivy to act as host. After all, she had tended the Castle Plum kitchen for way too many years to not know what to do. She walked Glistle around the corner to the dining table where the two spotted Fyn.

"Good to see you, Glistle," said Fyn.

"You, too. Lively crowd."

"Yeah, and they're not all here yet. I told my mother not to invite the neighbors, but she never misses an opportunity to invite someone to my birthday."

"Well, the more the merrier."

"Thanks, thanks for coming. Glistle, this is Ivy. The girl I was telling you about. Ivy—"

"We've met," Ivy said bashfully.

"Have you?" A little spark of jealousy made Fyn's voice pop. He knew Glistle was quite the charmer and usually had the popular girls attached to his hip. This time, he had Ivy.

"Getting off the cabby. We met on the rooftop sampling cracker hats at Plumlie's Puddings and Stuff."

"And you didn't save me any?" Fyn smiled.

From across the tiny yet jam-packed room came Mrs. Greeley's voice, "Fyn—come say hi to Mrs. Magmeade. My son—"

"I'll be back," Fyn rolled his eyes. "Work, work, work, saying hi to all these people. It's like a job, honestly." He put on a charming smile and spun around, "Mrs. Magmeade, hello!"

Ivy chuckled at Fyn's about-face. Standing with Glistle, she took in the room: dancers, foodies, and conversationalists. The laughter was louder than the music, and the conversations even louder than that!

They squeezed in at the table, elbow to elbow with other guests, and delighted at the family-style delectables piled high enough to block the view across the table. Ivy filled her plate: cheese bombs, purple squash, and honey barbeque brisket, Mrs. Greeley's signature dish. It was the talk of the table! That and the neighbor's bright, balloon-patterned, skin-tight suit.

"So where are you from? Oh—sorry, that's right. The slurry fields. Beautiful place."

"You think so?"

"Well, it is, isn't it? So, then you're royal?" Glistle said with some surprise.

Strangely, the questions that earlier had caused Ivy acute anxiety now seemed easier. Maybe it was the fact that she felt at ease with Glistle, or the volume of the party around them, or just something in the air in Belzebuthe, letting her know it was okay to be different; she wasn't anxious anymore.

"Well, sort of. I'm an orphan. My parents died young. My scrivenist, he wasn't the best at keeping tabs on me. I can't blame him though, right? Mixed in with all that slurry. It's no wonder I was difficult to find."

"So, you grew up in someone else's castle? That must have been… awkward."

She laughed. "A little more than that. Nectarine?"

Then, a young girl with jet-black hair in a bun topping her head sat down beside Glistle, her plate piled high. She was full-figured and wore bright purple-rimmed glasses that could be spotted from across the room. Her voice, like it was being projected to the heavens, was unusually loud. "You try the brisket yet, Glistle? Utterly fantastic!" she squealed.

Glistle chuckled and quickly introduced Ivy. "Ivy, this is Manone. Manone, this is Ivy."

"Ivy? Not Ivy Lovely, is it?"

"That's me," Ivy chuckled bashfully.

"I've heard about you! Brilliant what you did, turning bubbles to buoys! I imagine that you're a good friend to have—the way you came to everyone's rescue! It was really brave of you, battling the Queen and all!"

"Thanks," Ivy muttered from beside Glistle, head down. Glistle then whispered into Ivy's ear, "Manone's partially deaf in the right ear. Never really knows how loud she's talking. But she's great, one of the smartest girls I know. Knows practically everything there is to know about curse reversal. They call it pologies, but you'll learn all about that as a third year in your Potions and Pologies class."

Ivy nodded, grateful for Glistle's insight.

"Would you like anything else? I was going to grab myself a cranberry crumpet," Ivy said as she stood up, looking to make a polite escape.

"You do realize there's about a year's worth of cranberry crumpets right in front of you?" Glistle pointed to a pyramid of pastries.

"Right. But those look too pretty to mess up. As someone who spent her earlier years organizing those pastry trays, I'd prefer an extra from the kitchen. I'll be back."

On her way there, Ivy was stopped by a man in a tall hat who proclaimed himself to be Mrs. Greeley's distant cousin. He wound his conversation around Ivy until she felt a bit trapped, not to mention hungry for the cranberry crumpet.

Then Fyn called from a corner, "Ivy, Ivy, come to the kitchen. I need a hand."

Ivy interrupted the cousin's stream of words to say, in breathless relief, "Sorry! Duty calls."

She didn't even care if Fyn wanted her managing the scaldron for the rest of the evening. She glanced back and saw the man in the hat start in on the exact same conversation with a fresh ear.

When she got through to the kitchen, she asked, "What's going on?"

"There's something I want to show you."

"What is it? Where are we going?"

"Your first official meeting, of course!"

"What?" Ivy giggled.

While the party carried on in the dining hall, Fyn walked Ivy to the pantry in back. The tucked-away room, like a large closet, was painted a rusty orange. The wide plank floors were worn smooth and soft with use and a tiny window let light in—as much light as was to be had in Belzebuthe. A gang of sqwinches gathered on the floor, exchanging ideas and stories, laughing raucously while plucking elderberries and plums from the woven baskets on the floor. A young boy in a buttoned blazer preferred to lie down, chewing on chunks of ginger. All in all, there were seven sqwinches before her, including Fyn. It was an eclectic group, but all very bright and welcoming. Each member toted a patterned velvet pouch with feathers poking out. *The pouches must be quivers for quills*, Ivy thought.

"Guys, guys… quiet down! Come on! I want to introduce you all to a friend. This is Ivy. Ivy Lovely."

Manone gave her a little wave.

"Ivy Lovely," repeated a girl with pale skin and carroty red hair. "Fyn's talked of nothing but you. I'm Canna Casteele."

Ivy wasn't sure if Canna was teasing her or not. The way she flicked a braid over her freckled shoulder gave the impression that Canna was the kind of girl who knew how to use sarcasm.

"I like your jumper," said Ivy, a little cautiously.

Canna tugged on her suspenders, her signature look. They

were brown with small pins and had graffiti-like markings scribbled down the entire length of them. Ivy squinted to better decipher a word or two written in bold black ink on one pin. *Lucent Habberdash.*

"Is that a person or a spell?" Ivy asked.

"Favorite Quogo player. Quickest hands I've ever seen, and he's playing the first of next moon!"

"What are you all doing inside the pantry?" Ivy asked.

"We are the Quality Quills Club members every third day and just plain old friends all the others. Well, some of us more than friends. Isn't that right, Manone," the boy chewing ginger said as he winked. He had a large, midnight-blue tattoo on his right wrist; something that resembled the stonework of a castle. Ivy couldn't tell how far up the design ran because he wore long sleeves. "I'm Lennu. Fyn's said you have a knack for making magic accidentally."

Ivy smiled, "Is that what he's been telling you?"

A third boy spoke up, "And I'm Pedlum. Most talented, strongest, most liked by girls, most—"

"Most self-absorbed," added Canna, who then sat herself down next to Manone on a bumpy sack of potatoes. Pedlum was undeniably attractive. He had long, shaggy hair—Ivy's favorite length, like Fyn's—and large muscles. No doubt he was an expert in beast wrangling. And an expert in himself.

"Hayword!" Ivy belted, happy to see a familiar face nestled in the corner. There her classmate was sitting between two habbitries, each complete with a critter. His sketch work was open across one habbitry, and it took him a while to look up from his current sketch of razor-sharp teeth.

"Good to see you, friend! I didn't doubt for one-second you'd find your way here to Belzebuthe. Welcome! How's Humboldt enjoying it?"

Ivy nodded with a smile, "He's happy to be here."

Ivy and Fyn sat down, leaning against the open shelves, which held dry goods on one side and potion bottles and ingredients on the other. Fyn's eyes sparkled; he loved having his favorite people in his favorite spot. Ivy breathed deeply. She loved the scent of the dried herbs that hung from the ceiling: lavender, oregano, rosemary, and the more magical slurry, bitterfroth, and sourspout. The overall effect was like aromatherapy.

"There's a Quogo match next moon. Big stuff," said Hayword. "We were all just discussing our plans. Meeting at Manone's beforehand. You coming?"

"A match?"

"Have you not heard of Quogo, Ivy?" Glistle asked, appalled.

"Heard of it, yes, but still have no idea what it is," she said, shaking her head.

"Fyn's never been good at explaining it. He gets too excited. Quogo: The name originated back in the early 1600s. Short for 'quills on the go.'"

"Are you guys planning to play soon?" asked Ivy tentatively.

"Not us, the professionals! The one thing better than the QQC is the professional Quogo League. The season kicks off in the summer and ends early fall. Pre-season scrimmages are in the spring. Because of school, it makes it difficult to attend most matches, but the first one is coming up."

"As far as the QQC goes, I can't officially swear you in

until we are back at the Halls. But that doesn't mean you can't come to the scrimmages this summer."

"How does it work?"

Lennu chimed in, an expert on the sport and its players, "It's basically a duel between quills and their departed owners. There are endless rounds, and matches can go on for days. The room must have certain protections to keep the spectators and players safe. In Belzebuthe, the Quogo ring is beneath the Quill Keep. We call it the hex."

"So, it's a magical duel? Casting spells? How do you get a quill that isn't bonded to you to work?"

"All thanks to the liquid danger!" Manone answered loudly. "Absolutely potent. Nothing like waking up to the smell of straight danger. It gets the quills and spectres going, fighting to the death!"

"Isn't she great?" Lennu smiled at his love and her love of darker themes like death.

Fyn interrupted Lennu's reverie, "All retired quills hold the memories of their scrivenist, whether retired or renounced or turned tome. When used by a new person, the quill sort of summons the memory, or spectre, of its owner and operates out of that. So, two players duel; rather, their quills do. But the player can shape the game—depending on how much magic they know—but the biggest factor is who populates the quillusion."

"Quillusion?"

"I thought you said she was smart?" Canna directed this question at Fyn.

Fyn ignored Canna and went on, "Right. The magic of the match takes place in the realm of the quillusion, and the departed scrivenists appear as spectres. Like the spirit of the scrivenist who owned the quill." Seeing Ivy's eyes widen, Fyn reassured her, "Not a real spirit of course, but spectres do look pretty ghostly. It's cool to see the man or woman who once held the long-ago quill. It's the best way to learn about the history of magic and scrivenry, in my opinion. Facing these spells and creatures and whatever else in the realm of the quillusion increases the chance of your success in facing them in the real world. It's really fun. Really random."

Hayword sighed with delight, "Have you ever seen the vongunde dragon battle an exacto magno dragon? Practically impossible to see in life, but I documented that duel last spring—best match of the year! Hope to witness something like it with Habberdash!"

Superfan Canna chimed in, "His magic is unmatched!"

Lennu spoke up, "A lot really depends on the chemistry between the quill and the new user, and how much magic the Quogo player can coax out of it. Sometimes they are in harmony and the quill works really well, casting the right spells and blocks to win the duel. Sometimes not so good; sometimes terrible. You never really know the personality of a quill until you pick it up and try to use it. Plus, the advantage of being a player is that you are the only one who gets to hear the inner thoughts of the spectre—like the spells he or she is thinking, the methods, their train of thought."

Fyn concluded, "Anyway, the idea is to force the other spectre out of the boundary lines."

"And what do you get out of a match?" Ivy asked.

Fyn sniffed defensively, "Besides getting practice? Deepening your knowledge and awareness of magic? We, the Quality Quills Club, just like the professional Quogo League, play for quill keeps. Remind me to show you my collection."

"All those quills in the stairwell, when we were chasing after the intruder?"

"Yeah. Fortunate finds or wins."

Glistle coughed, "Or steals."

"Oh, quiet, you!" replied Fyn.

"Isn't it illegal to take possession of someone else's quill?"

"Not as long as the league players follow protocol—no banned quills, only quills from scrivenists happily turned tome, for example. Oh, and you have to be a member of the league."

"So, league players, but not Quality Quills Club players?"

"It's a little bit illegal for students, but we are all practically shoe-ins for the league when we are commissioned scrivenists," Fyn protested.

"But doesn't just being able to play around with any old quill make finally getting your own quill, being inducted into the Society of Scrivenists, less special?"

"Not at all. In fact, quite the opposite. In Quogo, you get to experience firsthand a quill's bond to its owner. We players can barely tap the possibilities of what a quill could do for its scrivenist! It makes me want my own even more."

"I see."

"You'll love it, Ivy. Watching a quill you learn new tricks. Honestly, I think that's the whole reason the mattelers are okay with it all. One for sport, and two, well—"

"Well, what?"

"Many fear the Dark Queen; some say she's close to uncovering Belzebuthe. There's been talk of it in the papers. That, and the Quill Keep break-in just the other day has everyone on edge."

"What do you mean, Fyn?"

"What I mean is, we've got to be prepared. We've got to practice. And so, we play."

Suddenly, Mrs. Greeley popped her head into the pantry.

"Up to trouble as usual, I see. Let's go, now. Up and out. We're about to do cake and presents and we need Fyn for that."

"A few minutes, Ma. Please."

"No! You're being rude to your guests. Some have traveled from as far as the edge of Dwarflin."

The teenagers exited the pantry reluctantly. The music had dimmed in the living room, and Mrs. Greeley led Fyn to a blue velvet wingback chair that took up most of the corner.

After the group had sung an energetic rendition of "Happy Birthday," Mrs. Greeley announced, "Time to open the presents."

Everyone gathered. Fyn was surrounded by presents of varying sizes. Some were so large Ivy wondered how they could have fit through the door. Some were tied up with brown paper, others jiggled mysteriously. There were more packages than Ivy had ever seen in her life.

Fyn began to plow through them—charmingly, but with determination. He opened an array of corked potion bottles tied with ribbon. Ivy felt her curiosity mount when he opened a package of mysterious looking bottles of inks and a brand-new proof pad. Then he picked up a box that looked like it had been wrapped in yesterday's *Scriven This.*

"Last minute wrapping, my apologies," shouted one of Mrs. Greeley's co-workers, an eccentric woman with brightly colored knee-highs. The box was surprisingly filled to the brim with water. Fyn fished out a pair of dark purple trousers, which immediately dried themselves.

"Soggy jogs! Been wanting a pair of these! Who told you? Thanks, Mrs. Dunbar. They would have come in handy several times during the school year." He shot an impish grin at Ivy.

The next carton was immediately recognizable to Ivy: Glistle's gift.

As Fyn opened the carton, he said, "Dilly owl eggs? Delicious. Ma—"

Fyn's mother clumsily grabbed the carton from Fyn. But she was too late. Before the box was even open, the screeches of the lumbuses drowned out everything. The siren-like noise was so loud that Ivy could feel it vibrating her teeth. The party was officially over.

CHAPTER EIGHT

FISHING FOR STARS

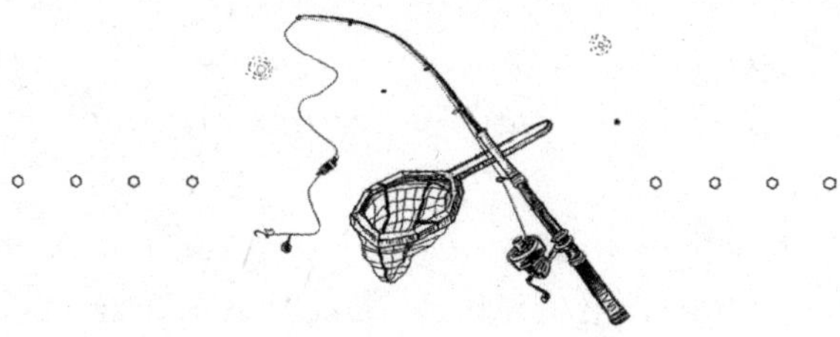

JUST when no one thought the lumbuses would quit, Hayword cast a species-specific silencing spell. Once quieted, the lumbuses were securely tucked back into the hall closet. Glistle had been pleased as punch with his present: he'd said that the gift of these creatures, commonly used as an alarm in other parts of Croswald, was in response to the break-in, but really it just suited his prankster nature. The Greeleys thanked Glistle a little insincerely, as Mrs. Greeley wished she could just send the horrible creatures back where they came from.

By then it was very late. Mrs. Greeley set to cleaning the kitchen, collecting jars of pudding and half-full glasses. Ivy brought in the dish that had held the pumpkin swirled brownies; not one left! They worked side by side—already Ivy felt comfortable with the way this kind woman ran her house.

"I appreciate it, Ivy," said Mrs. Greeley softly, sweeping her quill's magic across the floor.

"I don't mind at all. It's the least I could do to thank you for your hospitality."

"Think nothing of it, darling. Fyn and I both love having

you here. It's my joy to help a young woman out when she's in a pinch."

For a while, the only noise was the tinkle of silverware washing itself under a spell of Mrs. Greeley's.

"Did you enjoy your time, Ivy?" asked Mrs. Greeley.

"Very much!" Ivy smiled. "Except the ending seemed a little, er, abrupt."

"I can't believe those creatures are even louder than you kids! That Glistle is a real troublemaker! Good parents, not sure how he came to be."

Ivy smiled, "Everything was wonderful. Really, I had a great time. You are such a wonderful hostess."

Ivy glanced around. Guessing at Ivy's thoughts, Mrs. Greeley said, "I sent him off to escort the little aunties to their homes—they love Fyn's attention! He should be back by now, though. Probably out staring at the stars."

"I beg your pardon?"

"The roof, dear. He spends hours up there, especially loves to on his birthday. Go join him."

The roof? Ivy wondered nervously. Mrs. Greeley mentioned the roof so casually. It had to be more of a roof deck than just a *roof*, right? Ivy's fear of heights gave her pause, but she had yet to give Fyn a birthday gift and was eager for just the two of them to digest the evening. Really, just to see him.

"Can I help you with anything else before I go upstairs?"

"The box of streamers, dear. Drop it by my door, would you?"

"Of course."

Up Ivy went along the tiny, winding stairwell. At the top of the stairs, she entered her room—Mr. Greeley's old study was the highest up. Humboldt was snoring away, tuckered out by the exercise of cooking for the first time in a long while. *Lazy little critter,* she thought affectionately. She grabbed her parcel and walked to her window—it was cracked open and a chill air blew through. Not even letting herself peer down, she carefully climbed out, just hoping that Fyn wasn't too high up. The roof on the Tudor-style apartment building was wood shake and had shingles missing in patches. Others were coated in gray lichen that loved damp, sunless Belzebuthe. She followed the tracks left by Fyn's footsteps in the nighttime dew.

Ivy spotted Fyn on the spine of the roof, high above the streets, with the Quill Keep and the cabby deck off in the distance. His shaggy hair shone in the starlight. She climbed carefully to meet him, but now that she had found him her mind slipped to the fact that she was up on a roof. Her heart was pumping with fear. *You can do this. You're almost there. It's just like climbing the stairs; only no walls, no steps.* Ivy glanced back. *Not like climbing the stairs. Broken shingles and frantic pigeons.*

Fyn still had his back to her, both hands in thick gloves and gripping a long, thin fishing pole and a small, oval net. He had the same posture Rimbrick did when he would describe fishing for trout. Fyn looked calm as if he was prepared to sit in the same spot for hours waiting for something to happen, something that Ivy thought would never come. She couldn't help but smile, seeing him sitting there.

Finally, on the spine of the roof herself, she scooted toward him tentatively. Fyn smiled and grabbed her hand, helping her the last few feet.

"Careful there, Ivy. Are you all right?"

"I'm fine. What—what are you even doing up here?" Ivy

brushed off Fyn's concern.

"What am *I* doing up here? *You're* the one afraid of heights. You're practically as pale as a ghost."

Ivy narrowed her eyes at him. "I was looking for you."

"What for?"

"I brought you something. A gift. And something I baked myself. Well, Humboldt might have helped a little bit. Probably a silly idea, after your mother's feast, but at least it's warm. Aren't you cold up here?" Ivy shivered.

"This blanket's warm enough," he opened up the thick, green-and-blue checkered blanket draped around his shoulders to Ivy and she tucked under it, too.

Fyn held the fishing pole between his knees and unwrapped a small box to find a still-warm stack of griddlecakes. Beneath that was the book from Lie Buries.

"I know you love to read as much as I do, but I thought you might like to try some fiction for a change," Ivy smiled. "It's from Lie Buries."

"*The Boy Named Gu*," Fyn read the title, smiling. He flipped through the vibrant, holographic illustrations of the Hollow Shaft. "You'll miss me if I don't return from the Hollow Shaft this year, won't you? When the fourth years go to write biographies?" he teased.

"The story sounded interesting," Ivy rolled her eyes.

"Well, thank you, Ivy," Fyn smiled. "It looks like a good read."

Ivy wasn't entirely sure if Fyn appreciated the book. He appeared to be more into the blueberry griddlecakes he was chomping away on.

"How high up are we, anyway?" asked Ivy.

"Four stories."

Ivy worried in silence.

The sky was a sphere of fog above them. As if hung on silk strands just out of reach, stars glistened and shone brightly. Just like the real stars in Croswald, each was a slightly different shade of lightning—some pinkish, others yellow-green, still others blue. Each one had been crafted by one scrivenist hundreds of years before when Belzebuthe went from being an everyday town to one shrouded in secrets and spells.

"So, these stars, they aren't real? Glistle told me a little about them."

"Once they shielded Belzebuthe, the scrivenists found they missed the celestial bodies. They're made of moondust, the same building blocks as the stones in Croswald. Same as you, I suppose."

Ivy bit her lip.

"But now, they do more than just light up the dark town." Fyn paused and then asked, "Have you ever fished for a star before? It takes hours, and I'm not leaving here until I catch one."

"Fish for a star? That sounds impossible."

"Impossible?" he laughed. "Maybe in the rest of Croswald, but here it's very possible. The act of catching one is like wishing on a star, just in reverse. Meaning, you net a star, you get to help grant the wish inside, for whatever the star setter wished."

"Inside?"

"Yep, you twist them open—they're sharp and they sting and so you have to be careful, hence the gloves—and there's a little compartment within the star. The wish is usually a sketch or a bit of writing, and just by opening the star, you get to grant it. Small stuff, like a custom cape or a new proof pad.

Pretty fun—I like helping others."

"How does that even work?"

"The spell uses your magic to help manifest it for the wisher. Poof. Their proof pad just shows up. Actually, you saw the autographed Habberdash pin on Manone's suspenders earlier tonight?"

"Of course I did. I even asked about it."

"That was one of her wishes. An autograph from her favorite Quogo player. She was just sitting, sharing tea with her mother one day. The pin randomly made a splash inside her teacup."

"Lucky she didn't swallow it!" Ivy giggled.

"Right!"

"Never anything big?"

"Once I wished to get out of a sticky situation."

"You seem to be good at getting into those."

"Well, it was more of a, er, romantic situation, but the star wouldn't take the parchment. Just kept bouncing it out until I put another in!"

Ivy laughed in spite of a little knot of jealously forming in her stomach.

"I got a star to fill for my birthday, by the way. From Ma. She made me open it last. Do you want to help me set it free?"

He carefully opened a heavy wooden box lined with charred metal. The star was fist-sized and glowed a bright gold, lighting the whole roof. Fyn twisted the star open, wearing leather gloves three times thicker than Ivy's mittens, and quickly set his already-rolled wish into place.

"What did you wish for?"

"Can't tell you! Or else the star will disintegrate the

moment it settles in the clouds."

Fyn placed the sparkling sphere into his net.

"Together now."

The two gripped the net's handle and swept it in a full arc over their heads. The star glittered as it sailed up into the sky, slowing and settling over the next building.

"Here's to hoping this wish comes true," Fyn smiled down at her. "You can hold most stars in one hand, but they get bigger and more powerful the farther out they are. See that one?"

Ivy squinted at the brightest star—a pure white.

"That's the farthest star out, Star Solo. My father's favorite. It's the only star ever to appear on its own."

"Remarkable! How do you know that?"

"The star marker's map. Every single star is registered with the Star Shoppe. Some, the ones farther out, are named for the people who set them. Ma said my father would fish every birthday. Wouldn't stop till he caught one."

"I would think that everyone would be out catching or casting stars."

"It takes a lot of patience. A lot. They don't just come right to you."

Fyn and Ivy took in the beauty of the night sky. Ivy found something comforting in the bright stars that lit up their backdrop of fog. The Kindred Stone seemed to like it, too—she could feel its magic smooth out into a calm hum, less buzzy than usual.

"Can I watch you cast for one?"

Fyn smiled and responded by casting his pole in long swinging arcs, like a fly fisherman. The whipping cord was shimmering, as if it too was made of moondust. It was transfixing and only added to the beauty of the night: the soft whirring sound of the line, the light of the stars, being in good company.

I could stay like this forever. But of course, she couldn't. A line from Derwin's letter surfaced in her brain: "You must find the remaining two pieces of the stone and reunite them with the one you have now. It is your inheritance and our only hope of dethroning the Dark Queen. She is more dangerous than ever before."

"Fyn, how can I possibly stand against her?" Ivy sighed.

He knew exactly whom she was talking about. "Ma says that the most wondrous things, the most impossible of things, are often just ordinary things doing what they are best at. Think about a real star. They soar untouched and shine like diamonds, yet they are simply just balls of gas. The ordinary turned extraordinary."

He stopped casting and turned to her, "We just have to see the star inside of us. I think that's why the stars hang above Belzebuthe. They remind us that even in our darkest times, the bright spot in each of us can never be totally extinguished."

Fyn went back to casting for a moment.

"Do you want to play the question game?" Fyn asked Ivy. "I ask you a question and vice versa."

"All right. You go first."

"Okay. What was your favorite spell from last year?" asked Fyn.

"That's an easy one. The Celebratease. It would probably be quite nice to feel all that admiration for a couple of hours.

Even if it's just for a day."

"Must have been with Winsome? Last year, I learned how to create a Slippery Skin potion that allows you to slip through the smallest cracks. It tastes even worse than a Stop Motion potion. But it's pretty incredible stuff."

She nodded and giggled. Then, she asked, "Favorite dining hall?"

"The Uncommon Flicker."

"Didn't eat there at all last year. Our class always got out late on the other side of the Halls and the Flicker would already be full!"

"Yeah, you've got to try and get in there early. Favorite critter?"

"Humboldt. Duh. Best meal you've ever eaten?"

Fyn laughed. "Bramble's is tough to beat, but the brisket from tonight is up there. And the griddlecakes! Plumlie's pudding is pretty great, too. What about you?"

"Your mother's brisket makes my list! So good!"

"Favorite spot in Belzebuthe?" he asked.

"Hmmm. So far, I loved Lie Buries. I really want to check out the potions shop, though!"

Fyn cleared his throat and opened his arms wide.

"Oh, and here, of course!" she said. "This rooftop is pretty amazing. If only it were lower down."

Fyn chuckled, "Your turn."

"Favorite memory of your father?"

"Asking the tough ones."

"I'm sorry."

"No, it's okay. Some of my earliest memories are watching Quogo matches with him."

"What was he like?"

Fyn cleared his throat. "He left when I was small—only two. Ma thinks something terrible happened to him, but we never found out. She always says he was devoted to us. Busy with work. He was a gemologist for the Crownerie—their best one, so he worked long hours. Supposedly no one knew stones better than he did. Quogo was the only time he ever did anything for fun. He would have been able to tell me about that stone you have in your possession, Ivy, in your left pocket. My father could have told you everything about it."

Ivy grabbed her pocket furtively. "How did you know which pocket it was in?"

Fyn rolled his eyes, "You pat that pocket ten times a day, Ivy." He turned sharply to Ivy, his green eyes piercing her hazel ones. "You're she, aren't you? You're the one they speak of here in Belzebuthe. You're the true heir, the last of the Wanderers."

Ivy nodded, feeling overwhelmed by the truth of it.

"You know, my father was obsessed with finding the Wandering Family, the family cursed away from its castle and sent off to roam all of Croswald. I know because I've read his journals—his proof pads leading up to his disappearance were all about it."

Fyn's whole demeanor changed. Ivy could tell he was holding back tears of anger, of regret. She couldn't help but feel guilt for whatever happened to Fyn's father.

"And here you are, the end of the Wanderers." He hesitated and then said, "I have somewhere I need to take you."

Fyn led them, climbing down the fire escape, leaving the blanket and star fishing tools on the roof. They walked on a road headed out of the main shopping area, past the apartments and dwellings. Everyone else was asleep. On the edge of town, a low stone building rose up in the middle of the heather, all alone. Fyn led her inside. Ivy felt a chill run up her spine that had nothing to do with the cold. Someone had spray-painted "Wall of the Wandering" with a giant arrow pointing inside. Fyn led her through the doorless frame.

Inside, the abandoned cottage felt like an art gallery melded with a bulletin board that was run by a newspaper collector. The walls were plastered with articles on top of articles, sketches upon sketches, random scribbles, and words. Ivy read the headlines: *Wandering Curse Over After Nearly Two Centuries; Dwarf Still at Large; The Dark Queen Disrupts the Halls of Ivy Annual Ball.*

"What is this place, Fyn?"

"I thought you'd appreciate seeing Belzebuthe's dedication to finding your family. To finding you, Ivy. They knew that the Wandering Curse, however terrible it was, was the only thing protecting the last of the queenly line."

Ivy backed up, her heart burning in her chest. "Fyn, should I even be here?"

"It's all right. This wall is what's left of the home of Sigmar Soules, a Wanderer. This place was abandoned for generations, since the early 1700s. But once scrivenists figured out what had happened to the Wandering Family and its scrivenists, news of the Wanderers and their whereabouts was collected and shared here.

"Nothing excites a decent scrivenist more than solving a good mystery. Everything you see here, pinned to these walls, is a clue left behind: footprints in the snow, clothing hung slack on tree branches, portraits. Everything any scrivenist knows of your family is placed here. This was one of the biggest mysteries aside from who killed Princess Isabella.

"Kids at school, from outside Belzebuthe, are unfamiliar with the Moonsday prophecy, that the double moon was a vessel to hold Princess Isabella's power until the time came for a new true queen. But here we've grown up learning of the prophecy from our parents. So, while those at the Halls will know you as the girl who fought a queen, they don't fully understand who you are, Ivy, and what you mean to Croswald. And those few, select scrivenists who do know, will stay hush-hush until the time is right."

Ivy hardly knew what to say, so she remained silent, taking it all in. She approached the wall and set her eyes on an old copy of *Scriven This* pinned loosely, worn and wrinkled. It dated back to 1687. A headline, clear as day, caught Ivy's eye: *Wandering Family Still Lost.*

Fyn stayed silent, letting Ivy process everything. She unpinned an older article directly below the Wandering Family one:

Double Moon Returns

Last night, the moon's magnitude magnified in the same strange and unexplainable way that it did last year on the very same night. The moon is twice the size of a normal full moon and at least twice as bright...

And then she read one of the newer headlines still pinned to the wall:

Potions Master Claims to Have Seen the Wandering Family

And then another:

Winsome Monocle Declares the Wanderers No Longer Wander
The remaining descendant may be a student at the Halls of Ivy...

"So, this isn't like... a memorial?" Ivy's quiet voice cracked. Just thinking about the generations of her family that had perished while wandering, including her parents, made her unbearably sad.

"No, more like a puzzle, I guess. And a solved puzzle at that! When Winsome sent word back to the Town that the surviving member of the Wandering Family—you—had returned home to the Halls, Belzebuthe erupted in celebration. My mother said what started as a Moonsday celebration lasted for a week! Since the Wandering Family no longer wanders, the Wall has been changing."

He gestured to the end of the wall. A sketch of the Dark Queen at the Masquerade Ball was pinned there. Ivy shivered at the sight and her stone buzzed.

"What's she doing here?"

"The wall is evolving, trying to figure out how to protect you from her."

Ivy's heart flooded with warmth at the idea that this town full of scrivenists cared about her and wanted to help her even though they didn't know her.

"I—I don't know what to say."

Ivy walked by sketches of the ship in the ballroom. They were the most recent images and featured Winsome's face on the bow. It was strange to see the ballroom incident, which

Ivy had witnessed directly, amongst everything that was considered history.

They walked back through the sleet in silence.

QUINTON'S BREWS & HODGEPODGE

THE last few weeks had been great, so much fun with Fyn and his friends: QQC meetings at Fyn's place, and shared meals at Bramble's Fritters & Nosh on most afternoons. But the thing was, most of them had summer jobs, and there was only so much exploring Ivy could do on her own. She was steadily reading every book on Mr. Greeley's shelves. Many were on the subject of stones, but she had found out only a little more about the Kindred Stone. In Mr. Greeley's journals it was described as the only stone—perhaps mythical—that served as a magnifier of the wearer's powers. She knew about its origin, how Princess Isabella's magic had pooled into it, forming the first magical stone, but she hadn't known about how the double moon and the crystallization of other magical stones in the mines of Croswald were linked. But despite learning more about the stone, Ivy still had no idea where either of the two remaining segments could be hidden.

Ivy had received exactly one letter from Derwin. It had dropped into the Greeley's lott—a tiny copper box in their living room—two days before, and rather than tell her where he was or that Ivy could return to the Halls, Derwin just reminded her to read through the Greeleys' library, though Ivy never needed a reminder to read. He also promised Ivy that school assignments would begin in the fall, but she wasn't sure if she was looking forward to that or not.

More than just occupying her time, she also wanted to contribute to the Greeley household, and so she found herself finally daring to go into Quinton's Brews & Hodgepodge. She felt immediately intrigued by the place; especially after spotting the *APPRENTICE WANTED* sign in the right corner of the window. *They still need someone!*

A bell jingled as Ivy pushed through the arched door. The shelves were filled with vial after vial, jar after jar. Big bins of bulk ingredients were tucked low next to sloshing aquariums full of rare liquids and creatures. It was almost as good as being back in Winsome's upstairs laboratory. Ivy felt compelled to jot down notes and little details in her proof pad. She picked up a few items as she walked the narrow aisles. Nearly everything was unfamiliar to her, even after a year's worth of lectures with Winsome Monocle.

"What would anyone want with something like this?" she whispered as she held a bottle labeled *Broken Promises.* The bottle appeared to be filled with soggy notes torn in two covered in faded and illegible script.

By the time Ivy reached the far end of the first aisle, a short fellow appeared from a back room draped by a curtain. He poked his head around the corner to greet Ivy.

"Good morning, afternoon, evening to you! It's hard to say what time of day it is in Belzebuthe! What brings you into Quinton's Brews & Hodgepodge, home of potion masters, this morning? Or afternoon? Or evening, is it? Does it even matter?"

The thin, gray-haired dwarf was vigorously pumping Ivy's hand up and down, shaking her whole arm. His head, topped with a dull red pointed cap, came up to her waist. Wobbling, she reached to put the strange jar down as gently as she could while the handshake continued. But gently wasn't an option, and the jar ended up crammed between pickled willow weed and a box that had something steaming inside.

"Ah! Not many come in for that! I can see why you've put it back," he said. "But, not the right place for it!"

"I'm sorry. You startled me." Ivy was glad to have her arm back. She read the label while the dwarf reshelved the bottle. "What are broken promises used for, anyway?"

"Broken promises are one of the land's most bitter ingredients—great for a sundry of repellants. We have all sorts of ingredients here! Anything particular I can offer you?"

"Thank you, but I'm not in need of any today."

"How about an autograph? Would you like one? I'm famous, you know. Famously good at ingredient collection." The tiny man puffed with pride. Then he whispered conspiratorially, "My brother and I are the only reason that maga mushrooms can be found in Belzebuthe."

"Maga mushrooms?"

"The world's most potent fungi. Can amplify any spell or potion when used properly. And, my dear, it only grows in the deepest, darkest parts of Dwarflin, the dwarf forest, where a scrivenist has seldom ventured."

Ivy smiled at meeting a self-proclaimed celebrity.

"Oh, well, pleased to meet you. I've never met a *real* celebrity. Only the fake kind. Heard of Celebratease?" Ivy was potion name-dropping, hoping it would help her chances, knowing she had no experience other than the secret potions class.

"Heard of it? Hundreds of bottles of it stocked in back."

"I didn't quite catch your name. Quinton, is it?"

"No, little lady, Podge. Quinton's the owner, never comes in."

"Oh!"

"Now, how can I help you?"

"I heard you're looking for an apprentice..."

Podge's thick brow scowled together to form a unibrow. "You? An apprentice? You're not even yet a scrivenist. Have you any knowledge in creating an Elixir for a Mindless Whim?"

"Scattered minds aren't easily pleased, for a thought unplanned, all you need is one well-worth-it squeeze. A tincture to produce random, scattered, and spontaneous thoughts helpful for creativity. Ingredients include a combination of elder tree leaves and liver oil," recited Ivy, matter-of-factly.

Podge sputtered a bit in surprise. "Well, um, that's an easy one. What about the Beauty of Gryfe?"

Ivy's face fell and she shook her head. "I'm afraid not, sir."

"Sorry, dear. No can do. You're welcome to have a look around, though."

Ivy refused to give up. She moseyed up and down the aisles trying to devise a plan that might persuade the store clerk to change his mind. Surely, she could think of something. *A Revealavue? No, not that. I can't risk accidentally revealing myself to a stranger. Unpoppable bubbles? But what if that's too basic?* Ivy walked to where Podge stood on a stool mixing something with his scraggly beard skimming the liquid in the caldron.

"Do all dwarves have beards?"

"For the most part. Do you know many?" Podge peered at her, curious.

"The only other dwarf I know had a long beard, much longer than yours. It was the kind that would sop up all the liquid inside that caldron. A bright-ginger beard." Ivy added glumly, "He was a dear friend."

"A long, ginger beard, you said? Hmmm," Podge said thoughtfully.

After a pause, he yelled over his shoulder, eyes still locked on Ivy, "Hodge!"

"Right here!" Hodge popped up from behind the counter.

Hodge, nearly identical to Podge but with a dull green hat, looked at Ivy with curiosity as if studying her. While his stare penetrated her, Ivy allowed herself to hope a little.

"Hodge and Podge… you must have worked here for quite a while if Quinton agreed to name his shop after you two."

"We have indeed worked here for many years; however, the name is simply a coincidence. We're brothers, Hodge and I, if you couldn't already tell." Ivy had guessed—both dwarves, but Hodge was more rotund than his brother.

Podge continued, "We should say that, *yes* the store is in fact named after us. It's a better story to tell, wouldn't you say? But that sort of fiction is more the stuff of Lie Buries."

Hodge was far from being the chatterbox his brother was. He had crept over toward the window and was looking skyward. A shadow was passing—could shadows even exist in the fog?—and it darkened the room ever so slightly. Ivy's eyes followed his; it was one of those strange, dark, gray clouds. Then a sprinkling of snow came from the dark patch. Dull, gray snow. Not the bright white that Ivy was accustomed to.

"Weather has never been this strange," Hodge said under his breath as he draped the window shut.

"Nothing to worry yourself over," Podge said.

"Are those dark clouds common?" Ivy's stone buzzed.

Without any intention of answering her question, Hodge suddenly became eager to share a few more words than he had spoken during the length of Ivy's short visit. "Is it true? That you worked with old man Monocle before he passed?"

Ivy never knew when her reputation would precede her, and it always surprised her.

"Ginger beard. Celebratease potion. New girl in town. We dwarves know things."

He looked at Ivy strangely, placing a parchment down on the counter with purpose.

"Here's the agreement to the apprenticeship. Not much coin, but enough. Mostly restocking, but a good place for you to do your schoolwork when it's slow. We heard that you aren't returning to the Halls this year."

Ivy's jaw dropped. "How—"

"Like I said, we dwarves know things."

Chapter Ten

The Hex

IVY couldn't believe that summer was halfway over. Work at Quinton's that afternoon had kept Ivy later than anticipated: Podge had remembered that he needed potion recipes organized and old editions of *Potions Plus* magazine catalogued in the back. Basically, it was an enormous, sloping pile of paperwork that was the most tedious thing she'd ever done. She thought she'd never see the light of day—rather the stars—again. Ivy had missed the planned meet up at Manone's, and so she headed directly to the Quogo match instead with only minutes to spare.

Once she arrived at the Quill Keep, Ivy stared at the imposing building, a fortress-like brick structure with exactly zero windows. Ornate balconies framed solid stonework patterned to look like openings, but it was clear that no one was meant to enter without permission. A chill went down Ivy's spine: *Who could have broken into this building?* The Quill Keep towered like a lighthouse and kept the darkest, heaviest magic contained at its highest point. The entrance at the building's corner was narrow and midnight blue, but it grew wider as it stretched up. It made Ivy feel tiny. The wind whipped the fog around the corner from both sides.

Fyn was waiting for her outside.

"Thought I'd have to go find you!"

"How'd you sneak out without your mother catching you leaving?"

"Ma knows she can't keep me from Quogo. She knows exactly where to find me."

"Ha! Tell me why matches are here, again? Isn't this where—where—"

"Where the *bad* quills go?" Fyn made spooky wiggles with his hands as if Ivy's fear was laughable. "Yes, but we won't be spending any time in the Quill Keep. That's really just for mattelers, criminal historians, morbid tourists, and the like. And my mother. Gotta keep errant quills somewhere!"

Ivy hesitated.

"Like I said, it's not *in* the Quill Keep that we are going."

"Then where?"

With a flourish of his hairie, Fyn revealed a tiny door just to the left of the imposing entrance. This door was cut into the building's molding and framing, so it was almost perfectly camouflaged.

"Only visible to the discerning eye, but of course, everyone in town knows about the Quogo matches and exactly where they go on." Fyn rolled his eyes good-naturedly. "Come on! We're going to be late!"

The door creaked open just wide enough for Fyn to pass through. Ivy followed. She could tell instantly that they were traveling below the Quill Keep, surrounded by thick walls that absorbed all sound.

"Quogo is best kept underground. It's one of the many precautions," Fyn said casually.

What lay ahead of them were rickety wooden stairs that descended down into inky blackness.

"Only a couple stories! Easier to get to than the hex at school!"

Ivy gulped.

"Still not a fan of heights, I see," Fyn said, clearly amused at her discomfort.

"Still making bad jokes, I see." Since Ivy couldn't see how high she was, she pretended she was just walking the stairs at Fyn's house.

Ivy took in the sights and sounds as they descended the last few steps, lit by hairie lanterns. Excited scrivenists of all ages and stripes had gathered, and a thrum of conversation lifted up to them from a little sea of purple suits. The thick wooden planks that served as rafters held the space open, but otherwise the walls were earthen. Ivy judged that the hex, naturally shaped as a hexagon, was about fifty feet underground.

A stringy man at the bottom of the stairs called out, "Programs! Get your programs!" A yellow piece of parchment was thrust into their hands. It was, oddly enough, blank.

"Welcome to Belzebuthe's hex, where many retired quills have been resuscitated to demonstrate their power. Blood, sweat, tears, all of it." Fyn smiled hugely. He was in his element.

Then a strong, putrid smell hit her. Ivy had to cover her nose and she still gagged.

"What in all of Croswald is that terrible smell?"

"That's the enablement! The danger! See that tiny jar at the center of the mat? Well, I guess you can't—pretty busy in here. If you could see, you'd see a little bottle."

"Oh, right. I just didn't think it'd smell so terrible!"

"The fact that you can smell it so strongly only means the match is about to start!"

A second wave of the putrid odor hit her again: a combination of sweat, blood, and rotten meat.

"Trust me, it's worth it. Once the match starts, the smell subsides."

Then Fyn happily launched into an explanation of Belzebuthe's most popular sport. "There are three elements of Quogo. Before the players and their quills begin, the Castleton Stone is activated to keep the magic in the realm of the quillusion, rather than becoming real. Second, the enabler, the liquid danger to get the quills and spectres going, is released. Third, the spice marker—see it burning over there?—is set up. That marks the boundary of the hex, the border that the spectres have to stay within."

Ivy noted the beautiful Kelly-green stone at the center of the hex. The spice marker was a bundle of cinnamon and oak sticks that had been lit and then blown out. The marker smoldered in one corner of the hex, its smoke marking a hexagonal boundary and its scent gradually drowning out the smell of the danger.

Fyn ushered them to the closest empty seats—only two rows back. At the center of the room stood a man of medium height, but one with the kind of confidence and power that made him seem much taller.

"See there? That's Duncan Wurchester, a matteler. Pretty high up, too. But he refs Quogo for the fun of it. The best ref out there. This is the match that we've been waiting for to kick off the season."

To Mr. Wurchester's right was a young, wiry scrivenist with jet-black hair that stood up on end. On the left was an elderly scrivenist who looked more like a grandmother about to make cookies than duel. They each gingerly held quill quivers with great anticipation.

"Oh, look! There's Canna, Manone, and Lennu!" Fyn waved across the way.

"What about the others?"

"In here somewhere, I'm sure."

Ivy bit her lip, just taking it all in. The crowd was jittery. Mr. Wurchester swept his quill around the hex, testing the spice marker's barrier. The smoky boundary domed up over the hex.

Then the referee cleared his throat and shouted in a deep baritone, "Ladies and gentlemen, duelers and spectators, the time has come for our first match of this year's Quogo season. To my left, the esteemed scrivenist Everlee Fortune, one-hundred-twelve years' strong! And to my right, up-and-coming scrivenist Lucent Habberdash, with special expertise in poisons!"

Cheers erupted from the crowd, with Lucent Habberdash the clear favorite.

"How can she even stand a chance?" Ivy wondered, looking disbelievingly at the little old lady.

"Remember, if it were just a battle of sorcery or spellbinding or potion wielding, the most powerful scrivenist would always win. In Quogo, there is an element of randomness, of having to think quickly on your feet to use your own abilities and try and harmonize them with the quill in the ring."

"Half chance, half skill," Ivy murmured, her eyes flickering between the two players.

Lucent Habberdash's quick, clever eyes darted around the crowd. Everlee Fortune gripped her quills and looked as if she was talking to herself. Ivy spotted a familiar face across the room: Frederick Faddacky! She waved, wishing she could be sharing the experience with Rebecca as well, but he was deep in conversation with the scrivenist seated next to him.

"Look! They're about to draw." Fyn pulled her attention back to the hex.

Duncan Wurchester summoned the players to himself and drew a quill from each of their quivers. He nodded and said in a booming voice, "Fiddle Frontier and Yori Nori are the quills drawn! To your marks!" and exited the hex. Ivy felt the program twitch in her fingers; it had populated itself. The quill's strengths and statistics were being furiously written in the program, all derived from the quills' geers—the parchment note wrapped around each quill's stem.

"Ready? And... *begin*!" The matteler wafted an extra dose of the danger stink into the hex.

Each scrivenist commenced swishing quills and muttering spells. From the tip of Everlee's playing quill emerged a ghostly version of the quill's now-departed owner, Fiddle Frontier. The spectre was like a shadow of bluish light, but clearly a scrivenist, squat and rotund, ready to battle. Then Habberdash's spectre joined the first, this one a willowy young man, Yori Nori.

Each spectre had a spectre quill in hand, and Ivy saw that they imitated exactly the movement of the live scrivenists holding the real quills. Some movements Lucent and Everlee made were more effective than others. Lucent raised his arm, and so did his lanky spectre. He wiggled his quill and wrote his spell in the air, but the spectre just continued to proudly hold his quill high, unmoving. Ivy could see Everlee listening closely to a voice only she could hear, that of the departed Fiddle.

Fyn opened his program and remarked, "Doesn't look like Lucent's done his homework. Doesn't know his quill's history." For even more information, Fyn yanked a book entitled *Scrivenists of the Ages* out from his satchel and flipped it to Yori Nori's biography. "He's a dragon specialist!" He lifted his head and shouted at the hex, as everyone else seemed to be doing, "C'mon, Lucent! Let's see something big!" Then, to Ivy, Fyn said, "Most Quogo players do in-depth research, some even going to the Hollow Shaft, but looks like he's caught flat-footed. So much for Canna's crush."

Meanwhile, Everlee didn't seem to be doing much better. Rather than taking charge of the quill, it was quite the opposite: the quill was sparking and jerking her arm all about. Same with the spectre. Rather than listen to any of Everlee's calming spells, the quill increased its verve and began dragging her short, tubby spectre around the hex; Everlee followed after.

"Everlee Fortune is notorious for keeping even hyper-active quills! Most players edit their quiver before the game; that way, they have better control." Fyn was laughing now. "But look at her! No wonder we love her."

Also laughing with pleasure, Lucent clearly felt that he had the advantage. He gripped his fine white quill, confidently extended his arm toward Everlee, and chanted a spell. Rather than a powerful blast, as his movement suggested, a spurt of limp scales squirted from his quill's tip to rest on the floor. Ivy smiled widely and was a little glad to not be able to hear the cursing jag that Lucent went on.

Everlee's quill had kept her in the hex's bounds but was

now spinning her faster and faster at the center of the ring. Several minutes, which felt like an age, passed with only spinning and scale dusting. Ivy was laughing so hard that tears streamed down her face. The ridiculousness of it all!

"Let's see what you got, mister," shouted the woman, apparently an Everlee fan, next to Ivy. She was dressed head to toe in Everlee-inspired wear, topped with a gray wig.

Finally, a frustrated Lucent stood firmly planted to one spot, deep in thought. The young scrivenist swirled his quill, miming mixing, and muddling imaginary ingredients together. Yori Nori's spectre mixed a spectre potion.

"What's that he's got? What's he planning with that?" Fyn muttered.

They found out soon enough. Lucent turned with a confident smile, and he and his spectre dipped their quills in their potions and shouted a spell at top volume. From the spectre of Yori's quill grew an enormous, spirit-like dragon. Cobalt blue and at least twenty feet tall, its huge wings stretched out beyond the boundary, throwing wind up around the cavern and blowing Ivy's hair back. The crowd gasped and crowed with delight. Ivy was caught up in the beauty of the scene and felt like she was tottering on the edge of reality and imagination.

Nostrils smoking, the dragon lifted off, taking flight around the hex.

"Oh my moon! How is it beyond the boundary?"

Fyn shrugged but with a delighted expression said, "Some magic is too big to know any bounds! Really, though, as long as Yori and Fiddle stay within the boundary, game on! The Castleton Stone will keep it out of the realm of reality!"

The dragon sprayed a jet of ghostly fire down into the hex,

trying to trap Everlee's scrivenist. But she hadn't stopped whirling! Again and again, the dragon blew fire, but the blue flames missed Everlee and the spectre Fiddle every time. But then, Ivy saw it. The whirling was creating a gale-force tornado! The funnel took shape and grew, so that it, too, crested the top of the boundary. Now Ivy's hair was all in her face. The notes that countless scrivenists had been scribbling blew up and around, joining the tornado.

If she could have written in the wind, Ivy would have noted that even though the crowd was experiencing the Quogo magic, they weren't getting the full brunt of it. Clearly, the spirit scrivenists were being whipped around far more violently. And the dragon, too! His wings faltered in the face of the growing funnel, and eventually he too was swept inside the tornado. A shower of not-quite-real blue scales sprayed out into the crowd, and then they were swept back up into the gale.

Suddenly, Ivy could see a figure coming to standstill at the side of the hex nearest her and Fyn. It was Everlee and her spirit shadow, Fiddle. She raised her quill and brought it down in a strong, swift motion like she was swinging a hammer. With that motion, the storm came down with everything else along for the ride. The storm began to shrink, as did everything inside, including the giant dragon. Soon it was just about the size of Humboldt. Everlee let out a cackle. On the opposite side of the ring, Lucent used all his magical might to pull the dragon out of the storm; but even when he did, he couldn't get it back up to size.

While Lucent was fretting over his diminutive dragon, Everlee took the opportunity to blow the storm back up and knock Lucent and Yori out of the ring.

The crowd erupted in cheers and hollers and screams of defeat.

"Fyn! No wonder you love this enough to smuggle quills! Hilarious! Thrilling!" Ivy fumbled for her proof pad, now that the wind had died down. She just had to sketch that dragon while it was seared in her mind.

Fyn laughed along with Ivy, "I absolutely can promise that they are not always that funny." His voice got suddenly serious as he said, "Sometimes they can be quite terrifying. But nothing beats a match with Everlee Fortune! She must have the strongest grip in all of Croswald. Don't tell Canna I said that!"

"Ladies and gentlemen! We have a winner! Everlee Fortune." Duncan Wurchester held the grandmotherly woman's hand in the air.

Across the hex, Ivy saw Frederick jump to his feet.

"I'll catch up with you in a minute!" Ivy shouted over her shoulder to Fyn as she ran in and out of jolly scrivenists to Frederick. She tapped him on the shoulder.

"Frederick! Hi!"

"Ivy! I was just going to ask around for you. I'm so pleased you made it." He gave her a big bear hug. "Your friend has been very worried about you."

"I know, I know. I'm sure she is. I'm sorry. Could you give Rebecca a message for me? Gosh, it's good to see you! I wanted to write her, to tell her that I was here and safe, but I'm not sure how to get in touch. So it's so great that you're here!"

"Of course I can."

"Thank you so much! I've been aching to talk to her, to tell her I'm okay and just—just—*talk* to her!"

Frederick laughed, folding his program in half.

"Can you tell her that I'm all right? I've been staying with Fyn Greeley, a friend," Ivy was sure to clarify. "But I'm always thinking about her and wondering what she's up to."

"I promise you are on her mind, too," said Frederick.

o o o o

Ivy couldn't believe that the summer was coming to a close—not that it had been warm anywhere away from a hearth the whole time. But it was true. The Quality Quills Club had started to talk more about school than Quogo, and it made Ivy's heart ache to think about how much she'd be missing out. She tried to act engaged, but Fyn could always tell when she was sad and would often change the topic.

Lucent Habberdash had recovered from his embarrassing loss to Everlee Fortune and she, in turn, had lost to a rookie. The last match of the summer was between Habberdash and the rookie Beatrice Magpie. Canna could barely be sarcastic out of excitement and nerves for her favorite player.

The match proved to be even more exciting than the first, lasting nearly four hours. Beatrice stole the day with a disablement curse, which made Lucent's quill go as limp as a jellyfish. As the squiggling streamers and exploding confetti dropped from the ceiling to the crowd's delight, Ivy took it all in. It was the last match she would watch with friends until the next summer.

Ivy fidgeted with things she bought for Rebecca and scanned the crowd until she saw Frederick Faddacky.

"Ivy!" the jolly man exclaimed, "Rebecca insisted I bring this to you."

He pulled a lovely faux-fur stole from his satchel, and even better, a letter.

Ivy!

Really? A boy over your best friend? Happy to hear you're all right, though. Tell me they are treating you well. Frederick said he might see you again. I'm packing up for school–can you believe it? Anyway, if you're reading this, write back!

Rebecca

P.S. I thought you'd like this little number. The green lining is perfect for your hazel eyes! Frederick says it's freezing where you're at!

Ivy laughed out loud at Rebecca's characteristic energy and her thoughtfulness. Ivy gratefully took the quill and parchment that Frederick proffered and wrote:

Rebecca!

So good to hear from you, and thanks so much for the beautiful stole! No, I can't believe it's practically the end of summer! And really, Fyn's great but I miss you! He and his mother have been really good to me; Mrs. Greeley's cooking–her brisket!–is the best I've ever tasted! Oh, and I've joined a club... I think? What I mean is, I've made friends with some kids who are in a club. I wish I could be leaving here to the Halls with them in a few days. Miss seeing you every day. I know you won't be with Frederick much longer, so if I don't hear from you again until next summer, well, I hope your year is wonderful.

Ivy

Ivy sniffled. She tucked the note into the parcel she had brought for Frederick to bring to Rebecca. It was mostly fabrics and notions for the girl's fashion obsession: forever-fitting and water-resistant fabrics, stardust sequins, and shimmer lace.

"Tender girl, aren't you? Cheer up! Rebecca will be happy to hear from you. I must run to catch the last cabby, but don't be a stranger, Ivy." The kind scrivenist patted her arm.

All of a sudden, Fyn and Glistle burst back into view. They stumbled over, laughing at some inside joke.

"C'mon, Ivy! Time for some nosh," shouted Glistle delightedly. "Lennu lost! He bet Plumlie's for all of us on Habberdash. That's what he gets for showing off! I told him Magpie might be new, but she's brilliantly quick! So, are you coming?"

Ivy sniffed, trying to stuff down the thoughts of missing Rebecca, the Halls, everything in a few short days. "Sure, why not?"

Glistle shook his head. "Fyn, she's cute, but she's so emotional! It's only a game!"

Manone, Lennu, and Canna were all waiting atop the cabby deck, next to the Suitcasery, already delighting in Plumlie's. Pedlum arrived late, as usual, busy flirting with the Habberdash fans lingering outside the Quill Keep. Hayword was too busy packing up his creatures for school and getting organized, so he declined Lennu's offer.

"Tonight's match was crazy!" shouted Manone.

"Whatever! I'm a Habberdash fan for life!" added Canna bitterly.

"Man, he nearly had it!" said Glistle, delighting in a fudge-filled cracker hat.

Ivy leaned against the iron railing, looking over the enchanted, forbidden town.

Fyn came up behind her. "Are you okay? Pretty quiet since we left the hex."

Ivy turned towards Fyn. "Not really. At the Halls, for the first time in my life, I was welcome somewhere. I met you and Rebecca, made friends, and here I am: uninvited again. Just sort of hits a raw spot, you know?"

"Well, you'll always be welcome in Belzebuthe. And being

away from school isn't forever… I'll talk to the Selector when I get back; I'll ask her about your return." Fyn smiled, piling the pudding onto his spoon. "Don't forget, I used to be her chief informant."

"Ha! Thought you were the class facilitator."

"Same difference."

"Well, thanks for talking to her. It's just—I don't know, I guess I just feel like I'm missing something. Derwin sent me here to find the second segment of the Kindred Stone, and I've found nothing. It all just feels like, I don't know, pointless."

"That's his fault, not yours. Scrivenists are supposed to remember where they put things."

"Yeah, well, my scrivenist was lost at sea for too long. His memories were washed away with the waves."

As Fyn and Ivy stared back into the stars, Glistle brought a cracker hat for Ivy. "How about it? Going to give these fudgy things another shot?"

Ivy took in a deep breath. Before she could reach for the treat, one of the dark shadows above them grew larger as it descended. It littered its gray snow down on their heads, and Ivy felt it fit the mood. Then it touched down right in front of the Suitcasery. The three craned their necks over to watch the strange thing; Glistle even dropped the cracker hat over the ledge.

"Well, at least I don't have to open that one," Ivy joked weakly.

The cloud evaporated, leaving only dirty sleet behind.

CHAPTER ELEVEN

MOONSDAY

SUMMER was officially over. The other sqwinches in Belzebuthe, her friends, as Ivy had begun to think of them, had all departed in order to get school supplies and be in Ravenshollow for the Moonsday celebration. She was glad to have the distraction of work and the anticipation of studying once her Compass Startus began to populate itself with classwork.

She also loved the private assignments that Derwin had sent her through mendlott: "Describe the nature of the Kindred Stone" or "Practice levitating objects with and without a quill" or, the latest, "Sketch every phase of the moon from memory." She knew that these were custom built for her—she was the only one who'd need to know about the Kindred Stone for now, and the only scrivenist who was going to be able to perform magic without the direct use of a quill.

Belzebuthe was bustling—everyone getting ready for the holiday. This time the year before, Ivy had experienced her first Moonsday parade, complete with moonie pies. Even though it had been cut short by being chased by poking quills, it had been the best birthday she could remember.

For as long as Ivy could remember, Moonsday hadn't meant feasting; it meant work. Lots of work, tending the scaldrons alone in a sweltering hot cellar. It made going in to help Hodge and Podge seem like a breeze. She left before Mrs. Greeley was up and made her way down to the shop.

Ivy unlocked the door of Quinton's Brews & Hodgepodge and set about sweeping and tidying the shelves. She did her best to put the thought of celebrating Moonsday without her friends, of staying in Belzebuthe with only the company of busy adults, out of her mind.

By the time Podge came bursting through the door, Ivy had even cleaned up the back room—some experiment gone wrong.

"Oh! Hello, dear. Didn't expect you to come in!"

"Why not?"

"Well—the holiday! Nobody really needs potions today, and it's your special day! A happiest of birthdays to you, friend! I imagine you'll be doing something special for the big day."

Ivy smiled lightly in response. She had no plans, other than staying away from a Fyn-less home as long as possible. Podge waddled over towards Ivy with a small but hefty pouch.

"A little token for your hard work this summer. And an incentive to stay on with us as long as you can! We never dreamed we'd hire a sqwinch, but you've been a real treat."

"Is this a dwarf thing? Brums in old bags?" Her heart warmed at the memory of Rimbrick on their hill last year, but she had to stop herself from letting her emotions get the best of her. Ivy was touched by Podge's generosity, though she'd gladly give up all the coin in Croswald for someone to share her birthday with. "Thank you, Podge. Working here has been one of the best parts about living in Belzebuthe."

Podge smiled widely. "Now, shoo! Out with you. Go enjoy the day!" The little dwarf was pushing her out the door.

"Ha! All right then."

With one hand on the door, Ivy looked back at him a final time. "Will you and Hodge be celebrating the holiday?"

"With everything but beet ale," he grinned. Ivy did too. Podge continued, "I've got a bit of work to do, but don't miss the starguster parade! It puts the Ravenshollow hairie parade to shame!"

The festivities had begun in earnest: dancing and feasting in every home and spilling out onto the street. On Moonsday, Belzebuthe's typical darkness was punctured by hairie lanterns hung from every balcony and sparkling candles that lit the walkways. Even the stars seemed extra twinkly.

The wet, cobbled street that Ivy walked down reflected the colorful lights above: bright pinks, yellows, oranges, and purples. Then, with a shout, music began. A chorus of scrivenists wielded their quills and instruments made of magical sparkles floated above their heads, spouting forth jaunty, playful tunes.

Tinny roars took over the music for a moment, and the starguster parade commenced! The little motorbikes zoomed up and led the revelers through the street from above. The stargusters had lights hung from their handlebars and had been painted to glow for the evening. The drivers did little loop-de-loops in the sky while people below hooted. Ivy laughed and waved. Two of the stargusters were connected by a chain of hairie lanterns strung from a cord between them. The drivers smiled and waved as they skidded across the sky.

Ivy buttoned up her coat against the chill and followed the

parade, exploring the streets and shops on the way. Anything to avoid going back to an empty house. She made her way through the growing throng. Everyone chattered on, discussing the old double moon, magic, and more. As she walked, Ivy caught random bits of conversation from all corners.

"The Halls of Ivy opened again despite last year's Ball," said a thin-as-a-rail woman. "Can you believe it?"

From the other side of the street, an elderly man said, "It's a shame to miss the double moon, but Princess Isabella's power has left it and gone elsewhere."

Ivy ducked in and out of the crowd, eventually passing by Bramble's Fritters & Nosh, decorated brightly for the holiday with lanterns in the windows, wreaths on the door, and snow piled high in corners. The table where Ivy, Fyn, and their friends always sat was empty. As Ivy stared into the window, a little girl ran past in the reflection, giggling and tossing snow into the air, playing catch with herself.

Another conversation fragment drifted by: "I'd wait in that line all night. Tastes better than Spinner's Foam even!"

Ivy looked across the way to the voice. The line at the Melted Milkshake was out the door. Almost everyone in line had a smile and a lantern. Ivy tapped the shoulder of a bundled-up woman with her grandchild at her side. "Excuse me, but what's the line for?"

"Special Moonsday milkshakes!"

"Milkshakes in the cold?"

"Melted and sold in hot cups, of course."

The bright, colorful shop was no larger than the larder Ivy once lived in back at Castle Plum. The shop was below street level and curved purple bricks led to the entry. She could see the lilac and pink streamers and jars of candy inside. Ivy got in line and was grateful for how long it was—all the more to postpone going home. Besides, it was her birthday; a sweet treat was in order.

When Ivy got hers, the hot cup was almost too hot to handle. She wrapped it in her scarf and enjoyed the fragrance of the special moonie flavor: sweet caramel, nutmeg, and vanilla. Perfect for this snowy night. The luminous lanterns outnumbered the people, hanging from every gutter, every cranny, dressing the town in a colorful display of holiday lights.

She meandered through the streets, hot cup in hand. Ivy was unaccustomed to treating herself, but with the little pouch of unexpected brums in her pocket, she determined to go to the last spot in Belzebuthe that she hadn't yet explored—the Star Shoppe. Maybe she'd get herself her very own fishing rod. Make a birthday wish.

But when she got to the storefront, it was closed as usual. Even its display was dark, as all the lights and miniature stargusters they usually had in the window were being towed along behind the real stargusters in the parade.

"Rats."

Ivy made her way around the corner and into the alley. Perhaps someone was still in the shop and would let her in through a back entrance. Or maybe it was unlocked and she could let herself in just to take a look.

The alley was darker than the brightly lit street and the sounds of the raucous band faded. A wind stirred Ivy's skirt around her ankles, and snow flurries began to fall.

Then there was a strong whistling sound, followed by the clatter and rattle of metal crashing. Her curiosity and impulse to investigate lured her deeper into the alley. Directly behind Wally's Wardrobe, an entire garbage bin had been crushed and flipped on its side. Scraps of fabric were scattered everywhere. Ivy looked behind the bin, up and down the alley, trying to see what had tipped the heavy can. Nothing. *Strange.*

The wind swirled again, and Ivy looked up; a dark cloud spun above her. Her melted milkshake went flying through the air, splattering the bricks. She held her long jacket closed, protecting what was most important: her stone. The wind flew Ivy's satchel in the air behind her, pulling hard across her chest. Her hair was whipped into knots.

Then the dark whirlwind shot across to the opposite end of the alley, getting thicker and darker. It started to spin back toward her. Ivy braced for impact. But as she watched, she could see the storm lose energy. It touched down for a second time, slowed down sluggishly, and then dropped into a pile of slushy dark snow.

"What in all of Croswald—"

"A shade. Are you all right?" A gentleman had joined Ivy in the alley. He was a matteler, judging by his coat, and his dark beard couldn't hide his worried expression. His gray eyes reminded her of someone, but she couldn't place it. "And this one lasted longer than any other so far."

"What is a—a shade?" Ivy asked in a whisper.

"We aren't sure just yet, but I have my suspicions…."

Ivy waited for him to finish.

"We can't be sure, but the way they hurl themselves at the boundary, seeping through, they mean us harm. But the barriers keep them from lasting too long, from fully forming."

"Who are you?" she asked.

"Easel Leelangraf. Chief Matteler and Spellseeker."

Glistle and Gretta's father!

"You've got to be careful not to walk these alleys alone. Sad to say, they're not safe anymore."

Ivy protested. "This is Belzebuthe. Belzebuthe is safe!"

"Best to join the festivities, where you won't be alone, young lady."

They bade each other goodnight, and Ivy arrived late at the Greeley house. Mrs. Greeley was readying herself for bed, but as she heard Ivy walking upstairs, she came to greet her, albeit with a face plastered in facial mud, hair in a net, and in her peach nightie.

"Hello, Mrs. Greeley."

"Lonely, are you, dear?" she asked sympathetically.

"I am glad to have you for company. Just missing friends, that's all."

Mrs. Greeley tsked and then said, "Fyn asked that I wait and give you this on your birthday." She handed Ivy a package that looked suspiciously like a book. "Oh, and some packages arrived in the lott earlier today. All for you and in your room! Happy birthday, Ivy."

"Thank you!" Ivy called to the retreating Mrs. Greeley. Ivy was still unaccustomed to birthday celebrations; before last year, the only gifts she had received were books from dear old Rimbrick.

Humboldt rose to greet her. The nuzzle from his warm snout felt great on her cold feet. The hairies twinkled as she set them down. True to Mrs. Greeley's word, there was a small pile of gifts on her bed!

Ivy opened the gift from the Greeleys first. "*The Book of Bad Quills!* Oh, this must be everyone in the Quill Keep, Hum."

She flipped through the pages of the book. In long columns, scrivenists of all ages were pictured alongside their quills, and detail of their mischievous spells and dangers were recorded on the bottom half of the page. Fyn knew the book would tickle Ivy's thirst for history. She set the *Bad Quills* book aside and opened her next gift.

"Habberdash combat boots from Canna, Lennu, and Manone." Ivy smiled as she opened one paper-wrapped gift. They would be good for the days ahead that were bound to get colder.

A tiny potted violet sat on top of a box. She picked up the delicate plant and read the tag: *Ivy, Happy Birthday! I thought this flower was pretty, but not as lovely as you. Make sure to water it or you'll regret it! Glistle.*

Ivy found herself blushing at the compliment and then shuddering at the memory of Glistle's "gift" to Fyn. She sprinkled water under the delicate leaves immediately.

The small envelope was from Hayword. Ivy opened it and a letter and a set of porcupels fell out. *As many porcupines as I have, you shall never want for porcupels again!* Ivy laughed. The simple, useful gift reflected Hayword's personality.

Finally, Ivy turned her attention to a beautiful, dome-lidded box. It was the length of a lott, but the width of a Compass Startus. As she turned the wooden box over in her hand, she felt a little tumble inside it. She fiddled with the latch and, *pop*, the lid lifted. Ivy couldn't believe what she saw—Winsome's unlocker box! And his quill! She recognized the frayed, gold quill immediately.

Good news, read the note inside the box, *I've recovered Winsome's quill. I can think of no one better to give his things to than you. Happy Birthday, Ivy. Stay safe. D.E.N.*

Ivy teared up. Holding close to her chest the box Derwin had sent, she looked out her window—the stars were bright, but there seemed to be more and more of those shade things out and about. She didn't dare venture on the roof with them hovering, especially without Fyn. The chilly summer had given straightaway to an even colder fall, and snow was piled up against the buildings.

Too energized to sleep just yet, Ivy propped herself up on pillows and opened her Compass Startus. One official school assignment had populated itself! It was from her Magic Inside Creatures class: *Choose a critter, big or small, and in essay form, describe its behaviors, peculiarities, and any useful properties of its shell, nails, hair, etc.* Ivy knew exactly what to choose. She crept all the way back downstairs, careful not to wake Mrs. Greeley, to the coat closet opposite the front door. The lumbuses were in the exact spot that they had left them.

Ivy whispered the spell that Hayword had used at the party over the little carton—and then a quick *thank you, Hayword!*—and brought them upstairs. Back in her room, she gently picked one up and set to sketching and writing.

> *Lumbus: odd, if not downright creepy. A lumbus is encased in a palm-sized, smooth shell, much like a freshwater snail. The little orange-skinned creature that lives inside has oversized bony hands. When disturbed, they are impossibly loud.*

After looking it up in her Collectis, she wrote,

> *They grow in most moist places like mold–perfect for the Town–and they multiply rapidly in little mossy habitats.*

"Maybe they're kinda cute. Sort of," she said to herself. Thanks to Quinton's, Ivy knew without having to experiment:

> *Their dead, sloughed off skin is very valuable because it is the key ingredient in a classic potion for dramatically improved hearing. The duration depends on the potion's potency.*

When she felt satisfied with her sketch, Ivy turned to Derwin's assignment, which still glittered with wet ink from an unseen quill: *Find out all you can about the Occulyst.*

The definition in the Collectis was brief: *A repository for valuable things, populated and powered by magical Occulyst owls. Essentially a bank for scrivenists.*

"That's not very helpful, is it?" she said.

Ivy scanned Wembly's bookshelves, grateful yet again to be put up in what was essentially a tiny library.

"Ah, there you are! Just what I need."

An extremely dusty brown book had *The Occulyst: Owls, Oddities, and Other Odds and Ends* emblazoned on the spine. She dusted off the volume with her hand, then blew on it. A cloud of dust puffed up in her face and she sneezed. One lumbus moved, and Ivy held stock-still. *Don't wake up!*

Once she was certain the lumbus was still resting, Ivy cracked open the book to the middle. But before she could read a word, her eye fell on a small something that had been folded in the pages for who knows how long.

It was the size of a fingernail, smooth and polished, slightly oval like an egg. It was pearlescent and absolutely mesmerizing. On the narrower end, there were little etch marks around the perimeter. A soft golden line pointed from the pole down toward the little etch marks; as she moved, the golden line drifted around on the surface of the pearly egg. She couldn't touch the line—it was as if the line were projected from the inside of the sphere.

Ivy sank into her bed, gently pinching the little object and watching the golden line drift one way then the next. Her hairies dimmed. She hadn't realized how tired she'd become.

I'll finish the Occulyst assignment tomorr...

But before she could finish the thought, Ivy had drifted into a dreamless sleep.

Chapter Twelve

A Potions War

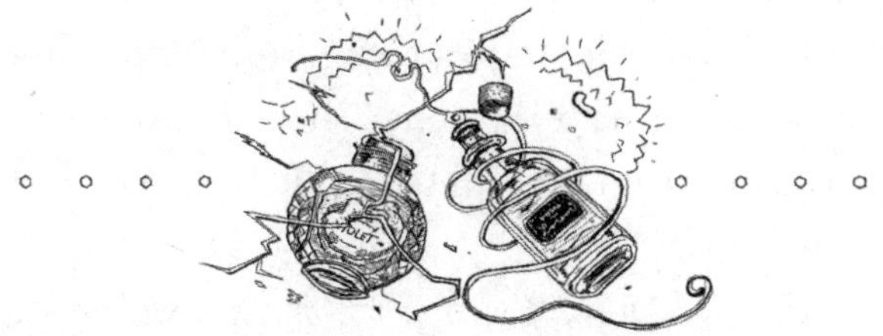

On a late fall morning, Ivy was uncharacteristically late for work. Her sleep had been deep and restful, yet also costly—now she had to run to work. As she rushed past, she could see that the Star Shoppe was empty as always, but its lovely, ever-changing display window held a handful of stars against an inky velvet backdrop. In the center, a miniature starguster was floating through the darkness and a tiny pair of animated puppets was star-gazing together. With a pang, Ivy remembered the nights on the roof with Fyn. *No! Think of potions!* She hadn't known it would be this hard to be separated from her friends, especially Fyn and Rebecca, for so many moons. No matter how interesting Belzebuthe was, no matter how kind Mrs. Greeley was, it still wasn't home.

Since the school year had started, the Compass Startus sitting on Wembly Greeley's old desk had been Ivy's major source of interest. Diagrams of creature innards from Professor Wrigley, sketching assignments from Professor Petty, glanagerie reading from Professor Night. Professor Derwin Edgar Night. Her scrivenist had apparently turned professor. Ivy had so many questions to ask him! She was relieved that he'd promised to visit Belzebuthe sometime in the winter moons, but she didn't feel like she could wait that long.

The other sources of light in her dark environment were conversations around the dinner table with Mrs. Greeley, cuddles with Humboldt, and learning from Hodge and Podge. Just like her tutoring with Winsome, she found that she learned best by watching them and imitating their expert mixing and making of potions.

Maybe there'll be a chipper dipper from Bramble's when I get in. The bright lemon flavor of the brothers' favorite teacake always put her in a better mood. *That or I'll get a new book from Lie Buries later.*

But the din from inside Quinton's erased any thought of cake or books or friends from her mind. The display windows were entirely clouded over in a noxious pink smoke. The windowpanes vibrated and Podge's shouts rattled inside.

Thinking they needed her help, Ivy barreled toward the door and threw it open. She leapt back just in time to let a dancing red magic cloud crackle and sparkle out through the door and down the street.

"What in all of Croswald?" she whispered. Ivy poked her head in to see Podge ducking and dodging as he clambered up a set of shelves.

"No! Not the Shrinking Swill!" he shouted.

But a cloud of tiny firecrackers enveloped him despite Podge's protests. As he shrank, his scratchy voice got smaller and smaller.

"Oh drat!" he squeaked, looking at Hodge venomously.

Then Podge, sweet tiny little thing that he was now, took a dark vial from the shelf where he stood. It was lucky that he happened to be where the smallest potion vials were and he could still lift one. Well, it was lucky for him, at least. He hefted the tiny vessel up and then threw it toward Hodge. It emitted a great volume of dark cloud, which gathered over Hodge's head and promptly began pouring down rain.

Ivy pushed back her brown hair, now soaking wet and hanging lankly about her face. She couldn't believe her eyes. Were Hodge and Podge fighting? With potions? And totally destroying the shop?

As if in reply to her thoughts, Hodge grabbed the nearest thing he could, a large swan-shaped vase with an elegant long neck. He swung it as hard as he could, but the neck slipped out of his wet hand and crashed on the wall left of Podge. The vase, instead of smashing into pieces, turned into a real swan, which commenced to honking and splashing in the mini storm. At least someone was happy about the rain.

Perhaps because of the *squonk squonk* of the newly arrived and uninvited guest, Ivy burst into laughter. But the hilarity was short-lived; she felt a splat of something oozy hit her square between the shoulders. A golden potion had been launched at her by a giggling Hodge. The rubbery material spread, quickly wrapping around her sides.

As she tried to yank the rubber off her shoulders, it pinned down Ivy's left arm. Although she wasn't meant to, she focused her mind (in the way she had come to know as the feeling of using her magic) to keep it from completely binding her. The Kindred Stone sparked away in her pocket as Ivy balled the rubbery stuff and threw it back toward Hodge. It bounced him directly on the chest, sending him tumbling back into yet another bookshelf, knocking all its contents to the floor.

Hodge's tail, which he most certainly didn't have moments before, wrapped around the rolling ladder and he was sent whipping around the room. Mischievously, Ivy sent a beam of magic to speed up the ladder, then turned to throw another bottle at Podge with a laugh.

"Ha! Just what I needed, thanks!" Podge said as he neatly caught the potion she'd thrown, downing it in one chug.

Podge went from pint-sized to larger than life in about ten seconds. Soon his head was pressing against the ceiling, with his shoulders stuck around the shop's joist. Ivy and Hodge backed up to get out of the way of his growing leg and knocked over another potion, one in a bottle shaped like a porcupel. In a puff, a scrivenist appeared.

"You have summoned me—what do you wish to document? Oh, my! A giant? Let's begin…."

And the scrivenist began furiously sketching the chaotic scene in front of him. His sketch was complete with the rain, the swirling clouds of magical dust, the spilled potions, the vocal swan, and now-giant Podge, whose head had broken through the shop's ceiling and into the apartment above. Straight into their dining room, from the sound of it.

A muffled, "Goodness gracious, Podge. Welcome! Spot of tea?" came through the ceiling.

Meanwhile, outside the store window, the hairie lights were glowing and flashing more intensely than ever. A sizable crowd was gathering outside. A whole slew of scrivenists—in addition to the potion one, who by now had faded, leaving only his notes—sketched the scene. The swan escaped, honking as it gained its freedom. Ivy hid behind a shelf, pulling the hood farther over her head, soaking wet and laughing in a corner.

"What's so funny? You ruined this place!" Hodge squealed.

"Me?! You two were well at it before I got here! Plus, you threw that rubber thingy at me first!" Ivy was hiccupping, she was laughing so hard. "Why the potions war?" With one last chuckle and a sigh, Ivy asked, "Is that some dwarf game? Or you two just being brothers, or what?"

"We've had a minor disagreement."

"Minor? Seems major, according to the mess. What about?" Ivy asked.

The giant Podge grumbled, "Oh, bother. This is going to take quite a bit of fixing."

Hodge drew out his quill and with a swish of his wrist the shelves were stacked back up and the potions began floating back into place. Hodge had pressed a bottle of pills into Podge's enormous hand. "Take only one, you big oaf."

"This, of all days, to leave the expeller at home!"

This comment of Podge's sent Ivy laughing again at all the ridiculousness. The hand disappeared into the apartment above, where Podge's head was. Gradually, the dwarf shrank back to his usual diminutive size.

"Well, that didn't go as planned, did it?" Podge was fairly cheerful, despite the state of the destroyed shop.

"What exactly *did* you have planned?" Ivy was by now very curious.

Podge sniffed, "Like Hodge said, we had a disagreement. A potions duel is the only dwarfly, logical way to settle anything."

"You are wrong, I tell you! She ought to know!" shouted Hodge. "Just because we know doesn't mean we meddle with her mendlott!"

"Know what?" Ivy questioned.

The two dwarves scuffled, just like boys on a schoolyard.

Ivy straightened up.

"Hodge! Podge! I'd say you'd best call it a draw. At least until we clean all this up!"

Hodge couldn't resist one more comment, unusual for the quiet dwarf, "We must let things unfold. She has a right to read that which is addressed to her!"

The two were clearly seething, and Ivy didn't know what to do but clean.

It took the three of them the entire day to restore the shop to its original glory, though now minus the dust. So focused were they on the task that Ivy didn't even notice the dwarve's lott rattling. Hodge and Podge glared at each other. Ivy walked to the lott and a mendlott popped out: a letter addressed to Ivy.

"Don't open it!" shouted Podge.

"Who is this from?" The envelope was silver, like her original invitation to the Halls of Ivy.

Both dwarves eyed one another knowingly.

Dear Miss Lovely,

Please return to school at once. All is well, and we'd like for you to resume your studies at the Halls.

Sincerely,
The Selector

Spelling

SITTING on a velveteen bench in a nearly empty cabby, Ivy bit her lip, nervous about her late start at the Halls. To calm herself, she read and reread the letter from the day before. Every time she read the letter, her heart leapt in her chest! As crazy—and fun—as the past moons had been in Belzebuthe, she couldn't seem to shake the loneliness, especially once her friends had left. And the Halls of Ivy, even before she knew it to be her ancestral castle, was the one place she had felt at home.

Ivy studied her schedule in the peace of her lonely back seat.

Second Year Class Schedule

Invisitaur Riding **Break of Dawn, once a week**
Professor Wheeler: Learn to catch, care, and ride one of Croswald's most indistinct and speediest creatures. Rain, shine, or snow, be prepared to ride the (mostly) invisible beast. Riding boots required.

The Magic Inside Creatures **First Hour**
Professor Wrigley: Learn the anatomy and magical properties of beasts and small critters. An in-depth exploration of creatures' most potent powers.

Magical Management **Second Hour**
Professor Royal: Without proper management, magic can be quite unruly. Learn to steward magic in this class through focus and the art of spelling.

Luncheon **Third Hour**
Enjoy a magically prepared lunch of your choice served to you by visiting master chef Duey Dummont, professors emeriti, or our wild-eyed Jester.

Settings in Sketching **Fourth Hour**
Professor Petty: Take your budding sketching ability around the Halls of Ivy to render tableaus and scenes.

Glanagerie Practicum **Fifth Hour**
Professor Night: Second years will dive deeper into the charmed spring water, using their real magical abilities to solve imaginary problems.

Hour of Discovery **Sixth Hour**
Venture, discover, and learn on your own. Let the halls lead you whichever way they wish. Choose to explore as much as you see fit or not the slightest bit. Do remember to stay on floors appropriate to your grade level.

Ivy tingled with excitement at the thought of being able to dive back into her studies. She could barely believe that it was safe enough for her to return; however, she wasn't about to second-guess the Selector's letter. But what would Ivy's friends and professors think of her quarter-term absence? The last time she had seen most of them had been at the Masquerade Ball. Ivy shivered at the memory. How much did they know about who she really was? She hoped that the time lapse had cooled her fellow students' curiosity. She didn't feel like answering a million questions about the Ball. Would they avoid her in hopes of avoiding a certain queen, too?

Chills coursed through her body, though it may have been a direct result of the snowstorm building outside the cabby. Her winter coat had been stowed away, but she did have Humboldt, whose hot breath cozied her feet, already in warmupps. She curled in a corner against a small frosted window. The cabby's typical rain had been supplanted by wind-whipping slush and snow—it was almost winter, even outside of Belzebuthe. Ivy held the dome-lidded box that Derwin had sent her on Moonsday. Just having Winsome's things brought her comfort. She wondered what she would learn at the instruction of his quill.

In addition, Mrs. Greeley had insisted that Ivy take whichever books she pleased as a parting gift. She hardly knew which ones to put in the trunk that Mrs. Greeley had given her, but she had taken with her the book about the Occulyst, the Crownerie handbook, one of Wembly's heavily notated books on the Wandering Family, and several others about stones.

With a lurch, they dropped out from the cloud cover momentarily and Ivy saw a glimpse of the Halls before her window clouded over again. Ivy knew that cabby rides were less than smooth, but this one seemed extra erratic. The cabby compartment began to quake, and then there was a huge crunch as the cabby grazed a turret and was spun around. The sudden shake caused the quill to flash, accidentally bursting open the overhead storage compartments and dumping a pile of clothes on Ivy's head. Then the whirling cabby crashed into the same turret lower down, having spun all the way back around. This time it crashed all the way through. The cabby beast had burst through one turret wall and was halfway hanging out the opposite one. Ivy had intended to arrive *at* school, but not *into* it.

Everything—teacups, eight passengers, books, benches, and one scaldron—was in a jumble. As soon as Ivy could untangle herself from laundry, she gathered Humboldt and her hairies and burst out of the little compartment's door. She panted, catching her breath as she took in the scene around her. They had crashed through Professor Royal's classroom. The same glorious windows overlooked the last of Ravenshollow's autumn color—soon there would be snow here, too. The tall indoor trees that held up the room's atrium framed the clearing at the front of the room for students to practice mastering magic.

Ivy's wild-eyed look was met with equally stunned expressions from the small group of second years studying Magical Management. Thankfully, they had been congregated around a back table on the opposite side of the room and no one was hurt. Though cabby travel was clumsy, crash landings always seemed to avoid crashing into people. Ivy could see that dust and debris had collected in her classmates' hair.

Hayword ran to see the beast out the front window. The beast was perfectly fine and continued making his storm, which had become an indoor-outdoor affair.

Next, Ivy heard a familiar voice.

"Ivy!" Rebecca rushed to hug her friend.

Although Ivy felt humiliated—standing in the center of the classroom, the obvious culprit of such disaster and sudden mess—she was relieved to see her friend again.

"Umbrellas, please!" Ivy heard Professor Royal command in her strong, beautiful voice. And like giant leaves, shiny black umbrellas drifted down from the ceiling.

Ivy gulped. She had a terrible feeling that this was actually the class she was meant to be in.

"Er, hello," she greeted the class that gawked in silence.

"Ivy Lovely," Professor Royal said, crossing her thin arms across her chest and smiling warmly, "I've been hoping you'd join us. Welcome back."

"Am I late?" Ivy asked the obvious. She was mortified. First day mortification was all too familiar for Ivy.

"No, rather, you're just in time," smiled Professor Royal, who had pinned back her softly curled hair. "Today's topic is spelling. Please, everyone back to your seats."

Ivy let out a little sigh of relief. It was a warmer welcome than she could have hoped for, considering her entrance. And she was so glad that Damaris didn't seem to be here.

But before she could finish the thought, a familiar yet unwelcome voice pierced the air. "You aren't going to let her keep *that* in class, are you? A scaldron?!" Ivy turned just in time to see Damaris mouth her favorite insult—*slurry girl.*

Thankfully the tension was shattered by an unexpected boom. Ivy's trunk was slung off the cabby's roof and hit one of the remaining walls. With a rumble and crumble of stonework, the cabby and its indoor snowstorm took off, as did the umbrellas. The cabby's magic repaired the wall as it departed, and Professor Royal used her Stone of Abrise to tidy the room.

Rebecca called for Ivy from a corner, motioning to the desk next to her.

Without hesitation, Ivy hobbled along with her things, Humboldt in hand.

"It's so good to see you. I missed you terribly," whispered Rebecca.

"Me too! Like mad. But I'm so embarrassed," replied Ivy, head down.

"What for? Before you arrived, Hannelore Lawler admitted she got lost on the way to class—for the tenth time! That girl is too quick for her own good! She's always rushing right past the door and missing it!"

"Soon she'll be able to control that Jessel Stone," said Ivy.

Hayword interrupted, "Hey, Ivy! Mind if I hold Humboldt?"

"Sure." Ivy smiled. "Thanks, Hayword. It's good to see you again." Humboldt loved the extra attention.

Professor Royal resumed her lesson. "As we were discussing, magic is a gift, my sqwinches and royals, a powerful gift that must be guided to serve you and not overrun you." She paused and then spoke again, "One of the most powerful abilities of scrivenists is that of spelling. In another school, spelling might mean putting together letters to make words. At the Halls, spelling means putting together letters to make words *to make spells.* Spelling is the art and craft of casting spells with your quill, class.

"You may wonder why, if you are a royal, you are privy to this spelling lesson. You'll never have a quill, so why bother? First, we must strive to understand not only our own magic but also the magic of others. Please take hold of a porcupel and do as I do."

Professor Royal waved her practice quill with a flourish and spelled with the tip: *studysesh for all.* The letters sparkled and twinkled in the air and dainty cups of piping hot tea landed on each student's desk.

"To warm you all up," she smiled as she spoke. "And you may need a sip as we practice spelling. Let's all try and conjure a cooling spell for the tea, shall we?"

"Can I spell a lock for that scaldron's habbitry?" snarked Damaris.

Ivy saw at least Hannelore and Hayword roll their eyes.

"Well, we appreciate your enthusiasm, but likely not, Damaris. Just as sqwinches learn basic techniques for managing stones, royals learn basic techniques for quills. This is one of the weeks you'll have to chalk up what you learned to enrichment. As a royal, I use a teaching quill or a porcupel, and though I'm more practiced than you are now, most of you scrivenists-in-training will surpass my spelling in the next few years."

Professor Royal had them open their Compass Starti.

"First off, penmanship is absolutely key. Even someone with a mind as bright as Hayword's might be hindered by terrible writing," Professor Royal sent him a playful look. "Your spellecution—how well you write your spell—absolutely dictates how successful your spells will be. The spell for cooling is simply *chill.* Everyone, practice writing the word *chill*, over and over, until you are absolutely confident. Go on! If you need a fresh porcupel, come see me."

The class set into writing, bodies bent over desks. When they were ready, they held up their porcupel and, mimicking the flourish of a true scrivenist, they wrote *chill* in the air over their cups.

Ivy got the hang of it quite easily but tried to downplay her ease with magic. She helped Colleen Holly slow her hand (she had to take off her crown) to round out the letters more smoothly. Their porcupels only sputtered dully, as compared to Professor Royal's. But nonetheless, enough magic was channeled so that about half the sqwinches were able to cool their tea. Rebecca had gone a little overboard and performed the spell nine times—her tea was ice cold.

"Ivy, you've done well with your work." Professor Royal leafed through Ivy's Compass Startus. Just like last year, it had expanded with her knowledge and had been growing increasingly thick since the fall term had begun.

"Thank you. I'm… happy to be back."

Professor Royal's hand rested on the wooden box with Winsome's quill and unlocker inside. "This is lovely. Perhaps safer in your trunk? And your trunk is probably better in your room," she said with a smile.

"Y—yes!" Ivy stammered.

Then the professor turned to answer Quincy Fryer's question about misspelled spells, leaving Ivy to her thoughts.

Chapter Fourteen

The Dorms

WITH Humboldt's habbitry and Ivy's trunk dragging between them, Ivy and Rebecca giggled and talked the whole way back to the dormitory.

"I'm so glad that we have a break for lunch! I don't think I could wait another second to talk to you! I've been *dying* without you here. Damaris is actually worse than ever, believe it or not, and the schoolwork is getting serious! Professor Wrigley assigns so much homework."

"Tell me about it! But what's he like?"

"Both weird and wonderful! Really knows his stuff. I've been missing my Hour of Discovery just trying to catch up!"

"Well, that will never do!" Ivy wiggled her eyebrows mischievously. "Now that I'm back, we'll do some real discovery."

"We'll see. I don't know if I've forgiven you for not coming home with me this past summer! *And* having an extended break without me!"

Ivy groaned, "Trust me, the past moons have been no holiday. Once school started, no one under a hundred was left in town!"

Rebecca laughed at Ivy's exaggeration—usually more Rebecca's style than Ivy's.

"But actually, if it weren't for the Halls and friends, I wouldn't mind never leaving there. It's really a remarkable place. Definitely beats anything else I've known."

"What's it like, Ivy? Frederick never really tells me about where he's from."

"Well, for starters it's always night. They have stars out your window, beautifully lit low-hung stars capable of granting wishes. Fyn and I fished for stars on his birthday. Then there's Hodge and Podge, the funniest duo you'll ever meet. They run Quinton's Brews & Hodgepodge, where I worked over the summer stocking potion ingredients and products."

"Is everyone there *really* a scrivenist? So many in one place!" Rebecca's eyes lit up like the stars Ivy described.

"Yeah, pretty much. Quills and all. And real-life Quogo, but more about that later on. I missed you terribly! The letter that Frederick brought from you was a highlight!"

"Frederick said you made a bunch of new friends… I hope I haven't been replaced!"

"Never!"

Once safely back in their dormitory, the same spot as last year only one level up on the second-year floor, Ivy placed her books on the shelf, along with the violet from Glistle. And Humboldt, happier than ever, sniffed out every crevice in the dorm room, searching for any tasty morsel.

"What's *that*?" Ivy's eyes widened as she pointed to an illustration in a textbook lying open on Rebecca's fluffy purple duvet. A rough sketch of a horned beast that stood upright was only half finished, unusual in a textbook.

"How funny to think I know more about invisitaurs than you, the best student at the Halls! We've been taking riding lessons, early in the morning, before class once a week. Part of being a second year! So far, it's just been 'catch 'em if you can' lessons. Half of the challenge is just finding them!"

"Why is this only half-sketched?" Ivy asked.

"To show that they are invisible most of the time. Really, you can only see them when the rain bounces off of them. No real color, just a shape in the rain. They understand everything you say. It's just a matter of finding one and convincing it to give you a ride! For those who have been lucky enough to find one, we end up with bruises all over! I never seem to know where the horns should be and always end up tumbling to the ground." Despite the bruises, Rebecca seemed thrilled. "I only wish the class met every day! It's too much fun!"

"That sounds so amazing, especially after being kind of cooped up."

"The only one who's had any consistent luck is Gregory Gershwin with his darn Weatheritall Stone. He can just spin out those puffs of rain cloud and see them better. I get the feeling that the invisitaurs are teasing us. They can see and hear from miles. They supposedly live all around the Halls."

"All over? You're kidding! Do they even like being ridden?"

"Supposedly they love it, but only when it's a seasoned rider, one that gives good back scratches. Not that I have any firsthand experience," Rebecca rolled her eyes.

Ivy giggled. "Ugh! You've had so much more fun than I have!"

Ivy began unpacking her trunk. The self-populating wardrobe now held uniforms in amethyst, one shade closer toward the traditional scrivenist plum than first years' periwinkle. She set her hairies beside her bed, and they were as dim as ever. Something about the cold in Belzebuthe had brought out the brightness in them. *Oh well.*

"I'm glad you feel bad about ditching me."

Ivy glanced back at Rebecca and grinned, "I didn't ditch you. I was staying out of trouble."

"Ivy, let's be real. Trouble always seems to find you."

Winsome's wooden box caught Rebecca's eye as Ivy unpacked it.

"Pretty. Is it new?"

"A birthday gift from Derwin. A collection of Winsome's things, like his quill, his unlocker."

"Oh yes! You must have thought I had forgotten! Open this." Rebecca thrust a large and primly wrapped package into Ivy's hands. "Croswald's most belated birthday gift. I tried to get it to you, but Frederick hasn't had time to get back to the Town. Happy birthday, Ivy!"

"You didn't have to."

"Of course I didn't have to. Open it! I made it myself."

It was one of Rebecca's amazing creations: an incredible dress. It was a blush gown with sheer fabric at the neck. The bodice and skirt had a beautiful pattern of sequins cascading down. The full skirt was actually a series of fabric panels shaped like the wings of a hairie.

"Rebecca! I love it!" Ivy gasped. "Did you use the stardust sequins I got you on this? They were for you!"

Rebecca just shrugged, "Considering your only other gown is, one, destroyed and, two, already worn, I thought you'd need something special for this year's Ball!" Rebecca beamed.

"Dressmaking is basically the only thing I like to do without magic. Except the hemming—that's so boring. I always have Frederick swing a quill at it to finish it off. Can't wait until I have my own quill!"

Ivy smiled and held the dress against her body. She took in the room and looked out the window. Across the chasm that separated the dormitory cliff and the castle-turned-school, the Halls' beautiful sapphire roof was speckled with bright white flurries. The Bitter Forest below looked frozen solid—*the only place colder than a summer in Belzebuthe*, Ivy thought.

"Well, now that you've unpacked and rested a bit, are you hungry?" asked Rebecca.

"I could use a bite."

Ivy grabbed the faux-fur warmer from her wardrobe. "By the way, thanks for this, too! It's really come in handy!"

"Well, someone's got to fill your closet! Something besides that old sweater!" Rebecca wrinkled her nose.

They bounded down the steps, their laughs puffing up into the cold air. Their leaps across the bridge slowed as they approached another group of students whose words drifted back toward Ivy and Rebecca.

"I don't know, he's just so, dark. Quiet. I really just miss little Professor Fenix, don't you?" said a sqwinch whose black hair hung to her hips in two braids. "I thought Night would get better with time."

The girl's friend, also a third year, judging by her grape-colored cloak, swung her arms around as she spoke. "How does crashing into a ballroom qualify him to teach anything?"

The girls burst into laughter.

"Then again, this might be the Dark Queen's new castle if

he hadn't come. Maybe he's brilliant!"

"Rebecca," Ivy hissed under her breath. "Who are they talking about?"

"Who do you think?" Rebecca replied. "Derwin!"

"Oh! With all this craziness I forgot to go see him!"

Ivy took off running, anxious to see her scrivenist in person, shouting over her shoulder, "I'll catch up with you soon!"

Rebecca hollered behind her, "Be quick!"

Ivy left Rebecca and raced in the direction of Professor Fenix's old classroom, brimming with excitement and about a million questions. Did Derwin even know that Ivy was back? What would he think when he discovered she was back from Belzebuthe without the second segment of the Kindred Stone? Were the Halls really safe for her now? She sprinted down the long, winding stairwell, running her hand against the soft, stone handrail. Just as she placed her hand on the handle of the door that concealed a room full of glanagerie light, Ivy felt a cool hand on her shoulder. She yelped and spun around.

"Selector!" Ivy said, shocked.

"Is something wrong?" The Selector cocked her imperious head. Her beautiful long fishtail braid—one loop for each year of governing the school and the Crownerie—hung over her shoulder and brushed the floor. She was cloaked in a sparkling gown, and her beautiful face was serene.

"I, I was visiting Der—I mean Professor Night."

"We need to talk."

"Now?"

"Now is too late. You should have come to my office first thing."

Ivy would never forget her first visit to the Selector's

pristine office, that time with Professor Fenix. Doubtless, the shelves with each student's magical Compass Individualis that reported the student's comings and goings, mischief and learnings, still lined the bookshelves.

"But I just got here. How can I be in trouble already?"

"That's the problem, Ivy. You're here. Come with me. It's important."

"But I—"

"Now."

Ivy stared at Derwin's door in the distance, yearning to speak with him. It had been nearly six moons since Derwin and Ivy last saw each other. The birthday gift was lovely (more of a stay-there package than a care package), but it wasn't the same as being able to ask Derwin questions about her family, have him mentor her magic, or guide her along through the crazy town that Belzebuthe was. That was what royal scrivenists were for, after all, weren't they?

Ivy followed the Selector as if being pulled by string. The Selector was a head taller than Ivy even without her crown that glowed iridescent silver. A mixture of disappointment, anger, and frustration stirred inside Ivy's heart.

As soon as Ivy entered, the Selector's door closed immediately. Behind her pearlescent desk was the dark gate and door that led to the forbidden Forgotten Room. Ivy bit her lip, nervous at the sight of it, half afraid the Selector might have her go inside, half afraid that whatever lay behind that door still needed to come out. But she couldn't allow her mind to wander there. Not now.

Ivy was surprised that the Selector's desk was empty; she expected to see her Compass Individualis fly off the shelf, open, and begin writing in itself, as it did when she was being disciplined. Instead, it was tucked away between countless other books.

"Am I not in trouble?" Ivy asked, surprised.

"Who invited you back, Ivy?" demanded the Selector.

"You did. I—I received your letter that it was okay to return. I've done all my homework, kept up with my reading. I am ready to be back."

This was met with silence from the Selector.

"I did no such thing," the Selector murmured under her breath.

"What?" Ivy's eyebrows drew closer together and her heart started pounding.

The two dragon statues on each side of the Forgotten Room's imposing door snorted smoke, seemingly unsettled by the upset look on the Selector's face.

"I want to be back here with my friends. I want to study. I want to be, well, I want to be home." Even as her brief sense of security evaporated, Ivy pleaded to stay.

"Ivy, I must warn you, you are in grave danger. There is something in our presence that cannot be trusted."

"What do you mean? If you didn't send for me, then who did?"

"Do you have the letter?"

"Right here, in my Startus."

Ivy pulled the book from her satchel and placed it on the marble desktop. The Selector took her quill in her pale hand and waved it over the letter in a small swirl as if she was pulling something up. As she did, a wisp of dark escaped the letter and wafted up into the quill.

"What was that?"

"Something dark. Something evil."

Ivy's eyes widened and her skin started to crawl.

"No one who wants you to remain safe would have sent this, Ivy," the Selector said sternly. "We haven't yet discovered how the Dark Queen gained access to the Halls. This means whoever allowed her in could very well still be giving her access."

The Selector paused.

"Professor Night and I believe you are in the queenly line, the true line from Princess Isabella, so we must assume that the Dark Queen will not rest until she gets whatever it is she's after."

Barely above a whisper, Ivy asked, "Do you think I fulfill the Moonsday prophecy?" She couldn't bring herself to say "queenly line" in front of the Selector.

After a minuscule pause, the Selector said, "Yes, I do. I will never forget the disappearance of the double moon. Your birthday, as it turned out."

Ivy had one other burning question, one she was too afraid to ask.

The Selector stared at her, almost into her. In her soft, calm voice she said, "You wonder why I disappeared at the Ball, why I left you and the other students."

Ivy's eyes were wide and glued to the Selector. She nodded in shocked silence.

The Selector sighed, "I had to disappear, though I did protect you from behind the scenes. I couldn't help you in front of her. She thinks I'm on her side, Ivy. I have to play the part, you understand. Otherwise, I cannot run the school and teach magic to you students, which provides Croswald's only protection from her. She mustn't be the only one who can wield magic! Selectors have been appointed by the Society of Scrivenists for hundreds of years just to ensure that."

The Selector drew a deep breath and continued, "Winsome did wonderful work with you last year. He believed in you when I didn't think you were ready. Now listen closely: If you leave these Halls, danger is waiting, lurking in the dark. Fortunately, because these Halls are your ancestral home, they can protect you even better than the average student. I will, of course, strengthen the spells protecting this sanctuary. I must insist that you remain inside and be cautious even within this place. Now that you are out of the Town, and people are beginning to know who you truly are, you must stay here."

Ivy nodded once. She couldn't imagine why she'd try to leave.

"It's a miracle you made it here alive, which is just further proof."

"Further proof of what?"

"That the Dark Queen wants you here. Be sure of it."

CHAPTER FIFTEEN

THE UNCOMMON FLICKER

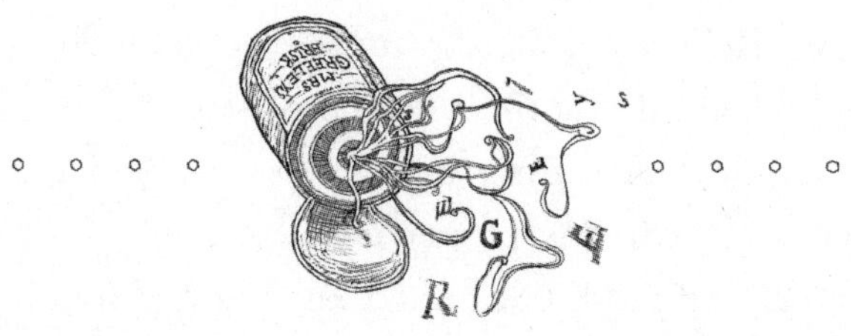

THE shock of the Selector's words had deeply unnerved Ivy. As she and Rebecca walked to the dining halls, a tumult of emotions wrestled in Ivy: a desire to stay at the Halls despite its not being safe, fear, and not a little bit of determination.

Like the Lolly Room and the Longbard, the Uncommon Flicker had a large horseshoe-shaped table. Unlike the other two dining halls, the inside resembled a tavern with rustic wood floors and high exposed beams. An enormous stone hearth narrowed as it reached towards the arched ceiling. The whole room was a little steamy, and Ivy couldn't put her finger on the fragrances: What were they serving? There were at least a dozen retired professors, all scrivenists, tottering in and out of the kitchen, pushing carts stacked with cylindrical tins.

"Um, Rebecca. Not much food in here, is there?"

An elderly woman with her ginger hair tied in a bun came to Ivy's right side. "Can I offer you a tin or can?"

She held out a tray piled precariously high with metal containers. Each had strange labels with swimming letters that swayed with the movement of the tray.

"Um… what are those?"

"New to the Uncommon Flicker, where the magic is uncommonly good and you'll need a flickering porcupel?"

"Yes?" Ivy said tentatively.

"Here," Rebecca grabbed a tin for each of them. "Thanks so much," she nodded at the retired professor.

"What kind of dining hall serves canned food?" Ivy whispered as the cart was pushed away.

"Not canned food, but tinned and canned food! Tinning and canning is the special spelling that these old professors came up with. It's a way to create the most delicious food, suited to every taste, while forcing the students to practice spelling techniques." Rebecca rolled her eyes a bit. "You'll notice there aren't a lot of crowns in here. Mostly sqwinches."

"I see that, but I still don't understand."

"It's one of those things you won't understand until you see it happen. Just watch."

Rebecca grabbed her porcupel, smiled mischievously, and picked up a can. With a flourish, she inked onto the label, *Mrs. Greeley's Brisket.*

The can popped open, going from shelf-cold to piping-hot. Steam poured onto her empty plate, like it was from dry ice. As it did, the unmistakable smell of Mrs. Greeley's signature dish wafted up. Ivy's mouth watered as the steam dissipated and revealed the piping hot meal.

"Oh my moon."

"Careful though. Needs proper spelling—look at poor Woodley."

The boy had wanted chicken soup but now had a clucking bird pecking at his otherwise empty plate.

"Check out Hadley Copperluck. She's a fourth year."

"Is that—is that a full Moonsday feast?"

"Yes! She manages to spell all the trimmings," Rebecca shook her head in admiration at Hadley. "There's barely room for her table neighbor's bowl of pudding!"

Ivy joined Rebecca in having the brisket—she was just realizing that she really was going to miss Mrs. Greeley, though she was over the moon to be back.

"How was Professor Night? Glad to see you, I'll bet."

"That's the thing!" Ivy said between delicious bites. "I didn't get to see him! The Selector pulled me into her office."

Rebecca raised her eyebrows, "In trouble already?"

"Not really. I'll fill you in later. I've never felt so hungry…." Ivy reached for a beehive biscuit.

When the meal was finished, the professors emeriti came back to collect tins, cans, and compliments.

Ivy turned to one and asked, "Is tinning and canning at all like spoken word spells?"

"To a degree, they are." The professor emeritus nodded approvingly. He brought out a Compass Collectis from underneath his cart and banged it down on the table. With one wave of his quill, the pages flew open to the exact entry. The professor recited as if giving a lecture, "'Spoken word spells, n.: Identifiable only by their invisible heaviness and small sparkles when shaken, these spells typically achieve small ends, like a refilling clobber coffee cup or a silencing spell. Scrivenists occasionally preserve common spells in this way to save a little time. However, if they are stored for long periods, the spoken word spells will grumble loudly.' But the tinning and canning spell differs quite significantly. If you have time, I can explain a bit."

"Once a teacher, always a teacher," Rebecca smiled.

° ° ° °

After sketching class, Ivy was a little nervous about finally seeing Derwin again and in such a public way. And as a professor! If only she had been able to see him earlier in the day. Were the other students allowed to know that Derwin was Ivy's parent's scrivenist? She walked in with her head down, following Rebecca's lead, and avoiding eye contact. Fortunately, the cavernous classroom was dimly lit and they could sneak by to her seat all the way in back, near to the aisle.

Gretta Leelangraf gave a little wave to Ivy as she crept by her.

"Hi!" Ivy mouthed. Gretta looked so tired!

Most of the class was already seated in the rounded room. At the center, upon the pedestal, was a glowing glanagerie bottle. The orange liquid in the sealed bottle bubbled and sputtered, quicksilver-like.

Derwin stood behind the lectern and, unlike Professor Fenix, he could be seen without standing on a pile of books. His lanky frame wore his scrivenist jacket well. He was holding a mug of Spinner's Foam in one hand and a textbook in another. A bit of the foam caught on his trimmed beard.

Ah, thought Ivy, *that's why his ideas in the bottle are shifting! Spinner's Foam will do that!*

"Greetings," said Derwin casually to the class, nodding in Ivy's direction.

Ivy only smiled, unsure if he spotted her in the back row.

With his mug in hand, Derwin walked around from the lectern to the glanagerie bottle on the pedestal in front of the class.

"Great news," he raised his glass as if about to give a toast. "Today's travels will be to a Spinner's Foam brewery. Spinner's Foam, as you know, is a peppy drink suitable for all ages that promotes the formation of ideas. Children benefit less from this drink, as they are already brimming with the magic of imagination. It's the old folks like me that need it more." He raised his eyebrows playfully and the class tittered.

"This imaginary brewery has belonged to the same family for generations, and it drifts on water like an oversized floating dock. As one who has spent a fair chunk of his life at sea, I cannot help but include water in the mix. The secret ingredient that most of you know is a nixbean for random creativity. The problem here, at this imaginary brewery, is that there is a loose bogdog roaming the floating factory, destroying the streamlined setup and production line. Bogdogs are often confused with wolves but they are, as you know, companions of the Cloaked Brood and have the ability to quickly turn to vapor. And a creeping fog is quite difficult to catch. You must stop the bogdog from flooding the factory, forever sinking it and bringing an end to the delectable drink! Any questions?"

Derwin dropped their names written on parchment into the bottle and the class was soon swept into the bottle in a cloud of glittering gold magic. They quickly set to their task.

The bogdog had chewed through the wiring to the brewery's mixers. Gregory Gershwin used his Weatheritall Stone to make sure the sun shone brightly, burning off any chance of the bogdog turning to fog. After a minor explosion in a back room—which had everyone stunned for seconds—Bobby Willcock and his Flameral Stone contorted flames into a wall around the machine room, keeping the furious bogdog at bay.

On the other side of the factory, Hayword used his endless knowledge of animals to coax the bogdog closer, just in time for Elaina Portal to wash it away with a giant wave, using her Wagua Stone. A great cheer went up, and then Caroline Blunder and her Fixeen Stone led the rest of the class in fixing the damaged equipment, using stones, porcupels, and a little elbow grease.

The class succeeded in saving the floating factory! It was a doubly successful glanagerie experience, in Ivy's eyes—after all, any glanagerie experience where Ivy actually traveled to the operator's imaginary world along with the rest of the class rather than on her own journey was a success. The students packed up their bags, ready for their Hour of Discovery.

Derwin returned to the lectern, quite pleased with his glanagerie concoction, and called out, "Ivy, you'll stay behind, please."

She gulped. As the students filed out one by one, Ivy approached Derwin. She felt a flood of mixed emotions: frustration that she'd missed the fall at the Halls, happiness to be back, guilt for not being able to do what Derwin asked, fear that what the Selector said was true. But one thought dominated: she had failed, almost forgotten, her task of finding the other pieces of the Kindred Stone while in the Town.

"I didn't find them. You must know that."

"First, welcome back, Ivy."

"Thank you, but the Selector just told me she didn't send the letter that gave me permission to return to school."

"I wondered, as we haven't yet caught the leak that invited the Dark Queen to the Halls…" Derwin mused. "But about the stone, we are getting closer, I'm sure."

"How can we be closer when I'm back here? I tried—"

"I know. I've read through your work and assignments." He rubbed his temples. "I'm afraid it's my terrible memory that's the problem. Borderline non-scrivenist, I'm sad to say. Water damage. I feel I can't even properly protect you: I sent you to Belzebuthe to stay safe. And yet here you are."

"But what do we do now? You said we had to hurry to find the missing pieces of the stone."

"Things will get better from here. I've discovered a way to use a glanagerie bottle to pull my memories more effectively. This bottle, this one right here," said Derwin, pulling a deep-blue glanagerie from under his lectern, "is a special glanagerie, a bottle that I've infused with my fractured memories. Some of the water was captured from the glanagerie I was trapped in. That way you can explore those lost memories and record for yourself better than I can relate them to you. I'm hoping this memory glanagerie might help pull out whatever is left after my imprisonment."

Ivy nodded, eyes wide.

"The good news is your missing the start of school makes for a great excuse to meet for tutoring. What do you say we start meeting once a moon for your Hour of Discovery? Too frequently can be too dangerous, too obvious."

Ivy smiled. "That would be wonderful. When do we start?"

"Tomorrow, Your Highness."

"You don't have to call me that," Ivy blushed.

"I will call you as you are," he insisted. "See you tomorrow in class, Your Highness."

"See you tomorrow."

Chapter Sixteen

The Magic Inside Creatures

THIS year's creature class was more in-depth, led by Professor Wrigley. It almost seemed like a part-of-a-creature class than creature class, as they just studied one component at a time. The room was opposite Ivy's Magical Management classroom, one level up from the room Professor Wheeler used for first years.

The vaulted ceiling in Professor Wrigley's classroom was at least twenty feet high, and, between the ribs of each arch, the ceiling was papered with a vintage motif of wild animals that featured dragons, dwarves, and floating bugs that looked a little like dandelion poofs. The dark wood of the floor was polished to a bright sheen. Ivy took special interest in the collection of hourglasses on a triangular shelf behind Professor Wrigley's desk. In each one, small neon-orange seedlings sprouted under an incubator of bright hairie light. A small sign beside the hourglasses referred to the seedlings as scufflings, blind critters that grow only as large as minnows but are kept for their air-clarifying purposes. She remembered that Winsome had sprouted these creatures, but that his constant explosions had suffocated most of them.

Professor Wrigley tottered to the front of his class and leaned against his desk, which was covered in thick pelts and claws and teeth. He was small and a little greasy looking. He grabbed a toothpick from the skull cup he kept for that purpose and began gnawing on it, his orange mustache moving up and down with his jaw. The desk was set in front of three Gothic windows that spanned the height of the room, much like those in Professor Royal's room. The panes of the glass were pockmarked and smudged—no doubt from more than one species of critter running amok.

"Sqwinches, royals. Imagine, if you will, a life that lasts a mere moment. That is the fate of this simple creature before you: the allergrim. Only days after its birth, it shrivels and dies. With the shortest lifespan of any six-legged creature in all of Croswald, they reproduce year-round."

He rocked back on his heel and stared into each of the student's eyes with a burning intensity. *This guy really loves his subject matter!* Ivy thought. Professor Wrigley withdrew a box from a desk drawer.

"Does that mean it is an unimportant life because it is so terribly brief?" He paused for effect. "No! Let me tell you. This little exoskeleton is of import to each of us.

"Does anyone in here suffer from hayflower fever in the spring? Yes, you two, keep your hands up. What about the sideways sniffles in summer? Yes, quite a few of you. Cats? Yes, keep your hand up. I could go on: reactions to lyceum nuts, or lind grass, or dust mites—many of us have allergies, some annoying and some debilitating.

"You there. The one with the cat allergy, come on up. Quickly now!"

Zake Sunder, a shy prince, shuffled to the front of the class where an orange tabby—the exact color of the professor's mustache—appeared and weaved in and out of the professor's legs. Professor Wrigley wasted no time and wrapped the cat around the prince's face, much to the boy's surprise. By the time the poor prince had wrestled it off, his face was swollen and his eyes were red.

"This species of allergrim was bred around furry, dandery animals. Cats, in particular. Pop it in!"

The professor held out a crisped-up shell of something that looked like it had been an insect at one time. When the boy didn't immediately eat the shriveled up allergrim, Professor Wrigley helped him along by stuffing it in his somewhat unwilling mouth.

"Crunchy! Sqwinches, get out your proof pads…."

With that, the sqwinches set to sketching and recording the transformation that took place before their eyes. The prince's eyes de-puffed and his breathing returned to normal.

Ivy let out a little sigh of relief for Zake; she couldn't help but remember all the times that she'd been humiliated.

Class wrapped a little early—apparently Professor Wrigley was known for that. He used the extra time to feed his creatures or collect more. As Ivy and Rebecca left, he was carrying on a heated discussion with Hayword about the merits of a vegetable diet for dungo dragons.

As they walked to Professor Royal's Magical Management class, they looked through the mullioned windows and spied a class of fourth-year princes jousting in the garden.

"You know, being a prince looks easy," Ivy murmured, thinking of all she had to learn ahead of her.

"It is! Any tough magic just gets shifted to your scrivenist," Rebecca sighed. "But trust me, the coursework isn't nearly as interesting as ours. Most royals are quite empty-headed." Rebecca sniffed down her nose.

Ivy laughed. "You are the only royal I know with a thing against royals."

"Ivy!" called a familiar voice from down the hall.

"Who's *that*?" asked Rebecca.

"That's Glistle. Hey!"

Beads of sweat dripped down Glistle's forehead and his shirt was torn. He jogged to catch up.

"It's good to see you back, Ivy!" Glistle lit up the hallway with his grin, offset by his dark skin.

"Good to be back. What happened to you?"

"Helping out Professor Wheeler."

Now Ivy could sec that the left leg of his pants had been ripped and there was a decent-sized scratch on the left side of his chin.

"Looks rough," said Ivy. "Oh, I haven't had a chance to thank you for the flower. Proud to say I haven't let it die yet."

"Happy to hear that!"

There was an awkward silence between the two of them. To stop it, Rebecca coughed, insisting an introduction.

"Oh! So sorry. Glistle, this is my best friend, Rebecca. Rebecca, this is Glistle Leelangraf."

"You must be Gretta's brother." The two did look alike, more so if Gretta hadn't been so frail looking. In contrast, Glistle was the picture of health. "We're in the same year as her."

"Oh, sure. Nice to meet you."

"Glistle's Fyn's friend," Ivy explained. "How is Fyn, by the way? I haven't run into him yet! Second day back already."

"He's been busy. Club stuff. Hayword told Manone about your entrance, though. Manone told Lennu, of course. And Lennu told Fyn, and well, Fyn told me," he chuckled. "Quite the entrance."

"Word certainly does spread fast." Ivy blushed.

"Anyway, Ivy, I was wondering if you were attending the Club meeting tomorrow afternoon. It's going to be a good one."

"A meeting about what?" asked Rebecca.

"You know, the Club," he said to Ivy and shot a sideways look at Rebecca. "Well, I've got to go. Gonna go catch up with Gretta. Bye, you two." Glistle winked and was off.

"What was that all about?" asked Rebecca.

"The Club? Just a group of Fyn's friends meeting to talk about old quills. I think I'm not supposed to talk about it."

But Ivy could tell by the look on her friend's face that Rebecca wasn't interested in the Club.

"That boy likes you!"

"Don't be ridiculous!"

As they approached the door to Professor Royal's room, Ivy was grateful to have the conversation end.

The Carriage Accident

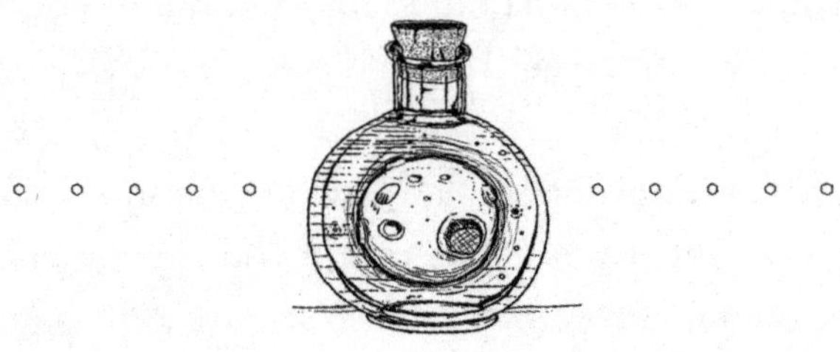

THERE was silence in the lustrous tunnel-like hall that led to the glanagerie classroom. No chatter of students before beginning class, no shuffling of feet, just the calm of the collective glanageries sitting peacefully on their individual shelves behind iron cages. Shades of purple and blue cast a luminescent glow. The water in each vessel was calm as if resting for the evening. It was, after all, nearly dinnertime and the bottles were peaceful for the moment, until instructed otherwise.

As the hallway opened up to the rounded classroom, Ivy spotted Derwin standing behind the lectern. He seemed intent on the memory glanagerie in front of him, currently glowing dark green. The glanagerie bottle bubbled and swished on the lectern, and Ivy caught sight of a distorted image, something that reminded her of a night sky over a forest.

Ivy cleared her throat and Derwin looked up.

"Is everything all right?" she asked, walking down the steps to him, nervous for her first memory glanagerie experience.

"Come around. I have something to show you."

Derwin took out the once soggy journal that Ivy had

pulled from a glanagerie world last year and rested it wide open on the lectern. It was Derwin's journal, where she'd first seen an image of the Kindred Stone. He set his quill free and allowed it to ink on its own. The quill was flipping and swishing in circles, sketching a scene of a forest and a steep road up a hillside and scribbling along the way.

Derwin looked at Ivy, concern radiating from him. "I believe I'm getting closer to knowing who the leak is, how the Dark Queen has been able to track you. The Halls isn't safe, but it's better that I can keep an eye on you here. It's pressing that we do this work while we still can."

"I wish this was easier—I wish you could just tell me where the other pieces of the stone are!"

Derwin looked incredibly pained, "Ivy, I haven't been the same since the Dark Queen cursed me into that bottle. A human isn't meant to spend sixteen years inside a glanagerie. I'm—I'm not the same man."

Ivy didn't know what to say.

"My sole purpose is to protect you, and I can't seem to find the Kindred Stone, the very thing that will do so, in my scrambled brain." He put his hand to his temple as if he had a headache. "Every time I train my mind or quill to the scraps of memory I do have, my brain is washed with glanagerie water, and all I can think of is boats, pirates, and the sea."

He shook his head as if to clear it. Ivy bit her lip, still unsure of what to say.

Ivy looked around at the room, "What happened to Professor Fenix, anyway?" she asked. "Is he all right? Did something happen that he left so abruptly?"

"You've heard the expression, 'Time heals all wounds,'

haven't you? I suppose you can say he and I traded places and he is now living peacefully on a top shelf. Don't worry, in a land of his choosing—bright castles in working order."

"What? You of all people should know it can't be good for him. He'll forget everything!"

"It was his wish. He never was a comfortable teacher, and last year's Masquerade Ball put him over the top."

"Derwin, does the Selector know you're offering this to me?"

"Some things are best dealt with discreetly," he said with a pointed look. "So long as you are exploring imagined space, these experiences will remain between you and me. She knows that you are catching up on glanagerie coursework."

Ivy nodded carefully. "I suppose no one who cares to protect Croswald can fault us for trying to find the other pieces of the Kindred Stone."

"My thoughts exactly. And to answer your very next question, I'll be right here watching over you."

"How—how did you end up in the bottle in the first place? When did you cross paths with the Dark Queen?"

"Perfect question for today. Rather than tell you, let's have you experience it for yourself. This memory is as real as the day it was imprinted, one that no amount of glanagerie water can shift. It's the day I found not you, but a letter."

"A letter? What do you mean, Derwin?"

"The bottle awaits, Your Highness."

The liquid in the glanagerie on the pedestal had turned as vibrant as moonlight. Ivy could see small sparkles, which must have been stars, lingering close to the neck of the bottle. As the liquid swished, a bright white sphere came into view—the moon—and prickly pines brushed the sides of the glass, occasionally magnifying as Ivy looked in on it.

"I—I don't know if I should. Can't you come with me?"

"I'm afraid I cannot. Remember, someone needs to supervise the outside, someone who cares enough to bring you back out," Derwin smiled wryly. "You, my young friend, are going to the day the double moon disappeared."

Derwin popped the lid with a grunt and slipped in her name on parchment. In an instant, Ivy was swept into a soft, billowing swirl of marigold. Derwin's determined, hopeful face was the last thing she saw before thumping against the stump of an overgrown tree. Ivy groaned and stretched.

"That was a lot more painful than my last entrance," she murmured.

Ivy lifted her eyes to a star-speckled sky. The moon was full and had a strange pulsing ring of light around it. *Not a double moon, but full...*

The tree overhead spread out like a tapestry, its feathery leaves keeping her shielded from the brightness of the moon. She focused on calming her breath. She knew by now that all she had to do was wait. As her eyes adjusted, she could see that she was on a sloping hill. There was a road above her, and giant evergreen trees dotted the landscape. She stood and stumbled over a long, deep gash in the dirt.

Then Ivy heard weeping. She gazed around quietly from her protected spot, and finally an outline of a figure emerged next to a tree opposite her. The figure nearby heaved his shoulders up and down. Her eyes had adjusted enough that she could see the face of the young man. It was a much younger Derwin. Ivy crouched as she watched him sink to his knees. Her heartbeat picked up and she followed the young man's gaze down the hill, along the freshly torn-up earth. The skid marks led to a crumpled carriage only a few strides in front of the scrivenist.

Ivy gasped. This was the scene of her parents' deaths. The carriage must have flown from the road at great speed and then met its end at a particularly grand tree which had been partially uprooted by the impact.

Young Derwin's quill sent a quivering beam of light to search the carriage. Rather than being able to pull out anyone who had been trapped inside, all the magic brought forth was a wooden box, the same box that she now had in her possession! Ivy watched, holding her breath as Derwin opened it; his face was illuminated by bright light, as if the moon itself were inside. With trembling hands, he lifted a note that lay within, tears streaming down his face. She could no longer take waiting in silence and stood to her feet.

Just then a crunching of gravel came from the road above. Ivy ducked back behind her tree. Derwin stood quickly from his crouch and wrapped the box with a bright strand of magic, then tucked it into his satchel. A midnight-black carriage was speeding down the road straight toward them. It came to rest on the road just above. A dark, slim figure emerged from the carriage, swathed in a gauzy black gown. The Dark Queen!

"Your Highness," Derwin said shakily, bowing deeply.

"Where is she?" the Dark Queen asked.

"I don't—I don't know what you're talking about."

"The child."

Ivy covered her mouth, trying hard to remain quiet.

"I only just arrived—my first hour of appointment as their scrivenist. There is no child, no survivors. The family has been in a terrible accident—all dead." He shone his light to the carriage.

"No child?!" The Dark Queen was incensed and gripped Derwin in coils of watery magic, lifting him from the ground to hover dripping in mid-air.

Winsome must have already gone with Ivy—herself! as an infant—to the slurry fields, leaving behind this gruesome scene. She felt like fainting, but Ivy steeled herself to go help Derwin, though she had no idea how she might do such a thing.

Derwin was tossed into the back of the carriage like a rag doll, and Ivy leapt up. Then the power of the memory swept her into the carriage with him and she found herself in a tight, barred compartment right alongside the scrivenist. The Dark Queen rode in the front compartment while a member of her terrifying Cloaked Brood drove.

Ivy could sense that her participation in the events unfolding was totally superficial. She couldn't change what was happening. No one but Derwin even seemed to notice that she was there. The scrivenist in her couldn't help but be fascinated by the magic of Derwin's special glanagerie.

"Can you hear me?" she whispered.

In direct reply, the glanagerie Derwin said a curt, "Yes. But she can't," he then turned back to the front of the carriage. "It's my memory, after all."

Ivy nodded and Derwin turned back to the front of the carriage.

"Where are you taking me?" Derwin demanded, gripping the bars that separated them from the Dark Queen. "I've done nothing wrong! We need to help those in the crash!"

"Them? They are dead! And they should be. My Brood

took care of that." The Dark Queen's aquiline features—all beautiful, yet terribly chilling at the same time—took Ivy's breath away. The Dark Queen threw a heartless, cold smile back at Derwin before pulling a heavy curtain shut. Her pure white, pointed teeth remained in Ivy's mind. She found herself digging her nails into the rough bench, pulling her body as far into the corner as she could, even though she knew that the Dark Queen couldn't see her. *She looks just the same, just like she did at the Ball!* And she emanated the same sickly smell, like stale water.

Derwin had cautiously pulled out the box from his satchel and held in his hands the most beautiful stone Ivy had ever seen. Opalescent and the size of a huge pear, it was pointed on top and rounded at the bottom; edges were cut into the stone to highlight its brilliance. It could be only one thing.

He ran his hands through his still-brown hair, standing it on end. He was in awe and terror, whispering to himself, "What am I supposed to do with this?" His brow furrowed in thought. "I was meant to join the ranks of the Wandering, the family that has been saved by its curse! The last in the queenly line… and the curse is what pulled me from their castle to them where they wandered! The child—the child's birth is what drew the Brood and Dark Queen near! But where can she be now? Her queenly blood… the Dark Queen won't stop until she spills it."

Derwin turned the stone over in his hands. "I can only believe she lives. The magic from the moon is certainly in her now." He looked at Ivy and intoned, "Keeping this stone from the Dark Queen, and reuniting it with the true ruler is our only hope. I have to escape before she discovers I have it."

Ivy wanted so badly to touch the stone in its full form, not yet broken into the thirds like the one she had in her pocket in the real world. She stretched her arm toward it, but the carriage hit a pothole and Ivy fell forward.

Then, still watching Derwin and the stone, she asked, "What are you saying, Derwin?"

"I'm saying that this right here, this stone… could the legend be true? That the Kindred Stone is real? The letter certainly says so." He held his quill over the stone. "I can feel its power magnifying even my own magic." His eyes were wide with discovery and wonder. Then his smile fell. "This may be the only thing that could save or completely ruin all of Croswald, our last bit of hope," Derwin's voice cracked. "I have to get this as far away from her as possible! I have to hide it!"

A fierce look overtook Derwin's mournful one. Ivy cracked a smile at his courage and determination. He pulled out his quill and performed a muffling spell; the air went thick and sound stopped traveling in the compartment. Then he sent a beam of light to the floor of the carriage, cutting an opening just the width of his shoulders. The gravel road flew by underneath them, a blur of stones and ruts in the dark.

"Umm, you can't mean to jump."

But then he did.

"No, no, noooo," Ivy whispered. With no other choice, Ivy took a deep breath and then dropped down between the wheels of the carriage. At least it wasn't as bad as jumping off a ship in the middle of a rough sea! She tucked herself into a ball and rolled. She had no idea it was possible to bounce on a hard-packed road, but apparently it was.

"Ow! Ugh! Eep!" Ivy yelped as she rolled to a stop. The

carriage disappeared in a rush.

Derwin helped her up. "Hurry! We have only a moment before she discovers I've escaped."

"But where are we going?!"

"The Crownerie, to the only person I know who can help me."

Ivy opened her mouth to cry out, but she didn't get the chance. Just then, with a swirl of gold dust, the images in the glanagerie world shimmered and faded. She was swept back up and out of the bottle, landing out of breath at Derwin's feet.

"Derwin! We were running from the Dark Queen—did she catch you again? Did you make it to the Crownerie? Who did you meet there? What happened? You have to tell me!"

Derwin held up his hands to slow Ivy down. "All good questions, Your Highness. I have no idea, other than I'm pretty sure the Dark Queen did catch me eventually," he smirked. "This is why we are using this tool—I've forgotten so much, almost as much as I myself was forgotten."

He sat at a desk and cracked his journal, motioning Ivy to join him. Poising his quill, Derwin said, "Now tell me everything you saw, from your perspective."

Chapter Eighteen

The Oath

AN energetic, booming voice called from down the hall, "Hey, Ivy! Ivy! Wait up!"

Fyn. Ivy stopped and smiled as she saw him for the first time since being back at the Halls.

"You're back!" He hugged Ivy immediately, happy to see her. "How's Ma been?"

"She's great! Things are finally getting back to normal for her at work."

All of a sudden, Ivy felt shy around Fyn. She smoothed over her hair and couldn't think of anything else to say. Perhaps it was the fact that seeing Fyn in his fourth year, mulberry-colored cloak made her realize just how much she had missed him.

"Good to have you back."

"It's good to be back."

Fyn chuckled, "And I heard about your arrival. You do make quite the entrance—one for the books! Not to worry though, only students from the Town will ever remember, thanks to the cloaking spell. And we all think it's absolutely hilarious. I can't imagine the look on everyone's faces!"

"It *was* pretty hilarious, now that I think about it." Ivy blushed.

"So, how's it going so far? Things all right?"

"Yeah, yeah, everything's great. Everything's good." Ivy smiled. "Just came from Derwin's, er, Professor Night's classroom."

"So crazy that he's teaching! So where are you off to now? Do you have plans for the rest of the evening?"

"I'm meeting up with Rebecca for some extra reading for our creatures class. Rebecca overheard Professor Wrigley telling Wheeler he was going to assign a pop quiz tomorrow."

"Ha! I'll bet she overheard him while up in the rafters, playing mink. That girl! For someone who despised her crown so much, she certainly doesn't hold back from transforming to snoop around somewhere. It's too bad you have plans because—"

Just then, a warm fuzzy thing embraced Ivy's leg. A little mink darted back through her legs, and leapt up, landing square on Fyn's shoulder.

"What did I tell you?" said Fyn, knowing instinctively who it was. The little mink jumped down.

"I only transform during the Hour of Discovery! Better a snooping mink than a sneak," said Rebecca, who materialized with a puff of glitter. "Where do you peabrains think you're headed without me? Ivy, aren't you coming to dinner?"

Ivy giggled. "Of course."

Fyn added, "Ivy said the two of you had plans to study tonight. I was just about to suggest something else."

"Suggest what exactly?"

"Sorry. Can't come. Members only," said Fyn sternly.

"Members? To play your silly game?"

Fyn looked at her with a start. "How did you know about," he lowered his voice to a whisper, "*Quogo?* And it's not silly."

Rebecca rolled her eyes, "Minks have ears, too. And, you can thank Glistle for spilling the beans. Secret meetings. A secret club. Count me in! I'm only upset you all didn't invite me to join first!"

"Well, it's all top secret. Gotta limit the members so it doesn't get out of hand. So we know that they can be trusted not to tell. So far it's only been kids from the Town."

"And Ivy! You know she'll tell me everything anyway."

"Fyn," said Ivy.

"Ivy," said Rebecca.

"Yes, we all know each other's names here."

"Fyn, of course Rebecca can be trusted. Please," Ivy begged, and Rebecca nodded eagerly.

Fyn let out a great sigh, "But matches are predicated on absolute secrecy!"

"And what else, having saved your life last year, must I do to prove my loyalty—besides swear I won't run and inform the Selector right now of your mischief? Clearly you aren't her little helper anymore. Oh, I'll bet Ivy doesn't know who the new 'you' is, Fyn. And how much time you spent training her last moon."

"Damaris Dodley is the new class facilitator," he said quickly.

Ivy did her best not to care.

"Fine," he huffed. "Without the other members' agreement, we aren't allowed to invite a new member. Club rules. But, I had a feeling you'd be tagging along, Rebecca, and so I've already got their permission."

"Why didn't you just tell us?"

"I like to have my fun, too."

Ivy was so happy to have her friend join the Quality Quills Club, she couldn't help but smile.

"Later tonight. We officially swear the two of you in. But first, how about some dinner?"

° ° ° °

After dinner that night, the hairies kept the dormitory bright. At least Rebecca's did. Ivy's hairies sputtered and fluttered, happy but useless. The clock ticked, and Ivy brought out *Quogo: The Card Game* to kill time and bring Rebecca up to speed while they waited. She spread the cards out, explaining the basics.

"First, we split the quiver—but you'll only play one quill at a time. Then we draw from the potions, spells, and pologies pile—three draws for three rounds with each quill. You hope that the card you draw matches your spectre's strength to beat your opponent one spell at a time."

"I can't imagine this being played with real quills!" said Rebecca, disbelieving.

"I can't imagine Fyn's Club games are as exciting as the *real* ones in the Town."

Ivy drew the card for Leela Vonteele: Her piercing green eyes stared back at Ivy. And Rebecca played Constance Court, whose mane of hair almost took over the whole card, but her long nose was her most prominent feature.

"Says here that Constance Court was a Chief Spellseeker back in the late 1700s. Constance could smell curses from over 200 miles away. Imagine what else she could smell?"

Rebecca drew a Strapping Sprout potion, good for growing a jungle in an instant. Since Constance had expertise in botany, Rebecca won the first round.

Ivy laughed, "Looks like Constance could smell the card I drew." She showed Rebecca her card: a Laughattack was worth only a single point. "Looks like I'll never be able to knock you and Constance out of the boundary!"

"This game's great! Can't wait to try out the real thing!" Rebecca sang as she pulled both quill cards into her quiver.

"Yeah, if Fyn ever shows up. What time is it, anyway?"

"Quarter past ten."

"We should be asleep! Especially if Professor Wrigley is planning a pop quiz tomorrow!"

But both Ivy and Rebecca were eager to play their next cards. Ivy flipped over a Slippery Skin spell; Rebecca, a pologies card.

"I'll take that, thank you! This pologie is an all-types counter curse, so you'll have to keep that slippery spell to yourself!" said Rebecca.

"Beginner's luck!" Ivy retorted.

Spellseekers stayed in Ivy's mind. They played for a while before Ivy asked a random question. "Hey, Rebecca, how much do you know about the mattelers?"

"The mattelers? They are like the magical secret police, I guess." Rebecca wrinkled her nose, "You know, Gretta and Glistle's dad is a spellseeker. It's a type of matteler."

"Right, Easel Leelangraf. We've met. Actually, on Moonsday, there was an incident—"

Rebecca interjected with excitement "DizzElixir! Another round to me, thank you very much! So, what's this about an incident?"

"Well…" Ivy hesitated.

"You know, for being a best friend, you sure do have a lot of secrets."

"It's just being where I was, there's only so much I really understand. There was this thing, a shade, that crashed down in the middle of an alley where I was walking—"

"Ivy! What were you doing alone in an alley?!"

"I know, I was exploring," Ivy went on, explaining the rest of the shade incident. "Anyway, Mr. Leelangraf was there, too."

They refocused on the game and drew their next cards.

"Aha! I win! I'll take that please," said Rebecca, swiping up Leela Vonteele and dealing the quill cards for the next round: Sal Switchstick and Gilligan Todd.

A knock sounded at the door. Ivy jumped up with her cards still in hand; Humboldt scuttled under the bed, his tail between his legs; Rebecca giggled.

Indeed, it was Fyn, and his grin was perfectly mischievous. He tossed each of them an empty quiver. Then Fyn pulled a chain up from his shirt: a small brass object with several cylinder spokes spun on the chain.

"What is that?" Ivy asked.

"The secret spiller. To ensure that the Club will be kept a secret! Good to see that you can't get enough of Quogo," he pointed to the cards.

"What took you so long to come?"

"Sorry. Damaris makes her last round at ten. The Selector always had me on a strict schedule when I had her job."

Fyn came in quietly and shut the door behind him.

"It's time to officially swear in the two of you. Here's how it works. You're to tell the secret spiller your deepest darkest secret. Should you tell anyone the details about the Club, our oath, or what goes on, every single sqwinch and royal in these Halls will come to know of this secret. And make it a good one! You have one chance at convincing the secret spiller that you're worthy." He held out the whistle-shaped brass charm to Rebecca first. "Make sure Ivy and I don't hear."

"Hard to think of a secret I haven't already told you," Rebecca narrowed her eyes at Ivy. But it wasn't long before Rebecca went to the corner of the room and whispered behind her hand into the little vessel.

"Now what?" Rebecca asked.

"Ivy's turn. Go on!"

Ivy looked at the secret spiller, unsure of what she should share. *What is my biggest secret?* It seemed she had so many: She was the rightful queen of Croswald, her family's scrivenist was the pirate who ruined last year's Ball (and was now a professor), and she was on a mission to recover the Kindred Stone. Yet Ivy somehow doubted any of these would be a secret for long, or even if they still were. She felt like last year she knew nothing, and then this year everyone knew everything. Everyone knew that she brought the Dark Queen down on the Masquerade Ball. Everyone knew that she grew up in the slurry fields as a servant. Damaris certainly wouldn't let anyone forget *that.* What could she possibly say into the little brass whistle?

Then she thought of something—something that, if spilled, would be disastrous.

"C'mon, Ivy! We're already late!"

Flustered, she whispered into the secret spiller. She took a breath and hoped she hadn't made a mistake. Ivy returned the little whistle to Fyn.

"Now, you'll recite after me. Stretch out one arm like you

are holding a quill, and then touch the secret spiller with your other hand. Together!"

Fyn spoke and both Ivy and Rebecca repeated:

He, she, who dare dart a quill,
Swears by the silence,
Or blood will be spilled.
We here, of the Quality Quills,
Engage with our members of our own free will.
Quills from our past,
Unsure what they'll cast.
Our promise to keep secret, above all, shall surpass.
To the potions and motions,
To creatures unknown,
The dangers, the quivers,
The darkest unknown.
To this, I declare, all secrets be still;
For I am a member of the Quality Quills.

"Wicked cool," muttered Rebecca. "So that's it? I'm a member now?"

Fyn laughed. "Not quite, but almost. Let's go!"

"Go where?" they asked in unison.

"You two are going to steal your first quills tonight. And then, we play them."

"Steal quills? From where?"

"Boulliquiste's!"

Ivy looked back at Rebecca, who was already jumping for her coat. Ivy, on the other hand, had her reservations. Ivy had never stolen anything in her life, other than perhaps a morning muffin, years back.

"Quite the habitual quill thief!" said Ivy playfully. Then more seriously, "I can't go, Fyn. I'm not allowed to leave the school grounds. What if there's something out there lurking like the Selector says? And besides, how are we even going to get out? The Halls' gate is locked until the morning." She thought briefly about the unlocker in her special box. She wasn't even sure how to use it.

"Being the Selector's assistant isn't totally without perks." He held out an enormous iron key with a heavy square head. "Ivory Lucky and I got to be quite friendly."

Ivy's eyebrows raised, and Rebecca said sarcastically, "Which Ivory Lucky are you friends with?" The school's locksmith—though some referred to her as a lucksmith—was well known for being split right down the middle—two looks and two different personalities.

"Ha! The right one, of course. The other plays by the books and doesn't ever lend a key."

Rebecca was already waiting at the door. "Ivy, come on!" she called. "Aren't you ready yet?!"

"I am," said a strong voice. Glistle popped his head through the door.

Fyn turned. "Who invited you?"

"I invited myself. I'm as much a Club member as you are. Oh, hey! My plant."

Fyn sighed and half smiled. "You gave Ivy a—never mind. None of your pranks tonight!"

Feeling more than a little torn and scared, Ivy took a deep breath and followed her friends. They slipped down the hall unnoticed. Down at the gate, the snow blanketed the bottom.

Fyn's key scraped as it went into the heavy lock. It was the same gate that had flown open the year before to let Ivy in. Ivy shivered, and it wasn't just the cold. The Halls were safe for her—so how dangerous could Ravenshollow really be?

Glistle brought Ivy out of her thoughts by nudging her.

She smiled. "You've stolen quills before?"

"What do you think?" he grinned mischievously.

"Ha! With Gretta?" Ivy felt like she'd have a lot in common with Gretta but just hadn't seen her much since coming back to school.

"Not really her thing." An anxious expression passed over Glistle's usually cheerful face.

They walked down the hill. Apart from the two pubs, most of the businesses were closed and several of the residences above the shops were already shuttered and dark. The cobblestone streets were bright with lanterns where hairies glowed with curiosity as they walked by.

It had been quite some time since Ivy had been back in the quaint town. In fact, the last time she was there she was quickly chased out by an army of flying writing tools. It was quieter, being that it was the middle of the night, but Ravenshollow's charm was the same—old wood buildings, tall and narrow.

Pairies of Hairies shone brilliantly, casting a glow across the cobbled street and highlighting Mr. Munson's All Things Scrivenist shop. *Oh, Mr. Munson. If it weren't so late an hour, I'd pop in and say hello and perhaps have a look around.*

Before they reached Boulliquiste's: All But Your Quills, the main street, Old Still Lane, led straight to the Crownerie. The shop was a dark, almost black brick, which set off its gold-lettered sign and the crowns that spun in its windows. This was where the royals received their crowns. She couldn't help but wonder who Derwin had gone to see there seventeen years ago. The shop itself was located at the entrance to the mine where the magical stones came from. Ivy stopped to take in its beauty.

"Pretty great, isn't it?" muttered Rebecca.

"I'll say. How could you not want a crown? Look at them. They're all so beautiful," Ivy muttered.

"Crowns are pretty, but I wouldn't change my scrivenist blood for a whole carriage of crowns."

Ivy chuckled and then looked back at the Halls. Its metallic blue roof shimmered beneath the moon. While her classmates were readying themselves for bed, she and her friends were on a mission, one that was breaking every rule in the book.

Fyn made a sharp turn into an alley, and Ivy almost missed it. *Hopefully no shades in this alley,* she thought. Ivy's worry set in. She forced herself to tune into what Fyn was whispering. Something about going down a chimney. He gestured to the roof.

"Tell me if I'm wrong, Fyn, but doesn't Bouvier Boulliquiste have a door?"

"Three: two here at the back and the shop entrance—"

"Then why, Fyn?!" Ivy interrupted. "Why the chimney?!"

"The chimney leads right into the showroom. You asked how we get in without getting caught. That's our way in."

"Are you sure we should be doing this?" Ivy asked nervously.

"You already have a quill, Ivy. I need one!" Rebecca chimed in. "It's your fault you got me hooked on that game… I want to play for real! Not just the cards."

There was a lonely roof ladder folded like an accordion above a full garbage bin and between clotheslines. Fyn wriggled the garbage's tin lid when the voice of a cross old man hollered, "Nothing else left in that bin, kids. I've been through it about four times today."

A grubby face appeared on the far side of the last clothesline. He nodded to the trash and then set about kindling a small fire in the alleyway.

Being the polite girl that she was, Ivy replied, "Oh, well, thank you for saving us the time."

"You ever try squirrel before?" he asked getting out a stick from his backpack. Then the squirrel.

"Er, no."

"Keep to yourself, old man!" interjected Glistle.

"Glistle!" Ivy frowned at his rudeness.

"Tastes better than the legs of a dilly owl. Certainly easier to catch!" The hobo returned his focus and, with shaky hands, he tended to his meager fire. Ivy couldn't help but feel sorry for the homeless man.

A little concentration from Ivy and the fire gleamed.

The man bellowed, "Would you look at that? This thing's been giving me trouble all night!"

Ivy smiled, happy to help in a small way.

"Got it!" yelled Fyn. He had hooked the ladder with a stick and pulled it down. Fyn gestured to them impatiently. One by one they climbed on top of the bin and onto the fire escape ladder that zigzagged its way up to the top of the building.

Ivy didn't let herself look down until she was securely on the roof, grateful that it wasn't anything as high as fishing for stars had been. Toward the back of the building, on the alley side, was a twisting brick chimney.

Fyn pointed, "So, this chimney leads straight into the showroom. Boulliquiste gets the quills from Norman Wrinkles at the Hollow Shaft. Of course, all dangerous quills go straight to the Quill Keep. Others are reserved for real Quogo games and players and non-scrivenist professors. Only the really ineffectual ones come here. He uses them for testing ink and all that."

Glistle interrupted, "Basically, the quills that end up here at Boulliquiste's come straight from Castle Plum, the least magical place in all Croswald." He winked at Ivy.

"So, the name All But Your Quill is—"

"Not exactly true. I guess you don't get *your* quill here—that only comes from Plumes and Fumes."

Glistle interrupted, "What Fyn really means to tell you is that the QQC always takes from the worst pile—the most boring quills," he rolled his eyes. "What I'd give to have one from the best bin, a quill with real pep. We are probably doing everyone a favor by taking the worst quills."

"I wasn't the best-behaved kid growing up. I was always slipping through people's chimneys. It was only inevitable that I'd find Boulliquiste's stash. That's when I started the Club," Fyn explained.

"I'll go first," said Glistle. "Catch you as you come down."

"No, you won't. I'll go first," Ivy insisted. The thought of Glistle looking at her from below made Ivy blush. Fortunately, the dark made her flushed cheeks difficult to see. Fyn tied a thick length of rope around Ivy's small waist, pulling tight on the final knot. "Too tight?"

"It's fine," she sighed. "All right, here I go."

Ivy sat with her bottom on the brick and scooted closer to

the edge before hopping in. She floated, her legs dangling. *This is perfectly fine. It's not that... high. But you better not drop me, Fyn Greeley!*

Fyn whispered down, "You're almost there!"

Ivy spotted the landing, full of ashes. Then her nose tickled. She smelled something burning! She wiggled and struggled to look down—her sash had dragged in the still-hot ashes and ignited!

Ivy yelped, "Ah! No!" and twisted to get a grip on the sash. She tried to brace herself using her legs on the chimney wall, but the rope kept giving slack and she fell—*plop*—straight down on her bottom.

"Ivy!" Fyn yell-whispered. "Are you okay?"

She sighed and coughed up some ashes. "I suppose. The fire's out, at least."

She could feel a little warmth through her layers, but Ivy had to admit her bottom was the most efficient and least magical way to extinguish a fire. She was covered in ash and soot.

Fyn pulled the rope straight back up. Ivy let her eyes adjust to the dark showroom. Boulliquiste's shop was just as she remembered, rows and rows of every kind of ink imaginable. But this time, she wasn't looking at the ink but at the quills.

"Coming down!"

Fyn, then Rebecca, then Glistle landed after Ivy.

Looking around, Fyn sighed, "Imagine if the professors dedicated classes to Quogo. You can sign me up to that class all day."

"Half of the fun is that it's against school rules. You and I know we're both better at breaking them than keeping them," scoffed Glistle.

"But Quogo every day?"

Ivy fingered one quill after the other, fascinated by the geers wrapped around each quill's shaft that revealed their departed owners' names: Lemont Brandish, Melodie Wink, Feeble Sourblast. However, the stories connected to these names were rather thin. Some even only had one spell attributed to them. The geers from more accomplished scrivenists, like Winsome's, were much more fun to read.

"Go ahead and pick a few."

"Really? It's stealing, Fyn. I already have Winsome's quill. I'll use his."

"These quills belong to no one now. Look around—so many! He'll hardly notice they're gone." Ivy looked around: The feathers were bent and out of shape, losing filaments, and limp.

"You'll be saving it from a life of rot, or testing inks!"

"I'll take this one! And this one! Oh… oh, and this one!" Rebecca blurted, holding out the last green quill like it was some sword. She was clearly choosing quills for their sparkle—Rebecca loved anything that glittered.

"Did you hear that?" Ivy asked.

There was a flutter as if a bird had been set out of its cage. Ivy whirled around—nothing.

Rebecca went back to digging through a bin under the varnished oak displays of glass inkwells and tester quills. Fyn and Glistle argued about the merits of a Quogo class. Ivy was unnerved, and so was the Kindred Stone in her pocket. It buzzed and sparked.

Ivy reached into another bin and pulled up a dull, navy-blue feather. A shadow fell across her arm and she jerked up, turning. A dark figure loomed at the door.

Ivy's cry alerted the rest of them.

"Somebody's coming!" Rebecca screeched.

Glistle dove behind an ink display, Rebecca hid beneath the stairwell. Fyn hid behind a corner wall. Ivy couldn't find a spot fast enough.

But then the figure disappeared, as quick as a shadow.

"Let's get out of here!" Rebecca grabbed her quills and hurried to the chimney.

"Quick! Back up! Glistle, you first. Then help pull up Rebecca—I'll push."

Ivy clutched a gray-blue quill—the exact shade of Lonefellow Loch—in her fist. There was no time to check its geer! Ivy poked her head in the chimney, feeling the warmth of the flame that had been put out. Rebecca shot Ivy down a sympathetic look, already being pulled up by Glistle.

"*Wait!* Don't leave me down here alone," Ivy hissed, as Fyn prepared to climb up.

"You're the smallest! Easiest to hoist!" he said, now only his feet visible.

As her friends disappeared up the chimney one at a time, Ivy backed up all the way against the wall. She tried to control her fear, smoothing out her ragged breath. Her stone had begun to glow. It was bright enough to be seen through her pocket. Ivy knew that her stone responded to danger, and it had to be reacting to whoever that dark silhouette was, the shadow that Ivy suspected was still here in the room with her. She crouched behind the nearest ink display while waiting for Fyn to call for her.

Then she turned back around to the mantel and the shadow had reappeared! In that instant, the fire in the hearth burst back into flame, making the back-lit figure loom larger! She couldn't tear her eyes away from where its face should have been: there were dark hollows where she should have seen eyes. Ivy sensed that the shadow, no taller than she, was playing a wicked game with her. Was this a shade up close? It couldn't be. No snow… and much more menacing.

Fyn tossed down the rope, but the shadow and flames were blocking her way. Ivy panicked, unsure of what was happening. She couldn't help but scream. Then another noise came from behind her, of shattering glass. Terrified at being surrounded, Ivy whirled around.

The homeless man was holding a rock in his hand, framed by the broken window. He gestured toward her and punched the rest of the windowpane out.

"C'mon, Miss, sounds like you need help. Careful you don't cut yourself."

Ivy reached out, gripping his wrists as he held hers. She planted her Habberdash boot on the window frame and with a sharp yank, he pulled her over and onto the street. The cold night air was a refreshing blast.

"Thank you!" Ivy gasped.

"Are you all right?"

"I am now. Thank you, thank you so much!"

"Returning a favor is all, Miss." He tipped his cap to her and went back to his brightly glowing fire.

"Ivy!" yelled Fyn from on top of the roof.

"Over here!" Ivy shouted back, catching her breath.

Fyn, Glistle, and Rebecca came crashing down the ladder.

"Let's go!" Ivy was already running. She glanced back at the broken window, feeling bad about the mess and the entire break-in situation.

They didn't hesitate for a moment, running back out of Ravenshollow, every window dark, and back up the hill. Fyn pulled out the key to jam it in the iron gate, but as soon as he put his hand on it, the ancient gate creaked open.

"Did you forget to lock it?" panted Glistle, disbelieving.

"I thought I did—whatever—it doesn't matter," hissed Fyn, leading them through and almost barreling straight into the Selector.

The Selector! And Damaris, looking more smug than Ivy had ever seen her. Rebecca yelped, and Ivy felt every muscle in her body stiffen.

The Selector extended her arm and held her hand out to Fyn with a look of disapproval. He knew what she wanted and placed the key directly in her palm.

"I'm terribly disappointed in you, Fyn. When Damaris told me to fetch your Individualis, I could hardly believe it."

Ivy sent daggers at Damaris, who grinned like a Cheshire cat.

"And you, Ivy. I believe I warned you, let you know what leaving the Halls might mean."

Ivy hung her head.

"Grounds duty for all four of you. This winter has come early, and it is your responsibility to keep all pathways clear of snow until spring."

The rest of the Selector's words—and Damaris's taunts—floated over Ivy. How had she talked herself into leaving the Halls? The trouble she was in now was nothing compared to the shadowy figure that had clearly meant her harm.

Deep into the night, the vision of the dark figure's

hollow eyes lodged in her mind, taunting Ivy and robbing her of sleep.

Back at the Ball

IVY and Rebecca had barely scooted into their glanagerie class on time; snow shoveling had taken far more time than anticipated, even using Loshes Washes. Ivy didn't know if she could take Damaris's smug face in one more class. Of course, Damaris wasted no time getting under Ivy's skin.

"Professor Night? This terrible cold has me thinking. Remember the Ball last year, the one that Ivy ruined for everyone? I still have nightmares about it. How do we know we are safe with her around?"

Ivy rolled her eyes. Damaris really wanted everyone to hate her. People hadn't been whispering around Ivy quite as much, but Damaris stirred the pot like it was her job.

But then Ivy looked around and saw most of the students nodding.

Hannelore leaned over to Ivy and whispered, "We know it's not your fault, Ivy; we're just scared."

"That's right," added Lila Reeves, her Ethereal Stone glinting in her crown. "Even Damaris knows it wasn't your fault. But I won't repeat to you what she's thinking right now."

What a burden Lila's mind-reading stone must be when

she was around Damaris.

Ivy raised her hand. "Professor? What if our next glanagerie experience was back to that night? The night of the Ball? So that we could have another chance."

"Yes!" piped up Rebecca. "I'd like a do-over."

The students murmured in agreement.

"Excellent idea, Ivy. We shall do just that." Derwin nodded.

Damaris looked crestfallen, then bored.

Derwin drew in a deep breath and closed his eyes, quill in hand stretched out over the bottle on the lectern. Then he opened his eyes and waved his quill over the bottle, which promptly began to glow with a purple and blue light. In the bottle were tiny dancing figures, all submerged in the water. The water rocked, as if in a dance, as distorted glimpses of long strands of pearls, partygoers, and peacock masks showed through. This was not just any masquerade; it was *the* Masquerade.

Smiling broadly at the students, Derwin gave the order: "Let's go, then. All of you." When the students hesitated, he reassured them, "Remember, this is not real—it's merely my imagination. You will be safe, safe to take risks and try new things. Damaris, even you! Those with a Wagua Stone, I encourage you to be creative with this ballroom full of water. Try to float the Dark Queen right out the window with your powers! That's what Waguas are made for."

The students laughed tentatively and began filtering down to the front of the circular classroom. Even Damaris. Derwin wrote each student's name on a piece of parchment, uncorked the bottle, and popped the parchment in. One by one, the royals and sqwinches were whisked into the bottle by a cloud of golden sparkles. Ivy steeled her nerves and was swept inside right after Rebecca and before Hayword.

When the dust settled, she found herself once again in the ballroom, deep underwater. She felt the weight of her wet gown anchoring her to the bottom. Her schoolmates waltzed underwater, oblivious to the danger they were in. This was the exact scene of her nightmares, and Ivy could feel her panic rising just as fast as the water.

Ivy shook her head to remind herself, *This is just a glanagerie.* She envisioned her classmates uniting and fighting together, and her fear subsided a bit.

"Rebecca!" Ivy yelled, still surprised by the power of her voice under water. "Rebecca…" Ivy's voice trailed off.

She saw Rebecca dancing with a handsome boy, the one she now knew as Pedlum. Why wasn't she helping? She seemed more a part of the glanagerie's scene than someone practicing magic within one.

Wait. She picked out more and more of her classmates—Damaris, Hayword, Lila. *This must be, yet again, a me-specific glanagerie bottle experience. Ugh.*

One thing was clear: The figures several feet underwater at the ballroom's floor were going to continue dancing and be of no help whatsoever. Her classmates twirled and twirled in circles as the Dark Queen's trance held everyone in her eerie, beautiful trap. But rather than focusing on helping her friends, as hard as that was, Ivy reminded herself that this was just a glanagerie. She couldn't help or hurt anyone. And she needed information.

Ivy heard the voice echo in her head—the same harsh voice, the same terrible words at the Ball.

"Care to say goodbye to your friends? Or your crown? Let's

have a little fun while you decide, shall we?"

More water flooded in. It was now so deep that Ivy felt crushing pressure in her ears. She surfaced and spun herself in the water to face the Dark Queen, her cream-colored dress wrapping uncomfortably around her legs. The woman stood at the top of the steps that led down to the pool that used to be the ballroom. The mask obscured her face, but the Dark Queen's abundant, long platinum curls hung loose over her elaborate, black lace dress.

Ivy's mind raced. In just a few minutes, Winsome would be unlocking the Forgotten Room. Though she could feel the familiar terror rising, she knew she had to fight it down. This was her chance to explore, to do something else, to learn.

As Ivy kicked toward the steps, she reflexively felt for the stone in her pocket—it wasn't in her ball gown, of course. But she tried to imagine it giving off its heat in the frigid water. *This is all imagination. I am in charge.* With that, Ivy changed her heavy dress to water-repellant soggy jogs, of course.

In real life, Ivy had denied the Dark Queen her "crown," mostly because she didn't even know what the Queen was talking about. Now, not only did Ivy know what she wanted, Ivy actually had it. The Kindred Stone (at least one piece of it) was the stone imbued with the blood of a righteous queen. That's what the Dark Queen was after, something to ensure her evil rule. Perhaps forever.

There was only one way to do the Masquerade Ball differently this time. She stretched her hand out to the nearest royal—Lila—and brought the crown toward herself through the water with her own magic. The energy of the magic sent bubbles and ripples away from the crown as it propelled toward

Ivy. *This will do,* Ivy thought as she waved her hand over the crown's stone, turning its lavender Ethereal Stone as white as a full moon. Ivy held it in her hand so that the Dark Queen thought that it was her crown.

"Fine! You can have it!" Ivy shouted with all her might, waving Lila's crown at the Dark Queen. "First, let my friends go, and it's yours. You have to show me they'll be safe."

With a curl of her finger, the Dark Queen whooshed the water away from the dance floor and up along the sides of the room, creating a thick wall of water that surrounded the dance floor. Though her friends continued their mechanical dancing, they were now also breathing freely in ankle-deep water.

"One wrong move and the water comes crashing down, wiping them away forever."

A snake-like surge of water wrapped around Ivy's waist and pulled her to the foot of the stairs, right under the Dark Queen's gaze. She watched the Queen's smile grow wider, exposing terrifyingly pointed teeth. A shadow she hadn't noticed before flickered behind the Queen, a shadow that was not her own. Before Ivy could focus on it, the shadow flitted off into the lightless hallway behind them. The wall of water swirled around them threateningly. The Cloaked Brood stood behind the Queen, fists clenched.

The Dark Queen extended her hand. "Give me your crown, foolish girl!"

"First, tell me why! You're the Queen—you're so powerful—can't you have any crown you wish?"

The Dark Queen remained with her arm stretched out, perfectly pointed nails reaching to Ivy, demanding the crown with her eyes. Ivy clenched Lila's stone behind her tighter, making it glow even brighter.

"I see you are a curious one. Dangerous thing to be, but let me humor you." The Dark Queen lowered her arm and shook her hair back. Her beauty was overwhelming but also cold and terrifying.

"Many years ago, there was another like you. Bold and brash, a brat just like you."

Ivy's fists tightened. *Listen to her speak. She can't hurt me. She's just a bit of glanagerie water gone bad after all.*

"And just like her, your fear will be the end of you. Give me the crown and you'll live. For now."

She's talking about Princess Isabella.

"Who—I mean, where did you come from? Aren't you in the royal line? The magic in your blood is more than this stone can hold." Ivy knew full well that she wasn't. But still, where *had* she come from?

The Queen's sharp blue eyes slowly blackened, as if ink were spreading across wet parchment. Now as dark and still as the depths of a lake, the Queen's eyes seemed to be able to see through her. Did she know what Ivy knew? Ivy tried to keep her trembling under control.

"I mean, you're so… so powerful, most high Queen." Ivy's voice shook. This, at least, wasn't a lie, though "most high" almost stuck in her throat.

The Dark Queen's eyes were now black almost to the edges, leaving only slivers of white around the huge, opaque irises. Ivy could feel a shift in the woman's mood; she became something less murderous, more proud.

"I *am* incredibly powerful. The engine, some say monster,

that feeds my power is never-ending." She raised her arms and lifted the wall of water that wrapped the ballroom and whirled it around into a globe. The giant ball of water spun in the center of the room, almost floor to ceiling. Shoes, plates, decorations were suspended in the water, and the dancers kept on dancing in their trance below.

It was beautiful and terrifying, just like her.

"When I met that girl, so long ago, she was curious, too. Also, like you, she didn't listen to anyone's guidance—she thought she knew best. But that's not why I could use her. Oh, no. Fear was the deepest undercurrent in her. Self-doubt, insecurity. That is the engine of which I speak. Look."

Ivy looked down at her dancing classmates. From the crowns of each of their heads came black wisps, slowly rising like weak tendrils of smoke toward the ball of water. With a start, Ivy noticed that the same sickly mist was rising from her own head.

"Fear," the Dark Queen cackled triumphantly. "I live for it!"

The wisps of fear continued to rise up and feed the swirling orb of water, which spun faster and faster.

"Her fear was a highway straight into her heart. I took her over, ever so easily. And fear, my girl, feeds not only me but the worst in you. In her. In everyone." The Dark Queen cackled again. "Empathy is drowned out by fear, leaving only self-interest. Courage is suffocated by fear, leaving only cowardice. Doubt and self-loathing grow larger. Anger, too, has its root in fear."

Ivy felt the truth in the Dark Queen's words, which made her heart even heavier. She fell to her knees. If Princess Isabella—almost a *real queen*—couldn't fight against this terror, who was Ivy to think she could? How would she escape this bottle, let alone find the rest of the Kindred Stone and set the world right? *I am nobody.*

"Just as she gave me a direct path to take her over, so shall you!" The Dark Queen continued to mock Ivy, but Ivy was stuck on the words "take her over." Could the Dark Queen possibly be telling the truth?

As if reading her mind, the Dark Queen replied, "Yes, her fear allowed me to inhabit her and bring out the very worst—the most advantageous—in Princess Isabella. When that idiot scrivenist yanked her from the bottle, he pulled us both out."

With that, she let the ball of water crash back down. The surge of water pushed up the steps, knocking Ivy forward. She scrambled up the stairs and, still clutching the crown, bumped right into the legs of the Dark Queen.

"The crown. Give it to me!"

With her last bit of courage, Ivy mustered, "If you're so powerful, why don't you just take it?! Go on, take it right out of my hand!"

And she did. The crown was ripped from Ivy's hand, cutting her palm. A band of dark water brought the crown to the Dark Queen's head. A fierce wind stirred, whipping the water into white caps. Thunder cracked in the ballroom. Ivy no longer had the strength to move, and she collapsed onto the steps.

A gust of wind blew her body back into the water. It was as if her body had turned to lead and Ivy sank down, away from the Dark Queen's eerie light, down to where her classmates were hovering around the ballroom floor, floating face down near the floor.

Everything went black.

With a gasp and a surge of water, the glanagerie spat Ivy back out into the classroom. She slipped and fell, back on her knees just as she had been moments before, but this time she stood up.

Coughing up spring water, she looked around. The entire class returned at once, dropping onto the floor like wet, dead birds. She hadn't been alone in the glanagerie after all! They had been there, too, just trapped and unable to break free. The Queen's trance had been too powerful. And Ivy knew at once what that meant: Had she done things differently at the Ball last year, all of her friends and her professors would be dead. Despite what she had promised, the Dark Queen wouldn't have set her friends free, even if Ivy had given her what she wanted. The idea made Ivy feel sick.

She felt Derwin's concerned hand on her shoulder and heard her classmates coughing back to life and clinging to each other. One look from Ivy, and Derwin understood what had happened. The expeller was already whirring her dry, but Ivy didn't wait for the expeller to finish; she rushed off to the restroom, leaving a trail of wet footprints behind her.

Rebecca rushed after her and found Ivy curled on the floor in a corner, crying.

"She would have killed us all," Ivy cried. Images of her parents, Princess Isabella, and then her friends struggling for air beneath the aquatic ballroom flashed through her mind. It all made her heart ache.

"It's all right, Ivy. We're all okay, thanks to you." Then Rebecca saw her hand. "Oh! You're hurt!"

"I'm all right."

Ivy was suddenly overwhelmed with gratitude. For the first time, she knew that resisting the Dark Queen had been right. That it wasn't her fault for "ruining the Ball." Really, she'd saved them. At least for the time being.

"What if things don't turn out the same way next time the Queen and I meet? How can I ever be prepared to face her?"

Then Fyn's words surfaced in her mind: *We've got to be prepared. We've got to practice. And so, we play.*

"I'm going to play," Ivy said determinedly.

"What?"

"Quogo. I want to play."

Rebecca nodded grimly.

The two made their way back into the classroom—everyone else was dry and chattering nervously. Except for Gretta, who stood alone.

Tears sprang to Ivy's eyes again as she spoke to her scrivenist: "You can be trapped in a castle, trapped in a scaldrony. Trapped by people. But the worst is being trapped by fear."

Quogo Below

A few days later, Ivy and Rebecca clutched their quivers under their cloaks and rushed down the hall toward Fyn, who was waiting impatiently. He leaned up against the balcony that overlooked the ballroom below, counting each minute of the Hour of Discovery that ticked by.

"Tell me, how is it that you two make it anywhere on time? Always late!"

"Easy for you to say! It was our turn to shovel the snow. *You're welcome,*" Rebecca replied a tad sarcastically.

"Well, we're here now! Can I play first?" Ivy asked impatiently.

"Calm down there, kiddo. We draw for who plays!"

The three walked along the ballroom and then up the stairs in silence, taking in the afternoon light that streamed through the windows. Most sqwinches were tucked up in the library's many nooks, reading for fun. Royals were practicing magic in the gardens, trying to sneak snacks from the dining rooms, or catching up on much-needed sleep.

They quietly pushed open the door of Professor Wrigley's empty classroom. The room was dark, the thick curtains drawn shut on the cathedral-like windows. The creatures in the room were taking advantage of the quiet hour and were napping in the customized bookshelves that held habbitry after habbitry. There was a small iron balcony that went around the room to give it a lofted library.

Ivy picked up a luminescent bottle of shorehorse scales.

Fyn's voice echoed up to the wooden timbers of the room. "We get to go to Lonefellow Loch and the Hollow Shaft next week. Part of the fourth year biographies project, you know."

"Who will you be studying?"

"Sigmar Soules."

"Oh! The Wanderer?"

"Yep. Hope I'll see a shorehorse at the Loch, but I doubt it," Fyn smiled. "You were the lucky charm for that one."

Ivy smiled, but his words struck a nerve. Fyn's fourth year. Her mood took a glum turn as she imagined school without him next year. Fyn would soon be off on new adventures of his own, and his adventures with Ivy would be long gone. She felt a sense of deep loss: The year was more than half over, she hadn't found the stone in Belzebuthe, and her home at the Halls was changing.

Fyn's voice brought her out of her thoughts. "Well, I know that the Halls will be *much* more boring without me," he said with a playful grin, trying to lighten her mood.

"What? Are you—" It was as if Fyn had read Ivy's mind. The very idea was disturbing, leading to her next thought, which also involved Fyn. Ivy blushed and scowled, but Fyn had moved on.

"By this time next year, I'll have earned my quill." He patted the embroidered feather on his jacket and continued,

"*My* quill. Think of how much fun we'll have then. Speaking of quills, are you ready to have a little fun? Follow me," he called, heading toward the ladder. "This way!"

They went up to the small iron balcony and walked along the perimeter past books and habbitries of all kinds. Some were empty and others had occupants. At one corner of the balcony, a small door was tucked into the shelves.

"What are you thinking about?" Fyn asked Ivy.

"Thinking about how we are spending this Hour of Discovery doing something kinda sneaky," Ivy said.

"I think I'd go crazy without the freedom of this hour."

Ivy took a deep breath, "I just hate to think of the Selector watching us right now. Surely my Individualis is open across her desk at this very moment recording what you're making me do. What you're making *us* do! Do you hear that? *What Fyn's making us do!*" Ivy shouted like she was engaging in a shouting match with the ceiling, which only responded with a drift of dust.

Fyn shook his head and grinned, like Ivy was the best sort of entertainment he'd seen in years.

"What's so funny?" Ivy asked, annoyed.

"Everyone knows that what happens on the Hour of Discovery is fair game. For the most part, any rule breaking is overlooked if it occurs during your Hour of Discovery. It's sort of like your Hour of Privacy. The Selector acts like she's blind to it, though I'm convinced she sees it all."

"Unless a Bearded Cloud obliterates it?" Rebecca interjected. Ivy nodded slowly in understanding.

"Ha! Yes, that's a possibility. Only with Ivy, I think, though," Fyn answered Rebecca. "Anyway, that's why all Quality Quills

Club meetings and matches are held during the Hour of Discovery and why your extracurricular activities with Winsome in his lair were okay by her. Thank goodness, because we've already had four matches this term."

"If only I had realized that sooner. I would have visited the Hollow Shaft during the Hour of Discovery and not gotten you in trouble last year."

"I'm pretty sure *that* would have still had us in trouble. Traveling to the Hollow Shaft takes considerably more time than an hour!" Fyn responded. "Anyway, what we are about to do is definitely not in the student contract—best kept hush-hush. Students aren't supposed to have quills, let alone play Quogo."

As they chatted, they came to the tiny door, emblazoned in bold, red ink with an intimidating message: *Critters of the dark dwell below. Beware. Enter at your own risk.* Fyn opened the door.

Ivy hesitated.

"Down there?" Rebecca pointed into a dark descending stairwell. "After we've just climbed all the way up here?"

Ignoring them, Fyn pushed on. There were more habbitries, a little hallway full of them. Like the glanagerie hall, these walls were cut with compartments, too. Each of these hosted a creature that needed to be kept from the light of day: bioluminescent moon jellies; a parakeet the size of a house cat; and a fangless, three-foot-long, Evernoughten snake.

"Do you always have your Quogo meetings in here?" Ivy asked, holding back in the doorway.

"Not a meeting… a *Quogo scrimmage!*" he whispered excitedly, hushing Ivy.

"In here, Fyn?" Ivy stared at Fyn blankly. "You're going to engage in a Quogo scrimmage *here*, in this stairwell. Do you realize the mess? The poor creatures—there's hardly room!"

"Yes! The creatures!" echoed Rebecca.

"Not here! Down below!" said Fyn with more than a little mischief in his voice.

Nervously, Ivy stammered, "But, wh—where is Professor Wrigley, anyway? How can we be sure that he'll stay away the whole hour?"

"He always spends his Hour of Discovery with beasts! Feeding, grooming, collecting," smiled Fyn. "Well, we're already late. The others are probably already down there and waiting. If they haven't already begun, that is."

"The others? Wouldn't we have seen them by now?"

"We arrive separately—several passageways lead down to the dungeon. All of us through one door would draw too much attention. This passage is my favorite, though. Takes us past some of Professor Wrigley's more interesting critters."

As they descended, Ivy peered over Fyn's shoulder for a glimpse of what was ahead. After the stairs, a long, dark corridor led to even darker corridors that were more interesting—and far more creepy—than she had anticipated. Just by the look of it, this web of passageways looked like a good place to get lost for a long time, or cast curses, or let loose stray beasts. Perfect for a secret Quogo scrimmage.

Water dripped from the ceiling, echoing and leaving small puddles along the earthen floor. The ceiling was too high to see. They stepped carefully over a fallen and shattered stone column.

"How do you even know where to go?" Ivy asked Fyn. "You can't see anything down here. It's only getting darker."

"Been here plenty of times before. Yeah, yeah, I think it's this way…."

"You *think*?"

"Are there rats?" Rebecca hoped not.

"You mean besides you?" said Fyn attempting to be humorous. It was not that successful. Rebecca's discomfort had caused her rump to sprout a long, thin tail. It whipped left and right, scraping the dusty stone walls just before beating Fyn in the back.

"So glad you decided to join us," added Fyn as he rustled in his bag, dodging Rebecca's tail.

"The pleasure is mutual," snapped Rebecca.

"This is how we get around," he said, holding something up.

"I can't see—oh, oh, I can."

A map of the lower level glimmered like gold leaf. Everything about the yellowed map was old-fashioned and aged, but the shimmer was gorgeous. It looked like the map was making its own light.

"It's called the Map of Olglarion. One of Professor Bingle's best."

Ivy's mind flashed to the strange little mapmaker who had lent her the map to the Hollow Shaft.

Fyn continued, "It shines only for those using it, but is invisible to onlookers. In the dark, you have to follow the steps on the map—see how it shows three strides forward and then left? It won't light the hallway or dungeon for you. You have to be staring directly at the map, you see. The minute you look away, total darkness."

Though the map was roughly drawn—its lines more like squiggles and boxes than the perfect-to-life sketches Ivy was used to creating—Ivy was impressed. And grateful. There were boxes that marked small dungeon compartments and jagged steps to mark stairwells. The pathway to where they were going was a brightly glowing line and it led to a large room near the center of the dungeon. It was marked with an *X*.

"Is that where we're headed?" Ivy asked.

"Yeah. Even with the Hour of Discovery on our side, we still don't want the wrong person to find out what we are up to. The walls are thickest down there, better to withstand any errant magic. It allows for more time to control any inopportune situation that may arise."

It was Ivy's turn to roll her eyes. "I can't imagine anything bad happening at Quogo!" She remembered with perfect clarity Fyn fighting off the intruder at his house in Belzebuthe. "To say nothing of your quill skills."

"Um, what goes wrong in Quogo?" asked Rebecca nervously.

"Well, so far we've only ended up with many bruises, three broken bones, and a couple of demolished bookshelves. No casualties as of yet."

Rebecca awkwardly laughed off what Fyn said, though she was undeniably rattled.

"This way," directed Fyn, staring hard at the map. They continued on, descending down, down, down in silence. Ivy lost track of how many flights of stairs they must have come down. Soon they could hear something like conversation echoing in the tunnels.

Then a room opened up into a poorly lit cavern made of rock walls and dark crevices. The room was huge and expansive. In the center, multiple bookshelves formed an uneven box-like border, resembling a handmade boxing ring. A handmade hex is what it was. Lounging around the shelves was a familiar group. It seemed all Quogo matches were held in dark places. Better to see the vibrancy of the quill's magic and the light of the ethereal spectres summoned by the quills. There were a few hairie lanterns on the shelves of the bookcases, just enough to illuminate the ring's boundaries and cast enough light on the sqwinches' proof pads.

"About time you three arrived," said Canna. "Manone's carved 'M <3s L' in every bookshelf, almost carved straight through one. We only have an hour! You must be Rebecca."

"And you are…?"

"Canna."

The two girls shook hands.

Each of the members carried a quiver. Manone was still actively using her quill to make the mark of her undying love in every surface. Hayword was organizing his quiver—he had only two quills, so he was just swapping them back and forth. Ivy wondered if he'd managed to snag quills that were beast-specific, their departed owners also animal lovers. Other members readied their proof pads, ready to sketch at any moment, eager not to let any lesson in magic pass unnoticed.

"Ivy!" Glistle ran up to greet her.

"Good to see you, Glistle. Do you remember my friend Rebecca?" As Ivy turned toward Rebecca, she realized that her friend, always the social butterfly, was already gone. Ivy was pleased to see that Rebecca had quickly started up a conversation with Pedlum, a third year. She had a thing for sqwinches with big, bulky muscles.

"Excited for your first scrimmage, are you?" asked Glistle.

"Nervous. But ready."

"Nothing to be nervous about. Worst that'll happen

is you lose the quill. Never had any casualties as of yet."

"Yes, Fyn just reminded me of that fact." But Ivy knew that if she lost Winsome's quill, she'd be devastated. She felt her velvet quiver grow heavier in her hands. It held only two quills: Winsome's tattered gold quill, still full of life; and the less vibrant gray-blue quill from Boulliquiste's. It had turned out to be from Lillie Almonde, a scrivenist who hadn't been able to discover much, but in some ways it was in better shape than Winsome's.

"Up close, they're unique, aren't they? There's so much to them. Almost like people."

"Which quills did you bring? What's that one with the pink tip?"

"Careful with it. This one's got a bit of an attitude." Fyn read from its geer, "This one belonged to Mergerta Molly Megermis," said Fyn, pointing to the name inscribed on the geer. "She tended to out-talk her opponents. Not bad for a Boulliquiste quill. Her powers of persuasion were next level. In life, she convinced a troll to swallow the head of a boar for fun."

"Sounds like she knew how to have a good time. So, I see the spice marker. And I don't doubt that Manone was able to secure the danger, but where is the Castleton Stone?"

"Oh, that. We don't have one yet."

"What? How do you expect to keep the spells in the realm of quillusion?"

"Working on getting one! But remember that these quills are *weak*. I doubt we even need it," Fyn shrugged.

Lennu called out impatiently, "Are we going to get on with it or what?"

The nine members aligned themselves around the bookshelves, on the inside of the hex. Fyn held up the pouch that held the QQC's names on parchment, ready to draw. He held it out to Lennu, who pulled out a scrap and called out, "Pedlum!"

Rebecca jumped to her feet, squealing in delight. Pedlum walked proudly to the center of the hex.

"Ivy," was the next name Lennu called.

"Me?"

The group responded by cheering Ivy on. Fyn hopped down and over, pushing Ivy to the center. Lennu gestured for Ivy and Pedlum to hold out their quivers. He drew a quill from each.

"Ivy Lovely plays Winsome Monocle. And Pedlum... Hosstash Vertusse!"

"Um," Ivy stammered, "I'd rather be a spectator."

"Your name's been drawn, Ivy!" Fyn replied. "Weren't you practically begging to play?"

"Well, yeah... but I—I just can't give up this quill, Fyn. Not even for fun. It's Winsome's! Can't you draw again?"

"Who says you'll lose? One rule of the Club is that you never back down when called upon. No exchanges. Plus, you trust Winsome, don't you? You know your quill master better than anyone here."

"Pedlum, go easy on her now," winked Rebecca, edging closer to Ivy's corner.

Ivy had no choice but to play. She crossed the smoking spice marker boundary and came to stand opposite Pedlum.

There was no more time to think. A liquid light pooled out from the quill in her hand. And then there was an almost life-like, blue-light Winsome before her. Ivy squealed: no reaction from Winsome.

"Winsome, can you hear me?"

He could not.

"Am I supposed to do som—"

But before Ivy could finish her sentence, an ethereal, red-tinted bottle went soaring past her head, chucked by Hosstash and aimed at Winsome. It shattered against the ground by Winsome's feet with a puff of smoke. Light-as-Air potion! Ivy and Winsome began to hover!

Even though floating, Ivy felt herself sync with Winsome. She could hear his thoughts almost as well as she used to hear him muttering to himself. The words, *flint, blood orange,* and *coal* fluttered up in Ivy's mind. *Some type of explosion potion*, Ivy realized in a flash. The moment she thought it, Ivy raised her quill, and she and Winsome hurled the magically concocted potion at Hosstash. All in the realm of quillusion, the spectre glass shattered and its contents sizzled up from the floor, rising up into hundreds of banging firecrackers. Hosstash leapt and bobbed and ducked but managed to keep himself in the boundary.

The rest of the group set to writing, their porcupels moving a million miles a minute.

"That all you got?" sniped Pedlum.

He and Hosstash conjured a Slither McSerpent spell and a trail of tinted-green sparkles snaked around Winsome. The green cloud grew and whipped itself around his wiry body. Winsome yelped in surprise, but his yelp quickly morphed into a hiss.

Ivy's face was hot with emotion, as she didn't know whether

to be more curious or furious with Pedlum for using a Slither McSerpent spell.

"Hissssssss!" Winsome managed to say, a long, forked tongue flicking out of his mouth. His arms shrank and his skin began to take on a greenish hue. If Ivy didn't move quickly, her spectre wouldn't have arms to swing a quill.

Let's turn him into a rat, Winsome, Ivy thought and raised her quill. Ivy's idea mixed with Winsome's expertise and with a puff of smoke, Hosstash was more rat in an instant than Rebecca had ever been. The spectre rat squealed, and the snake-like Winsome lunged for it. For a moment, Ivy was afraid that Winsome might actually eat his opponent, but the rat ran across the boundary in a frenzy.

Once the boundary was broken, the spectres dissipated, leaving only the players panting and laughing.

"We have never had a quill or spectre powerful enough to chase another right out of the ring, all because of fright!" sang out Manone.

"Good on you, Ivy!" shouted Lennu.

Ivy was breathless—she could hardly believe she'd won.

"Next time I'm not taking it easy on you, Ivy," Pedlum puffed.

But Ivy could tell he was bluffing. Reluctantly, he handed over his quill, with its broad green-yellow feather.

"All that Hosstash Vertusse is good for is snakes, anyway."

"Really?" remarked an interested Hayword.

Glistle won the next round against Canna, but Fyn and Lennu didn't get to finish their match as they ran out of time. Teasing and playing all the way back up from the dungeon toward dinner, the QQC arrived back in Professor Wrigley's classroom with only a minute to spare.

"Let's get some grub! I'm starving," said Glistle.

"I'll catch up in a bit," Ivy said as she made sure her new quill was tucked neatly into her quiver, and her quiver into her jacket pocket. She wanted to check and see when Derwin wanted to meet next.

But before she made it to the glanagerie classroom, she bumped into Derwin in the hall.

"Hello, there! You certainly had fun in the dungeon, didn't you?"

The two locked eyes.

"How do you mean?" Ivy inquired.

"Quogo scrimmages are never a safe idea. I imagine you've gathered as much. But it's a brilliant way of practicing magic."

"You're not supposed to know. Hour of Discovery is private."

"Yes, well, it's unfortunate you and I share a mind at times. No privacy when it comes to a royal and her scrivenist, Your Highness," he shrugged.

"Don't call me that here!"

"Sorry. Tell me, how did old man Winsome perform this afternoon? Couldn't quite get the details! But not to worry, linked scrivenist-royal minds don't violate the secret spiller agreement," he reassured her in a low voice.

"Well, I won my first quill," Ivy announced proudly. "Hosstash Vertusse—apparently an expert in all things serpentine. Would you like to see it?" Proudly, Ivy reached for her satchel.

"Collecting quills can become rather addicting. Although entirely illegal for sqwinches, I'm afraid." He admired the quill briefly and then said, "Always have been a fan of Quogo. Never heard of a Hosstash Vertusse, however."

INVISITAURS

IT was pitch black when Ivy heard the scratching sound. The sky was dark and moonless, and dawn hadn't yet begun to seep in at the horizon.

Scrritch. Scrrrriiiiitch.

Ivy cracked her eyes open and peered around the room. On the nightstand between their beds, beside Rebecca's books—*How to Best an Angry Dragon* and *Dragon Training and Management*—and Ivy's sleeping hairies, lay Winsome's quill poking out of her quiver. Out of instinct, she picked it up and with Ivy's soft touch, the quill sparked a little as if it, too, sensed something in the hallway.

Then she heard the sound again, the scratching outside her door. Rebecca was sleeping soundly, Humboldt snoring away. The noise had definitely come from outside their room, and now not only was the quill twitching, but the Kindred Stone had begun to glow and quiver. Ivy sat bolt upright. The room was dark, but the floor at the foot of the door was darker still, like a bottle of ink had spilled and was seeping under the door.

Ivy jumped up out of bed. The ink spill stopped and then retreated. *Not Damaris and her nasty pranks again?* Ivy was too curious to stay in bed. She quietly left the room, Winsome's quill in hand, closing the door ever so softly and stepping into the dormitory hall. The hairies went from a dim glow to a bright curiosity that lit the hall, shadows dancing from the stone beams that lead the narrow arches to soft points at the top.

Then a shadow moved at the end of the dark hall, disappearing around a corner. Ivy held the quill out like a sword and dashed after whoever was sneaking around; but once she had rounded the corner, the shadow was gone. Ivy didn't know whether to go up or down the large stone stairs that spiraled in front of her. She ran to the columns that held up the stairs, looking up and down.

Suddenly Fyn's head popped out—he was doing the same thing as Ivy.

"You scared the wits out of me!" hissed Ivy.

"Careful where you point that thing." Glistle popped his head out from behind Fyn. They hopped down the stairs quickly, and Glistle gently pushed down Ivy's hand, which was pointing Winsome's quill straight at his head.

"You'll poke somebody's eye out." Glistle cocked his head, staring at the wilting feather. "So, what are you doing out in the hall so late?"

"I should ask the same thing of you!"

"And I should ask you, too, Glistle. Are you following me?" asked Fyn.

"Yes! You might have thought you were quiet, but I'd know your clomping around anywhere," Glistle shrugged. "I thought you might be going for another quill run at Boulliquiste's. What are *you* doing?"

"I don't know. Just—just got a feeling."

"You weren't outside my door just now, scratching around?" asked Ivy.

"What? No! Is that why you're up?" asked Fyn.

"Yes, I thought I heard something. Are you sure it wasn't you?"

"Who, Fyn? Trespass on another level? He wouldn't dare break school rules!" Glistle said sarcastically.

Fyn rolled his eyes, but then said to Ivy earnestly, "No, it wasn't me."

"It wasn't me, either," insisted Glistle.

"What time is it anyway?"

"Half past three."

"Did you find anyone?" Fyn queried.

"Not a trace. It just felt like I was following a shadow."

Ivy began to feel a bit silly. Of course in a dormitory of this size another student might be up. Midnight snack, bathroom run, restless night of sleep. But Ivy couldn't be too cautious. Not after the Selector's warning. And that shadow in Boulliquiste's.

"Well, isn't this a party?" grinned Glistle.

"You should get back to bed," said Fyn, hushing Glistle, who spoke too openly, too loudly.

"We better all go back before anyone finds us roaming about," Ivy whispered. "By anyone, I mean Damaris. I've had enough of her getting me in trouble."

○ ○ ○ ○

A few hours later, Ivy had to drag herself from bed again. Professor Wheeler's Invisitaur Riding class was just too, too early. But on the terrace outside the grand entrance, the rest of the group seemed rambunctious enough. Beautiful winter floram blossoms that clung to the rails were glimmering gold. At least Fyn and Glistle were in charge of the snow shoveling that morning, though they'd be as tired as she.

Rebecca had warned her that the hike to Professor Wheeler's barn was a long one, but Ivy certainly didn't expect to go out nearly as far as she had to catch the cabby to Belzebuthe. The invisitaur barn was tucked against the side of a hill in an oak grove. It was a picture-perfect spot, the way the snow shone mystically on the barn's wooden shingles.

"Not a full class, is it?" Ivy asked.

Rebecca turned to Ivy, her breath puffing like a cloud, "Only half of the second years cared enough to wake this early. Not everyone is interested in learning how to ride invisitaurs. At least not at this hour."

Ivy was shocked to see Damaris as part of the crew.

Following Ivy's eyes, Rebecca said, "She has a massive crush on Glistle. Sometimes he helps with demonstrations."

"Let's begin our lesson by admiring these magnificent beasts." Professor Wheeler was gazing out behind the class in the empty frosted field. His silvering hair was neatly parted to the side, and he wore his scrivenist jacket with riding pants and boots.

Confused, Ivy looked around before whispering to Rebecca, "I don't get it."

"What?" she whispered back.

"Where are the invisitaurs?"

"In the field. Roaming."

"Roaming where?"

"Over there," Rebecca pointed. "Ivy, remember? They're

invisible."

Professor Wheeler led on, "Remember, invisitaurs are sensitive beings. Their skittishness is second only to their invisibility as far as trademarks go. This is why invisitaur riding is greatly assisted by terrible weather. Falling rain and snow help outline their physical forms. And, oh, what a sight, let me tell you. They have the speed of one wearing a Jessel Stone, instinct far better than any human, the loyalty of a scrivenist to their royal, and occasionally the personality of a jester. They have a knack for juggling humans. They are lean, muscular beings with the capacity to lift an entire tree with ease. Needless to say, we as riders are but feathers on their shoulders."

Ivy squinted over the horizon. Her fellow students were only half listening to Professor Wheeler, tightening their boots or, in Damaris's case, looking for Glistle. Suddenly, Ivy felt an awareness wash over her: tall, lean, fast, invisible. The mysterious creature that had carried her to safety and the cabby had to be an invisitaur! She gripped Rebecca's hand in excitement, almost crushing it, but Professor Wheeler wasn't finished yet.

"We've spent the last lessons observing the beasts—rather their footprints—and trying to make contact. Today you'll learn about the hook."

"The hook?" Ivy asked tentatively.

"As we have spoken on numerous occasions, the most difficult feat in riding an invisitaur is the hook—the moment you catch or lure the invisitaur to allow you to ride. Like fishing, you never really know when they're going to bite until they do."

"Bite?" called out Woodley Butterlove nervously.

"Like you tear into every loaf of bread," snickered Damaris.

"Why are you even here, Damaris, just to be mean?" Ivy shot back.

"Oh, look. It seems as though I've annoyed Woodley's girlfriend."

Ivy rolled her eyes and then turned out to the field. Now that she knew what she was looking for—the creature that had saved her—she was even more interested in the class.

"Look!" she whispered to Rebecca. "There's one!"

"What are you talking about, Ivy? They are invisible."

"Yes, but just look!"

Ivy could see hot breath melting snow in the oak branches. She saw tentative, curious footprints approaching the class and then backing away. Then she saw the thin layer of snow being scraped together. A giant snowball flew through the air and hit Damaris right in the back of her unsuspecting legs.

"Hey!" She whirled around with an accusing glance at Ivy.

The class stifled giggles, not wanting to be on the receiving end of Damaris's wrath.

Ivy shrugged and smiled, "Wasn't me."

Then she felt the air around her warm and she looked up.

"Is that you, friend?"

A reassuring pat on her head came down.

"Good to see you again," Ivy whispered to where she assumed the invisitaur's head was. It then swung her up and above to rest on his shoulders. Ivy returned the pat.

"Ah, you see, Miss Lovely has captured the heart of Silius."

"He has a name? How can you tell which is which?" asked Ivy from above.

"You get used to reading the heat shimmers around their

bodies on cold mornings like this. Silius is the biggest and fastest, the head honcho. Good job, Miss Lovely."

"How did I do it?" Ivy was totally clueless.

"Invisitaurs hear your heart, not your voice. You called to it and he accepted. Silius must know you have good intentions."

"That explains why Damaris has been snowballed," Rebecca announced jokingly. "Seems like they were taking it easy on her."

"Professor, are you going to allow her to speak to me that way?" Damaris shot a snowball at Rebecca's head and missed by a mile.

"Girls. Girls. Please, pay attention. Fighting can startle them, and you don't want them to jump on top of the roof. Not just yet."

Quincy Fryer asked, "If an invisitaur can jump so high, and they are strong enough to lift a tree, what's the point of containing them in the barn? Can't they just bust right through it?"

"We don't. The barn is their cove, their home base. Just like horses, they enjoy their total freedom paired with the coziness of a stall. Typically, they bound around the school grounds all day. You just don't notice unless you know how to look."

"They're funny, aren't they?" Hayword said.

"Complete clowns, but they're fast as anything. And, of course, excellent hiders. Part of your final will include a massive game of hide-and-seek." Professor Wheeler looked delighted as if nothing could please him more.

"I'll allow those with a Weatheritall Stone to practice the magic of their stones. Summon a light snow and it will reveal the bulk of the invisitaurs' bodies in the field. Also, remember: kindness and gentleness are key! Have good intentions or you'll never get a hook!"

Gregory Gershwin summoned a rainstorm—beyond the gentle snow that the professor had recommended. The storm flooded the sky over the field and Silius took off to romp with Ivy astride his shoulders. Ivy couldn't help but squeal. He was just so fast! As they frolicked—leaping over dead logs and the stream in the center of the field—Ivy caught glimpses of other beasts, their fur glistening with the spelled-warm rain.

The invisitaurs were tall and bow-legged. They leaped up and dangled from the tree branches overhead; then somersaulted down little hills. Tall, steer-like horns curled up to the sky from their bulky heads. Their snorts left behind giant clouds of hot breath in the rain. Laughing with delight, Ivy hugged into Silius tightly.

"They all look different!" marveled Hannelore Lawler as she ran in and out of the now-visible beasts. Her Jessel Stone made her almost as fast as the invisitaurs.

"Same frame, but yes, different in their expressions, their heights, the way they move, and their character!" shouted Professor Wheeler in return.

Some students were struggling to attract the invisitaurs to them. Other sqwinches were sketching away like their porcupels were on fire. Half of the class darted through the air, experiencing the ride in its fullness. Quincy Fryer was out riding through the nearly frozen school pond, halfway back to school. Hayword was dashing through the woods.

From his bullhorn, Professor Wheeler yelled tips on slowing the beasts down, everything from stroking the rough fur between their horns, to whispering compliments, to offering to bring doughnuts to the next class.

Eventually, all those who had been able to hook an invisitaur calmed their steeds down. Upon Professor Wheeler's instruction, they were able to form a line and walk their beast in an easy rhythm around the meadow. Damaris and a few others were unsuccessful in hooking an invisitaur and, as a result, dismissed themselves from class early. The others bobbed up and down, laughing and giggling, enjoying the winter breeze. Professor Wheeler then hooked one himself—a favorite of his—and proclaimed that they were hitching rides back to the Halls. As they approached, through the hallway windows they could see students heading to the library for one more read before school. Their sleepy eyes popped open when they saw the six riders floating past.

At the entrance of the Halls, Professor Wheeler gave out feedback and reading assignments. Hayword was beside himself. Ivy's ride Silius helped her dismount by picking her up by the collar of her school cloak and swinging her down gently to face him. She stood still, drenched and looking up toward the creature's face. The rain on its fur was now turning to ice in the winter's cold.

"I met you earlier this summer, didn't I?" she asked, unsure of how much the invisitaur could understand, if anything at all.

The beast tossed its head gently in agreement and grunted.

"You saved my life.... Can I ever thank you enough?"

The invisitaur patted her head and, again, Ivy thought she saw him nod his head ever so slightly.

"I hope to meet again, Silius."

Then Silius was off, loping around the pond, shaking off the ice as he went back toward the barn with the rest of them.

Chapter Twenty-Two

Shadows, Spices, and Scaldrons

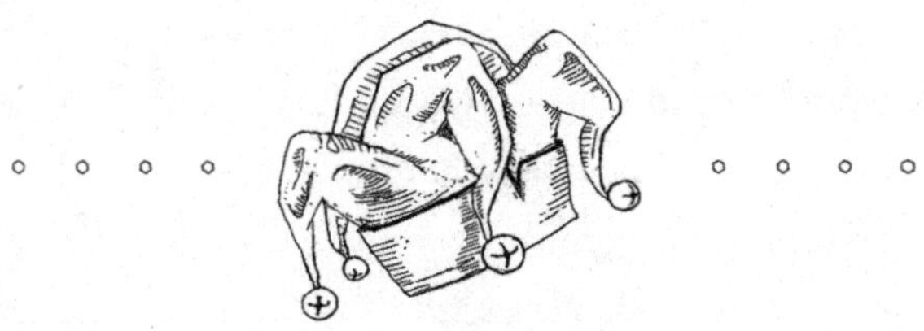

THE leaves outside of Professor Wrigley's windows were now beginning to bud yellow-green. Just enough spring light filtered through the windows for the lessons. The topic was hairies, Croswald's indispensable source of lighting. Most of the students looked like they were struggling to stay awake, clearly of the opinion that hairies were hardly enough to warrant an interesting discussion, let alone a second-year lecture! Even the Castle Plum had plenty of hairies within its magic-less boundary. The class was full of exaggerated yawns, twiddling porcupels, and passed notes.

Ivy's faintly glowing hairies were even less interested in the discussion than was Damaris Dodley, if such a thing were possible. Ivy had wondered why Professor Wrigley had insisted they bring their hairies at all.

"Please turn to page 128 in your textbooks. Ivy Lovely, would you lend us a voice, please?" Professor Wrigley gestured for Ivy to read the passage beneath the close-up hairie diagram, which illustrated hairie wings, feet, and toes.

Even though it wasn't totally natural, Ivy was becoming more comfortable with the idea of reading aloud and letting her voice be heard. She wasn't sure if it was the support of her classmates—her friends—or if it was the fact that she had so much more practice wielding a quill, but she was coming into her own.

Ivy cleared her throat and read the tiny script, "Hairies are pint-sized, fine-haired critters whose hair glows in response to human conversation, particularly gossip. Hybridized in the late 1600s, these creatures cannot live in the wild but thrive in close quarters with scrivenists especially. Less commonly known as lanternbugs, fully grown, hairies are the length and width of a snap pea. Hairies are related to fairies but don't have their independent will nor charisma. They come in every hue of the rainbow and have the ability to shift their color according to mood on Moonsday. The tradition of using hairies for natural light dates back to their hybridization. Harry Visbillow discovered that they much preferred the safety offered behind glass over the freedom of the open world. This is very unlike their fairy cousins. As far as we know, hairies are some of the few creatures able to understand human language. Their vocal cords are far too simple for complex expression, though some are known to chatter. However, their eardrums are enormous and highly developed."

"Class, look at the diagram of this nosy creature. This hard spot behind the ear is actually a very specific bone used to detect the vibration of speech." The Professor shook his head in admiration.

"But *why* do they like to be contained, when there is so much to explore?" Hayword Nesselton insisted on asking. "What kind of life can a hairie have behind glass?" He paused, summoning courage, "I mean, how can they breed?"

A titter spread through the class at the idea of breeding.

"Why do they prefer containment? The warmth of the lanterns and the company, Hayword. To each his own. And a correction, if you will: hairies do not *breed.* Every several years, during the warmest moon, they *multiply.*"

Then there was a rattle and the squeak of old metal above. No one else seemed to notice, but perhaps because Ivy was already attuned to the upstairs doorway she craned her head up. There was Westin, the Beast Keeper, on the tiny walkway that wound around the upper bookshelves. He was pushing his cart full of habbitries, each with a creature. As they squeaked and purred and growled, classmates looked up.

"Am I late to the party?" he called with his croaky, toad-like voice. The wheels of his cart wiggled, screeching as they turned the corner. Westin announced casually, "Caught you all a classmate."

Professor Wheeler glanced at his roster, then back up at the Beast Keeper: "Gretta Leelangraf?"

Ivy gasped. She hadn't noticed that the bundle of amethyst fabric lying on top of the cart was actually a person.

"Poor girl is fast asleep. Messing with something she shouldn't, judging from the tears on her dress," he admonished.

When he arrived at the top of the brass spiral stairway, Westin locked in his cart to the railing with a metallic clang, stood on the back, and spun down the stairs. At the bottom, the cart unlatched and rolled straight to Professor Wrigley.

Westin wasted not a minute longer and unleashed his extra-large expeller. The creature flitted about in delight, sucking up a dark vapor from Gretta's soiled dress.

The expeller coughed and gagged, but Gretta slowly sat up, blinking. In her fist, she clutched a rough sketch. It looked like a person wrestling with a shadow, but Gretta crumpled it and quickly shoved it into the folds of her dress.

"Not the first time this has happened," Westin reassured the still fumbling Gretta as best he could. "But try and focus on your classwork—that way you won't get in over your head with a… a whatever this was."

Ivy sent a small smile to Gretta, hoping to reassure her. But Gretta wouldn't meet her eyes. Disconcerted, Ivy looked to Rebecca, hoping that she'd have some insight, but Rebecca was completely still, quiet as a mouse. The memory of how she and Ivy had met overwhelmed her; just the sight of Westin and his cages made Rebecca feel uncomfortable. She sank low in her seat.

Unfortunately, Damaris had noticed Rebecca's discomfort as well.

"Oh, Beast Keeper? Perhaps you should stay for the remainder of class. This one," Damaris pointed at Rebecca, "loves to turn into all kinds of rodents."

"I haven't had an accidental transformation since last year!" Rebecca cried out.

"My apologies for disrupting your class, Professor." Westin nodded and excused himself.

But as the Beast Keeper made his way out the main door, Ivy caught sight of a glass vitrine with a bit of a black cloud floating within it. It looked like a ball of dark, angry cotton.

She couldn't help but call out, "Excuse me, but, that bottle there. With the little raincloud…."

Westin stopped the cart, its wheels screeching. "Yes?"

"I've never seen anything like it before," said Ivy. Or had she? "On your cart, that is." Her mind flashed to fishing for stars with Fyn on his rooftop, the storm in the alley Easel Leelangraf referred to as a shade, looking out onto clouds that were the exact color as this puffball. Black in the center, the cloud's edges faded to a light gray, occasionally sparking like an angry balding hairie.

"Oh, dear, a bit off topic, I suppose," added Professor Wrigley.

The students finally perked up. Something dangerous, perhaps? More exciting than hairies, at least.

"What is it?" sounded the voices of several.

Professor Wrigley was unable to refrain from an impromptu lecture. "This is a newly discovered creature, something that many of us are working on describing and understanding. Definitely ephemeral, potentially insidious, and not from around here. No formal name yet, but we've been calling it a shade."

It is *a shade!* Ivy perked up, listening closely.

"How did you catch it?" asked Hayword.

"The Tempest Poultice to break it up, and a Stay-with-It spell to catch it and keep it from dissipating, as they have every other time. A valiant, collective effort with the Beast Keeper, my potions, and the matteler's wisdom. Class, dial to S and open your Compass Collecti. You'll see that the entry for shades grows by the minute."

It was true; the description grew before their eyes:

Shades are localized to the Town.

Those words faded and reappeared as:

Shades are primarily localized to the Town, though one has recently been caught at the Halls of Ivy. It is unknown whether they have agency of their own or are controlled by another being's intent. They appear to have storm-related powers but...

Professor Wrigley picked up the glass with the bit of shade and shook it. A storm thundered inside, hurling tiny bolts of lightning. Fortunately, the Beast Keeper's habbitries were magic proof. But the lightning and clouds rattled threateningly. Ivy's stone buzzed in her pocket. *Danger.*

"Slurry girl's scared," said Damaris, eyeing her.

Ivy did her best to ignore her malicious classmate.

After class, Gretta left quickly, heading in the direction of the dormitories, and Ivy and Rebecca huddled together while they made their way to Professor Royal's room.

"The shade—Mr. Leelangraf said that it's the Dark Queen hunting for the Town. Do you think that could be true?!"

"I don't know, Ivy. But we've got to get to Magical Management. Let's talk about it at lunch. Maybe you'll feel a little better when you have something in your belly."

The shade left Ivy feeling like she had a puzzle to figure out. Maybe she really should have stayed in Belzebuthe? No. Safe wasn't an option. After all the harm the Dark Queen had done to her family, to all of Croswald, and how her family and Winsome had sacrificed for her, she would fight. But how? She would find the remaining pieces of the Kindred Stone. Ivy could barely focus on the lesson—even Professor Royal noticed how poor her spellecution was. Then Didley—the bird that swooped through the Halls to announce the beginning and end of classes—squawked and the hour was over.

Rebecca led the distracted Ivy to the Lolly Room. Ivy was in no mood for the Jester and his jokes and high spirits, but Rebecca had a craving. When they arrived, the bright colors and merrily spinning parasols failed to lift Ivy's spirits. To make matters worse, the stone hadn't calmed down since seeing the shade in the bottle. Ivy had to fold her skirt over itself to hide the light emanating from her pocket. The conversation at the tables was raucous and the smell wafting from the long buffet tables was wonderful! But Ivy could barely work up an appetite. Something just felt wrong.

"Look at you. You've lost your color," said Rebecca as she popped a grape into her mouth.

Ivy felt the magic in the Kindred Stone amp up.

"What?"

"Ivy, you're as pale as the Jester's pinstripes! Are you all right?"

"I still have that shade on my mind." Ivy listlessly spooned carrots onto her plate.

"It was terribly unnerving, wasn't it? And that stuff with Gretta," Rebecca said as she loaded the plate up high with cauliheaders, potatoes, and dilly drums.

Ivy just nodded, resting her satchel at her side to hide the stone's light.

"It's going to be okay, Ivy. If anything, shade or something else, I'll make sure that you're safe. I'm prepared to claw some eyes out!"

Ivy giggled, "I believe it, you adorable mink."

"You laugh. But it's easier to maneuver around when you're

smaller."

Ivy chuckled again, "I do think Fyn may have a point in the Quogo thing. I feel like I'm getting more familiar with wielding a quill—so much more than in just class alone."

"Me, too! I'm looking forward to the next scrimmage."

Lunch was nearly over. Ivy watched out the window, finally digging into a delicious spring stew. A light rain started to feather down onto the budding leaves of the trees in the Halls' gardens.

Ivy looked over at the Jester who was hovering over Bobby Willcock's side of the table. The Jester held up his childish cards chest height, demanding that the meek boy play. Bobby flicked a puff of smoke in the Jester's direction, like Humboldt would. When the Jester persisted, Bobby set one of the playing cards on fire. The Jester hopped and waved the card in a frantic effort to put it out.

The Jester then turned to Ivy and Rebecca, foisting his favorite card upon them. "You Are What You Eat!" was written boldly on the top.

"In the mood to play, girls?" The Jester, clad in his usual ridiculous get up, waved the card in front of them.

Rebecca rolled her eyes and whispered to Ivy, "He'll leave us alone faster if we do. I'll handle this one—more accustomed to changing shape than you are."

She grabbed the card. With a poof of glitter, Rebecca became a cauliheader. Ivy had worked with the pint-sized creature many times in Castle Plum: about the size of a sweet potato, cauliheaders grew tender florets from their heads. Ivy had always been careful to let the florets grow to full length before harvesting, that way it was no more than a haircut for the critters. But Helga on the other hand….

Ivy couldn't help but smile at Rebecca. Her shiny black eyes were wide set on the round, lumpy body that Ivy could have easily held in her hands. Then the little cauliheader began to roll around like a ball, knocking over glasses and rolling through plates of food. Their dining mates jumped back, laughing.

"Strong for being so small, isn't she?" Bobby Willcock chortled.

One royal squawked as a plate of rice showered her dress.

Amidst the cauliheader chaos, Ivy spotted a dark stain against the wall leading to the kitchen. *Wait, not a stain, a shadow.* It was right behind Woodley Butterlove and Elaina Portal. Ivy quickly stood and walked over. The shadow disappeared into the kitchen, just like the shadow under her door!

Ivy quietly pushed open the door and entered the kitchen. An enormous fireplace with an iron chimney rose from a furnace at least fifteen feet wide. At least two-dozen scaldrons were housed there, cooling down from the lunchtime roar. A small nook, bright and fragrant, housed colorful spices in large apothecary jars. Their labels were jotted down in the Jester's erratic hand: green pepper, turmeric, and rose petals. Pots and pans of every imaginable size hung from a rustic, copper pot rack connected to the ceiling—fully stocked.

Out of habit, Ivy turned to the fireplace, where a brick arch framed the scaldron habbitries. One scaldron gazed at Ivy with its bright red eyes framed by a scaly brow. Smoke emanated from the little cooker mouths. Well, some were rather large—some six times Humboldt's size. The one farthest to Ivy's left shook in its cage, flapping its steel-gray wings anxiously and throwing its head back and forth like it was battling a toothache.

"Are you all right?" she whispered to the creature, kneeling down to it.

Oh, how that moment reminded her so much of Humboldt! Ivy knew there wasn't room for another scaldron inside her tiny little dorm, but if she could have, she'd have cared for all of them like she did her fire-breathing friend.

"Have you got something sour in your mouth?" asked Ivy. She cocked open the cage and tickled the underneath of its long neck. It burped a little soot onto her face, but she knew just how to handle him. Beside the first, a second scaldron wriggled in its cage, trying to get free. Then another habbitry cage went flying forward and down to the ground; another tipped sideways.

"Aaaah! What's going on with all of you?"

Suddenly, Ivy smelled something incredibly pungent wafting from the little scaldron's burps. Spices. Sage, rosemary, and something sparkling green that made her think of Hodge and Podge. Whatever it was, it was strong. And it was making for some upset scaldrons.

"Oh no…." *Someone did this on purpose.* Ivy's Kindred Stone buzzed wildly.

One after another, the scaldrons began spitting and spraying. Fiery snot and saliva sprayed out and Ivy took cover. She could not believe that her reintroduction to scaldrony was just as disastrous as her last experience with Helga. A decade of being a scaldrony maid, and she hadn't had this much trouble. Then the poor creatures began to flame out, burning up whatever had been stuffed in their mouths to incinerate.

The kitchen was getting hotter and hotter, and the herby

smoke made Ivy's eyes burn. Then to her dismay she saw that the butcher's block countertop across from the habbitries had caught fire. Orange flames licked at the table. Out of the corner of her eye, she saw a shadowy figure rise up. It was a dark, featureless shadow, just like the one at Boulliquiste's! Before she could shout, the shadow slipped out of the kitchen.

The fire was spreading steadily—she had to move fast. Ivy crawled on her belly, releasing one habbitry latch at a time. For the upper rows, she had to hold her breath and close her eyes, feeling with her fingers for the hinges. The smoke was almost unbearable. She turned and tried to remember a watering spell, but she could barely see, let alone think.

"C'mon! This way," Ivy choked out, pushing two scaldrons who had become listless along toward the door. The flames leapt up behind them, growing in intensity. Ivy didn't know how she'd open the door—she didn't want flames to burst into the dining room, or to have the fresh air drive the fire into a true frenzy.

Just then, the Selector burst in. She swept her quill in some kind of fire-dampening spell. The flames evaporated instantly, leaving behind only dark piles of soot and a nearly destroyed kitchen.

Chapter Twenty-Three

Quo-no

IVY didn't think she'd be able to make it to the scrimmage. The explanation to the Selector had been long and painful. No, she didn't know what the shadow had been. Yes, she had been the one to let all the scaldrons out. Yes, she would assist the Jester in refurbishing the kitchen over the next few weeks.

But now, inside the dungeon, that all felt moons away. Ivy felt the stone in her pocket get so hot—or was it cold? That strange sensation that was both. It wasn't buzzing, but she could feel it gathering energy as if pulling it from the air in the widespread cavern. Its weight was a comfort to her. Funny to think that she and Rebecca had the only gems in the room. But most of the Club had no idea about hers.

Glistle flashed a playful grin tinged with wickedness from across the crude hex. His and Ivy's names had been drawn for the day's match.

"If you think I'm going to take it easy on you just because I might like you a little, you have another thought coming," he said, wiggling his eyebrows. If Ivy could have looked up, she would have seen a small frown on Fyn's face.

But Ivy laughed, "Didn't get the memo? No need to take it easy. I'm the quickest draw this Club has ever known. Right here!" she pointed at herself playfully. "Quickest hands." Ivy tossed Winsome's quill into the left hand and back to her right like she was a juggling act. "Quickest feet," she scampered forward and then back as if fencing. Then, she shook her quiver at him tauntingly, "Quickest quills!"

"Have you got a Jessel Stone hidden in that pocket of yours?" Glistle teased, setting Ivy's nerves ablaze. *Not a Jessel Stone,* she thought.

"All right, you two, time to draw quills," said Fyn.

Glistle walked up to Fyn and held open his quiver. Fyn shoved his hand in and pulled up a shiny black quill. From Ivy's quiver, Fyn drew Winsome's quill.

Ivy pushed down her nerves and lifted the quill, pointing it in Glistle's direction. How different she felt with only a few Quogo matches under her belt. Her quill collection was growing doubly as fast as her confidence; and yet, despite each new spectre and quill she added to her quiver, she preferred to have Winsome's feather drawn. The deep connection she and Winsome shared was a bond greater than anything else she'd find in the hex. Ivy squinted as she concentrated, waiting to start. *Don't let me down, Winsome.*

Glistle, on the other hand, stared at his black quill with blank unrecognition. For a moment, Glistle wondered how this unfamiliar quill had ended up in his quiver. He gazed at the black feather, brushing his fingers along its soft vanes. But loud cheers distracted the eager player, and Glistle gripped the quill tightly. *You look like a winner,* he reassured himself. It gleamed attractively.

"Hope this is quicker than the last scrimmage, over by dinnertime," said Pedlum, who already had moonie melts on his mind.

The players took their places on opposite sides of the hex. Ivy bit her lip.

With that, Fyn called out, "Go!" and the match was on.

With a smirk, Glistle brought up his quill. But then he looked at it and dropped the slender, inky-black implement straight to the dirt floor. It felt like the quill had bitten him!

Ivy wasted no time. She summoned Winsome's apparition with a flick of her wrist. And there he was! Well, almost. Just the sight of her dear mentor, even if just in blue light, was enough to make tears spring to her eyes everytime. It was even more meaningful knowing that she'd never be able to visit his tome.

She blasted a burst of ghostly bubbles from Winsome's quill toward Glistle, which sent his quill floating into the air. Glistle jumped up to catch it before it drifted away. Once he had retrieved his quill, he cast his spectre. The remaining bubbles bumped and jostled the materializing spectre but didn't quite knock it out of the hex.

Glistle's spectre was of an oily looking scrivenist: long limp black hair, fair skin, all in ghostly light. The Kindred Stone began thumping in her pocket, as if it were a disembodied heart. Ivy glanced down, and even she could see the glowing stone casting a bright spot in her dress. She limply cast more bubbles at the creepy scrivenist, trying to buy time. Her mind was rushing, but for some reason she was too scared to form the spells she knew she needed. She couldn't even remember what the spells were.

Then Ivy noticed that she couldn't hear any of Winsome's

spectre's thoughts, just silence. He just stood there, with his quill hanging limply. *What's he doing? You've got to focus, Winsome. Come on, concentrate!*

Glistle did seem less gleeful than he had at the beginning of the match, but his competitive nature pushed him on. With a look of wariness, he raised his quill and wrote the spell for a rainstorm in the air, the script sparkling for a nanosecond. In response, Ivy and Winsome's spectre wielded a shielding spell that would keep them both dry.

What emerged from the tip of the oily scrivenist's quill was no rainstorm. Blue magic kept spilling and spilling from the tip of the mysterious quill as the creepy spectre began to write his own spell in the air. Flowing script was being carved into the weak smoke boundary. Ivy felt glued to the floor. There was a murmuring, like a brittle winter wind in the Bitter Forest. The script wasn't quite legible: Ivy chased the glowing words with her eyes. They shimmered into clarity: *I bring into being an–*

"It cannot be!" These words came from a voice that Ivy recognized.

"Winsome, is that you? Are you—are you talking to me?" she asked.

"Run!" Winsome's voice urged.

She was familiar with overhearing his spellmaking—a benefit of playing Quogo—but this was different, like the spectre of Winsome was having actual thoughts instead of the quill remembering Winsome. It was like a real Winsome versus the canned version she usually heard.

"Run?! What about you, Winsome? The match?"

"Run. You cannot remain here!"

Ivy felt her feet tingle. Then Winsome's spectre, apparently of its own volition, crossed the boundary in hopes of ending the game. Ivy focused her attention on the slithery scrivenist before her, still a spectre. The opponent's spell script was continuing across the air: *I bring into being an orbis. Break her bones; use her for stew, sweet orbis; I challenge you. Let the magic she wields be left unspoken, her soul be harmed and deftly broken. The taste of her blood a fair token.*

The spilling light was pouring itself into the mold of a creature, a huge creature. The sqwinches had never seen anything like it. For a moment it stood still, letting the group take in what was taking shape before their eyes.

The creature's legs, thick as tree trunks, were wide set and bent as if ready to pounce at any moment. It was pumping one thick fist into the other palm menacingly. Taller than any human, it wore a torn tunic. But the skin on its massive limbs was bumpy and sinewy, like a toad's. The most terrifying part, though, was its enormous head. The ogre-like creature had a massive underbite with fangs that jutted up from its lower jaw. Its nostrils were just slits in the skin; so were its ears. Under a heavy, ridge-like brow, its tiny, beady eyes were flitting back and forth around the room.

"Oh, dear," Hayword muttered in sheer and utter shock. "An orbis."

Then it drew in a breath through its slit nostrils, a breath that Ivy could feel like wind, as if it was sucking all the oxygen from the room. A grin slowly spread across its face. The thing was cleverer than Ivy had given it credit for. Rather than look for a spectre to battle, it turned directly to Ivy.

"What?!" hissed Fyn. "It's like it sees her! It's not possible!"

With a terrifying growl, the thing lunged at Ivy! With a

yelp, she dodged under it. But it sniffed again and spun to face her.

Ivy shouted, staring up at the oily spectre. "Debnick! It's Daryl Debnick!"

Fyn was already pushing Ivy behind himself. "Come on! Everybody, do your best to slow this thing down! Get out your best quills!" He shot a lick of flame from a yellow quill at the beast.

The Club set to work, desperately trying to get their stolen, borrowed, or otherwise inherited quills to cast as many spells as they could: Canna turned the dirt floor around the beast's feet into wet concrete; Pedlum sent a burst of sparks that showered over the orbis and everyone else in the hex.

Ivy looked around the room for anything that might help her. Then she set her eyes on a potions kit by their satchels. Hurriedly she grasped the kit and struggled to open it with her shaking hands.

The orbis lashed out again at Ivy, its fists easily puncturing the smoking boundary. Then, terrifyingly, its clenched hands with their disgusting nails lost their blue light. As slowly as the light had pooled to create the spectre, it was now draining out, leaving behind dirty fingernails, then thick fingers. The orbis was leaving the realm of the quillusion and becoming real.

Two gigantic brown fists connected to arms of blue light pounded at the floor, sending the border bookshelves flying across the room and over Ivy's head. They shattered into broken timber and splinters. She scurried to the furthest corner of the room with the kit. The orbis's nostrils flared as it tried to pick up her scent again.

Manone recovered from her shock and began uttering pologie after pologie, spell undoing after spell undoing, but Debnick's spectre just stood there smugly. Nothing Manone did mattered!

"What's happening?" screamed Canna. "This isn't fun anymore!"

"Someone, help me destroy this quill!" shouted Glistle. "Set it on fire or something!"

"That's impossible! It's magic. Fire doesn't put out magic!"

"Where did it come from?" yelled Lennu.

"That can only be the quill stolen from the Quill Keep!" shouted Manone.

"Oh, snap!"

"We need to protect Ivy!" shouted Fyn.

The orbis, now fleshly up to its massive shoulders, inhaled deeply and turned to Ivy. A silvery strand of drool dripped from the corner of its mouth.

"Rebecca! What are you waiting for? Use your crown," yelled Canna, who ducked behind a bookshelf.

Immediately understanding, Rebecca transformed herself into a perfect replica of Ivy, scent and all. Confused, the great beast swiveled its head from left to right, Ivy I to Ivy II.

"We've got to run!" Ivy shouted, remembering Winsome's words. Like an ordinary spectre, Winsome had vanished once the flimsy boundary had been broken through—if only Debnick's would do the same!

As they ran toward one of the tunnel's entrances, they were forced to split into two groups and dashed down separate tunneled hallways. Fyn, Ivy, and Glistle went left. Hayword, Pedlum, Rebecca (Ivy II), and Manone went right. Lennu and

Canna were pushed aside by the orbis, which then ran full-bore toward the small tunnel on the right and rammed its half-spectre, half-real body through the tunnel.

"Whatever you do, Glistle, don't let go of that quill!" Ivy shouted as she ran.

"Faster, Ivy. See if we can help them lose the orbis!" Fyn yelled.

As they ran through the dark tunnel, they could hear the giant beast following the other group, knocking holes in the walls the size of boulders and completely bursting through cellar doors and arches. The cloud of dust was pushed through the tunnels and nearly blinded them.

With a crash, they met up with the other group—the tunnels had run together and were headed straight back for the hex.

Ivy was relieved to see Rebecca, but not so much to see the orbis, which was lumbering along behind, surprisingly nimble for its terrible size. At the sight—rather scent—of the real Ivy, the orbis fell into a momentary confusion and the group darted back into the cavern that housed the hex. Ivy and Rebecca headed to opposite sides of the room while the others cast magical blocks and shields as best they could. But recycled quills and sqwinches were no match for an orbis—a long-extinct beast that was now very, very real. Nothing of the quillusion remained, no hint of blue light. Only oily, grotesque bumpy skin, brown teeth, and putrid breath.

Ivy was frozen to the spot and was shaking so badly that she dropped the potions kit that she forgot she'd been holding. Its corner hit her foot and the sharp pain forced her out of her fear. Looking down at the popped-open kit, she spotted a vial of sorcslurry glowing vibrant purple. For all the time Ivy had spent hidden behind the slurry at Castle Plum, she never thought she'd be at all excited to see the magic-diffusing plant!

The orbis roared and threw its arms wide, sending the remains of the shelves flying. The cavern walls vibrated: soil shook down to the floor, and then several large rocks came loose and tumbled down. The dreadful creature honed-in on Ivy, no longer confused by Rebecca's transformation. But the erratic glowing of the Kindred Stone in Ivy's pocket had swelled into a steady shine, helping her think through the chaos of the room.

Ivy grabbed the glittering vial of sorcslurry and then hurled the rest of the potions kit at the orbis's head, shouting, "Over here, you big oaf!"

For anyone else, the blow would have knocked them back. But for the orbis, it was just a tap. The creature grinned its terrifying smile and began to drool again.

She slowly backed up to the wall, finding her way to a staircase that led up. Ivy climbed carefully backwards, never taking her eyes off the orbis.

"Ivy!" Fyn called. But Ivy ignored him, intent on her plan.

The orbis tracked her, moving as slowly as she did, clearly confident that it was about to feast on the last of the queenly line. Ivy steeled her nerves and waited until the orbis's horrid breath was hot on her face. At the fifth step up, she was eye-to-eye with the creature. It snuffed her scent in.

"Hungry?" she panted.

The orbis roared again, opening its wide mouth and exposing rotten teeth and a brown tongue. Ivy kissed the vial of sorcslurry and then hurled the tiny vial straight down its throat. The moment the vial hit the back of its mouth, its growl was cut short. The small vial exploded violently with a pulse of Ivy's magic.

There was a resounded boom and flash of light. More rocks fell down, one knocking Fyn down, who was following close behind the orbis.

When the dust settled, all that was left of the orbis was the skull of a boar, a rat heart, pond scum, and one long jagged tooth. All that was left of the hex was crushed potion ingredients and splintered boards. All that was left of the bold Quality Quills Club was scared sqwinches.

"I quit," said Hayword Nesselton.

"I double quit," added Manone.

Fyn looked at Ivy, who returned his gaze in silence.

Rebecca walked closer. "I quit, too. This is too dangerous."

Glistle came next with the quill in hand, "What do we do with this?"

"Give me that, Glistle! We all know what happened when you last held it," Canna shrieked.

"Okay, okay," he said shakily, handing the quill over. "Seriously though, what should we do with it? We can't tell the Selector—she'll wonder why we have it. I don't want it!"

"I wouldn't mind collecting that reward, though..." said Canna dazedly.

The shell-shocked group stumbled their way up and out. The only conversation was terse conferring, trying to decide the best way to dispose of the mysterious black quill that had somehow found its way into Glistle's quiver.

Chapter Twenty-Four

Dungeon to Den

IVY had dropped the black quill at Derwin's lectern, sealed in a box with a dampening spell and an anonymous note. Canna had been dissuaded from her desire to claim the reward. Derwin, in turn, had delivered the quill straight to the Quill Keep, where the mattelers were working on the mystery. Glistle and Fyn had been able to learn that much from their parents. No one knew—yet—that a group of sqwinches had unleashed Debnick's spectre in a game. Their quills were tucked deep into their quivers and their quivers deep into their closets.

Since sending off the black quill, the Club members hadn't met eyes in the halls for weeks, let alone played the game that had become more terrifying than fun. Ivy felt like the air between them was thick with emotions, mostly blame. Fyn blamed Glistle for the quillusion; Hayword and Glistle blamed Fyn for organizing the Club; Manone blamed Hayword for not knowing how to kill an orbis despite his beast knowledge; Canna blamed Fyn for not having a Castleton Stone; Ivy blamed herself for having royal blood. At the center of it all was a deep cold fear: They were terrified of the orbis and the fact that it nearly escaped into the Halls. The fact that it had nearly killed Ivy.

Ivy was looking forward to Settings in Sketching—she'd grown accustomed to Professor Petty's brusqueness and her grouchy moods. After all, sketching had always been one of Ivy's favorite activities, even before school. Professor Petty knew that Ivy was the most practiced in the class, but that didn't mean she was any kinder to her. Nonetheless, Ivy enjoyed the second year course, which took them all around the castle.

Ivy and Rebecca made it into the classroom right before Didley cried out. The last of the spring afternoon's light was seeping through the windows of Professor Petty's room.

"I wonder where we'll be off to today," whispered Rebecca.

"Don't bother taking off your cloaks, class!" said Professor Petty in her shrill voice. "Gather your proof pad and one or two porcupels. Follow me!"

But rather than head back out the door, Professor Petty turned around and yanked open a small door behind her desk. A small door much like the one in Professor Wrigley's class.

"Uh-oh," Ivy looked at Rebecca.

The snaking line of students followed the hefty woman around a corner, ducking into a low flight of stairs and down a poorly lit hallway. At the bottom of the stairs on a small landing, the professor whipped out the familiar Map of Olglarion. Even the professor needed assistance around in the dank dark. Ivy and Rebecca knew in that moment exactly where they were headed: the dungeon.

Neither spoke a word as they snaked through the corridors that led to the hex.

When they entered the final tunnel, Professor Petty

exclaimed, "My goodness, what in all of Croswald happened in here?" The tunnel was pockmarked by the orbis's fists, and rubble lay piled up everywhere. The QQC had been too nervous to return to the scene of chaos they had unleashed, but Ivy now wished she'd had had the presence of mind to clean up before they ran.

At the entrance to the cavern, Professor Petty stopped in her tracks; the line behind followed suit, crashing into each other as they came to a sudden halt. The cavern was in terrible shape, even for a dungeon. There were rock chips and shattered boulders all over the ground, and pieces of bookshelves everywhere. Scrape marks scarred the ceiling, and dispelled potion bottles and ingredients pooled in a giant footprint.

"Goodness! Careful where you step."

Ivy bit her lip, staying close to Rebecca, looking around at the mess she knew she caused. Then Professor Petty whipped out her quill and began taking care of the mess. The rocks and walls were put back together; the bookshelves reassembled. Apparently, there was nothing to be done for the potions ingredients, as all their magic had been dispelled or spoiled.

"Well," Professor Petty huffed, "I suppose a tableau is a tableau, no matter how untidy." She pushed the potion ingredients toward her reluctant expeller.

"Clearly," added Damaris, who always felt the need to make her presence known. "Whoever was here last should be punished!" Ivy wasn't sure if Damaris actually knew that she and Rebecca were part of the reason the dungeon looked the way that it did or if she was just being her snobbish self.

"Class, this is where we will sketch today. The dungeon chamber. A bit of a lesson as to what this dungeon was once used for. Back before the Halls became a school, the Halls belonged to a family of huntsmen that was cursed seven generations ago. Before they were cursed, they wrangled the wildest beasts—specifically dragons—in these chambers.

"I've brought you each a vial of inklink. And how convenient that the scene you'll be sketching today looks so much like a crime scene. Class, inklink is often used for teledetecting. The magic of this ink is that it can go beyond what the scrivenist or sqwinch knows that they are thinking, to what they might be sensing. In this way, scrivenists explore clues, inklings, and hunches just through the process of sketching the scene. It's very helpful for mysterious scenes and dark places. Inklink captures more than your mind can record, things that you have not personally witnessed. The more practiced you are at magic, the deeper you can pull. The more information will surface."

The class sat cross-legged around the freshly swept floor, readying their proof pads to sketch as Professor Petty handed out small pots of inklink.

"Ivy, what are we going to do?" Rebecca hissed.

"I don't know!" Having the orbis so fresh in their minds—they could recall the smell of its breath—was going to make sketching this scene without incriminating themselves difficult indeed.

"Get to it, Ivy!" shouted Professor Petty. "Rebecca!"

The two were forced to begin work, despite the fear that their memories would reveal their involvement. Ivy concentrated hard on the room before her. Her hand moved swiftly, and a flurry of rough outlines and shapes began to form. Professor Petty hovered over the students, walking back and forth as she watched their proof pads begin to fill. Classmates spoke in hushed tones and porcupels scratched away on paper.

"Do you think they'll figure out what happened, that it was us?" Rebecca asked nervously.

Ivy stared at her drawing: figures had started to emerge. "This is our first time using inklink—I doubt anyone is that powerful yet. Plus, if we sketch anything incriminating ourselves, we can just chalk it up to being something outside of our memory, something we had nothing to do with."

Rebecca groaned, "If they do find out, my mother will be furious! She'll squash any idea of me studying scrivenry any longer." Rebecca's mother had only recently come around to allowing her royal daughter to wield a quill, thanks in large part to Frederick Faddacky.

"Focus your memories on before the match! Before the you-know-what broke out. Then we'll worry about getting in trouble if it happens. But the more we talk about it, the more it'll be fresh in our minds. Okay?"

Rebecca sighed. They both turned their heads in worry, sketching silently. Ivy couldn't help herself: She allowed her mind to be drawn into the moment right before that fateful scrimmage. She drew the members of the Quality Quills Club preparing for the match. *Me and Glistle in the hex, Fyn. Rebecca. Canna. Manone. Hayword. Pedlum. Lennu. And a tenth member? One too many.* Ivy went to erase the extra person, which proved to be impossible. She nearly wore a hole in the piece of parchment, trying to erase her mistake. The extra person was hunched on a boulder, farthest away from the hex. Unlike Ivy's other renderings, this person was all in shadow—almost as if he or she was made of a wisp of smoke.

Ivy glanced over at Rebecca's sketch. Rebecca had trained her mind on the moment that the QQC had entered the room: the bookshelves all lined up as the boundary, the match not yet started. The shadowy figure was nowhere to be found in Rebecca's rendering.

"Are you all right?" Rebecca asked, seeing Ivy's hesitation.

"Who's that?" Ivy asked, pointing to the lone figure in the corner of her own drawing.

Rebecca looked from the sketch up to the corner where the boulder stood and pointed. "Um, are you sure you aren't just drawing *her*?"

Ivy looked up with a start. Up on the boulder sat Gretta Leelangraf, sketching steadily in the dark.

"What's she doing all the way over there and all alone?"

"Professor instructed we sketch the angle we like. That girl always likes to be by herself."

"Yeah...."

"Ivy, what's bothering you?"

Ivy changed the subject abruptly, "I just feel terrible that the Club is broken up because of me."

"It's broken up, Ivy, because it's dangerous and illegal to be playing games that can go wrong without the proper protocols. We shouldn't have been playing in the first place, especially not without the Castleton Stone! Plus, it's not your fault that Glistle picked up that quill at Boulliquiste's!"

"But did he? I just don't think that Debnick's quill could have ended up there! Everyone in the Town was looking for it; even Boulliquiste would have known from checking his stock." Ivy's mind flashed to the shadowy figure in the ink shop. After a pause, she said, "Maybe the quill ending up in his quiver was a fluke thing. Right? I mean, the orbis couldn't actually have been sent to hunt me, could it?"

Ivy could tell that it was difficult for Rebecca to give the reassurance she was seeking. Instead, Rebecca smiled tightly, nodded a little, and quietly continued sketching the broken patches of cobblestone.

But then, true to her nature, Rebecca spoke up, "Wrong. It *was* sent to kill you, Ivy. With the Selector and Derwin here at the Halls, you're safe. But Quogo might be a way of inviting danger into the Halls. There's a reason there are rules and boundaries and mattelers at matches. It's controlled by more experienced players than the nine of us. We're lucky it was only an orbis and nothing worse."

"What could be worse than an orbis?"

"Who knows, Ivy? Isn't that the point of the game? The dangers? The quivers? The darkest unknown? Imagine for a moment what you might not know."

"Fascinating!" said Professor Petty from over Ivy's shoulder, nearly scaring the wits out of the two girls. "It looks like you have sensed that a game of Quogo was once played here. Good spot for it, I must say. However, the boundaries look fairly rudimentary, so it must be early in the game's history."

Ivy nodded, eyes wide, throat dry.

As the girls finished their sketching, the shadow in Ivy's drawing only became more mysterious, like it wasn't a person at all, just a wisp of darkness itself, unattached to any being. Ivy thought of the dark figure inside Boulliquiste's. The one in the Jester's kitchen. Even at Fyn's place, the break-in. Was something following her? Watching her? Ivy's rendering only became more haunting. She kept her mind trained on the moments before the game, but soon she had to stop sketching; she couldn't stop thinking about Winsome.

"Rebecca, you know how I told you I heard Winsome speaking? During the scrimmage?"

"Yeah?"

"It was more than just hearing his thoughts… Winsome was talking to me."

"You mean you heard him uttering the spells and such?"

"No, I heard him talking *to me.* He told me to run, run away from the orbis. He could somehow sense what the spectre was summoning, like he knew what was about to happen."

"What? That's impossible." Rebecca lowered her voice to a whisper, her head almost touching Ivy's, "I know you loved him, Ivy, but he's dead. Not even tome, just gone."

"Hi," a timid voice interrupted them. It was Gretta, her proof pad closed tight and tucked under her arm. The first word Gretta had said to the girls in moons.

"Oh! Hi. How are you?" Ivy smiled awkwardly, covering up her sketch.

Gretta smiled and said, "Good," but the dark circles under her eyes told a different story. She tugged her right sleeve down over her wrist, hiding a cut on the top of her hand.

Rebecca eyed Gretta a little suspiciously and said, "Nice to see you, Gretta. Now, tell me, how is it that you pop in and out of classes as you please? Seems to me you miss class as much as you make it."

Gretta shrugged her thin shoulders faintly, speaking in a whisper, "I always finish my work. Glistle helps."

Rebecca pressed on, "If Ivy or I miss a minute, lost in the

Den or just a bit of exploring, we're written up faster than a scrivenist can sketch. Do you know how many pathways I had to clear of snow this term?"

But Gretta changed the subject as she turned to Ivy. "Um, I overheard the last bit of your conversation…."

"And?" said Rebecca.

"I believe what Ivy said, that she heard Winsome's voice." Ivy had never seen the shy girl seem so determined, though Gretta's voice was still soft and whispery. "He may be dead, but his spirit lives and he watches over you. Powerful scrivenists appointed to royal families can sometimes remain connected, a little like strands of magic that continue to attach a scrivenist to his or her royal after their natural life. I think especially for you, Ivy, your, um, situation would increase that bond, until you've recovered what's yours, until you take back the crown." Gretta shuddered, a dark expression coloring her face.

"How do you know all of this?" Rebecca demanded.

"Are you okay, Gretta?" Ivy asked, concerned.

"Yes, fine. Just tired. I guess I mean to say, things don't always make sense, but Winsome talking to you does. My father is a matteler—we talk a lot about magic, about curses, about detection, at the dinner table."

Rebecca was not convinced.

A very fatigued Didley fluttered into the cavern and squawked weakly.

"Poor thing. I dare say he had to hunt for us down here. Class dismissed," announced Professor Petty. The class wound its way out of the dungeon classroom, comparing sketches and talking about the beasts that they'd caught glimpses of. No sketch was as complete as Ivy's, with Rebecca's a close second.

As Ivy, Gretta, and Rebecca emerged into the hallway, they were met by Glistle and Fyn. Gretta and Glistle exchanged awkward glances before Gretta scurried off.

"Your sister's real weird, you know that?" said Fyn.

"Shut your mouth. Or I'll give you something that'll do it for you!"

Fyn caught a glimpse of Rebecca's proof pad. "What were you girls doing back down there?"

"Class."

"What?"

"Inklink in the dungeon," Rebecca said with a meaningful glance.

Fyn looked worried.

"I'm calling for a QQC meeting. Not a match, but a meeting," said Ivy.

Fyn raised his eyebrows, "But where, Ivy? We can't go back down there anymore."

"You're right. How about we try someplace new?"

"Like where?" Glistle jumped in.

"I know just the spot," said Ivy, who grinned at Rebecca. "Meet in the Den for today's Hour of Discovery. It's important."

o o o o

Ivy didn't know how she'd feel returning to Winsome's secret classroom for the first time since the year before. On the one hand, she couldn't wait to surround herself with all the potion ingredients, the view, and the memories. On the other hand, she worried that it may all just be too much to handle, especially in front of a group.

As they left Derwin's glanagerie class, their last of the day, Ivy wondered again if she should ask Derwin about the orbis, but he was occupied with Damaris, who was complaining about something or other. *Next time*, Ivy said to herself. She still wasn't used to having a scrivenist to trust. Plus, he seemed so busy lately.

On the way to the Den, the Halls' library, Ivy and Rebecca caught up to Lennu and Manone.

"You guys coming?" Ivy asked.

They smiled, happily following in line. Turning the next corner, they bumped into Hayword who, between Derwin's classroom and the Den, had managed to pick up a habbitry for each hand. No words were spoken, but he jumped in line, following the members.

As the nine sqwinches filed into the library, they passed stacks and stacks of beautiful books, several stories high. Other students were hard at work, and the ladders were swaying side-to-side busily. Mistis, the librarian, was restocking shelves as usual. Ivy led them straight back to the smallest study room in the expansive library.

Once in, they closed the door of the *A.B.C.R.O.O.M.* (All Bugs, Critters, Rodents, Or Odd Monsters) behind them. The same loveseat upholstered in bug-themed fabric crowded the tiny room. *Thinking Outside the Walls: Creative Strategies When You Feel Stuck* by Winsome Monocle was the only book in the room that wasn't about creepy, crawly creatures, and the only one that had kept jumping off the shelf last year. Now, it rested on the shelf as stationary as any other book.

"This? This is your brilliant idea, Ivy?" asked Lennu. "Lock us all in a reading room the size of a closet? No thanks."

"Are you claustrophobic?" Rebecca asked.

"I just don't like it!" Lennu sputtered.

With a flick of Ivy's wrist, the books cleared themselves, stacking neatly on the floor and revealing the secret door at the back of the shelf. Another flick of her wrist and the door popped open and the dark hall stretched out before them.

Her friends were dumbstruck. This was the first time she'd practiced magic so freely, other than in front of Rebecca and Fyn, but she figured that the cat was out of the bag since the orbis's rampage.

"How—what?" asked Canna, rarely at a loss for words.

"This leads to Winsome's chamber," said Rebecca in a hushed voice. She smiled at Ivy appreciatively, knowing how much it took for Ivy to share this special place with them.

"Well, I'll bet you're glad one of these habbitries has hairies, aren't you?" said Hayword.

"What's the other one got?"

"Never you mind."

Hayword distributed hairies and cautioned, "Gentle! They'll be skittish without their lantern, but they'll happily perch in a hood or scarf."

"Up the stairs at the end. That's right," Ivy said as she watched Glistle make the first step up.

"What *is* this place?"

"A secret classroom. I spent most of last year studying up here with Winsome, my family's scrivenist. You know his spectre pretty well by now." Ivy's mind wandered to Winsome's quill, stuffed down deep in her quiver, in the farthest corner of her wardrobe.

"What was your family's scrivenist doing here?" Manone

was eager to know.

Ivy wasn't sure how to answer that yet.

The winding staircase led up to the door, and Ivy prompted Glistle to push it open. The heavy, wooden door revealed the high-ceilinged, cluttered laboratory, jam-packed with potion ingredients. Winsome's desk behind the door was still piled with End Letters while the stench of the Wandering Curse repellent still lingered. Ivy pulled back the burgundy draperies to reveal the breathtaking view of the lights of the neighboring castles beginning to illuminate, the stars above twinkling in the twilight, and the Dark Queen's imposing castle in the far-off distance. Just like the first time that she had seen the room.

Once the QQC had their fill of the view and the *oohs* and *ahhs* dropped off, Ivy cleared her throat.

"I've decided to call a meeting because, well, we shouldn't avoid each other anymore."

"Who's avoiding?" asked Pedlum.

"Oh, come on," replied Fyn.

"Professor Petty just held her class where we play Quogo. We should be grateful that she cleaned up the mess without really piecing together what happened!" said Rebecca. "We should never play again."

"Well, there's not enough room up here," said Hayword.

"I was thinking that we could meet up here privately until we find another place to play."

"*If* we ever play again," said Canna.

"No playing!" Rebecca shouted.

Fyn interrupted. "All right. So, what do we do now? We can't risk an orbis or anything like it. Not for Ivy's sake and not for ours. If not for Ivy's quick thinking, it would have destroyed the Halls and it would have been the end of the Quality Quills."

"The Quality Quills Club *has* ended!" snorted Canna.

"The end of a club? Is that what you're worried about?" shouted Manone. "It could have been the end of our lives! I'm out!"

"You can't be out, Manone. We just have to be more careful," begged Lennu.

"Can we play the card game instead?" Rebecca suggested.

"That's for amateurs!" countered Pedlum.

"Real amateurs!" echoed Glistle.

"Well," Ivy said, her conviction building, "the Dark Queen is plotting something. And I think that as the QQC, it's our job to protect not just our members but everyone else, too. We have to equip ourselves to fight."

"What? Do you think the mattelers need help from sqwinches? Hardly!" scoffed Manone.

"And when did it become our job to protect the entire student body?" chimed in Pedlum.

"To the dangers, the quivers, the darkest unknown… you swore to it!" cried Ivy.

"Well, I'm removing myself!" shouted Manone, her booming voice even louder than usual.

"You can't," pleaded Lennu.

"See you when I see you," said Manone, as she made a dramatic exit.

"Manone! M!" Lennu shouted after her, then turned to the rest of the Club and whimpered, "I think I just went through my first break-up," when she didn't look back.

"Even if we never play again, we have to find out how that quill made its way into Glistle's quiver," said Ivy. "Glistle, can you remember anything?"

Glistle shook his head, "I already told you. I swear I've never seen the thing before. Not at Boulliquiste's, not in my quiver before play, never."

"Hmm, you do count your quills quite often. How could you not see it?"

"You should talk, Fyn!" Glistle shouted. "I'm serious. It just—just appeared there."

"Do you think someone planted the quill to attack Ivy?" asked Rebecca hesitantly.

"How is that possible? I never let the quiver out of my sight." Glistle opened his jacket to reveal his quiver neatly tucked into his jacket. "It'd have to be a ghost. But *Fyn* pulled it from my quiver—"

"From *your* quiver!" Fyn shot back.

Something stirred in Ivy's mind, but she couldn't put her finger on it. With a heave, she brought her satchel up onto Winsome's beaten up workbench and dumped out the contents: a boar skull, a rat heart, now-dried pond scum, and one long jagged tooth that was so sharp it could easily puncture skin.

"Ivy, where did all of this come from?"

"This orbis. Don't you remember? This is what was left when I threw the slurry down that disgusting hatch. I thought maybe it might help us in the future. Too bad we don't have Winsome to ask his advice."

"But you do have Derwin," said Rebecca.

Hayword immediately reached for the tooth, longer than his fingers. "So large! It has to be from an anchelor."

"These must be the main ingredients Daryl Debnick used to create the orbis. When you fed it the slurry, it counteracted the magic and turned back to its original form," said Fyn. "A vile pile of junk!"

"Anything in the Collectis about the orbis?" suggested Canna, who was already spinning through hers.

"Well, not much. Debnick kept his later work for the Dark Queen quite secret."

Pointing to a page, Canna quoted, "'The elements of the orbis potion are unknown, but mattelers continue to work on the case. The difficulty remains that to study an orbis, you'd have to create one.'"

"I've seen one of these before in a textbook," said Fyn, lifting up the tooth. "Hayword's right. It's an anchelor's incisor. Water-dwelling, right? They are extinct now, so these teeth are terribly difficult to come by. They are typically only found deep in Lonefellow Loch."

"I'm so glad they are extinct," shivered Rebecca.

"Right! Me too. And I'm glad that there aren't orbises running around anymore. Nothing for them to do, once the queenly line was gone."

"Isn't the orbis somehow related to the Cloaked Brood?" asked Fyn.

"Yes. That's what I've read," said Hayword with confidence, as he pushed his glasses up his nose.

There was a pause in the conversation.

"What do you do with this stuff?" asked Fyn.

Hayword's hand shot up. "Dibs on the tooth!"

"Don't be ridiculous, Hayword. What we need to do is hold on to it all. This information, it's important somehow," Ivy insisted.

"You want to conjure your own orbis? And you're calling me ridiculous?" Hayword asked Ivy querulously.

"Let's definitely not do that. But in the meantime, keep that tooth away from me. It's bad enough luck that I have a cursed quiver," Glistle shuddered.

Ivy had never seen him so out of sorts.

A BOOK OUT OF PLACE

OUTSIDE, a storm on the horizon was building, black clouds gathering over Ravenshollow. Didley, with his high-pitched squawk, flew in and out of the classroom walls, alerting all students to remain inside: A Bearded Cloud storm was nearing the Halls of Ivy. Students were sent back to their dorms early. Ivy rushed from the library to meet Rebecca back in their room.

As she walked across the blustery bridge from the castle to the dormitories, Ivy saw the pointed windows of the student rooms cut into the cliff glowing in the growing dark. Students were warm in their school robes, hairies alight, and conversations carried through the corridor. At first, discussions of the latest potion and crushes outweighed talk of the weather. Even so, the sconces on the stone walls shook, and the conversation was punctuated by the thunder and young princesses (and a prince or two) shrieking after every crack of thunder. The wind whistled down the dormitory halls. A small crowd of royals and sqwinches had gathered in Gregory Gershwin's room. Even though he wasn't technically supposed to do magic in the dorms, his Weatheritall Stone couldn't help but create a little tropical sunshine in his room. After a particularly wild bout of thunder and lightning and the following screams, Rebecca rolled her eyes.

"Oh, brother, they sound worse than a barrel of lumbuses. Someone should tell them it's only bad weather!" Rebecca closed the door to their own room firmly.

But Ivy knew that a Bearded Cloud wasn't just bad weather, no matter what her classmates thought. One student had just been proclaiming that Gregory's crown could set the storm spinning off in another direction. If only it were that easy. Ivy shivered, half from the cold, half from remembering the Bearded Cloud that she and Fyn had barely survived on their way back from Lonefellow Loch. If it hadn't been for the shorehorse and Ivy's magic cushioning the landing, she and Fyn would have surely been goners.

Ivy finally opened the glittery invitation that had arrived three days prior and had been resting on her nightstand; *You're Invited to the Annual Halls Masquerade*, it read.

"Can't believe it's almost that time again. Can't believe I'm invited back." Ivy paused. "It's a beautiful invitation."

"And I can't believe you finally opened that!" Rebecca ventured to guess why Ivy had taken so long, "Are you nervous about the Dark Queen's coming to the Ball, like last year?"

At that moment, thunder boomed. The erratic brightness from the storm's lightning made threatening shadows bounce around on the girls' walls. Rebecca watched the storm outside the window as intently as a Quogo match.

"You could say that," Ivy muttered.

For a brief moment, Ivy's mind wandered to Fyn. *I wonder what Fyn's thinking right now–Bearded Cloud flashbacks*,

I'll bet. He'd better be staying inside!

Ivy nudged Humboldt, sleeping at the foot of her bed. "Hey little cooker, mind turning up the heat?" The scaldron gladly obliged, snoring a little louder, and his breath was soon warming the room.

"Tea?" Rebecca was pouring herself a cup of studysesh. "So much school work to be done! Honestly, I'm grateful for the early night. The dragons that Professor Wrigley has us studying: so much talk of scales and ash in class, I'm just so afraid I'll sprout wings and start smoking at the gills." She rolled her eyes. Rebecca hardly ever transformed by accident these days.

Ivy grinned and shivered at the same time. "Tea would be wonderful." Then as an afterthought, she added, "I've got a lot of thinking to do."

"Here you are. Warm as mittens."

Ivy sat up in her bed and grabbed the cup of tea from Rebecca's hands. She took several slow sips, and the undeniable fragrance of tinglemint and rosemary immediately cleared her head. It was just what she needed to work out the chaos that was this school year. Really, it seemed that the Bearded Cloud was a perfect expression of how crazy their second year had been so far.

"What's that you're reading?" Ivy asked.

"*Northern Dragons.* Not exactly for Wrigley's class, but something Frederick recommended. When you live with them, and it's your family business, and your scrivenist is dragon obsessed, it's kind of inevitable. They're incredible beings."

"What's it like to have a dragonry at your castle?"

"They squash mother's gardens, burn holes in the stonework, and shake the turrets." Rebecca giggled.

Ivy laughed, "And do your parents not care?"

"Father loves it. Frederick gave me and my sister riding lessons last summer. It's too bad you missed them. I broke my arm twice and it gave my mother a near heart attack. But Frederick mended me, no problem."

"Sounds like fun," Ivy said, and smiled.

The illustrations in *Northern Dragons* were in true scrivenist fashion. Brightly detailed sketches demonstrated the various stages of growth of the exacto magno dragon, its skeleton, how it looked to scale next to a person (twice as tall, with a wingspan double that), and more. The wings in the picture shimmered burnt orange and red, just as they did in real life. Ivy imagined the whoosh and shush of the wings in flight, and how the dragon's hot breath could do far more than cook a griddlecake.

"Remind me what it was like, Ivy," said Rebecca, pausing for another sip as she looked out their narrow Gothic window.

"What what's like?"

"The Bearded Cloud."

"Oh. Pretty much like that!" she pointed outside. "But worse. Worse than the orbis, honestly. Flying through it, I was so terrified I didn't think it could get any worse. But then it did. I'd never wish it on anyone. While we were being thrown around in that hurricane, we saw terrible things. When you're swept up, it's impossible to imagine a way out."

Rebecca had spun open her Compass Collectis to the definition. She read, "'Horrible visions may force victims to relive the most frightening moments of their lives or may forewarn of future evils.'"

Ivy nodded. "For me, it was Helga, then wolves, the Dark Queen."

"Wolves?"

"Yes, maybe one of Fyn's fears," Ivy mused. "But it was so hard to decipher what was real and what wasn't when I was swept up inside. It's just a big, dark tempest."

"A thrashing abyss!"

"Yeah. I didn't think I was coming out of it." Ivy looked out the window again. "What's it doing here, though? Do you think the Dark Queen has anything to do with it?"

"Isn't she supposed to stay away from the Halls?"

"Maybe, since the Ball, the Dark Queen feels like she can force her presence here."

Rebecca shrugged and opened her proof pad to sketch designs of skirts and blouses, something she did to relax almost every evening.

The thought of the Dark Queen having full access to the Halls of Ivy made Ivy's stomach churn. She gulped some more tea and grabbed her proof pad. Opening it to the sketch from Professor Petty's class, she traced her drawing with her finger. There was something so familiar about that shadow in the corner. She had definitely seen it before. It was the same one she'd seen in the kitchen and at Boulliquiste's, but it was more than that.

Ivy lay back in bed, staring at the ceiling, thinking of the orbis incident and how she would have forced that beast right into the Bearded Cloud if she could. It was going to be a long, long evening. From where she lay on the bed, Ivy rested her eyes on her books across the way. One metallic title popped out to her: *The Girl with the Whispering Shadow*, Gretta's book from Lie Buries.

Ivy sat up with a start, her head cocked and alert.

"What's the matter, Ivy?" asked Rebecca, as Ivy made her way across the room.

"This book! Where did this book come from?" she asked.

"I thought it was yours."

"This book belongs to Gretta. Has anyone been in here, Rebecca?" Ivy looked back at her.

"Just you and I," Rebecca replied cautiously. Humboldt growled. "And Humboldt. Although, now that you mention it, I forgot to tell you that the door was open when I got back. Lucky Humboldt's lazy and didn't try to escape. I just thought you or I didn't close it properly. But do you think someone was in here?"

Ivy grabbed the book off the shelf. She flipped through the pages quietly, an awareness slowly dawning on her. The shadow.

"It's Gretta," Ivy muttered.

"What?" asked Rebecca.

Chills coursed through Ivy's body, the small hairs sticking straight up on her arms. Rebecca tightened her robe, rubbing her folded arms.

"Ivy, what are you talking about?"

"Look!" Ivy thrust her sketch and the open book to Rebecca. The similarities between the hunched shadow in the cavern and the one in Gretta's book were undeniable.

"Oh my moon. And what is this place?" Rebecca turned the book back to Ivy.

Ivy turned it around and looked. She had been so focused on the shape of the shadow, of the chills it gave her, that she hadn't even taken in the book's setting. Ivy dropped her teacup, and it shattered on the stone floor. She grabbed the book back.

"It's the Quill Keep!"

Rebecca gasped, "You mean where that terrible quill was stolen from?"

Ivy nodded, already opening the door. "She showed me

this book over the summer—she wrote and sketched this! This means that it's been her who's been causing havoc everywhere I go."

It was all clicking into place in Ivy's mind. *It was Gretta who stole Daryl Debnick's quill. It was Gretta who snuck the quill into her brother's book bag, and it was Gretta who—*

"Ivy! Why would she want to hurt you? Whoever brought the quill from the Quill Keep to our Quogo scrimmage meant to kill you!"

"I'm not sure. We have to find out. We must confront her!"

Ivy went for the hallway, but Rebecca caught her by the robe.

"Listen! If you think this is true, I can't very well let you go looking for death."

Ivy held up the book. "Rebecca, this is the story of a cursed, tormented girl! I think that Gretta might be as confused as we are. Look, Rebecca." She showed her friend the sketch of a tired girl who wore an expression of fear and bewilderment.

Thunder shook the very cliff that the room was carved into at that moment.

"I know this doesn't look good for her, Rebecca, but I think Gretta's in trouble!"

"What?"

"Rebecca, what if this book is Gretta's way of calling for help? Don't you see? It may look like a fantasy written by a very deranged girl at first glance, but all of these incidents really happened. She's trying to tell us something! C'mon!"

Ivy gripped the book and raced to the dormitory stairwell. Gretta's room was at the end of the hall: Ivy knew she was disobeying the order to stay in her room and that this one was likely to be documented within her Compass Individualis, but the moment was too urgent for rules. Rebecca followed, hollering at Ivy to stop.

"You're going to get us expelled, Ivy!"

"There won't be a school to get expelled from if we don't help her!" she hollered back.

Ivy found Gretta sound asleep in her dorm. Her roommate, Hannelore Lawler, was reading a textbook quietly in bed. To say she was surprised to see Ivy and Rebecca burst into her room was an understatement.

Breathless, Ivy managed to get out, "We—need—to talk to—Gretta."

"She's been asleep for hours, I'm afraid. Honestly, I have no idea how she's able to sleep through a storm this bad. She sleeps through everything."

Ivy tapped Gretta but was unsuccessful at waking her.

"Gretta, wake up!"

Her sleeping face looked fitful, purple circles under her eyes discolored her smooth caramel skin. Her lips were pale.

"Let her sleep! She might not be feeling well."

"Here, help me carry her," Ivy said to Rebecca, ignoring Hannelore.

"Where are you taking her?"

"To Derwin. Professor Night."

"The glanagerie professor? What for?" Hannelore was bewildered.

"You hold her up on that side—"

"You aren't supposed to leave the dorms!"

But they were already off, leaving Hannelore to fret

behind them. Ivy and Rebecca hobbled along the hallway with Gretta weighing on their shoulders. The lights were flickering on and off.

"Wait." Ivy broke another rule and temporarily buoyed up Gretta's body—even though Gretta was tiny and had lost weight in the last moons, the two girls needed a little boost. They reached the common room that led to the bridge.

"Ivy, Derwin is back at the Halls. The only way to get to school is to cross over. We can't go out there. We have to wait until the weather calms!"

"We have to. The storm isn't going to break for hours, and look at her: She's ill! He'll be able to help us!"

"Well, in addition to being incredibly dangerous, leaving our room is against the instructions of the Selector! And—and can't you hear it outside? We'll never make it across!" Rebecca said.

The door from the common room to the bridge slammed open, harder than a carriage crash.

"Absolutely not," said Rebecca. "Listen to me for once. We'll blow right off that bridge! You're mad!"

"Figuring this out, helping Gretta, is the only thing that will get the Dark Queen and this storm away from the Halls! Whatever is cursing her has to be a part of it!"

With that, Rebecca knew she had to follow Ivy. They stepped out onto the windswept stone while the rain pelted against them sideways. Ivy could tell that the center of the storm wasn't over them yet. They would have to rush across. A giant bolt of lightning lit up the sky, touching down somewhere in the gardens beyond the Halls.

"Gretta has no shadow, Ivy! Look!"

The flashing light illuminated Ivy and Rebecca's shadow, but Gretta's silhouette against the cold, stone wall was strangely absent—like they were carrying nothing at all. Ivy felt rigid with fear but knew she had to press on. Rain lashed at them, and they were instantly as wet as if they had been swimming in the ravine below.

"Are you ready? On three, we run!"

"Ivy!"

"One."

"Ugh! You make me crazy!"

"Two. Three!"

The limestone was more slippery than ever, and Ivy was never more grateful for the chest-high old stone railings. She led them hunched down low to the side where they would be most protected from the wind.

Rebecca shouted over the wind, "Great! So now we are practically crawling? This will get us there fast!"

Ivy had to laugh. It was ridiculous. But just then the clouds darkened, swiftly becoming thicker and blacker than they had been a moment ago.

"Hurry!"

Ivy's vision was obstructed by the wildness of her hair, whipping her face and twisting into countless knots, but she pressed on, walking backwards, hunched by the wall, and carrying Gretta under her arms. Rebecca stumbled and almost fell. The entrance to the Halls of Ivy was only sixty feet away, not too far, but at that moment it seemed impossible to reach.

Rebecca and Ivy inched their way along, their slow progress against the wind taking every bit of their effort. The clouds got darker and closer, and they could no longer see the arched door into the castle on the other side of the bridge.

"Stay close to the wall! We have to feel our way across!" yelled Ivy. She had to scream just to be heard, even though Rebecca was just inches away.

The girls were grasping hands, making a seat for the limp Gretta. Ivy's fear was pulsing like a heartbeat, beating out of her chest. She had to fight to focus on what she was doing: helping Gretta, and hopefully messing up the Dark Queen's plan.

The storm surged, and out of the black cloud above them came four even blacker horses towing a carriage, barreling straight toward the bridge. Ivy could see the horses' nostrils flare and the froth flecks at their mouths. The matte black carriage could belong to only one person. Rebecca shrieked, but Ivy knew better.

"Just keep moving! It's not real!"

Rebecca was frozen to the spot, but the carriage barreled through her, pure wind and fog.

"Nothing in the cloud is real! They're only fears. We have to keep going; we're almost there!"

Ivy knew that Rebecca was scared out of her wits. Another gust came up and Ivy lost grip of Rebecca's hands. She fell back, holding Gretta on top. Her long brown hair was tangled with Gretta's curly black hair in a soggy, suffocating mess. She struggled to sit, protecting Gretta by tucking her against the wall.

But where was Rebecca?

Ivy called out. Her friend! Had she turned to crawl back the other way? Had she been blown off the bridge?

"Rebecca! *Rebecca!* No, no, no! Where are you? Rebecca!"

What have I done?

But Ivy's search was interrupted by a pack of wolves descending from the top of the dormitory cliff. *Not wolves! Bogdogs!* They snarled and howled, and Ivy couldn't help but try and scoot away from them. She scraped back and pulled Gretta along with her. The pack of bogdogs tore down the slope to the bridge and hit the girls with a puff of cloud.

Hot on their tails was the next fearful vision. A fiery-red tail lashed its way through the air over Ivy's head. She couldn't help it and let loose a shriek. Ivy tried to get as small as possible and huddled with Gretta against the wall.

The bridge itself shook, and Ivy was forced to look up. A bright flash of shimmering red was over her. Then it swept up and above her—it was a dragon!

It landed on the bridge with a thump and its tail lashed the edge of the banister, sending a capstone flying over the edge. Ivy screamed. The dragon swept up and around the bridge, disappearing for a moment down into the ravine.

Ivy stood, grabbing Gretta by her wrists. But before she could even try to move toward the Halls, a sweep from a bright wing knocked her down. This was no fear-based vision—this dragon was very, very real. And so were the talons the size of candlesticks that gripped her and Gretta's arms.

With a heave they were in the air, going higher and higher. They dropped and rose with each pulse of the leathery wings that beat up and down. The dragon let out a terrifying call and swept up into the sky, only to dive down dramatically. The dragon looped around the bridge upside down, blowing bright fire into the darkness. That's when Ivy knew the dragon was Rebecca! Rebecca, a fully grown exacto magno dragon.

With a swoop, she flew back toward the Halls, ramming

into the entrance. Their crash nearly blew the doors off their hinges and the two girls and the dragon skidded in on the marble floor. Dazed and breathless, Ivy turned to the dragon.

"Well, that was close!" Ivy tried to act cool, as if she and her friends hadn't just nearly died. "You did great, friend."

Rebecca couldn't reply; she just batted her fiery red eyes.

Splitting Shadows

REBECCA began to shed scales and transform back into her natural body. Meanwhile, Ivy waved her hand over Gretta and herself, drying them; no sense in their getting a cold, especially as they'd already broken a dozen rules. Once they were warm, she struggled against the wind to shut the door and waited for Rebecca to be herself again.

"That was absolutely brilliant!" Ivy crowed.

Rebecca shook back her honey-blonde hair and smiled, "I couldn't stand that wretched storm for another second. But who sleeps through a Bearded Cloud, for star's sake?"

Gretta's head lolled. No natural sleep was this deep.

"Quick thinking on your part—smarter than a typical dragon. But let's go. We've got to get her to Derwin."

They rushed down the hallway, flanked to the left by windows that typically looked out over the ravine and dormitories—now the view was all storm. Lightning rattled the windows and shapes rumbled in the dark clouds. As they passed each of the arched windows, terrible visions chased them: Helga again with her frying pan, the bogdogs, and even an orbis! Rebecca screamed at that one. They ran past classrooms,

Ivory Lucky's key room, and the balcony that overlooked the ballroom. As they rounded a corner, Ivy plowed straight into the Selector.

"Girls! What are you doing out of your dorms?"

"We had to!" Rebecca replied.

"You could have been killed! Ivy, you of all people should know the dangers of this storm."

"Selector! You've got to help her! Please." Ivy shoved Gretta toward the Selector.

Gretta's black curls lay flat against her head. She was sweating so profusely that it was almost like Ivy had never dried her. Her skin looked bloodless, and her mouth was twitching like she was trying to shout out in a nightmare.

"I think—I think she might be cursed," Ivy whispered.

"Come," said the Selector and threw open the doors to her office.

With a wave of her quill she pushed everything on her desk to the side where it hovered midair. Ivy noted with her last shred of humor that the Compass Individuali on the Selector's desk—busily writing in themselves the deeds and misdeeds of the evening—were hers and Rebecca's. Of course. But why not Gretta's?

"What happened to her?" the Selector asked brusquely as they laid her body across the marble desk. "Something tells me you are the one who got her in this mess, Ivy."

"No! Really! She was like this in her room," Rebecca insisted. "We're friends. We went to visit her—"

"Selector, I think it has to do with her shadow."

The Selector turned to Ivy slowly. Her gaze was steady, but unreadable.

"I know it sounds crazy," Ivy stammered, "but she—she doesn't have a shadow!"

The Selector brightened the hairies and gently lifted Gretta's arm. On the wall behind her chair, the Selector's arm and hand were casting a clear, strong shadow, but it was as if she were holding nothing. There was no shadow from Gretta's arm. Nothing.

"And there's something else. I've been seeing this dark figure—in sketches, that day in the Jester's kitchen. Could it be—"

"Her shadow's been cursed."

The hairies were now glowing crazily in response to this discussion. The Selector opened her hand and Gretta's Compass Individualis flew into it. She scanned the slender raisin-colored volume, shaking her head.

"I should have known… she's hardly made a single discovery all term." The Selector paged through the volume quickly. "Yes, it has to be."

"Has to be what? Is she going to be okay?"

But with that, Gretta's eyes flickered and she whispered hoarsely, "The storm, a storm is coming."

Ivy responded, "The storm is here, Gretta. Wake up! Oh, Gretta, come on!" Ivy shook her.

As she spoke, the Selector opened an antique cabinet behind her desk, uncapped an unknown potion bottle, and waved it under Gretta's nose. Gretta went from fitfully sleeping to groggily wakeful. She looked around the room in fear. Then the Selector pulled out potion ingredients and began mixing something together in a beaker.

"When you are sleeping like this, Gretta, do you dream?"

Gretta looked at the Selector tearfully, "I wouldn't call them dreams. The worst kind of nightmares!"

"Always the same thing?" Ivy asked, letting her own experience of dreams lead her questions.

"No! Never. Always somewhere terrible, where I'm doing something terrible, but I always wake up in bed. My roommate says I never leave—I've even bolted the door! But..."

"But what?"

"When I wake up, every terrible thing I've dreamt I've done comes true. I tried to tell you, Ivy! Like this storm! I dreamed I was summoning it. Oh, I just don't know what to do. I'm so scared! So tired."

"Look at this, Selector!" Rebecca pulled out Gretta's book.

"Gretta," Ivy said softly while the Selector looked at the book, "are you saying you dreamed of everything in that book, *The Girl with the Whispering Shadow*?" Her mind flashed to the page that showed the Jester's Lolly Room, a quill being swept into a student's quiver.

"And more. Those were the clearest," Gretta whispered, too ashamed to let the Selector hear. "That cursed quill... I think I'm the reason it was in Glistle's quiver, why it left the Town at all. Oh, Ivy—I didn't mean for any of it to happen!"

Ivy's face paled. To think that the reason an orbis was brought back to life, to kill, may have been her classmate!

"Ivy, it's like I'm somebody's puppet and they're controlling me with an imaginary thread. I would never hurt you! I've tried everything! I've tried to find a way to tell you, Glistle, my father. Anyone! That's why I left the book in your dorm room. I couldn't speak of it, but I drew and wrote everything I could remember with my pseudopen!"

"You remember everything that happens clearly?" the Selector inquired.

"No. It's just… I keep scraps of it, like distant whispers. I hardly even remember falling asleep. And when I wake up, I'm bruised where I should be bruised in the dream. Singed, bleeding, or soaking wet sometimes," Gretta cried.

"It is as I thought," said the Selector to Gretta. "Drink this." The Selector turned to Ivy and Rebecca and said, "Gretta's shadow has been cursed. A whispering shadow is a rare spell, but I know how to set her free. When she drinks this, her shadow will be called back to her—it's going to be frightening, but nothing you can't handle after the Bearded Cloud."

Gretta drank the black potion and gagged. Her tummy started rumbling loudly, her ears stinging. Her body shook.

"Who would want to curse her shadow?" Ivy asked.

The Selector raised an eyebrow, "Who do you think?"

"But why? Why Gretta?"

"Shadows are sneaky—sly little things. Useful and able to accomplish tasks without drawing attention to themselves."

At that moment a chill fell over the room as if a bit of the storm itself had entered the Selector's office. The hairies flickered and dimmed, having just been at their brightest. Ivy could sense their fear. The stone dragons over the entrance to the Forgotten Room went from smoking disinterestedly to snarling and blowing streams of fire.

Across the floor, a shadow slunk. It was as if something dragged the thing by its heels across the stone. The shadow's fingertips gripped the floor, trying to pull itself back out the door. Ivy and Rebecca leapt back, and Gretta screamed.

"No! I don't want it! I want no part of it! Keep it away!"

"It's all right. You'll be safe, Gretta. We have to bring you together before we can sever your connection forever."

Gretta couldn't help but writhe; she'd been so tormented she couldn't take one last thing. But then the shadow's feet met with Gretta's, and no amount of kicking would shake it off. Gretta was weeping.

"No! Nooo! Please!" she cried.

"Be still! Ivy, help her to be still!"

The Selector pulled the Kallegulous Key from under her robes and instructed Ivy and Rebecca to brace themselves on the opposite side of the room. Ivy had a fleeting thought, wondering why the key was with the Selector and not Ivory Lucky. *This is no time to ask,* Ivy thought.

"I will sever the shadow, then lock it in the Forgotten Room. It's no easy task, so I'll need your cooperation, Gretta. You'll need to hold perfectly still."

The miserable girl nodded assent, but the shadow had a mind of its own and kept thrashing.

"Ready?" And the Selector raised her pure white quill and quickly wrote a spell—the words shimmered over the connection point of girl and shadow and then disappeared before Ivy could read them.

With a ripping noise, the shadow tore itself from Gretta and flew around the room like a gleeful ghost, sending the room into total blackness. The Selector threw open the door to the Forgotten Room, and its torrential wind filled the office. The Selector wrote another spell in the air—the only light in the room apart from the dragon's fire—forcing the shadow into the chamber.

The shadow rode the sparkling spell toward the large door, where the dragons were fully flaming now, but at the last minute it just spun off, riding the wind to the other corner of the room. Then, before anyone could move, the shadow dipped down and slid under the door.

"No!" The Selector shouted. It was the first time that Ivy had seen her lose her composure.

The hairies gradually came back to light, but the four in the room were still. The wind from the Forgotten Room swirled until the Selector shut the door. No one knew what to say.

Except, of course, Rebecca. "Um, excuse me, but did that cursed shadow just take off?"

"Severing a shadow is much more challenging than it may seem, Rebecca. While not capturing the thing is unfortunate, the important thing is Gretta's health. Left alone, the curse of a whispering shadow is lethal. It will slowly and steadily drain the very life of the one cursed. Now that it's been split, the shadow can't drag Gretta into its dirty business."

Gretta shuddered and then spoke slowly, stretching her arms, "You know, I do feel a little better. My head is clearer than it's been in… in… I don't know how long. How long have I been cursed? I feel like I've been hearing that whisper in my head forever."

"Considering your condition, too long. Gretta, this is important. Have you ever been in contact with the Dark Queen? Or her Cloaked Brood?"

"No. Never!"

"Well, what about the Masquerade Ball?" Ivy hated to bring up that terrible night, but she had to.

The Selector interrupted, "Are your parents aware of

the situation?"

"I haven't had the energy to write to them. I wanted to fix it on my own. I'm just so ashamed."

"Your being cursed is nothing to be ashamed of, Gretta! The shame belongs to whoever cursed you! And besides, we all need help sometimes," said Ivy, gripping Gretta's hand in firm reassurance.

The Selector flipped through a couple of pages of Gretta's book. "Stealing a quill from the Quill Keep? How much of this is real?"

"Oh, well, I, er, I—"

"Where is this quill? It's extremely important to give it to me now."

"It's safe!" said Rebecca, "Back at the Keep."

"That's good," the Selector said. "But next time, don't try and fix everything yourselves. I am here for you, girls. Luckily, no one was hurt. That storm—so terrible! Ivy is the first to survive it twice."

Rebecca was holding up Gretta's arm while Gretta looked at her curiously.

"What are you doing?"

"Look! Still no shadow!" Rebecca looked at the wall lit by hairies in wonder.

"Removing a shadow is extremely dangerous—it comes at a cost. You'll join the ranks of the very few who have lost their shadows entirely, Gretta. You'll see that it doesn't affect your life in a day-to-day way. Unless you work with dwarves."

"Dwarves?"

"They see it as a mark of having worked alongside dark magic."

Gretta's caramel skin, just now gaining back its color, drained again.

The Selector locked the Forgotten Room and placed the chain with the Kallegulous Key back around her neck. Before turning around, murmuring to herself, she said, "As long as it leeched onto Gretta, the shadow had limitations like a puppet on a string. A whispering shadow always seeks freedom; and by cutting it loose from Gretta, we gave it just that."

"That doesn't sound good," muttered Rebecca.

The Selector turned to face them. "The storm is passing. Go straight back to your rooms. Do not speak of this to anyone until we have located the shadow. No sense in worrying other students about something that will likely not hurt them. Please walk Gretta to her room. Her strength is still much diminished."

The girls huddled together as they half-ran back to the dormitories. The night was still windy and the rain came down—but the storm was no Bearded Cloud. They walked Gretta to her door.

"Ivy, Rebecca," Gretta whispered, "The curse started before this year. I know it did! I was sick before then. I think the Dark Queen got to me before. Let me show you."

Gretta pulled them into her room where Hannelore Lawler was sleeping soundly. Gretta shut the door behind them and woke only one hairie. From under her mattress, she pulled out a crumpled wad of sketches. Quietly the girls smoothed them out on the bedspread.

"There were these, too," she showed them.

Each was of the Masquerade Ball, from the perspective of the sneaky shadow. One in particular caught Ivy's eye; it was of the shadow's hand pulling open the grand door at the castle's front entrance. Beyond the door, a matte black carriage awaited. From the carriage stepped a stunning woman clad in head-to-toe lace. A woman with an elaborate black mask and wild platinum curls.

"Don't you see? I let the Dark Queen into the Halls!"

Rebecca gasped, and Ivy knelt on the bed, her hands shaking as she leafed through Gretta's tortured sketches.

The Occulyst

THINGS at school had been calm ever since the Selector split Gretta's shadow. Early spring rains had passed, and the late season was fragrant with blooming flowers and calm weather. But Ivy didn't trust the quiet. Club meetings (but no games) were back on schedule and, with the date so soon, talk of the Masquerade Ball started to fill the school. That, and summer plans. The major highlight for Ivy had been the final for the invisitaur class, an elaborate game of hide-and-seek that had taken the better part of a morning. Ivy had won handily.

There was a beautiful sunset out of Winsome's laboratory window that evening, complete with swirls of blue-purple and lilac. Ivy and Rebecca had been practicing their sketching techniques for several hours, and yet, there was still much to study for final exams.

Rebecca sighed, "Winsome really knew what he was doing. I get so much done up here."

Together they were working on an assignment for Professor Petty: They had been all over school collecting items for the still life sketch, part of their final. An ancient book, a pot of dried-up ink, two talons, curlicues from the grounds' ivy, a half-eaten muffin from the Longbard Dining Hall, and four giant glass potion bottles lay upon Winsome's cluttered laboratory table, ready to be sketched.

Rebecca's focus drifted, and she began sketching a fetching dress with cap sleeves, a high neck, and a full skirt complete with pockets.

"You know the Masquerade Ball is tomorrow night. Have you given it any more thought?"

Ivy's hand stopped moving and she looked at Rebecca.

"Thought?" she repeated, staring at Rebecca but thinking only of the Dark Queen. "I *have* given it thought and, well, I'm not going."

"Not going? Why not?"

"You've heard the talk. Everyone's wondering if I'm going. Really, they're hoping I'm not. I can't ruin it for the second time in a row."

"I'll be *livid* if you don't go."

Ivy laughed. Rebecca's expressiveness always made her mood lighter. "Feel free to stay, but I've got to go catch up with Derwin."

"More memory glanagerie?"

With a nod and a hug, Ivy was off.

Feeling a little deflated by memories of the Masquerade Ball and a conviction that evil was lurking somewhere around the corner, Ivy was less upbeat than usual. "Hi, Derwin. How was your day?"

"Longest yet. But it's good to see you."

"Did the Selector tell you about the shadow?" It was the first time they'd been alone in weeks.

"Indeed, she did."

And just like that, questions tumbled out of her mouth, "So Gretta gets cursed by the Dark Queen, the shadow gets loose, and now we can't do anything? Does this mean the Dark Queen won't have access to the Halls anymore? Can her plan be so easily ruined?"

"You don't seem convinced," prompted Derwin.

"Well, that's because I'm not. Seeing that thing, that shadow, escape didn't exactly make me feel warm and fuzzy."

"Well, what advice I can offer is that the Dark Queen can meddle with all she chooses to, Ivy. I'm sure that she didn't intend for you to discover the curse, but I'm equally certain that it accomplished—at least in part—what she intended. Splitting Gretta's shadow means it no longer has a tether. Free to do evil far and wide."

Ivy nodded slowly. "That's what I was afraid of."

"But at least Debnick's quill is safe." With a pointed look Derwin let Ivy know that he knew she was involved in the drop-off of the quill. "The mattelers aren't quite satisfied with what they've discovered, but it will have to do."

He led them to the podium.

"Now, Ivy, the school year is almost at a close." He tapped the royal-blue glanagerie in front of him. "These are the last dredges of what I can remember… I don't know if I have any other memories cast into this bottle," Derwin's voice was rough with emotion.

She stared into the vibrant bottle: What first looked like a grove had narrowed to a focus on what appeared to be a deranged tree house, lit by a bright moon.

"Every one of these sessions has been building to this, Ivy.

With that shadow on the loose, we are running out of time."

Her curiosity and the thrill of it all overcame her nervousness. "All right, but will you be coming with me this time?"

"I'll be there in spirit."

With a pop of the lid, Ivy was swept inside. The darkness around her was as if her eyes were still glued shut. Only the light sound of the wind swaying the tree leaves, coupled with the crunch of woodland beneath her feet, assured Ivy she wasn't in the Halls of Ivy anymore.

"I've come so far. It's got to be close!" said a tired voice.

Ivy's eyes slowly adjusted. The source of the voice was of the younger Derwin. He hurried ahead, trudging up the mountain in his worn leather boots, the same that he had been wearing the night of her parents' death. Ivy followed closely behind, questioning his every step like a nagging child. "What are we looking for out here, Derwin?"

"The Occulyst. Wembly split the stone—some dwarf magic!"

Ivy gaped. Wembly could only be Wembly Greeley, Fyn's father.

But Derwin pressed on urgently before Ivy could say anything. "And now I must hide the pieces!"

"Where? Where will you hide them?"

"The Occulyst. At least one there."

"But surely won't the Dark Queen find it there? It's just a—just a *bank*." Her mind flashed back to the assignment Derwin had sent her in Belzebuthe. But the details escaped her; she could only remember the little pearl spinner she'd found in the pages of the Occulyst book.

Derwin turned to her slowly and said, "But I have a plan. You do know how the Occulyst works, don't you? His owls are the only beings capable of hiding matter in thin air."

"But should we really be out in the open here? What if the Dark Queen finds us?" she whispered, looking back over her shoulder again and again, as they pressed deeper into the forest.

As Ivy looked back again, she barreled into Derwin. He stumbled but caught himself.

"Sorry! It's just so dark out here. Where are we, anyway?"

But he was too focused to notice her apology. "Mount Promises."

They continued on in silence up the steep grade. The dark forest gave way to sparser bushes and rock outcroppings. Near the top, they had to scramble over boulders. But then Derwin stopped suddenly, and Ivy stopped behind him, afraid.

They were at the summit. An enormous, ancient tree towered over them. Its roots were as thick as barrels and snaked over and around the boulders. Giant leaves the size of Ivy's head lay in drifts around the trunk and cascading roots. The thick, brown, gnarled trunk was as wide as a house, and its low branches spread wide.

As Ivy's eye followed the line of tangled branches, she saw an elaborate tree house with rooms suspended throughout the tree. Some of the rooms hung precariously out over the edge of a cliff. To say that the little cottages in the banyan were nestled in the tree branches would be an understatement. The branches had grown around the cottages, snugging them in toward the trunk. Owls hooted in the dark, soaring above and around the tree.

Ivy couldn't resist the urge to ask, "Are we going—are we

going in there?"

"Yes. Home to the Occulyst," muttered Derwin. "Come. There isn't time. We've got to make the most of what we have. For all of Croswald, let us hope he's here!"

Derwin hurried, taking care not to trip over the webs of roots and vines on the uneven ground.

The round door at the bottom of the tree was just like a plump owl body, the two tempered glass windows above it just like wide eyes, and the tiny awning over the door like a beak. Derwin and Ivy pushed through, hunching over to fit, and found a man tittering to three owls perched at a small dining table as he spread their seed across the length of it. Hairies flitted about in golden birdcages that hung from the ceiling at varying heights. Owls and Occulyst looked up in surprise; they weren't accustomed to people bursting in.

The Occulyst was not at all what Ivy had expected to see; in fact, he was quite the opposite. He was a thin-faced man with limp strawberry-blonde hair that hung in locks around his shoulders, but his wide eyes were warm and kind. Strange, but not in a bad way.

"Welcome," he said with some surprise, brushing feathers from his red jacket, adorned with bright golden buttons.

"I need—I—," panted Derwin.

"You need help," said the Occulyst. "Up you go, my little dearies," he said to his feathered friends. "Take some to go, but there's always more. Don't worry! Maybe even some shortcake later."

The owls fluffed their feathers and hopped or flew out of the room.

"I'm in need of a vault, an invisible vault."

"The only kind we have here. What is it you wish to place?"

Derwin opened up his satchel and held out the faceted stone in his fist; it was a twin to the one Ivy had in her pocket. Rather, the triplet.

The Occulyst peered over his glasses.

"Where did you get this?" he said, hushed. "It looks like it's been cut. I've never seen a stone like it."

"Only where it needs to go matters. You cannot imagine what this stone means to Croswald. The Brood is coming for it as we speak."

"Follow me." The Occulyst spun and walked over to a ladder that led to a narrow porthole at the top of the room.

The room above was round and surrounded by connecting wooden arched doorways. This one, like the room below, had open gilded cages where hairies flitted about brightly. The occasional owl popped into the cages, making them swing recklessly. The Occulyst opened the door directly behind them. This led into another room. Ivy just hoped it wasn't one of those that hung out over the cliff.

This room had burrows in the wooden walls—some in the tree's trunk and branches that ran through the wall. As they walked by, owls poked their heads out in curiosity. The Occulyst tended the burrows as he passed by, clucking softly and adding feathers and bedding to each.

Around the next corner, the Occulyst opened a door into another cottage, ushering both Derwin and Ivy inside. At the center of this round room was one of the Occulyst's signature birdcages. Ivy remembered the sketch from Mr. Greeley's book, but the cage in front of her was captivating: Its bright golden sheen was the focus, and the edges of the room faded to darkness. The cage was slightly shorter than Ivy and it hung on a thick chain several feet off the ground. The metal bars of the cage were delicate, more like gold wire, and strung with beads.

Derwin walked up to the cage, entranced. "Is that a Stone of Abrise?" he said, pointing at a deep purple stone.

"The power to lift objects," nodded the Occulyst. "Portal Stone and Hellexor Stone beads, as well. But believe me, it takes more than pairing those three stones to make this work." The Occulyst puffed with pride, "These girls are the most magical birds in all of Croswald. Most wise. The nesting stones, the beads, are already reacting to the power of the stone you've brought," the eccentric man gestured to the piece Derwin held. "Strange."

"It's a bit warm in here." Derwin began to sweat nervously.

"Occulyst owls require a certain temperature to hatch."

"Hatch?"

"Otherwise known as banking. This cage, one of many, is where the transportation takes place."

Derwin's blank look prompted the Occulyst to continue, "First, you'll set the valuable inside the birdcage. One of my fluffy little friends will disappear your treasure and will shortly hatch an egg."

"The treasure will be stored in the egg?" Derwin asked.

"Of course not! What kind of vault is an egg? A baby owl will be hatched from the egg, an owlette that will possess the power of summoning back your item. Your compass will hatch with the owl. With this compass, you will be the only person able to find this owl and the only person able to request the summoning of your item."

"So, it just—it just disappears?" Derwin peered into the

empty birdcage.

"More like dematerializes. Well, that's how it usually works. In the case of *that*," he pointed to Derwin's tightly clenched fist, "your guess is as good as mine. There's a lot of magic in that—"

"Yes." Derwin cut him off.

Ivy could tell that every muscle in Derwin was tense.

"What if it never comes back? What if it disappears forever?" Ivy asked in a panicked tone.

"It's better gone forever than in the hands of the Dark Queen. Her lack of Princess Isabella's true magic is the only thing stopping her from ruling forever."

Derwin stepped forward. There was a flutter as a small white owl came down into the room from a high-up window. It circled, peering at Derwin and the Occulyst. The Occulyst smiled and nodded. The bird flew into the cage.

"This may take some time. The compass for your item," the Occulyst pulled out a small, pearlescent object from his pocket, "will look a lot like this one."

The tiny oval had a dial that swiveled and then pointed strongly upward. So familiar. Then the scene started to shimmer, just like it did when the glanagerie memory was coming to an end.

"Wait! I need to see more!" Ivy begged Derwin.

"How does the compass…" Derwin's words were already fading.

The next thing she knew, Ivy had been dumped out on the floor of the glanagerie classroom.

As soon as she could, Ivy choked out, "But Derwin, Wembly Greeley! He cut the stone?"

A light came into Derwin's eyes, "Yes! I knew I had held

his name close for a reason. My mentor scrivenist. It's why I sent you to his home. If only he were still here!"

Ivy ached for the same thing! Then, with a jolt, she remembered the little round object in the Occulyst's hand.

"Derwin, we have to get to the Occulyst. I think I have your compass."

Chapter Twenty-Eight

The House in the Tree

When Ivy opened her dormitory door late that night, she was greeted by Rebecca's soft breathing and Humboldt's snores. She tiptoed to her bed and was surprised to find the gorgeous sequined dress that Rebecca had given her for her birthday hanging on the outside of her closet. A magenta mask, which complemented the gown's blush tone, was on the hanger, too. Ivy had to cover her mouth to catch her laugh. Rebecca was certainly determined to have her go to the Ball! Then Ivy's eyes welled up with tears. She couldn't believe she had such amazing friends! As much as she wanted to be at the party, she knew what she had to do. She tore a page from her proof pad and wrote:

Rebecca,

You are simply the best. I wish for nothing more than to be able to wear this amazing dress and dance the night away with you! But everything we know and love is threatened. I know where the next piece of the stone is–I have to see if it's still there before it's too late. I'll be in touch soon, I promise. If luck's on my side, I'll be back before the Ball.

Please don't be mad. Oh, and could you look after Humboldt while I'm away? I'm sure Hayword wouldn't mind watching him if you'd rather drop him off. Thanks!

Ivy

Ivy went to her books and cracked open *The Occulyst: Owls, Oddities, and Other Odds and Ends.* There, in the pages of the book, lay the tiny little pearl that she had almost completely forgotten about. It was definitely an Occulyst compass—the same as she'd seen in the glanagerie. She was only beginning to understand Derwin's connection to Wembly Greeley, but this just had to be Derwin's, the one for the Kindred Stone! She slipped the compass into her pocket alongside her stone and pushed her worry down. She laced up her Habberdash combat boots, buttoned her cloak, stuffed her quiver into her cloak's inner pocket, and then sneaked out into the hall.

Ivy dashed as quickly as she could back to Derwin's classroom. She couldn't wait to leave for the Occulyst's immediately, as they had agreed!

But just as she reached Derwin's door, Ivy heard voices echoing up from the classroom. Instead of bursting through the room, she hesitated.

"Listen! What you are doing here is not safe! The water in a glanagerie is not to be tampered with! Don't you remember what happened the last time a princess with magical blood was swept into a glanagerie alone?" Someone angry, someone Ivy didn't know.

Ivy crept in, careful to keep to the dark shadows in the tunnel.

"I've made sure it was safe! There is no better way to pull out my memories!" Clearly Derwin.

A third voice, familiar to Ivy, said, "Now, Derwin, be reasonable. It's our job to supervise magic and make sure that everything is for the benefit of all of Croswald. I know as well as you do that what you are doing is important. Come with us to the Town, just for a day or so, to make sure that this glanagerie is safe for her. We cannot afford to jeopardize the future of the throne. And then there is the issue of Debnick's quill."

"Can't it wait? Just for a few days? I have something extremely pressing to—"

The first, gruff voice interrupted, clearly leading Derwin up the stairs and out of the classroom. "Up and out, Night. Transport is already waiting on the roof." *A cabby.* They were fast approaching the tunnel, coming right toward Ivy.

Ivy had to move! It was too late to go back out into the hall—they'd see the light. She saw Derwin's eyes brighten with recognition as they approached: He saw her. He swung the door to the tunnel open a bit further, creating the perfect deep shadow for Ivy to hide in. Ivy squeezed in the pocket of darkness and held her breath, all the while hearing Derwin try to negotiate.

"It's important!"

"Derwin," said the voice that Ivy now recognized to be Easel Leelangraf, Glistle and Gretta's father, "we will be back soon! Just enough time to analyze the bottle and then…."

Their voices drifted off, but Ivy stayed put. Again, she was on her own. Her scrivenist was off on one adventure, and here she was about to embark on a completely different one. But she had to go. And she had to go immediately.

Once out on the grounds, she breathed a little easier. Ivy wove her way through the garden's grand topiaries, up the hill, and to the empty barn.

"Are you here?" she called. "Hello? Silius?" No reply.

Ivy circled the field, but all was quiet. Down the hill, windows at the Halls of Ivy were beautifully illuminated from within—especially the ballroom. Ivy could see silhouettes of party streamers, balloons, and giant floral arrangements being set up for the next day's Ball. The jingle of metal, perhaps of a lantern, brought her back to the present. Ivy followed the sound, quietly walking around the corner of the barn, through the double sliding doors and into an open stall, the olive-green door pushed back. And there was Fyn, slouched in the drafty stall with its leaky roof, fingering one of his quills.

"Fyn! What are you doing out here?"

"Ivy?"

"Are you all right?"

"Of course I am."

"Well then, what are you doing out here instead of in bed?"

"I couldn't sleep. I was just sitting out here, thinking, looking up at the stars." He pointed to the hole in the roof over their heads. Something about it framed the stars just perfectly, blocking out the light from the Halls. "I'm graduating soon. Just can't believe that's it. I was just thinking my father would be proud, and it made me start thinking of the stars."

"Oh. Graduation. Right." Ivy sank down beside him inside the stall, her back against the stained wood. "I've actually been thinking about your father, too."

"Really?"

"Yes. I think he may have helped Derwin hide the Kindred Stone."

"What?!"

"From the way Derwin talks about him—the young Derwin in the glanagerie, I don't think the one out here remembers your father much—but it seems like Derwin knew him quite well. Did you know that he was Derwin's mentor scrivenist in the Town?"

"Mother never mentioned that!"

"Anyway, I think it was your dad who helped Derwin split the stone, your dad who helped hide it from the Dark Queen."

Tears sprang to Fyn's eyes. "How do you know this?"

"And I think I know where one of them is. Mount Promises."

"The Occulyst?"

"Yes." Ivy pulled out the little eggshell compass.

"Ivy, where did you get that?"

"This has to be the reason Derwin sent me to your house."

Under the stars, Ivy filled in Fyn on the glanagerie scene, and on finding the compass in Belzebuthe in his father's study.

"I'm going with you. If my father had any part in hiding the stone, I have to help, too."

"But the Ball?"

"What's a ball without you, Ivy?"

Ivy blushed.

Then Fyn thought aloud, "It could take days to get there on foot."

"Well, who said I planned on walking?"

At that moment there was a loud boom and the wall they were leaning on shook. Then there was another boom.

"What the—" muttered Fyn.

But Ivy ran outside and she saw exactly what she was looking for: nothing. That is, nothing until she squinted and saw the shimmer of heat emanating from her favorite invisitaur. And from the sound of it, it seemed as if it was playfully head-butting the barn.

"Hello, friend! I need your help." By now, Fyn had joined Ivy and she continued, "We need to get to Mount Promises as quickly as—"

Before she could finish her sentence, she was swept up onto Silius's shoulders and Fyn was below, looking around, back and forth, at his eye level for her.

"Ivy? Ivy!"

She giggled, "I'm up here."

Within seconds, Fyn was tossed up, too, onto another invisitaur's shoulders.

"Do you know each other?" Fyn asked.

"Silius and I go way back. Don't we?" The beast patted her foot, and she returned the affection by giving his invisible neck a squeeze.

o o o o

The gentle rocking of the invisitaurs' steady pace—back

and forth, back and forth—lulled Ivy and Fyn into a dream. They stopped for boysenberries and spring water occasionally, and Ivy lost track of time. The sun rose and then set again. The Masquerade Ball would be in full swing by now, but it seemed farther away than the many miles it really was.

The two invisitaurs cradled Fyn and Ivy in their invisible arms for the second half of their journeys, like newborns. As they approached Mount Promises, the slope steadily increased, going from a stroll to a hike to a partial mountain climb. The invisitaurs took it all in stride, and the sqwinches barely noticed being transferred from one arm to another as the beasts grabbed hold of roots and pulled themselves up rocky ledges.

There was a small plateau at the top of the mountain. Fyn's invisitaur gave him a quick shake and then dropped him on the ground unceremoniously. Sleepy Fyn tottered and fell clumsily on his bottom, then just lay back on the boulders. The invisitaur nudged him and snorted, and Fyn sat up, yawning.

"All right, all right, I'm up," he said, brushing twigs and moss from his hair, barely staying upright.

Silius, however, handled Ivy like a precious jewel. He set her down softly.

She turned to him appreciatively, murmuring, "Thanks, Silius."

But apparently, she had been gazing up into space: A large, lumpy hand spun Ivy around to correct her. She could feel Silius' breath and sense his smile. She crinkled her nose and laughed, "Sorry about that!"

Just as it had in the glanagerie, the landscape at the narrow top of the mountain gently sloped downward to the base of the enormous Occulyst tree and its tangle of thick roots. As Ivy looked on, it was harder and harder to tell if the house or the tree had come first. She saw the rounded dwellings rise up into the leafy foliage far past where the moonlight allowed her to see.

"The Occulyst," Ivy breathed out. She turned back to speak in the direction of Silius's grunt. "We're hoping this won't take too long. Wait for us?" Her hair blew back with his next grunt of warm air. She couldn't help but smile, sensing the comfort of her friend close by.

The windows that peeked through the branches were aglow with a warm light. The details of this magical place were much sharper in real life than they had been in the glanagerie. The sounds of the wind in the tree clearer, the scent of the damp earth more vivid.

"I've always wanted to come here. Been most places in Croswald, but I guess I've never had anything worth depositing." Fyn smiled wryly as the two walked closer to the tree.

Now that the invisitaurs had settled back for a quick nap on the rocky ledge, the rustle of birds flying in and out of the tree returned. Ivy could hear the sound of giant wings flapping, of owls hooting in the moonlight. One swooped down behind them, not quite brushing them but stirring the air all around them. Then it lifted up into the branches and ducked in through one of the windows, which were mostly round holes open to the night.

"Quite the owl infestation here, isn't it?" Fyn joked, his main way of making a nerve-wracking situation lighter.

Now fully under the canopy, Ivy and Fyn peered up into the branches of the ancient tree. Giant owls, tiny owls, short owls, tall owls were silhouetted in the light of the moon. They were perched on the high-up branches, as curious about their visitors as their visitors were about them.

"From here, they just look like regular owls. Who would think they have the ability to dematerialize treasure or make invisible, undetectable vaults? Just think of the loot they hide!" crowed Fyn. "Family fortunes! Heirlooms! Secret inventions!"

Ivy laughed. "They probably hold a lot of pretty boring stuff, too. Spell notes, land deeds, mementos."

"Old letters from lovers."

They both blushed.

The two walked slowly, in wonder, and twigs and leaves crunched underfoot.

Ivy pulled out the tiny Occulyst compass from her pocket where it had been. Previously, in Belzebuthe and at the barn, the dial had just spun lazily around, alternating directions. Now the dial stood at firm attention pointing straight toward the door in the tree.

"Supposedly this compass follows the tail feather of the owl it was hatched with—the dial is made of the same stuff." She hesitated. "It's telling us to go in."

"Well, are you ready?"

"I guess so. I just don't know what I'm going to do if it's not there. I'm kind of scared that it's not. What if someone's already taken it?" The lump in her throat made it impossible to talk.

"If it's not there, we'll figure it out, Ivy. We won't stop looking." Fyn squeezed her hand. "Plus, there's no bank more secure. Invisible vaults that can only be revealed and unlocked by creatures that can't be tempted nor caught. Even the Occulyst can't summon an object without a compass."

"Yes, but the Occulyst did say he didn't know how the stone's magic would interact with the owl's magic."

Fyn paused and then said, "So tell me again, *why* couldn't Derwin just tell you where this piece was? And why didn't he just come and get it himself? And why isn't he here now?"

"I heard the mattelers talking to him before I left; I hope he's not in trouble. They took him to Belzebuthe, to make sure the memory glanagerie was safe. Besides, he hasn't been the same since being trapped in the bottle. The glanagerie water erased his certainty around the stone. The memory glanagerie was helping him remember as much as it was helping him tell me. As far as the stone goes, he says it's mine, that the stone should only be with me." Ivy could hardly believe the words as she said them.

"Still," Fyn shook his head, "Professor Night can barely be called a scrivenist—a horrible memory, abandons his royal, teaches her nearly nothing, and directs her towards danger? All I'm saying is, this could be a trap. I'm pretty sure that the Selector wasn't joking when she warned you about the dangers of leaving the school grounds. And with that shadow now on the loose—we're too far away from safety! The reason I come with you on these hair-brained adventures, Ivy, is to look after you. If your scrivenist isn't going to, somebody should!"

"Hardly. You love it."

"All right. That's maybe a little true. But honestly. Mostly to protect you."

"And a little bit to find out why your father had an Occulyst compass from Derwin, right? Let's go."

The glossy leaves above were low and narrow, making a

little garden tunnel toward the arched doorway. Ivy reached out toward the door in front of them, acting more confident than she felt. She pushed it open and stepped in; Fyn followed. Ivy felt the familiar thrum in her veins: a mix of nerves and excitement, worry and wonder, just like when she dove into a glanagerie. Because of the last experience in Derwin's bottle, there was an overwhelming sense of *déjà vu.*

They stepped into the little dining room. But, rather than being greeted by the kindly Occulyst, they found the room empty but for a few owls who perched on the rails of the chairs around the dining table. They looked up as if Fyn and Ivy had just interrupted their nocturnal chat.

In the corner, the little kitchenette lay still; a self-cleaning spell apparently had finished hours ago, but a half-eaten dinner remained on a cold plate.

"Strange he's not here," Ivy whispered.

"Maybe he's sleeping," Fyn said. "It's late, you know."

"Maybe," Ivy replied, unconvinced. She looked up into the hole that led to the upstairs room.

"So, where to?" Fyn asked.

Ivy hesitated. "Fyn, without the Occulyst knowing that we're here, it's trespassing."

"Ivy, the Kindred Stone, rightfully yours, might be in one of these vaults. It's not the time to sit around and wait for permission."

"It's just—I don't know, Fyn, something just doesn't feel right. Something's off." There was an icy coldness—Ivy remembered the inside of the treehouse being warmer; better for hatching, the Occulyst had explained.

"Ivy, we're in a treehouse miles and miles away from school, against school policies, and the closest thing to neighbors are hundreds of strange old birds. Of course things don't feel right. We've already missed the Ball—all our friends are dancing right now."

"You're pretty upset about that, aren't you? We'll definitely be back for graduation." Ivy certainly hoped what she said was true—graduation was two days away.

"I'm only saying that I didn't leave the Halls of Ivy, travel all this way, for you to start doubting yourself. Whatever it is you saw, whatever it is that brought us here, let's go and get it. No need to wait for an introduction."

"But what if something happened to him, Fyn?"

"Then it's good we take a look around. Be sure he's all right."

"Yeah, that's right. If we do bump into him, we'll just tell him we came and we didn't see him, and we were worried. Worried about a man we never met, who's guarding the most sacred stone in all of Croswald for a family friend," Ivy scrunched her nose; listening to herself was like listening to a story straight out of Lie Buries. Who would believe it?

"Sounds convincing enough," Fyn smiled mischievously. "Let's follow that compass."

Steps cut into the wood led up to room after room after room—they squeezed through small trap doors and doorways. Little portholes to the night sky peppered the walls, and owls of every imaginable color and size popped in and out.

Countless owl nests were notched into the old banyan tree's thick trunk. As they worked their way up—always following the compass—delicate, golden birdcages became the centerpieces of each room. They varied in size, but each had stones on the tines of the cage, delicate little gems that made the cages even more jewel-like. Unlike the nests, the cages were empty.

Fyn walked up to the nearest birdcage, placing his hand through the golden opening.

"Fascinating!" He said as only a rapt sqwinch could.

"So, you know the basics, but when I was here with Derwin—"

"In the bottle, you mean?"

"Yes. This is where the transport or hiding or vaulting—whatever you call it—takes place. In the cages."

"Look," Fyn nudged her. "Compass says go left."

They tiptoed up the stairs on the left as quietly as possible, fighting the noise of the creaking wood. Their shadows cast by gentle hairie glow stretched along the wood-paneled sidewalls. More owl cubbies than ever lined the walls—some rimmed with gold—and tiny doors led to more chambers. More owls.

"Hello? Is anyone here?"

Silence, but for the flap of a few wings.

"Ivy, look out this way," Fyn said, brushing past and pointing outside.

She followed and popped her head out the window. They were high up now, and the view into the tree was lovely. She could see the other chambers branching off, lighted windows sparkling in the tree.

Ivy glanced at her compass again, which was now pointing back down the stairs.

"Is this a joke?" Ivy voiced her irritation.

Fyn shrugged. "Birds fly."

They walked into the next dimly lit interior; in this room, like all the others, any furnishings—chairs, lanterns, ladders—were made from the wood of the tree. Some of the nests had inhabitants, but most were out hunting. Still no Occulyst.

In the next room, there was a small twin-sized, four-poster bed slanted in the corner. Sketches of owls covered every cranny on the wall. There was a side table with little artifacts, mostly eggshells and feathers, scattered on the table.

"Something must have happened to him," Ivy worried. "He wouldn't just abandon his birds."

"The owl, Ivy. Concentrate on why we came here."

Then Fyn voiced the worry they both had, "What if the owl's not coming to you because you're not Derwin? What if the compass won't work without the original owner? That thing is just taking us on a wild goose chase."

"A wild owl chase," Ivy corrected Fyn.

But Fyn was beyond his capacity for patience. "It seems like that compass is pointing out here." He stuck his head out the largest window. Then he started to climb out onto the limb.

"Don't be ridiculous! You could fall! Plus, we shouldn't split up." Ivy tugged on Fyn's leg: He was nearly halfway out the window. "And there's no way I'm going out there."

"You keep searching inside. Don't worry. I'm not going far."

Ivy stared at Fyn, mouth slack. He was serious.

"Be careful," Fyn said good-naturedly as he climbed out.

This high up into the tree, the foliage was so thick that not even the moonlight shone through. Fyn quickly disappeared into the darkness, the hooting of disturbed owls the only hint of where he was.

Then, a loud sound frightened Ivy. Her first thought: *Fyn!* But the crack came from inside, from a room somewhere below. She raced down the ladder that popped out the bottom of one curvy cottage and then into the next cottage on the second floor. In this room, there weren't any nests in the wall, but there was another giant gold birdcage with elaborate curlicues, almost large enough for Ivy to stand in. It was the same one from the glanagerie! It swung gently as it hung several feet off the ground. The walls of the room looked charred, which made the cage sparkle even brighter in the hairie light.

Quickly, Ivy spotted the source of the sound that had drawn her down. At the top of the cage there were several wooden dowels that stretched across, giving the birds a place to perch and hoot at each other. One dowel lay split in two and had a flustered looking, completely enormous owl sitting on half of the broken perch. Aside from looking momentarily foolish, the giant white owl was magnificent. Its wings were specked gray and the tips had a pattern that looked like tiny eyes on repeat. It hopped over to Ivy and its yellow eyes locked on her hazel ones.

The stone buzzed in Ivy's pocket. *The owl!* Her eyes jumped down to the compass and it confirmed what she was thinking. The dial was locked on the creature. Ivy shifted to the left, and the compass moved to stay steady on the owl. To the right, same thing.

The owl flapped its wings as if to take off. Though it stirred up the air in the room, the giant bird only hovered an inch or two before Ivy stumbled over herself to catch it.

"Look at you. Are you who I've been searching for?"

The owl continued to stare into Ivy's eyes.

"You can't fly, can you? Too big? What do we do with you now?" She hefted the creature into her arms with a grunt, a ride that the owl regally accepted. *The Occulyst would be very helpful right about now.*

As Ivy backed up, a low creak sounded from behind her. She turned. There in the doorway was the Occulyst. The strawberry-blonde, thin-faced man was the same as in the glanagerie bottle, just older. And yet something was different. He was less energetic, less enthusiastic. Like there was less color in his face, and he stood at a distance from his dear animals. One small owl flew in to land on his shoulder.

"Go!" he shooed it off, waving his hand irritably. "Shoo!"

A chill fell on Ivy. Was it because she was trespassing? Or because the Occulyst seemed different than he had just a day ago in the bottle? Of course, when Derwin had visited, the Occulyst was a much younger man.

"Hello," he said solemnly.

"You don't remember me, do you?" Ivy questioned. She remembered every word of their conversation.

The Occulyst's eyes widened, not unlike his feathered friends, and he cocked his head to the side. "Should I?"

"I suppose not."

"I'm sure you haven't been here before… one must meet another to remember," he said, wriggling his bony finger. "I see you've found a friend." He motioned to the owl in her hand.

The Occulyst removed the winter white owl from Ivy's arms brusquely, holding it carelessly.

"Careful with her," Ivy urged. The owl flapped its large wings frantically, trying to escape the Occulyst's grip. Even all that desperate flapping didn't lead to flying, but it did succeed in setting itself free. Ivy was grateful the owl had a little extra heft to cushion the thump upon landing. The Occulyst hoisted up the owl again.

"Why don't we try setting her inside this cage here," the Occulyst said in an oily tone. "Perhaps some magic will take place?" He shooed the rest of the owls out.

Don't you know? Ivy thought. So strange. He shoved the owl into the cage.

"Is—is everything okay? I couldn't find you in your chambers," Ivy ventured nervously. "Don't you usually greet guests at the door?"

No response.

Ivy pressed on, "Also, I thought you'd want to know that I came to retrieve an item locked away, but not by me. By my parents' scrivenist many years ago. His name is Derwin Edgar Night? Perhaps you remember him. And, well, he sent me here."

"Ah yes, I remember him very well. This owl, it must be guarding something incredibly large—perhaps a stone?"

"I beg your pardon?"

"Owls tend to reflect the magnitude of what they hide."

Ivy fell silent. How could she know how much to share? The Kindred Stone was still in her pocket—who could she trust with the knowledge that she was searching for another segment of the same powerful stone? But hadn't he himself helped Derwin hide the stone?

The tiny compass in Ivy's hand kept its point on the owl that waited expectantly, eyes locked on Ivy. She turned and steadied the cage. The fluffy bird settled into the bedding at the center of the cage and the light in the room magically dimmed. The stones on the cage's wires brightened in a flash and then settled into a dull glow.

"Give it your compass; that's how this works. Set it down with the bird."

Ivy could swear she heard an edge of impatience in his voice, but when she looked over, his face was calm. She hesitated. If only Fyn were here instead of searching the tree's limbs for an owl she had already found. She wanted him to be there, to witness what would happen and to help her.

"Don't be shy all of a sudden. It doesn't suit you."

Ivy glanced from the tiny compass in her hand to the owl's wide, wise eyes. Those eyes reassured her. She was in the right place, with the right compass. She was meant to do this. She held out the compass toward the bird, and it bent its neck down as if showing her where to place it in front of her. Ivy set it down. The compass still had its dial pointed straight to its originator. The giant white owl pecked once at the compass and it dissolved into a tiny pile of pearlescent dust, which swirled around the owl once and disappeared. The owl flapped its wings and settled deeper into the nest.

After a few seconds, the owl flutter-hopped out of the nest, leaving behind a huge owl egg. The luminescent egg was speckled in a grainy pattern of brown, white, and mint green.

The top half began to crack. A beam of golden light shone through, and Ivy's eyes lit up almost as brightly. *Crick. Crack.* Small pieces flecked the floor.

But then, unexpectedly, the egg collapsed into its own emptiness. There was nothing inside. Not even a baby bird. No treasure. No stone. It was just a pile of shell.

Ivy panicked, "Where did it go? What happened to it?!"

The Occulyst turned sickly white. "Impossible."

"What happened? Where did the compass go?" she

repeated.

"It's gone," he uttered, seeming deflated. "Nothing inside. This isn't supposed to happen!" The Occulyst knelt quickly to sweep the inside of the cage, pushing aside the nesting twigs and fluff with frantic hands.

"What's going on?"

"Either the vault has been compromised," he paused for too long, "or whatever it is you seek to protect, to recover, is too powerful to come back out. Perhaps you are not the right one to do it. But if not you, then who—"

But Ivy knew in her heart that she was the right one.

"Compromised? By whom?" Ivy thought of all Fyn had said. *A trap.* Could this be a trap?

A mist swirled into the room and around the Occulyst's feet. A low growl emanated from behind him, and three terrible bogdogs materialized. The only other noise was the flap of dozens of owl wings, all in a frenzy, fleeing the premises. Ivy picked up her owl and backed up against the wall.

The three bogdogs parted. They had dragged in a limp figure with them. *Fyn!*

But it wasn't Fyn. It was the Occulyst wearing the same deep red jacket adorned with golden buttons and everything! Ivy yanked her gaze up to the Occulyst's face, the one she'd just been talking to, but in his place there stood another person entirely.

The Dark Queen.

Chapter Twenty-Nine

The Empty Nest

THE Dark Queen stepped out of the shadows toward Ivy.

"That was you? The whole time?" Ivy shook.

In response, the Dark Queen transformed herself back into a semblance of the Occulyst and then let the figure fade away, like the image dissolved in water, to reveal her true face again. Or was it her true face? Ivy had no idea. She only knew that the lithe blonde woman was the same person she'd danced with at the Masquerade Ball the year before.

"The Occulyst," Ivy whispered, looking at the unconscious man, limp as a rag doll. "What did you do to him? Leech off of him like you did Gretta?"

"Gretta's a fool. You see, when you helped your little friend out, you freed my spawn, my shadow. The shadow knew just how to draw the Occulyst into my trap. Put a few of his *special* owls in danger, and he came running," the Dark Queen's cruel voice filled the room.

Ivy was speechless. How could she have known the wreckage that setting Gretta free would cause?

"Before you say anything else, know that the shadow's work isn't done. You silly scrivenists, you think you can keep me away from that Town. Where do you think it's headed next? Where do you think *I'm* headed next?"

"There are spells. Protections. You'll never break through!"

"You see, that's where you've helped me immensely. Now that the shadow doesn't have to wait for that foolish girl to return home and disappear when she wakes, it knows not only how to get there but how to squeeze through the shielding spells and disguise itself as only a shadow can."

"I don't believe you!"

"What you believe doesn't matter. It's what I know that matters." She stepped closer to Ivy. "And I know that you are here for the very same reason that I am, for the Kindred Stone—the only reason I've let you and Night live this long."

With a jolt, Ivy realized that the Dark Queen didn't know that the stone was broken apart into three sections. Not yet anyway. She believed the whole thing was hidden by the Occulyst.

"Well, you saw as well as I did. The egg was empty! What's your plan now?" Ivy was so overwhelmed her voice cracked with emotion. She was grateful that she was stuck holding an enormous owl—if not for that, her knees would have buckled to the floor. How could she come this far and get stopped, maybe killed? Had all her sessions with Derwin been for nothing? What if he had lost the rest of that stone and it was gone forever? How had the Dark Queen known Ivy would come here? Had she really compromised the safety of Belzebuthe by setting the shadow free? Silent tears coursed down Ivy's colorless face.

The owl turned its head slowly to her, its intent yellow eyes boring into her. It tried to flap its wings, struggling a bit. *Do you want to get down? Are you going to go fight her?* Ivy thought sarcastically. But the owl continued to flap until Ivy finally set it down in the birdcage. As quickly as it could, the creature fluffed and fluttered, until it was settled. Then it set its eyes back on Ivy, locking in. *Are you trying to tell me something?*

Ivy saw that the inside of the birdcage was twinkling ever so slightly. She didn't mean to, but her hand reached inside as if by magnetism. She felt the soft down of the owl's feathers and stretched further back, underneath the beautiful bird. A glow of golden light emanated as she did. But then Ivy felt something unusually cold and hard in her sweaty palm. She gasped.

The Kindred Stone.

She felt the smooth, sharp facets on one side and the jagged roughness where it had been split. In shock, she almost let go and felt the stone soften as if it were fading away. Ivy tightened her hand into a fist.

"I knew it!" the Dark Queen crowed. "It's there, isn't it? I tried to pull it out myself and couldn't. You've done me a great favor," she sneered.

The woman extended her pale, bony hands to Ivy. Each finger had a large ring on it, and every stone was shaped into a point like a row of studs. She clicked her rings together impatiently, "Hand me the stone. Now. Pull it out!" she yelled angrily.

Ivy couldn't let go of the stone—what if she never found it again? And she knew she couldn't give it to the Dark Queen!

The Dark Queen scowled. "Give it to me," she demanded.

"No!" said Ivy, refusing to let it go.

In her anger, the Dark Queen's skin started to sheen over with sweat. No, it wasn't sweat. It was water. Water poured from her skin down onto the wood floor. The water spilled into the room, soaking the hem of Ivy's cloak and covering her boots. Ivy didn't let go. She couldn't! She bit her lip and held tighter. The cage swayed over the water.

"Very risky of you to deny me. And with such tone! I'll tell you one more time: Give it to me."

"No," Ivy repeated quietly. She trembled and tried not to breathe in the sickening smell of the Dark Queen's water. She couldn't give in to her fear.

"I thought you might need a little convincing," the Dark Queen muttered. With one wave of her stud-encrusted hand, a wave of water rushed towards Ivy, crashing over her head before retreating. She choked and gasped, just barely able to keep her hand under the owl. The Dark Queen remained mostly dry even as the water collected as if in a bubble around Ivy. The wood of the cabin was creaking and groaning.

The second wave brought a floundering Fyn into the room. When the wave retreated, he gagged and coughed and looked around frantically.

"Ivy? What's going on?!"

He was bound by aquatic rope, winding his hands behind his back and forcing him against the wall. Ivy almost dropped the stone rushing to help him but caught herself in time.

"Let him go," Ivy demanded.

"So long as you pull the Kindred Stone out and hand it to me," ordered the Dark Queen. "The boy will live."

"It doesn't belong to you," Ivy yelled, half crying, half terrified. "Like the throne doesn't belong to you!" Ivy's tone strengthened.

"Ivy, don't listen to her! Don't give it to her!" Fyn pleaded, before a thread of water, thick as an eel, wrapped itself around Fyn's mouth and nose like a gag.

"You let go of that stone, I let go of his life." The Dark Queen's calm was unnerving.

Fyn struggled, but the watery ropes pulled tighter. The water level rose. Its volume threatened the little cottage structure: the walls cracked, and water flooded out, but the Dark Queen kept pulling it back. The dark water swirled around Ivy's legs.

"No!" Ivy shouted, awkwardly twisting her body around, half floating in the water, keeping one hand clenched under the owl's now-wet feathers and the other gripping the birdcage.

Fyn's eyes had closed and his fists slowed as if he were falling asleep. Ivy panicked as she watched his face turn pale. He was fading, losing consciousness. Drowning. She felt the stone in her pocket pulling toward the piece in her hand as if it yearned to be reunited. They throbbed in unison.

"Fyn!" Ivy cried.

She couldn't watch this! How could she make a decision like this? Ivy clenched her eyes shut. Water sloshed around her face and she gripped both stones: one hand around the stone in her pocket and the other in the nest. A jolt of energy sprang through her. She kept her eyes tight as the water came up over her entirely. *Please.*

"Do not underestimate my desire to kill him right in front of you," said the Dark Queen, her voice loud below water.

Ivy closed her eyes tighter at the sound of the evil Dark Queen's voice. A blanket of cold descended upon her and pinpricks of light appeared behind her closed eyelids. She was in Belzebuthe. Ivy turned her face toward the hand that was clenched around the stone. She was in the night sky, among the stars. Vibrant visions of stars, fishing on the rooftop, talking about Star Solo with Fyn, flooded her. "It's the only star ever to have appeared on its own," she could hear Fyn repeating in her mind. *Of course!*

She knew where the second segment of the Kindred Stone was in that moment, how its unique, unparalleled magic had taken it from being stored in an invisible, immaterial vault to somewhere even safer. She needed to get to Belzebuthe.

Ivy let go of the stone, but reclenched her fist, pretending she still had it in hand. She struggled to get up out of the water, and opened her eyes. The stone dematerialized. She turned to Fyn: his listless body below water. *I have to do something!* Then Ivy saw the secret spiller dangling from Fyn's neck.

"We've got to be prepared. We've got to practice," Ivy said to herself slowly. "And so, we play."

An idea sparked in Ivy's mind and her stone went from erratically sparking in her pocket to thrumming strongly.

Seeing Ivy's hand clenched tight, the Dark Queen leered.

"Send away the water! And I'll give it to you," Ivy demanded.

The water receded.

"And set Fyn down. Him, too," Ivy gestured to the Occulyst.

The Dark Queen obliged but said, "All right. No more demands; give me what I came for."

With every fiber of strength in her body, Ivy faced the Dark Queen. Her clenched fist was glowing with the force of her anger and magic—as if she actually was holding the stone.

In a low, almost muted tone, Ivy said, "I am a member...." She lowered her voice even more, "I am a member of the Quality Quills Club."

"What?" demanded the Dark Queen, cackling.

Now Ivy bellowed bravely, *"I am a member of the Quality*

Quills!"

A bright light shot out from the secret spiller around Fyn's neck and swam through the water like a sparkling snake accompanied by a piercing, hissing voice: "The Town's name is Belzebuthe! The Town's name is Belzebuthe!"

With that, a clear understanding of exactly where Belzebuthe was and how to get there came into each person's mind, the long-hidden knowledge as searing as a knife.

The Dark Queen was thrown into confusion by the shrill noise of the secret spiller. Suddenly, dozens of owls flew back into the room, descending with ear-splitting hoots, pecks, and a frenzy of feathers. Ivy dropped and covered her head.

The Queen shrieked, "She doesn't have the stone!" But owls kept dive bombing and flapping at her, making it near impossible for the Queen to move.

The Occulyst grabbed Ivy's hand and the enormous white owl and pulled them toward the window by Fyn. The three jumped out onto a branch, and the Occulyst led them down a complicated path of limbs, ladders, and leaves.

Ivy could hear the Dark Queen recover and cackle as she descended down through the tree, "Belzebuthe! A secret no more and safe no longer!"

Hearing the Town's name roll off the Dark Queen's tongue made Ivy's stomach churn.

"Take care of them!" she commanded her bogdogs harshly. "Belzebuthe calls."

"Hurry, this way!" the Occulyst said in a hushed tone.

Once they were on the ground, Fyn looked at the secret spiller in disbelief. "Ivy, what have you done?" Fyn looked at her, and pain filled his face.

Ivy clung to him, hugging him so tightly he nearly lost all breath again.

"The Town's name was your secret? Now it's—it's not safe! Do you realize what you have done?"

"I'm sorry, Fyn! I had to do it; I had to. We need help. You were dying! Plus, she already knows where the Town is."

"What?"

"The shadow! She told me. It knows how to get there, and now that it's unleashed it will lead her straight there. This way at least everyone knows she's coming. They can help us!"

"The Town's name is Belzebuthe! *Belzebuthe. Belzebuthe...*" The whistle's shriek had dwindled to a whisper and it slipped down off the mountaintop, down through the trees, headed straight for the Halls of Ivy. Ivy doubted for a moment that she had done the right thing.

"Do you have the second stone?"

"No!"

"No?"

The Occulyst broke in. "You have to go! You must beat her to the Town!" The Occulyst's demeanor was as Ivy remembered it: concerned, kind, accommodating—if a little urgent at the moment. The Occulyst opened a hatch that led under the tree's roots.

"Go!" he said and disappeared with the owl in tow. "Belzebuthe needs you." The Occulyst slammed the trapdoor closed behind him.

Ivy grabbed Fyn's hand and ran to where Silius had been resting. She could tell by Fyn's leaden feet that he was still terrified. Confused. The sky was still pitch black, but Ivy could tell that soon the sun's rays would break through. For the moment, though, it couldn't get any blacker. Fyn and Ivy ran, their breath labored. Ivy's throat was painfully cold; and Fyn, despite his usual strength, fumbled with each step. Ivy held him closely, trying to get their legs in sync. He needed rest, but there was no time for it. Ivy jumped over divots in the dirt and climbed over the tangled roots, but the weight of Fyn's body was slowing her down immensely.

"Silius!" Ivy yelled, desperate. "Silius!" she cried even louder when they cleared the cover of the tree and neared the rocky outcropping.

"Ivy," Fyn panted, trying to quiet her. He clenched his side; he felt like he might have broken a rib. "What—where? What are we doing?"

"We have to get to Belzebuthe! I saw the star. Star Solo. I know where the Kindred Stone is!"

"My moon, it can't be the star, Ivy?!"

"It's the star, Fyn!" Ivy said. She couldn't help but smile. "Silius!"

Suddenly, a large growl sounded and mist collected at the base of the tree behind them. The bogdogs! The beastly dogs had caught their scent and were after them. Their menacing fog swirled behind their pounding paws. Ivy panicked, knowing there was no way they could outrun them. She staggered backwards with Fyn, still supporting most of his weight. With a squeal, Ivy stumbled back.

But then Ivy felt Silius' hand on her, swooping her up.

"Get Fyn, too!"

Silius tossed Fyn to his friend and they were off.

"I thought you'd left us," Ivy squealed, catching her breath.

Ivy could feel Silius's heart pounding. He was scared, too.

They flew down the hill, faster than was safe. The invisitaurs tucked Ivy and Fyn under their arms—uncomfortable but secure—so they had more mobility, leaping down boulders, jumping over hedges. Owls soared overhead, shrieking and keeping watch.

The two invisitaurs rappelled down the other side of the mountain with Fyn and Ivy on their backs.

"Due south is quicker to Belzebuthe," Fyn said. "Wait, how do I know that? I've only ever traveled home in a cabby!"

Ivy looked guiltily at him. "Are you all right?" she asked.

"Been better. Keep coughing up pond water, but I'll be all right. Just needed time to catch my breath is all."

The invisitaurs made it down the mountain and picked up their pace to a sprint through the field below.

Ivy shouted across to Fyn, "I think I'm understanding something. She needs the stone more than she needs me dead."

"What do you mean, Ivy?" Any color left in his face drained out.

"What I mean is, she could have killed me at the Ball. She could have killed me back there, but she's waiting, waiting for me to find the Kindred Stone."

"You don't think she knows it's been broken into pieces?"

"No. And we might be able to use that to our advantage. After I find all the pieces, the whole Kindred Stone, that's when she'll come for me."

The journey to Belzebuthe was long and hard. They stopped only for water.

After the morning sun crested the mountains, Belzebuthe came into view. The town they should never have been able to find without a cabby was right there before them, mist- and mystery-free.

Chapter Thirty

Star Solo

THEY burst through the fading fog into town, leaving their invisitaurs in a glen to rest. Fyn led Ivy through a series of winding shortcuts. Almost everyone in Belzebuthe was attending the pre-season Quogo match between Vegal Squeal and Margo Dupree—it had started the night before and had stretched to the early hours of the morning. As they ran, Ivy saw that the spell, the clouds that concealed Belzebuthe and made every compass beside the Collectis spin, was shifting. Dark patches were above them, but so were thin cracks of morning light. Ivy was sore from riding the entire night and caked with mud from the journey, but there wasn't even time to stop and think.

"Did we beat her here?" Ivy asked hopefully.

Fyn shrugged and ushered her to the charming storefront of the Star Shoppe. They urgently burst through. The arched door swung open and hit the wall, bouncing back so hard that Ivy bruised an elbow.

"So sorry, Ivy! Are you okay?" asked Fyn.

"Fine," she nodded, rubbing her elbow and letting her eyes adjust.

Ivy was taken aback by the shop's interior. She had expected to see a precious store full of star memorabilia, but it was an abandoned space, dark and empty. It seemed as if the cozy, inviting display window was the exact opposite of the dank and tiny room.

The center of the floor was woven from thick jute, like a giant basket. A sconce on the moist, drab wall by the door dimly illuminated a pale, pearlescent maximum capacity sign: *Sized Right for Five Generously Sized Scrivenists.* Another slightly larger sign above that read, *Only Way to Go Is Up.* The letters trailed up and off to the right. The walls were outfitted with pipes of all sizes, corroded and in different shades of gray and rusted orange.

"Fyn, what *is* this, a literal hole in the wall? We don't have time for this! We have to find the star!"

"Trust me, Ivy. That's what we're doing."

"The stars are up there!" Ivy pointed up and out to the sky.

Fyn replied in a hushed tone, "We're going to need transport up, gloves, and a few essentials."

Ivy closed her eyes and envisioned holding the second stone, feeling its jagged edges, the warmth at her fingertips, the magic shining out in between her fingers. Every inch of her could feel it. It was there, in the star. It had to be there.

Fyn ushered Ivy into the center of the room. Then, surprisingly, the edges of the woven mat they were standing on curled up and became the walls of a basket. Ivy looked around in wonder. Slowly, at a snail's pace, the basket holding the two was lifted up, up, up. As they went up, a golden shaft of light pricked the darkness and then grew brighter. Illuminated imprints of stars glowed beautifully on the walls as they passed.

Everything fell to silence, aside from the rattle and jangle of the platform making its way up the chute like a hot air balloon.

As the moving platform finally settled into place on the top story of the building, it was evident what was casting such a warm glow. A long wall was dotted with all sizes of stars: some the size of buttons, others like a bar of soap or really large grapefruits. The glow was so beautiful, it felt like everything in the world was in harmony, and for a moment Ivy forgot why she was there.

There were countless maps of constellations, figures of a full, half, and double moon glued to the walls. The place sold constellation quilts, maps of Belzebuthe's magician-made sky, fishing gear, gloves, and boots.

Still gazing at the sparkling wall, Ivy muttered louder than she intended, "It's incredible."

"Remarkable, really," called a soft voice. Ivy turned to see that Harriet Smiles was walking unsteadily towards her, slow as their start. "Are you interested in a star?"

"We are."

The proprietor had bright eyes that always held a twinkle. Her hair was swept up into a blonde bouffant that framed her sweet face. She was wearing her characteristic red lipstick. Coincidentally, she had a small, star-shaped beauty mark on her cheekbone.

"Would you like to make a wish? You can either fish one down, thereby granting another's wish. Or you can set a new one. Stars have the capacity to grant a wish of varying size: a first kiss, visit a tome. The larger the wish, the larger the star and, of course, the larger the price."

"Thank you so much, Ms. Smiles."

"Harriet. Please call me Harriet."

"Harriet. I'm sorry, but we really are in a huge rush. I wish I had hours to spend here but I, er, I have seconds. We're only interested in the Star Solo."

"Star Solo, did you say? Why, no one's asked about that star in years. No one's been able to come close to dislodging that star from its perch. Even if you could get close, it's likely to be even hotter than a typical star. It might even take your quill hand, a fate worse than death."

"Please, it's important that we get to the star."

Harriet smiled pityingly and then hurried about the shop, getting two pairs of her thickest gloves, a net, and a casting line. Fyn pushed a pouch of brums across the counter.

"You and your father were my best customers for a while."

Fyn squeezed the shopkeeper's hand and turned to Ivy.

"Put these on, Ivy," he handed her the smaller gloves. "And if we get close—"

"*When* we get close."

"Best of luck," Harriet said. "Oh, and steer clear of those troublesome shades. Those strange things just keep getting worse. Some hiccup in the cloaking spell I hear. Horrid things are scaring customers away!"

Harriet led them to the windows where there was a balcony that stretched across the building's narrow width. With her bright green-and-white flecked quill, she dimmed the display stars and handed Ivy a map to the constellations. The inky-black paper rolled out to reveal each of Belzebuthe's stars in miniature. Set at the center top of the dome was the Star Solo. It was significantly larger than the other stars on the map, and higher set, like a brum floating above the other pricks of light.

"How do we get to it?"

"The starguster. Pay by the hour." She pointed to the balcony, where a fleet of funny little contraptions awaited. The small, reclined bicycles had four wheels: two large wheels in the back on either side of the low padded chair and two small wheels near the front by the pedals. The metal frames were rusty, of course, from the Town's weather.

Ivy sank into the seat, leaning back and stretched her legs out to reach the pedals.

"Now, pull the shield down, dearie."

Ivy did as Harriet instructed and reached above and behind her head to pull the glass visor down to cover her body.

"You'll be able to hear each other if you speak right into this," she pointed at a star-shaped tube.

"Do I just—just pedal?" Ivy asked.

"Yep," said Fyn. "Ready?" He smiled at her reassuringly, and then gave her a push out into the sky.

Ivy pedaled the starguster frantically, seeing the lights of the hairie lanterns on the still deserted streets below. The starguster zoomed up.

"Slow down, Ivy!" Fyn was chasing her tail on another starguster.

Ivy backed off pedaling and noticed that the air was thicker than it should be, but pleasantly so, almost as if it was water or gel-like but still easy and smooth to breathe. Slowing down gave her the chance to look around. She was at the level of the lowest hung stars, and the light from them bounced off the shield, enhancing and distorting them. The fog provided a velvety backdrop for the bright stars, giving each a hazy halo.

"This. Is. Magical."

The setting was serene; thousands of stars shimmered as they pedaled by. Fyn grinned. Ivy pedaled by stars, steering close with the hand rudder at her side. The stars varied in color, brightness, and size. Some twinkled and flickered, while others shone steadily.

Ivy looked wistful. "Are these all wishes, Fyn?"

"A lot that people want to change, Ivy." Fyn looked sad for a moment. "More wishes than scrivenists below, even."

Amongst the stars and fog, the large black masses floated around, bumping like overinflated balloons.

As she sailed past a pink star, Ivy felt a dark, blobby cloud bump into her starguster. It pushed her close to a bluish star that scraped by her visor and sparked. The shade then dissipated in a wet poof.

The shades were definitely lower and blacker. It seemed as if the farther up they pedaled, the more active they became. The big black masses bounced off of them like buoys, floating like balloons and blocking starlight momentarily. There had never been this many!

Ivy spread the map to check their direction. She looked up and there it was: the star named Solo, dead ahead. Its light was growing steadily brighter as they approached, and Ivy felt the stone in her pocket tremble.

"There it is!" Ivy pedaled up, and Fyn followed close behind. As they climbed higher and higher, Ivy's ears began to pop.

"Yeahhh!"

They doubled down, pedaling as fast as they could to the upper and outermost edge of Belzebuthe's sky. Here they could see even better the cracks that widened by the second. The Croswald sun crept in, dampening the shine of Belzebuthe's stars.

Ivy got there first, pulling the starguster as close as she could to Star Solo.

"Don't worry! I've got it, Fyn!"

"Careful, Ivy! The shades are blowing closer!"

Ivy threw back the shield; she could almost reach the star. The stone segment in her pocket was buzzing steadily. She could see the stone shine through her skirt and cloak. Ivy felt like the stone's energy was helping her lift out of her seat, urging her to reach for Star Solo. She stood suddenly, and in her excitement, she caused the starguster to wobble. The whole frame and seat were wet from the shades, and Ivy's boot slipped. She fell, but not before she grabbed Star Solo with both gloved hands. She screamed and fell through the thick air in a slow-motion fall. She brushed by a nearby star, and it singed through her cloak and burnt her arm.

"I got you!" Fyn was right below her, shield pushed back. She dropped quickly into his lap. "Your arm!"

"The star! The star, Fyn! I've got the star!" She ignored his concern.

In Ivy's hand, the shell of the star disintegrated, leaving behind a bright white and gleaming stone!

"Oh no!" Fyn redirected Ivy's attention. A fleet of shades was barreling toward them, sizzling as their wet bodies touched stars.

"Ugh, not now!"

"We have to get down!"

Fyn directed the starguster down and pedaled for all he

was worth.

Chapter Thirty-One

Battle for Belzebuthe

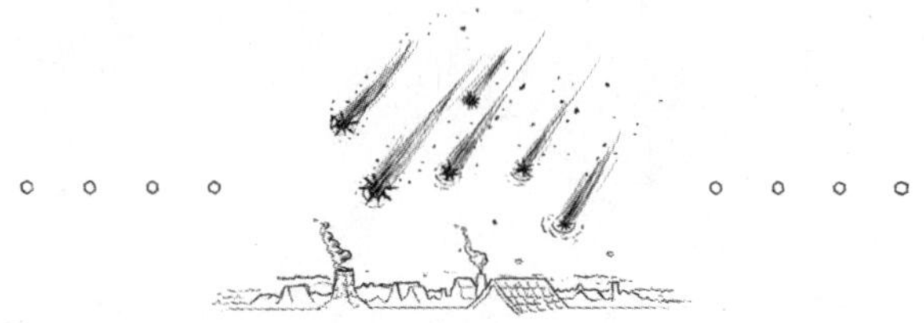

FYN carefully lowered Ivy down onto the ridge of the Suitcasery. As Ivy steadied herself on the uneven shingles, looking out over the cabby deck, Fyn pedaled to the perfect landing spot (or so he thought): the notch between the roofline and one of the blackened chimneys. The landing wasn't graceful—the air was thinner down in town—and he lost one small wheel and dented the other. The chimney took the brunt of the damage.

Fyn hobbled on the angled rooftop back to Ivy, careful not to slip in the slush. The conveyor belt from the cabby deck was still, the ticket booth closed, and the whole of Plumlie's cart all buttoned up.

Shades, Fyn worried. The big clouds darkened to gunmetal gray. As the stormy clouds festered and began to block the sun, all below grew eerie. But as for Ivy, she hardly noticed. She couldn't believe she held the second piece of the Kindred Stone in her hand.

Closing her eyes, she felt just like she had in that moment at the Occulyst's, but now she could keep it in her hand! Her hand! The radiant stone was smooth and faceted on one side where its opalescent colors flashed. The other side, what had been the inside of the stone before broken into pieces, was like jagged quartz. Two parts of a giant pear-shaped stone that had been cracked into rough thirds. The crystal sparkled brilliantly in the light of the breaking day. The first stone in her pocket glowed impossibly bright, lighting up her dress. It levitated, lifting a fold of her skirt, as it moved toward its long-lost counterpart.

"Meant to be together," Fyn said. Then he glanced at Ivy and blushed.

With a quavering voice, she whispered, "I just can't believe we did it. We found it. Why do you think—why hasn't anyone fished it out of the sky before?"

"Hmm, I'll bet it was still in some sort of dematerialized state from the Occulyst's owls. You unlocked it, Ivy. You did it," Fyn smiled. After a minute's pause, he grew serious, "But, Ivy—"

"What, Fyn?" Ivy asked distractedly, comparing the two segments of the Kindred Stone in her delicate hands and trying to piece them together.

"The shades, Ivy."

Ivy didn't have a chance to respond because she felt, more than heard, a thump right behind them. Fyn and Ivy spun around; it was as if a cloud had fallen from the heavens and landed in a pile of snow. No longer just cloud shaped, the shade was standing tall as a figure. The shade's bulbous limbs were made of dark stormy cloud, and snow spun off of them. No features distinguished its shadowy face.

Ivy shook in her boots. As if he were a ventriloquist, Fyn spoke quietly, mouth barely moving. "Maybe if we don't move, maybe it won't see us."

The thing whistled at them so loudly it could shatter an eardrum.

"Maybe not. We run, Ivy. Right now."

Fyn and Ivy scuttled away. However, on an angled rooftop covered in slush, they could move only so fast. A huge gust blew them off their feet, knocking them onto the pointed edges of the rock-hard shingles. Ivy gasped and hurried to get back up.

The shade suddenly dissipated into a diffuse black cloud, shaking gray snow down on the two. Then, within the blink of an eye, it transformed into a great wind, circling the chimney and blowing Ivy and Fyn back. Standing, they raced along the spine, looking for any place to escape the shade's intensifying wrath. The wind churned up the wood roof shingles as well as the starguster into a miniature tornado.

"Duck!" yelled Fyn, his hand on Ivy's back.

The shade slung the starguster at Fyn and Ivy's heads. They dove facedown, flat against the sloped roof, just in time to avoid the starguster-turned-missile moving faster than it ever had. They heard the poor cycle burst apart into pieces as it hit the ground below.

With another gust, they were shoved closer to the edge of the roof that overhung the cabby deck. Ivy clung to the shingles with one hand, the stones in her other, and closed her eyes against the flying debris. Then there was a crack of thunder. Startled, Ivy loosened her grip on the stones, which was just enough to allow the next gust of wind to knock them from her hand.

"No!" Ivy screamed as the two stones plummeted to the deserted cabby deck below. They were glistening like twin fallen stars. Images of the stones' two-year journey to her flickered through her mind.

Her dread was punctured by Fyn's call. "Ivy! Come on, pull yourself back up!" She had slipped farther down the roof and her legs dangled over the deck, fifteen feet below. But Ivy couldn't even be afraid of the height right then: She was so horrified that she had dropped the stones, the only things that could save them from the Dark Queen! And it hadn't even taken the Dark Queen to shake them out of her hand, just some miniature storm.

She tried to banish the thought of Derwin's sacrificing everything to protect the things she'd so quickly lost. Snippets of the old-fashioned script in the letter Derwin had found with the stone floated through her photographic mind.

> *What magic remains of a beloved heart is safeguarded by the double moon. The only thing that offers hope to this world lies within this box: a stone pure and bright. A fraction of the powerful queenly magic reverberates in this crystal form.*

The queenly magic. The same magic that was in her blood.

The snow turned to sleet and Ivy slipped farther. Fyn was holding her under her arms.

"Ivy! You have to pull up. Come on! It's coming back!"

"Let me go, Fyn!"

"*What?* No. Not happening!"

"The stones, Fyn! I have to get the stones."

"You'll break your legs! Don't be ridiculous!"

Ivy's stubbornness shone through the sleet.

"Let me fall, Fyn," she demanded. "Trust me." It was really her magic that Ivy was asking he trust. For the very first time,

Ivy was wholeheartedly trusting it, too.

He refused, but Fyn's decision was made for him.

Ivy felt her body temperature rising. Images of her parents, the wreckage, the evil Dark Queen, the Ball—all fuel for Ivy's inner magic. Fyn felt the heat coming off her, first just strange and somewhat comforting, but then uncomfortable, then painful, the increasing heat too much to bear. Its intensity was like touching a star with bare hands. He had to let go.

Ivy fell, landing feet first in the snowdrift pushed up against the Suitcasery. Her legs buckled and she rolled backwards, scraping her knees and elbows on the dirty cabby deck. She held still for a moment, grubby and still steaming from her heat, checking over her body.

In that moment of stillness, Fyn couldn't help but fear the worst.

"Ivy!" he grunted, breaking off a piece of rain gutter and using it to slide down to her, dropping the last five feet.

Ivy took a huge, heaving breath before Fyn could reach her. He helped her stumble to her feet. As soon as she stood, Ivy turned and threw her body over the stones just behind them.

"Are you out of your mind? Are you all right?" Fyn shouted. Then looking at her lying over the stones, he added, a touch sarcastically, "Maybe put them in your pocket this time."

She did so as she said, "I'll be fine." The shade on the roof dove down and split in two, one a cloud sending sleet over the whole deck, and the other a tornado that took off, flying its foggy frame around rooftops and launching loose shingles at them.

"We need to get help, Fyn!"

The howling wind increased.

"Who? Everyone's at the Quogo scrimmage. Plus, what could we say? Belzebuthe has never been under attack! Who'll believe us?"

"How else do we stop it? These shades will tear this place to shreds," yelled Ivy. "We have to try, Fyn!"

The entrance to the Suitcasery was blocked by the staguster wreckage.

"Quick!"

Fyn grabbed Ivy's hand and ran with her to the opening where the luggage entered the chute. Hoisting Ivy up on his shoulders, he yelled, "Open the hatch!"

Dozens more shades dropped from the sky. Their thunderous bodies were creating a cataclysm of extreme weather. Ivy climbed through the hatch and helped pull Fyn up. It took both of them to pull the wooden hatch down, closing it behind them. Once closed, it rattled wildly on its hinges.

Fyn shouted, "Go, Ivy, go!" as he held the handle, using his whole body to keep the door shut. He stayed at the door while Ivy scooted forward.

Ivy jumped down on the stock-still conveyor belt and over piles of tattered, abandoned luggage. She tripped and skidded on her knees, her skin shredding even more against the rough metal. She slammed through the next door and was out in the copper gutter, scrambling down in the interior of the building.

"Go! Go!" Fyn's voice called out from behind her, "Keep going!"

"I can't slide any faster!" Their voices echoed in the empty building.

Ivy burst through the next room and into the apartment where she had interrupted the family of scrivenists and their snoring grandpa as she chased her satchel so many moons ago. The family may have been at the Quogo scrimmage, but the old man was snoring reliably.

"Wake up!" she yelled. "You've got to get out of here!"

The old man woke and peeked out the window. Wearing only his plum pajamas, he followed Ivy as she rushed to the first-floor atrium. Ivy could hear the sound of brick tumbling down, windows shattering, and furniture flying from above. Looking up, she saw several shades banging around against the ceiling, whipping up a storm in the building. With relief, she spotted Fyn's shaggy head up at the top floor, in the middle of a terrible lightning storm. He was yanking at the pulley system for the conveyor belt.

What is he doing?!

"Fyn!"

He finally wrested the rope from the pulley, knotted it around the stone balustrade and twice around his waist, and jumped off the balcony.

Ivy screamed.

Fyn rappelled down the walls, jumping lightly as he lowered himself on the rope. He landed safe but soaked at Ivy's feet.

"What? I'm not afraid of heights." He smiled at Ivy. "Here," he motioned to the grandpa whom Ivy had led down. "Hide in the cellar behind the stairwell until this blows over. We'll be back before you finish your nap." Fyn helped the gentleman inside.

"We have to get to the hex! We have to warn the others." Ivy envisioned the first hex she'd ever seen, so far below the

Quill Keep.

The two burst outside. The entire town of Belzebuthe had been overtaken by miniature storms. Tornados were touching down, shattering glass storefronts and breaking up the cobblestones from the beautiful streets. The Plumlie's cart was airlifted from the cabby deck and then smashed into the newspaper cart below, its *Scriven This* papers and puddings whirling around in the wind. Shades were dropping by the dozens. Though they appeared light as air, each touchdown was like an earthquake.

Where they had just been flying, a tiny crack of sunlight broke even wider, spreading and splintering across the entire sky. The edges of Belzebuthe's protective sky began to shimmer with light.

"Oh no," was all Fyn could say. "It's happening. It's actually happening."

"We need help! The mattelers, the Club, they should be here. Why aren't they here? Derwin. Someone!" shouted Ivy.

"C'mon. We have to get down to the hex. It's soundproof, and they probably have no idea what's going on out here!"

The two grabbed hands and ran toward the Quill Keep. Fyn shot magic from his quill to push open the tiny door down to the hex. The door snapped in half—not what he intended. He grabbed the larger of the two pieces of door and sat down on it.

"Get on!" he gestured to Ivy, urging her to sit behind him.

"What?!" But realizing they had no time to waste, no matter how strange the idea, she hopped on. Fyn shoved off, pushing the door down the rickety steps like a sled.

"Aaaah!" Ivy couldn't help but scream as they careened up against the sidewalls, almost flipping over twice. Her heart skipped a beat. They traveled down the many flights of stairs, finally crashing into the Quogo arena. The participants were clearly weary, and half of the bleary-eyed spectators were sleeping. Fyn's bellow woke them.

"Belzebuthe is under attack!" he yelled.

Some of the spectators jumped up, including Duncan Wurchester and other mattelers. But the players kept fighting weakly, clearly nearing the end of a long battle and having little left to give.

Then the shades began blustering down toward the hex. The mattelers rushed up the steps with magical quickness, battling the shades that were busting the steps into splinters as scrivenists ran. Fyn and Ivy followed back up the stairs, almost out of breath.

Just as they made the last step, the stairwell faltered for the last time and crashed down below. Half of the spectators were still stuck at the bottom of the Quill Keep!

"No!" Ivy screamed.

"Don't worry, Ivy," Fyn tugged her along. "They aren't helpless—they are some of the most powerful scrivenists in Belzebuthe. They'll find a way to get out and help us. For now, we follow Wurchester!"

From the crowd pushing out of the Quill Keep came a familiar voice: "Fyn!" Mrs. Greeley rushed to them. "What are you doing here?!"

"Ma, the Dark Queen's on her way," Fyn blurted. "We have to stop her from destroying Belzebuthe!"

"The Dark Queen?" Mrs. Greeley's eyes opened wide. "Come up with me, quickly! I'll need help securing the Quill Keep. If any of those quills get out…." She shivered. "They think Debnick's quill was bad, but they have no idea! Hower Class, Wilford Buddrat, Leslie Stoot—some of the worst! Just saying their names make me weak in the knees."

Mrs. Greeley used her key to open the Keep's main door, and the three shoved it closed before a shade could sweep in.

She turned to the two of them and said, "I've heard a terrible rumor, speaking of dangerous quills, that you two had something to do with Debnick's quill being returned." She arched an eyebrow at them. "I met with Derwin while he was with Easel, coming into Belzebuthe. But now, not a moment to spare! We will work our way from the top—most dangerous—to the bottom, dears. Come on!"

They dashed after Mrs. Greeley, who was speeding up a blocky, rectangular staircase that wound around the inside of the narrow tower keep. The restricted quills floated peacefully in aquariums built into the limestone walls along the way. Then the limestone stairs wrapped around to the next level.

"The mattelers'—offices—are?" Ivy panted.

"Yes! On the Keep's hidden floors. I believe Derwin's here now—they are still questioning him!"

Near the top, many stories up, they passed the cracked aquarium with the brass nameplate that read Daryl Debnick. Ivy bit her lip. What if things worse than the orbis lurked behind each of these? What seemed to be peaceful, beautiful feathers floating in colored water could become destructive so fast.

Mrs. Greeley fumbled with the keys on her ring, searching for the right one.

"No time!" Ivy tried to even out her breath and drew out

one of her stones.

"So that's the stone they speak of," Mrs. Greeley muttered in disbelief.

The aquarium in front of her held a broad white feather that was speckled with tan and black spots. Ivy drew her arm back and, looking side-to-side, asked her team, "Ready?"

The Greeleys nodded, and Ivy struck the glass with all her strength. The stone rang out as if it had hit a gong, and for a moment, Ivy was afraid that she had cracked the Kindred Stone further. No, the stone was strong in her hand. Water spurted from the cracked glass, and Mrs. Greeley quickly grabbed the quill.

"Nice work! On to the next!" Fyn always managed to be cheerful in the most dangerous environments. "What are we going to do with these, Ma?"

"On the third level, there are safe boxes. Impossible to open once shut—no keys. No spell is strong enough to open them, meant only for emergencies. We have to take them there!"

"Why not keep these terrible quills in there always?"

"Can't learn from them that way!"

They worked their way down, cracking cases and collecting quills. Unexpectedly, Derwin came rushing out of a dark-paneled door Ivy hadn't noticed hidden in the shadows.

"Ivy! What—what are you doing here?! You shouldn't be here!"

Three, no, four mattelers—all in uniform—brushed past the group and down the wraparound stairs. The stamping of their boots reverberated, setting the quills they had collected to buzzing wildly. Fyn did his best to smother them in his coat.

"Derwin! Help Wisteria with the quills," shouted Easel Leelangraf over his shoulder.

From the back of the group, one of the mattelers yelled, "Less than five miles away. She's bringing some unnatural force with her!"

The Dark Queen, Ivy surmised. *And the shadow?*

The mattelers burst out, slamming the door behind them, to join the fight against the shades. Ivy was relieved to see her scrivenist, no matter the circumstances. She ran to him and clutched his shoulders.

"Derwin! Oh, thank the stars that you're here! The shades—it's awful!"

Derwin quickly looked Ivy over, upset that she even had a few cuts and scrapes on both her elbows and knees. To be sure, he asked, "Are you all right?"

"I'm fine. Oh, it's so good to see you!" Ivy instinctively hugged Derwin tightly.

Mrs. Greeley interjected, "From what I hear, you're quite fond of putting the girl in danger! What kind of scrivenist allows their royal to enter a glanagerie world alone? Are you out of your mind, scrivenist? She's just a child! *The* child! I overheard *everything*!"

"Wembly would have done the same, Wisteria! But yes, we do have to get them out of here. Somehow the Dark Queen now knows how to find Belzebuthe."

Fyn and Ivy shot each other a look.

"And she's looking for Ivy. We have to leave immediately!"

"No!" Ivy said. "We have to do something! All of us! Locking away these quills isn't enough! And Derwin, I—we found the second stone! It was in the stars! Your hunch was right! It was here in Belzebuthe the whole time! Here—"

Ivy reached for her pocket, but Derwin stopped her.

"Don't! Listen to me, no matter what happens, you keep those stones safe, do you understand? Without all three pieces, the Kindred Stone's magic is only as powerful as any other stone. It's not powerful enough to challenge the Dark Queen. Keep it hidden. And we've got to get you and your friend out of here!"

"We want to help, Derwin!" Ivy insisted, drawing Winsome's quill and clutching her quiver.

"Yeah, we're here to help!" said Fyn, revealing his quiver, too.

"We have to stop her, and we're not leaving without a fight," said Ivy, putting her foot down.

"Ivy. This is no glanagerie experience. The Dark Queen is headed this way!"

"Are you asking me to run?"

Derwin thought for a second, adjusting himself to the idea of letting Ivy stay. Then he said, "Fine! But stay with me!"

They reached the third floor and slammed all the dangerous quills they had just collected into one toxic safe box. Then a rumble shook the building. Then another. Something was pounding the side of the building. They dove behind a railing, Derwin shielding them as best he could. The wall of the tower ripped away with a cracking sound, the limestone crumbling down into a pile of rubble.

Outside, the mattelers were flashing their quills at the shades with some luck. But the dark-gray monsters only continued to grow in intensity, barreling through brick as if it were soft as a cloud. Outside Bramble's, Ivy spotted Easel

Leelangraf—both his height and dark curls made him easily discernible amongst the fleeting crowd—and he was sending spell after spell from his dark-blue quill. Just then, a lamppost went soaring past. Ivy could swear she saw the look of horror on the hairies' faces as they flew by. Duncan Wurchester caught the lamppost with his magic, his face dripping with sweat as he kept the object levitating over the old man from the Suitcasery.

"How did he get out?" But as soon as Ivy asked, she guessed that the cellar had been blown open by the shades. Not that she should have been too worried about the grandpa in the first place: he thrust and parried with his quill, sending beams of sunshine and lightning bolts around the shades.

"Hurry up! Take cover!" shouted Duncan. The force of the wind carrying the lamppost was too strong for him to hold. Seconds after the man took cover in the rubble of the Keep, Duncan released the lamppost from his magical grip and it shattered on the ground.

Ivy shouted over the storm, "What *are* these things?"

Derwin replied as they ran to the Town's center, "The mattelers just discovered that they are remnants of a curse that the Dark Queen has been casting at Belzebuthe, trying to break through the shield!"

"Would some kind of pologie work to dissipate them?" Ivy asked, watching Fyn spell *Dry up!* over and over, to no avail.

"Hmmm," Derwin furrowed his brow deep in thought. "Perhaps a simple Reversible Rain pologie may be the perfect antidote for the shades. Can you remember the spell? 'Reversed and then cursed, but then curses reverse.'"

"Of course. Professor Royal."

Derwin tested out the spell on a shade that was spinning

toward them. It worked! The rain that the shade had been flinging out rewound back into the shade. Who knew that rain could go up instead of down? The shade grew lighter, fading up into the morning sky that could be seen between the mass of shades.

"I always knew you were a good scrivenist, despite the memory loss!" Ivy cheered.

Derwin smiled. "Thanks for the reminder! Let's go!"

As they went, Fyn, Mrs. Greeley, Ivy, and Derwin each cast the Reversible Rain pologie, spinning the shades back where they came from. At Belzebuthe's center, serious scrivenist faces were drenched with sweat. Derwin hurried to let them know the Reversible Rain pologie was working.

The shade storms that had been gusting and spinning and throwing gray snow every which way were thrust back, one at a time. Mrs. Greeley squinted, unaccustomed to the bright sun. But amidst the diminishing storms Ivy spotted something wonderful in the distance. An exacto magno dragon—bright orange-red—was cutting through the clouds. But it wasn't just the dragon. No. The Quality Quills members were all in tow, hollering to help.

"I don't believe it, Fyn. Look! The dragon! It's Rebecca!" Ivy grinned.

Fyn looked up, astonished. "They knew to come because of the secret spiller! Ivy!" He turned a grateful look toward her. "You're brilliant!"

Glistle and Gretta were each gripped by the dragon's giant red claws. Lennu, Manone, Pedlum, and Canna were all sitting comfortably in a line along its long neck. Hayword held on for dear life to a scaly tail that whipped in the wind. It dipped lower, between chimneys, and past the Melted Milkshake. As it swooped down, its extended wings brushed balconies, and Gretta and Glistle lifted their feet so as not to get caught on a chimney.

Huge gusts from the force of the dragon's wings had forced the shades to spin away, but not for long. Even more shades dropped from the clouds, bringing with them hurricane-like winds, rain, and hail. Rebecca the dragon turned in midair. She was too large for the Town, and her tail whipped and lashed the sides of already-shattered buildings. Quickly, Rebecca set down Gretta and Glistle while the other members jumped down to the ground.

"You all came! You're here!" Ivy exclaimed.

"Of course we did, but no time for a chat!" said Canna, who flashed her quill at the oncoming shade. The feather, red as a flame, forced the shade back. A second shade barreled towards them, this time with enough force to cause her quill to fly.

Ivy ducked out of the way.

"Use the Reversible Rain pologie!"

"Right behind you!" yelled Hayword.

Alongside the mattelers, the Quality Quills Club members were out in full force, brandishing their borrowed quills.

Rebecca wasn't her dragon self for much longer. After shrinking back down to human, she ran to Ivy.

"Rebecca!" Ivy shouted, relieved to see her best friend. "I'd say welcome to Belzebuthe, but there's no time for it!"

"What kind of friend just leaves her friend to go to a ball by herself?!"

"I know, I'm sorry! Please don't be mad."

"I'm not really. More worried! We'll talk later!"

At that moment a spiraling wind went rushing between

Rebecca and Ivy, knocking them both off their feet. Even though Rebecca was still in her original form, her fiery breath remained, and she burned a hole in the nearest shade with a shot of blazing breath.

They were gaining ground! Between the mattelers and the Quality Quills Club, most of the shades had been reversed. Ivy should have felt triumph, like that which she saw on the faces of her friends.

But a familiar eerie feeling was upon her. *The shadow.* It had to be near. Both stones in her pocket were buzzing crazily. The bright morning sun darkened, and a darkness fell across Belzebuthe.

There, in the center of Belzebuthe, was the shadow that had once been Gretta's and now was clearly the Dark Queen's, more terrifying than ever. The dark silhouette moved like smoke, changing shape and rising above them, as high as the buildings. Gretta shook, standing close behind her brother, who narrowed his eyes.

The shadow raised its arms and swept them through Belzebuthe's sky. Stars began dropping from above, crumbling to dust and burning up as they hit the ground. As each star hit, a burst of light exploded against the cobbles, and wisps of wishes disintegrated into thin air. Several landed near enough to quills to have their wishes granted: a bicycle popped up, a song played. But most were just crushed wishes—shattered scrivenist dreams.

A hush fell over the fighters. It looked as if the Dark Queen would conquer Belzebuthe handily without ever even showing up in person.

The damp cobbles beneath Ivy's feet kept causing her

to slip. Even so, she stood and faced the shadow, holding Winsome's quill outstretched. Her heart felt like it was going to thump out of her chest.

Fyn joined. "What do you say we make that shadow disappear with the dark? Ready your quills!"

Ivy smiled, seeing the Club members lined up alongside Fyn, quills in hand.

Finally, all nine members surrounded the Dark Queen's shadow, daring to draw near. They formed a boundary around the shadow, like a Quogo hex. The mattelers stood alongside them. The shadow cackled.

Fyn shouted loudly, over the whipping wind of the shades, *"To the potions and motions"* and sent a vomiting potion straight into the shadow's gut, causing it to shrink temporarily.

Hayword grinned, *"To creatures unknown"* and spelled a barrel of snakes at the shadow.

The rest joined in: *"The dangers, the quivers, the darkest unknown. To this, I declare, all secrets be still."*

Ivy grinned, "I'd better take it from here—no need to spill any more secrets today!"

Fyn grinned, "Tell her, Ivy! Go on, tell her who you really are."

He winked. Ivy's eyes glimmered. Deep down, Ivy knew who she was: a slurry girl turned royal, an orphan denied her family's right, with the magic of the moon settled inside her, and now, the newest and proudest member of the Quality Quills Club. Her new family.

She spoke loudly, deliberately, *"For I am a member of the Quality Quills!"*

A full-out Quogo battle commenced—not a duel between

two scrivenists but a cacophony of spirit fighters. Distractions. Spectres and spells clouded the circle, and the shadow turned side to side, confused as to how to fight so many. Rebecca transformed into a shade, giving the shadow a taste of its own medicine!

The mattelers joined the fight, brandishing their quills powerfully. Several attempted to spell the cracks in the boundary to close up. Others brought townspeople into safety. As the battle raged, the only safe place seemed to be outside Belzebuthe. On the outskirts of town, mothers and their children hid behind ancient pines, watching as the haze and fog surrounding Belzebuthe lit up.

The cloud cover of Belzebuthe cracked again loudly, further opening and crumbling, allowing for even more late morning sun to seep in. The shadow howled and cackled and stamped down its foot. With a whoosh, all at once, everyone in Belzebuthe was thrown backwards away from the shadow. Not a single soul was left standing.

Ivy struggled to get up: She couldn't! Something was pinning her in place! She looked around in a panic. Everyone else was in the same predicament. Each was pinned like a bug by their own shadow. Most had lost their quills and quivers in the blast, and they couldn't get up—Winsome's quill was all the way back by Gretta and Glistle. Arms and legs flailed. The shadow laughed and brought down more stars as it grew even larger. It shot the stars at the townspeople like weapons.

Gretta had been stunned just like the rest. Instinctively, she tried to scramble away from the shadow like a crab. She quickly discovered she could, because she had no shadow to pin her down! Quickly, quietly, as stealthily as the shadow that had dominated her year, Gretta crept back to Winsome's quill, sticking out of a gray slush mound like a pin.

The shadow was roaring and approaching Ivy, kicking in shop windows as it went. Gretta gritted her teeth and ran straight to her friend.

"Ivy!" Gretta screamed as the wind blew hard enough to take their voices away. She pressed the quill into Ivy's chest.

Ivy took Winsome's quill in her hand. She had never seen a more beautiful thing in her life. Bewildered, she looked at Gretta, "How—"

"Now!" screamed Gretta. Then a huge gust blew her back.

Ivy turned her head back to the shadow, her body still pinned at her feet. She struggled up and took as strong a stance as her awkward foot placement would allow. Ivy held out Winsome's quill with every fiber of strength in her, shaking in defiance.

The Dark Queen's voice rang out through the shadow, filling the whole sky. "Do you honestly think a dead man's quill could defeat me?"

"No. But I can!" Ivy shouted into the wind.

She swooped Winsome's quill in a giant circle and the dust and chunks of fallen stars started to rattle on the ground. She had the sensation that Winsome's warm, gnarled hand held hers and they swept the quill together.

"What's happening?" Gretta cried from behind Ivy.

The rattle soon turned to hovering stardust, then shooting stars whirling around with the arc of Winsome's quill. The re-ignited stardust turned brighter and brighter, sweeping around the shadow like so many slingshots. The shadow roared and swung its arms, beating some down, but the star bits just rose back up into the galaxy-like swirl. Slowly, bits of stardust began to come together, re-forming stars.

The two stones in Ivy's pocket were prickling her leg, responding to the stars and their magic. Ivy held them in one hand and strained her quill with the other. Wherever she whipped Winsome's feather, the stars followed, and the shadow tried to keep up. Over to Bramble's, back to Quinton's, back around the perimeter of Belzebuthe. Left and right, front and back, Ivy swirled the stars around the shadow. The shadow responded with more wind, more rain, and more darkness.

Ivy gripped both hands around both stones and the quill. Finally, Ivy spelled on the fly, *Shine bright, sweet stars; Come together; Rid our world of the shadow forever.* The words crackled from the tip of the quill and sparked in the sky.

Like an explosion, the largest ray of light anyone had ever seen shot from the tip of Ivy's quill. The brightness completely shattered Belzebuthe's barrier and overwhelmed the Dark Queen's shadow. A white-hot heat swirled around the shadow's darkness, and the shadow itself splintered, cracked, and burst into millions of dark particles no larger than grains of salt.

Chapter Thirty-Two

The Rubble

IVY held Fyn and Rebecca's hands as they walked through the debris of the Town. The pharmacists from the apothecary tended to the walking wounded—dozens of townspeople had been hit, bruised, and burned by crumbled buildings, flung lampposts, and cast-down stars. The mattelers were working on a magical rebuild of the Quill Keep and other critical buildings, making sure everyone was safe and accounted for. The midday sun shone so brightly that nearly everyone had to shield their eyes.

Ivy wept, and so did Rebecca. Even Derwin had tears coursing down his face. The town of Belzebuthe was no longer safe, no longer a secret place. No longer even much of a town. The Dark Queen's shadow had destroyed it so thoroughly that no one could ever imagine its being the same again.

Even so, Derwin managed a choked, "Good work, Ivy—I always knew you had it in you. Proud of you."

Duncan Wurchester rushed over to where Ivy and Derwin were standing and shouted, "Kids and quills?" Duncan pointed an accusing finger at the members of the QQC. "Was it you kids who stole Debnick's quill and started this mess in the first place? Never did find the perpetrator. I don't care who you are, you have no right—"

Standing a head taller than Duncan, Derwin interjected sternly, "These kids saved our lives. If it weren't for those quills, we'd all be dead."

The matteler didn't seem convinced. "That may well be—we will investigate it further. For now, Derwin, your assistance is required at the Keep."

Derwin nodded his goodbye to both girls.

As they watched the men retreat, Rebecca chimed in. "So, this is Belzebuthe?" she asked in awe. "Glad I got to see it, even if in such a sad state."

The two girls walked to Quinton's. The shop's building still stood, but the contents had been entirely hollowed out. It was as if the potions shop had vomited out all its contents onto the street in a toxic sludge.

"Ivy," crowed Podge. "You're safe!"

"Not just safe, but she saved us all," said the usually quiet Hodge. They all embraced.

Podge, taking in the scene, said mournfully, "These potion ingredients represented hundreds of years of collecting, even more knowledge. She will not stop until she has absolute power."

"This is the end of magic itself," grieved Hodge.

"It can't be!" Ivy cried.

After helping his mother to their house—it still stood, though everything breakable inside was shattered—Fyn wandered to the Melted Milkshake. Manone was crying in Lennu's arms. Their first-date spot had been completely blown out. The ground in front of the destroyed sweet shop was flooded with salmon-colored slush. The sight of shards of broken glass, roofs ripped from the tops of buildings, and debris cluttering the cobbled streets was devastating.

Spotting a destroyed orange cart turned upside down, Canna, with her eye makeup streaming down her cheeks and bruises all over her forearms, cried, "Plumlie's!"

"We nearly died," Manone muttered under her breath, leaning into Lennu's shoulder, horrified.

Hayword hurried over, his knobby knees weak and shaking.

"Gu—gu—guys! Glad to see that you're all right! And, holy critters! Not sure which was scarier, that shadow or the shades—both so unpredictable! I swear on my menagerie, I'll never quit the Club ever again!" Hayword kissed his quill like he was married to it, grateful for the feather like never before. "And Rebecca the dragon?" Hayword stammered. "I've never seen her look so beautiful! I'm totally realizing that girls with Hellexor Stones and love of animals are totally my thing."

"Take it easy, pal," cautioned Pedlum.

"Yeah, well, speaking of predictability—one thing about that shadow was for sure. It wanted *in*. It wanted to end this town," stated Lennu, before whispering into Manone's good ear, "You doing any better, M?"

She nodded wearily, and Lennu continued to rub her back.

Canna said seriously, "Fyn? You know things that we don't. You have to tell us."

After a moment's pause, Fyn told them everything—about the Occulyst, about Ivy's not only having the queenly blood that the orbis chased but being the moon child. About her lifting the curse of the Wanderers, and about the search for the Kindred Stone.

"You mean… Ivy should be Queen?" Manone was in shock. "The last of the Wanderers?"

"You mean I'm friends with a queen?" Lennu said. "I always knew there was something cool about that girl!"

"The rightful Queen…" Hayword mused. "Wow."

"You knew this all along?" Canna asked sharply.

"I didn't know about the stone and Star Solo. But I did know about Ivy. I just—I thought she needed protecting. And well, I'll be gone next year, and who knows where the scrivenist apprenticeships will be taking place now?" He gestured to the ruin around them. "I'll need you all to look after her while I'm away—even those who are graduating. She needs all our help protecting her."

"Seems like she's pretty good at protecting herself," said Lennu, still in awe of the morning's events.

"Of course. I'm just saying, if she's ever in trouble"—the thought sent a shiver down Fyn's spine—"be there."

Manone, Pedlum, and Hayword nodded enthusiastically; Lennu murmured, "Of course." Canna gritted her teeth and bobbed her head once.

After a suffocatingly tight group hug, the members of the QQC split off to check on their families and homes. Fyn climbed over rubble and looked around, but he couldn't spot Ivy. *Where had she gone?* He did spot Gretta and Glistle in deep, worried conversation with their father outside Bramble's Fritters & Nosh.

Fyn approached with his own concerns. "Mr. Leelangraf, Sir. Will Belzebuthe ever be the same again?"

"The shops and homes, fortunately, yes—in time. However, the cloud cover was hundreds of years in the making and the protection spells are all out of whack—no promises there. If we all contribute, we'll all have a roof over our heads in no time. But Belzebuthe is no longer a secret, I'm afraid to say."

"And what about the stars?" Fyn asked urgently. "They're all gone now." *Gone like my father.*

Glistle and Gretta stepped aside as their father drew in Fyn, putting his arm around him.

"This is the end of the era of safety for scrivenists, Fyn," grieved Easel. Any color left in Fyn's face drained out. "But we must keep hope, just like the stars taught us to. You should head back to the Halls, son. All of you kids. Let the mattelers handle it. You've got a graduation to attend."

Passing Quinton's, Fyn peered inside, looking for Ivy. He spotted Rebecca just in time, right before she used her last scrap of energy to transform back from an expeller who was slurping up the potions mess. Back in her original form, she looked queasy and worn out.

Fyn ran to her, giving her his arm to hold.

"Ivy's not with you?" he asked, concern coloring his voice.

Rebecca shook her head worriedly.

"I think I might know where she is."

They turned and walked until they reached the edge of town.

Ivy was alone, tears flowing down her face, inside the hut with the Wall of the Wandering—rather, what was left of it. She was curled at the foot of the crumbled wall, parchment mixed with stone roof all around her. She was still gripping Winsome's quill, which was decidedly less perky than it had been, and the Kindred Stone pieces in her pocket.

"Ivy!" crowed Rebecca.

Fyn and Rebecca bent down and embraced Ivy.

Rebecca squealed, “Don’t just go off on your own like that!”

“Sorry. I don’t know. I guess I just needed some space to think about things. I can’t help but feel that everything that happened out there is entirely my fault.”

“Ivy, you can’t think like that,” insisted Rebecca.

“You saved us all,” Fyn exclaimed. “You’re a hero! The entire town is grateful to you.”

“Are you sure about that, Fyn? Belzebuthe is no longer a secret. Everything’s changed.”

“Scrivenists should not have to practice their magic in secret,” Fyn said, shaking his head indignantly.

“But I led the Dark Queen here.” Ivy sighed.

“Oh, Ivy. You’re too hard on yourself. You saved Gretta. Do you not give yourself credit for that? And then you defeated the shadow!” Rebecca insisted.

“Yeah, well, I couldn’t have done it without you two. Without the Club.” Ivy looked up and said, “Without Gretta. How’s Gretta?”

“She’s all right. A little shaken, but she’s in good hands. She’s with her family,” Fyn reassured Ivy.

“Oh, good. That poor girl. What she has been through this year alone….”

A silence fell on the three of them. Ivy fidgeted with both pieces of the Kindred Stone in her wounded hand—she couldn’t shake off the layers of guilt weighing on her like one of Mrs. Greeley’s winter coats. On the one hand, she felt proud to have accomplished Derwin’s mission—to have found the missing second piece. On the other, Belzebuthe was destroyed. *Is this worth it?* She thought long and hard.

"What do you plan to do with those?" Fyn asked, eyeing the stones. "Store them with the Occulyst?"

"Are you kidding? After what happened last time? Plus, I doubt he wants to see us again. Not after we practically destroyed his place. I'm beginning to think that, wherever I go, I bring a lot of bad luck."

"Excuse me?" Rebecca interrupted. "Maybe if you hadn't run off on me, I'd know what in the world you were talking about!"

"I'm sorry! The Occulyst. I'll tell you after I get some food in my belly."

"I'll only forgive you if you promise to never exclude me again. What are best friends for, if they don't know all your business?"

Ivy chuckled, "Deal."

Fyn looked up with a start. "Graduation's tomorrow."

Ivy muttered, "Oh. Right."

Rebecca cut right through that conversation.

"What is this place anyway?"

"The Wall of the Wandering," Ivy answered. "Well, it was… what's left of it, anyway." Torn newsletters lay crumpled on the ground; wrinkled sketch work was like patchwork on the wall. She reached for a newsprint, split down the middle, and read silently to herself.

Seeing the headline, *Could the Moon Child Be Alive?*, Fyn mentally responded, *Very alive, and I might kind of love her. I'm going to miss her.* Fyn turned to hide the tears forming at the corners of his green eyes.

"What will they do now? The scrivenist world as we know

it is all in shambles," said Ivy while scrutinizing story after story.

"Well, magical restoration is quite fun—a specialty I might be interested in, in the fall," said Fyn. "We should start heading back to the Halls. Update the Selector."

"Let's head back. But first, the rebuild begins here," Ivy said with new confidence. She held up Winsome's weary quill.

"What are you doing, Ivy?" Fyn asked.

"Rebuilding people's hope."

The debris and news articles swirled with dust back to their original spots. Fyn's and Rebecca's eyes watered as they coughed up the soot. Using Winsome's quill, Ivy contributed to the wall for the very first time: *The moon child was here.*

They left the rubble of the wall, hand in hand.

Chapter Thirty-Three

Graduations and Goodbyes

IVY had never been to a graduation before. She wasn't sure she even wanted to now. The class of fourth years—Fyn, Manone, and Lennu included—sat in rows in the ballroom, and she and Rebecca leaned over the rail on the balcony. Back at the Halls of Ivy, the chandeliers were as bright as could be, and sparklers sent out glittering words soaring overhead, *Hoorah!*, *Congrats!*, and more sizzled midair before fading.

To Ivy, everything seemed a little like a charade. She was still in shock from the battle with the shadow. And the Selector had just informed them that scrivenist apprenticeships would continue in Belzebuthe—it made her wonder if the Selector really knew how terrible the Dark Queen's intentions were. Ivy stared at the Selector, who was leading the ceremony from the front. She tried to focus on what the Selector was saying about graduating, but it was difficult when Ivy had so many questions for her.

It was impossible to know which cap belonged to Fyn until his name was called and he made his way towards the stage from the third row. Ivy clapped, less enthusiastically than she should have. She already missed her more-than-beloved friend. All Ivy knew was that she wasn't prepared to spend an entire school year—two more years!—without Fyn's passing her in the halls, adventuring beyond the castle gates, or damaging the dungeon during Quogo. She'd break into Boulliquiste's again if it meant he would stay. Meanwhile, Fyn shook hands with the Selector, who handed over a quill certificate.

Loud cheers erupted as the last name was called.

The Selector smiled beautifully, opened her arms, and said, "And to this, I add, may your magic bring you ever more delight and your mind grow in wisdom."

Purple caps were thrown high. And the crowd began to jostle.

"There's Pedlum! I'll be right back, Ivy." Rebecca was off.

There was a tap on Ivy's shoulder. It was Gretta, and she looked wonderful—her curls were perfectly bouncy, her caramel skin glowed, and she seemed well rested.

"Hi, Ivy." Gretta smiled hugely, happy to see her.

"Oh, hi!"

"Listen, I just—I wanted to say goodbye and, well, I didn't feel right leaving without seeing you first. Any plans for the summer?"

"Spending the summer with Rebecca, finally."

"Well, I hope you have a great summer with her and her scrivenist. Lots to learn, I'm sure. My dad's here to pick up Glistle and me. In a *carriage*, now that secret travel is a thing of the past." Ivy looked over Gretta's shoulder, where Glistle and their parents waited patiently. Glistle smiled at Ivy from near the grand door. "I'm just looking forward to a summer I don't sleep through."

"You know, I never got to thank you properly, Gretta. After everything you've been through, to come back like that and face your fears, it's inspiring. If it wasn't for you, well, you saved my life. And you saved the lives of many scrivenists. So, thank you for coming back."

Gretta smiled, holding out her hand for a shake.

Ivy grinned widely, pulling in her friend for a huge hug instead.

"See you next year, Ivy."

"See you. Oh, and Gretta?"

"Yes?"

"Can you thank your brother for the stinking violet for me? There's nothing like returning home to a room that smells worse than, well, a stinking violet."

"Ugh! That sounds just like him."

Ivy waved to the Leelangrafs, but when she turned to go, she found that the Selector was waiting patiently right behind her.

"Selector! You startled me."

"A talk is in order."

Ivy took a deep breath and followed the train of the Selector's robe.

Once inside the Selector's office, Ivy braved asked the question she was terrified to pose: "Is this the moment where you tell me I'm not welcome back again?"

She watched as her thick Individualis struggled to squeeze out of its snug spot, float its way across the room, and land with a thump on the Selector's large desk.

The Selector read from Ivy's Individualis—now significantly larger than last year's—in an emphatic tone,

"Breaking into Boulliquiste's, stealing an invisitaur, skipping class, leaving the school grounds unattended, risking the safety of the entire student body," she paused, her concern growing, "and unveiling the secret world of scrivenists!"

Ivy squinted and said, "So I'm not invited back then?"

"Ivy, what were you thinking?" The Selector finally looked up at Ivy as if in need of some explanation.

"I know, I know. I'm sorry. I was only trying to help."

"I understand why you've done all that you have—to protect Croswald. It's honorable of you, but dangerous. You cannot keep putting yourself in harm's way." Ivy was relieved beyond words.

"You know, Selector," Ivy paced from side-to-side. "I think I'm beginning to understand something."

"And what's that?"

"The Dark Queen needs the Kindred Stone."

The Selector listened silently, her eyes narrowing. Then she turned over her palm, revealing the Kallegulous Key, bold and silver. Ivy looked at her quizzically.

"You cannot fool around on adventures and risk the Dark Queen's taking possession of the stone if you slip up. You're not just risking your life; you're risking the entire Kingdom and whatever harmonies are left. I offer you this Kallegulous Key—"

"To the Forgotten Room?"

"The Forgotten Room—where no one will remember the stone but you."

"You're saying hide it there?" It was strange that the Selector had begun to keep the Kallegulous Key around her neck.

"It's not safe while you sleep, not safe sitting on a nightstand, hidden in a boot, tucked away in a trunk, buried in your pocket…"

Was that just a lucky guess? She might be right; after all, the Dark Queen now knows I have at least one of the stones. Where safer to keep a Kindred Stone than where all have forgotten it even exists?

Ivy nodded her agreement and the Selector handed the key over to her. Ivy approached the gate that protected the Forgotten Room's door. The dragons smoldered above as Ivy lifted the key to the lock and turned it. There was the familiar rush of wind as the door opened and Ivy stepped inside, gripping the key tightly.

The scent in the room was familiar—old parchment, dust, and ink—but the room itself was a lot emptier without the bulk of Derwin Edgar Night's things. Ivy looked out the window, watching students as they were surrounded by loved ones. Giant, festive bubbles floated up, up, and into the clouds. She walked deeper into the room, searching for the perfect hiding spot for the stones.

She came across the space where Derwin's desk and all his books and possessions had been. Ivy walked to the center of the space. Towering stacks of books and forbidden spells and curious instruments on either side made the space that she stood in seem extra empty.

A lone, dusty book lay near the wall. Ivy knelt and brushed the cover off; it read, *The Words of the Wandering.* She had a flash of a memory from nearly two years ago in Mr. Munson's shop, a book with words that faded away.

But now there was a note just inside the endpapers. *For you,* it read. *Visible to only the roving group.* Ivy cracked the book open and could see every word and sketch that had been hidden inside.

Acknowledgments

Thank you first to all of Croswald's new readers—I'm forever grateful to each one of you who took a chance on an unknown author and for your continuous support! I also want to thank my editor, Jessie Chatigny. You are magic and I was meant to meet you. Thanks for helping to shape this story into the best possible version. And to Daniela Barrera, this book's very first reader (aside from my mom!), thank you for connecting me with so many new readers all over the world.

Gratitude to the entire Resn Global team: Greg, D, Charlie, Cam, Wade, Rachel, and Dan. Everything you create is magical and so Croswald. Also, a special thank you to Miriam Lacob Stix and Lynette M. Smith: your edits were amazing.

Thanks to my brothers who constantly inspire me in ways they probably don't even realize. Brian, thanks for your help naming the occasional potion! I lost my grandmother while writing this book—she's the inspiration behind Harriet Smiles: a small character, but a very special one. She gifted me my brightest star, my mom. Mom, thanks for believing in me from day one. And Dad: dream, dream, dream. You've always encouraged me to dream big. Z, my husband, thank you so much for letting me fall even deeper into Croswald for so many hours on end.

Lastly, thanks to Ivy Lovely for teaching me to be brave—I'll be forever grateful that I had the courage to finally cross my own slurry field.

About the Author

D.E. Night lives, dreams, and writes in South Florida with her family and her menagerie. The four-book Croswald series is her first. She draws inspiration from silver-screen storytellers, magical imaginings, whimsical creatures, and steampunk art. A day spent daydreaming and writing—preferably to the sound of a rainstorm—is her favorite kind of day.

Spellbound by Croswald?

The complete series is available wherever books are sold and at DENight.com, where all copies are signed by the author. You can also read the first chapter of Book III: *The Words of the Wandering* on the author's website. Please post a review at your favorite online book retailer or on Goodreads!